"You feel so

She drew in a long, shuddering breath. "Reed, you know anything about me."

"This is all I need to know." His hands weren't gentle as he dragged her close and pressed her back against the kitchen counter until their bodies were fused. The quick sexual tug was so compelling, dragging him down, down, until he was drowning in the taste of her, the feel of her, warm and willing in his arms.

He heard her sigh as her arms came around his waist, and he was lost. Lost in a kiss that spoke of hunger, and need, and a desperate desire to take and give until they were both sated.

He plunged his hands into her hair while he ran hot, wet kisses across her forehead, her cheek, her jaw, before returning to her lips. The most compelling lips he'd ever tasted. He wanted, more than anything in this world, to fill himself with her. And he knew, though it was nothing more than a few kisses, he could easily cross a line.

RAVES FOR R. C. RYAN'S NOVELS

LUKE

"Ryan creates vivid characters against the lovingly rendered backdrop of sweeping Montana ranchlands. The passion between Ryan's protagonists, which they keep discreet, is tender and heartwarming. The plot is drawn in broad strokes, but Ryan expertly brings it to a satisfying conclusion."
—*Publishers Weekly*

MATT

"Ryan has created a gripping love story fraught with danger and lust, pain and sweet, sweet triumph."
—*Library Journal* starred review

"Ryan, aka author Ruth Ryan Langan, takes it to the next level in the first book of her new Malloys of Montana series...Fans know that hot Montana men are Ryan/Langan's specialty (the McCords series, anyone?), so get cozy in your favorite reading nook and enjoy!"
—B&N Reads Blog

"Beguiling...Touching and romantic, Ryan's portrayal of a city slicker falling for a cowboy delves into the depths of each of their personalities to find common ground in their love for the land. Readers will eagerly anticipate future installments."
—*Publishers Weekly*

"4 stars!!! With tough, sexy cowboys set against the beautiful, rural landscape of Montana, Ryan's latest is a must-read."
—*RT Book Reviews*

THE LEGACY OF COPPER CREEK

"Solidly written romance. Rich, layered, vulnerable characters in Whit and Cara, coupled with strong chemistry and intense heat between them, proves Ryan does the contemporary Western love story well."
—*RT Book Reviews*

"If you're looking to lose yourself in a fictional family that will steal your heart and pull you into the thick of things, this is the book for you. *Copper Creek* is where a wayward soul can find a home and have all their dreams come true."
—**MommysaBookWhore.com**

THE REBEL OF COPPER CREEK

"A winner. Ryan writes with a realism that brings readers deep into the world she's created. The characters all have an authenticity that touches the heart."
—*RT Book Reviews*

THE MAVERICK OF COPPER CREEK

"Ryan's storytelling is tinged with warmth and down-to-earth grit. Her authentic, distinctive characters will get to the heart of any reader. With a sweet plot infused with family love, a fiery romance, and a bit of mystery, Ryan does not disappoint."
—*RT Book Reviews*

"Full of sexy cowboys and a Western feel that is undeniable…
A well-written, fun story that I really enjoyed."
—NightOwlReviews.com

JAKE

"A must-read…cozy enough to make you want to venture
into the wild West and find yourself a cowboy…And if you
haven't read a Western romance before, R. C. Ryan is where
you should start."
—ReviewsbyMolly.com

"Wonderful characters who quickly find a way into your
heart…a glorious picture of the West from one of my
favorite authors."
—FreshFiction.com

JOSH

"There's plenty of hot cowboys, action, and romance in this
heady mix of a series that will leave you breathless."
—*Parkersburg News and Sentinel* (WV)

"A powerfully emotional tale that will connect with readers…
Love a feel-good cowboy romance with a touch of suspense?
Then pick up *Josh*."
—RomRevToday.com

QUINN

"Ryan takes readers to Big Sky country in a big way with her
vivid visual dialogue as she gives us a touching love story

with a mystery subplot. The characters, some good and one evil, will stay with you long after the book is closed."

—RT Book Reviews

"Engaging...Ryan paints a picturesque image of the rugged landscape and the boisterous, loving, close-knit Conway family."

—Publishers Weekly

REED

REED

R. C. RYAN

FOREVER

NEW YORK BOSTON

Copyright © 2017 by Ruth Ryan Langan
Excerpt from *Matt* Copyright © 2016 by Ruth Ryan Langan

Cover photography by Claudio Marinesco. Cover design by Elizabeth Turner. Cover copyright © 2017 by Hachette Book Group, Inc.

Forever
Hachette Book Group
1290 Avenue of the Americas, New York, NY 10104
forever-romance.com
twitter.com/foreverromance

First Edition: April 2017

Forever is an imprint of Grand Central Publishing. The Forever name and logo are trademarks of Hachette Book Group, Inc.

The publisher is not responsible for websites (or their content) that are not owned by the publisher.

The Hachette Speakers Bureau provides a wide range of authors for speaking events. To find out more, go to www.hachettespeakersbureau.com or call (866) 376-6591.

ISBNs: 978-1-4555-9166-4 (mass market), 978-1-4555-9167-1 (ebook)

Printed in the United States of America

OPM

10 9 8 7 6 5 4 3 2 1

ATTENTION CORPORATIONS AND ORGANIZATIONS:

Most Hachette Book Group books are available at quantity discounts with bulk purchase for educational, business, or sales promotional use. For information, please call or write:

Special Markets Department, Hachette Book Group
1290 Avenue of the Americas, New York, NY 10104
Telephone: 1-800-222-6747 Fax: 1-800-477-5925

For my third son, Mike
The soul of an artist
The heart of a builder
And for my beloved Tom
Who treasured the unique gifts of all his children.

REED

PROLOGUE

Glacier Ridge, Montana—Twenty Years Previous

Hey now, Frank." Burke Cowley, the white-haired fore-man at the Malloy Ranch, caught his boss, Francis X. Malloy, storming out of the big, sprawling ranch house shared by four generations.

From the look on Frank's face, it was the final straw in a winter that had been filled with tragedy, after the shocking accident on a snowy road that had taken the life of his son, Patrick, and Patrick's beautiful wife, Bernadette, leaving three sons without their loving parents.

"Where are you going in such a hurry?"

"Reed's missing."

"What do you mean, missing?"

"Yancy called him down for supper, and he never answered. Matt and Luke went looking for him. So did Gracie. They searched the house while Colin and I went through the barns. He's nowhere to be found. Colin said the last time he saw Reed he was saddling up old Nell, but that was hours ago. Damned fool kid said he just wanted to be left alone. Colin thinks he was heading up to the range shack on the north ridge, since that's the last place Reed spent time with his pa."

"And Colin couldn't stop him?"

"He tried. You know how hotheaded Reed can be. He dug his heels into Nell's rump and that horse took off like it had a burr under the saddle."

"Hold on. You're not thinking about heading up there now?" Burke held up a hand. "You can see the blizzard heading this way."

"You think I'm blind?" Frank Malloy's eyes burned with a terrible raging passion. "I've already buried a son. I'm not about to lose a grandson, too."

"You get inside. I'll go." The ranch foreman spun around and headed toward the barn, giving his boss no time to argue.

By the time Burke had saddled his horse and bundled into heavy winter gear, Yancy Martin, the ranch cook, stepped inside the barn to hand him several wrapped packages.

"You could be trapped up there a few days. Here are some roast beef sandwiches. Reed's favorites. And a bottle of whiskey for you. To keep from freezing, and hopefully to keep you from throttling that little spitfire when you find him."

"Thanks, Yancy." Burke shoved the supplies into his saddlebags before pulling himself onto the back of his trusty mount, Major.

The cook put a hand on the reins. "I know Reed's done a stupid thing, but he's been missing his folks something awful. It's a heavy load for a kid to bear." He paused. "I know he's a handful, but that ornery kid has a way of sneaking into my heart. You bring Reed home safe, you hear?"

Burke nodded and pulled his wide-brimmed hat low on

his head. Reed may have been rebellious and reckless as hell, but he had that same effect on all of them. Despite all the trouble he could cause, they couldn't help but love him. He had a kind heart, and as his grandmother, Grace Malloy, was fond of saying, he was like an old man in a boy's body. In so many ways, Reed was wise beyond his years.

"You know I will, Yancy. The good Lord willin'."

As horse and rider faced into the storm and started across a high, sloping meadow, the old man found himself thinking about the terrible crash that had happened weeks ago on a night like this. The death of Patrick and his wife, Bernadette, on a snowy Montana road had left a void that would never be filled. Not for the Malloy family, and especially not for Patrick and Bernadette's three sons, twelve-year-old Matt, ten-year-old Luke, and nine-year-old Reed, who were floundering in a world rocked by the sudden, shocking loss of their parents.

"Stay safe, Reed," the old man whispered fiercely. "At least until I can find you and tan your miserable hide."

For hours Major plodded through drifts that were now waist-high, before the outline of a mountain cabin loomed up in the darkness.

Burke unsaddled his horse in the shed behind the range shack, grateful to find Reed's mare, Nell, already contentedly dozing. Tossing the saddlebags over his shoulder, he trudged around and let himself into the cabin, bracing for the encounter to come.

Reed Malloy sat huddled in front of the fireplace, where a couple of stingy tree branches gave off a thin flame. He'd shed his boots, which lay in a puddle of melted snow by the door.

The boy's head came up sharply. Seeing the fire in those

eyes, Burke bit back the oath that sprang to his lips. The last thing the kid needed right now was any more fuel poured on the flame that was burning so hotly in his soul.

Without a word Burke draped the saddlebags over the back of a wooden chair before heading outside, returning with an armload of logs.

"What're you doing here?" Reed's jaw jutted like a prize-fighter's.

"Getting out of the cold." Burke deposited the logs beside the fireplace and set the biggest one over the flame.

Crossing to the table, he tossed aside his parka and began removing the packages from his saddlebags.

When he saw the boy's gaze dart to the wrapped sandwiches, he took his sweet time unwrapping them. He walked to the tiny kitchen counter and filled a coffeepot before placing it on a wire rack over the open fire. Within minutes the little cabin was filled with the rich fragrance of coffee boiling.

"Good place to sit out a storm." Burke glanced over. "You hungry?"

Still frowning, Reed shrugged.

Taking that for an answer, the old man placed the sandwiches on plates and handed one to Reed before settling into a rocker in front of the fire and easing off his boots with a sigh.

For long minutes the two ate without speaking, listening to the hiss and snap of the fire on the grate and the howling of the storm as the wind and snow buffeted the walls of the cabin.

"They sent you here, didn't they?" Reed set aside his empty plate.

"I volunteered. Everyone back home is worried sick." Burke calmly continued eating.

"I don't want you here. I came up here to be alone."

"You could have skipped the drama and just gone up to your room."

"Right. Where I'd have to listen to Matt and Luke jabbering all night long. Luke telling us to just suck it up. Matt telling us we have to put on a good face so we don't add to Grandpop Frank and Gram Gracie's pain. Easy for him to say." Reed hissed in a breath. "But what about us? What about our pain?" He turned away, but not before the old man saw the look of abject misery in his eyes.

The old cowboy took his time, choosing his words carefully. "I know you're scared, son. It's tough that you had to learn the lesson so young. Life's not fair. Never has been. Never will be."

"Gee. Thanks for nothing." Every word sizzled with hot anger.

"I'm not going to sugarcoat things, boy. I won't bother to tell you that pain will go away soon. It won't." Burke heaved a sigh. "But I will tell you that one day you'll wake up thinking about something besides the loss of your ma and pa. Not tomorrow. Not the next day. But one day it will happen. It's the same with all the tears that right now are sticking in your throat, threatening to choke you every time you swallow. One day, out of the blue, you'll find yourself chuckling. Or laughing right out loud. It'll catch you by surprise, but it'll feel good, and you'll do it again. That's the way life is. One day your heart is so broken, you can barely breathe. And the next day, you find a reason to smile. Maybe just a little reason, but it'll be enough to lift you up. And before you know it, you've gone more days smiling than crying."

"I've got no reason to smile. Not now. Not ever."

"You say that now. But you're one of the lucky ones, Reed." Burke turned to the boy. "You've got a powerful love of this ranch, this land, and especially the cattle. I've seen it since you were no bigger'n a pup."

Reed couldn't deny it. He loved this ranch with an all-consuming passion. He loved the land, the cattle, the wildness of this place. And he had dreams. Dreams he'd shared with his parents, of making their herds the healthiest and demanding the highest price ever. The Malloy Ranch would be a name respected around the world. He wasn't sure just how he would make that dream come true, but this much he knew. If being willing to work harder than anybody, if giving up everything others took for granted counted for anything, he would make it all happen.

And the key was the cattle. He didn't know the how or why of it, but the feeling was so strong, he was nearly consumed by it.

But the loss of his parents left him feeling alone and crushed by the weight of his loss.

The boy turned to the old man. "Did you ever lose someone you loved, Burke?"

The foreman stared into the flames, his eyes shrouded in secrets. His voice lowered to almost a whisper. "I have. I've been where you are now, son."

Something in the quiet tone of his voice had the boy holding back any more questions. Instead he sat, absorbing the heat of the fire and the warmth of understanding he could feel vibrating from the tough old man beside him.

Burke Cowley was the man every wrangler on the Malloy Ranch turned to in time of need, whether it was doctoring a sick cow or calming a cowboy during a crisis. He could be as tender as a new mother when treating a wrangler's injuries and as vicious as a wounded bear when crossed by some drunken fool who didn't follow orders. Burke could work circles around every wrangler on the Malloy Ranch and still tend a herd all night in a raging storm. If this tough old cowboy could survive a powerful loss, Reed felt the first tiny flicker of hope that he'd make it through the raw pain that burned like the fires of hell in his heart.

Like the man said, maybe not tomorrow. But one day.

Still, Reed sensed a storm raging inside him. Bigger, stronger than the one raging outside the walls of this cabin. Pa used to say he'd been born with it; it had been there simmering inside him from the moment he gave his first lusty birth cry. Unlike his older brothers—Matt, who was always in control, and Luke, a rolling stone who loved nothing more than a challenge—there was just something inside Reed, the tough, determined youngest of the family, that set him apart.

But first he would have to learn to put aside this terrible grief and tame the temper lurking inside him. He sensed that if he didn't learn to tame it, this emotion could take control, and that he would never allow. If anything, he wanted to be in control of his own destiny.

He knew one thing. Nothing would ever take him from this place and the cattle. Not even the loss of the two people he cherished more than any in the world.

CHAPTER ONE

Malloy Ranch—Present Day

After more than a month in the hills that ringed the ranch, Reed Malloy looked more like a trail bum than a member of a successful ranch family. His hair hung to his shoulders. His face was covered in a rough beard. His clothes were filthy.

He unsaddled his mount, tossing the saddle over the rail of the stall before filling troughs with feed and water. In the stall alongside him, his uncle, Colin Malloy, did the same.

That done, the two men trudged toward the house, noting the line of trucks.

"As usual," Colin said with a laugh, "I see Matt and Luke and their wives manage to never miss a meal."

Both of Reed's older brothers were building homes on Malloy land and currently divided their time between the new construction and the family ranch. The bulk of their time was still spent here, but because of the size of the ranch, nobody felt crowded.

Reed was grinning at the noise level as he scraped his

boots before stepping into the mudroom. He hung his jacket and hat on hooks by the door and rolled his sleeves before pausing to wash up at the big sink.

In the doorway he stood watching as the familiar scene unfolded. Yancy Martin, ranch cook, was lifting a pan of cinnamon biscuits from the oven. The wonderful fragrance filled the room.

Reed's grandparents, Frank and Gracie, were seated on a sofa across the room, sipping coffee. His great-grandfather, Nelson LaRou, a once-famous Hollywood director, now retired, who was called Great One by all the family, seemed to be enjoying the heated conversation between Matt and Luke, who were standing nose-to-nose while arguing over the best grazing lands. Matt's wife, Vanessa, and Luke's recent bride, Ingrid, along with Ingrid's little sister, Lily, continued setting platters on the big trestle table, oblivious to the noise. Malloy Ranch foreman Burke Cowley stood to one side, grinning and sipping his coffee, without saying a word.

Matt turned to Reed. "Finally, somebody with a brain. Tell Luke what you told me about the south ridge pasture."

Reed crossed the room and helped himself to a mug of steaming coffee. "Sorry. It's been a long morning. While you guys were still thinking about getting out of bed, Colin and I made the long trek from the hills after riding herd on a bunch of ornery cows for the past month. My backside aches, my stomach is grumbling, and I'm not getting dragged into a family feud."

"We're not feuding. Hell," Luke muttered, "if we were, fists would be flying."

"Not in my kitchen." Yancy drained a platter of crisp bacon and handed it to Ingrid.

The others merely chuckled.

"We're having a...lively discussion." Matt set down his mug with a clatter.

"And I'm having breakfast before I starve." Reed turned to Yancy. "Is it ready?"

"All ready." Yancy began tossing flapjacks onto a huge plate. "Get it while it's hot."

As one, the family began gathering around the big table, with Frank and Gracie at one end and Great One at the other. Matt and Vanessa, Luke and Ingrid sat on one side, and Lily, Reed, and Yancy on the other.

Ingrid's sister, nine-year-old Lily Larsen, had adopted Great One as her very own grandfather and glowed whenever she looked at him. The old man accepted her hero worship as a sacred trust and had completely lost his heart to this tough little tomboy.

As they passed the platters of bacon, scrambled eggs, flapjacks and syrup, as well as toast and cinnamon biscuits, the conversation turned, as always, to the family business.

Frank turned to Reed. "I'm surprised you'd leave the herd in the middle of the season. How did Colin pry you away?"

Reed took a moment to savor Yancy's light-as-air pancakes before turning toward the ranch foreman. "Burke sent word that if I didn't take a break soon, he'd hog-tie me and haul my..." A glance at his grandmother had him pausing to remember where he was. He might swear like a wrangler when up in the hills, but here at home, he was respectful. He added lamely, "He'd haul my hide down the mountain himself."

Frank turned to Burke. "What's this about? You know it's do-or-die time for Reed."

"True," the foreman said. "But even a dedicated cattleman needs time away from his herd so he doesn't forget how to be civilized."

Luke looked up. "Are you saying our little brother is going caveman on us?"

At his remark, the others laughed.

Burke nodded. "Take a look at him. Hair to his shoulders. Beard longer than Father Time's. He's been spending so much time in the hills, I wasn't sure he was even human. So I suggested he take a few days here. I'm sure the wranglers can keep his precious herd safe that long."

Reed ducked his head and continued eating.

It was no secret that he was pinning a lot of hope on a herd he was raising on the north ridge, using no antibiotics to enhance their growth and feeding them only range grass. Since he'd begun experimenting with his special herd back in his teens, he'd never once seen a profit. In fact, if it hadn't been for the family picking up the cost, he would have had to give up on his dream years ago.

But now, he was feeling even greater pressure to succeed.

On his last trip to Italy, Matt, the family's designated business manager, had managed to swing a deal with Leone Industries, a successful, well-respected multinational conglomerate. They were willing to take a chance on the fledgling green industry, hoping to corner the market on naturally raised beef. For the first time since he'd begun his project, all Reed's years of backbreaking work promised to pay off. Not only could he repay the debt he owed his family, but he could also bring their already successful ranch business into the future.

"They're looking healthy." He turned to his uncle, who'd accompanied him on his predawn ride. "Wouldn't you say so?"

Colin nodded. "We did the usual weigh-in, to see if they're keeping up with the herd getting antibiotics and enhanced feed. So far, they're matching pound for pound."

"That's great." Frank turned to Matt. "Think they'll be ready for shipment after roundup?"

"If Reed says they'll be ready, they will be." Matt smiled at his wife. "Maybe Nessa and I will go along to make sure they arrive safely."

"Very noble of you, bro." Reed nudged Yancy, and the two shared a grin. "I'm sure, while you're in Rome, you'll be forced to spend some time at Maria's villa and sip a few bottles of her family's wine." At the mention of their family's friends and clients in Rome, Vittorio and Maria, the family smiled.

"Just to be sociable," Matt deadpanned.

Around the table, everyone shared in the joke. Matt had been promising his wife a trip to Italy when their new house was completed. And in truth, no one else was willing to volunteer. Most of them preferred life on the ranch to international travel, even if that travel meant enjoying some exotic perks.

"I need someone to drive me into town today," Great One announced.

"What time?" Reed helped himself to seconds.

"Noon. I have an appointment with"—the old man stared pointedly at Colin—"Dr. Anita Cross. She wants to check my heart."

Colin knew his family was determined to find out all they could about his romance with the town's pretty young doctor. He was just as determined to keep that part of his life to himself. At least for the time being. And so he deflected Great One's comments with a joke. "Did you tell her you don't have one?"

At Colin's comment, the others chuckled.

"This is your last chance to have an excuse to see Dr. Anita, sonny boy."

"Sorry, Great One." Colin shook his head. "You know I'll take any excuse to spend time with her, but it's my turn to take up the Cessna."

The family routinely flew across their land to check on herds, outbuildings, and far-flung wranglers, to assess anything that might need their attention.

Reed polished off the last of his eggs. "I don't mind driving you, Great One. While you're seeing the good doctor, I'll load up on supplies and maybe even stop by the Pig Sty and have a longneck with the locals." He shot a grin at Burke. "Is that civilized enough for you?"

"Just so you don't spoil your appetite for supper." Yancy circled the table topping off cups of coffee. "I'm planning on grilling steaks."

"With your special twice-baked potatoes, I hope." Frank reached for a pitcher of maple syrup.

"You bet." Yancy ruffled Lily's hair before adding, "And chocolate torte for the ladies."

Grace was all smiles. "You just said the magic word, Yancy."

"I thought that'd make you happy, Miss Grace."

Later, as breakfast wound down and the family members made ready for the day, Luke elbowed his younger brother. "I suggest you shave and have Yancy cut that hair before you go to town, or nobody will recognize you. But I'm glad you're the one stuck taking Great One to town. I'd rather watch paint dry than have to spend hours twiddling my thumbs in Glacier Ridge." He shook his head as he turned away muttering, "Nothing ever happens in that place."

Reed halted the ranch truck next to the entrance of the Glacier Ridge Clinic and hopped out, circling around to the passenger side to assist his great-grandfather.

After breakfast he'd taken a seat in the yard while Yancy gave him a haircut, a chore the ranch cook had gladly taken on since Reed and his brothers were kids. Then Reed had shaved his beard before taking the longest shower of his life.

Burke had been right, he thought. He was feeling almost human again.

The minute they stepped inside the clinic, the medical assistant, Agnes, hurried over. "Hello, Mr. LaRou. Dr. Anita told me to take you into exam room one."

She turned to Reed.

"I'll call you when Dr. Cross is finished here."

He patted the old man's shoulder. "Have fun."

Great One slanted him a look. "Don't I always?"

Reed was grinning as he climbed into the truck and drove slowly through town. Knowing Great One, he'd soon have the entire staff mesmerized with his inside stories of Hollywood's rich and famous.

He spotted a vacant parking slot halfway between the diner and Trudy Evans's shop, Anything Goes. Minutes later he started walking up the street, enjoying the sunny day as he glanced in the windows of all the buildings that made up the little town of Glacier Ridge.

He paused to wave a greeting at one of the customers in Snips, the local beauty and barber shop, and almost missed the blur of motion that dashed past him and darted into the street.

He was still grinning, but his smile was wiped away when he realized that the blur was a red-haired little boy wearing a superhero cape, legs pumping, arms swinging as he raced headlong into the middle of Main Street.

"Hey. Hold on there." Reed dashed after the little guy and scooped him up just as a driver in a delivery truck leaned on his horn and veered to one side, barely missing the boy.

Reed's heart was thundering when he realized how close he'd come to witnessing a tragedy.

He carried the boy to the curb before kneeling down, still holding on to his wriggling bundle. "Didn't your mother teach you to stop and look both ways?"

"Mama?" The boy shoved round owl glasses up the freckled bridge of his nose and looked around with a puzzled frown.

"Yes. Your mama. Where is she?"

Suddenly the sunny smile was wiped from the cherubic little face, and the boy looked close to tears. "I want my mama."

"Yeah. So do I." Now that the danger had passed, Reed's famous temper flared. What kind of mother let her kid run wild? "Now let's find her."

When the little guy tried to wrench his hand free, Reed picked him up to keep him from dashing back into the street. As he walked along the sidewalk, he was peering into the window of each shop.

Within minutes a young woman sailed out of the doorway of a shop, her eyes wide with fear. "Kyle. Kyle. Where are...?"

Seeing her son in the arms of a stranger had the words dying in her throat.

"What are you doing with my...? Where did you...?"

"In the middle of the street. Isn't he a bit young to be running loose without someone looking out for him?"

Reed hadn't meant to be so harsh, but the thought of what could have happened had the words spilling out in a much rougher tone than he intended.

"My fault completely." She held out her arms and Reed handed the boy over.

She buried her face in the boy's hair. "Oh, Kyle. You scared the wits out of me."

Reed studied the mother and son. It was easy to see where the little boy got his hair. Hers was a tangle of wild copper curls, falling past her shoulders and framing a face so pretty he couldn't stop staring.

"I was flying, Mama."

"Yes. I see. But you know better than to go in the street."

"Cars can't hurt me when I'm Super Kid."

She took in a deep, shaky breath. "That's what I get for going along with your game." Over his head she met Reed's disapproving look. "Thank you. I'm grateful you were there to save him. I'm Allison Shaw—Ally—and this is my son, Kyle. He's four."

"I'm almost five," the little boy corrected.

"He's almost five." She stuck out her hand and Reed was forced to accept her handshake, though he was still feeling less than cheerful about a mother who let her kid tempt fate.

"I guess almost five can be an...imaginative age."

"If his imagination was any stronger, I'd have to clone myself to keep up."

That brought a grudging smile to Reed's lips. Or maybe it was the tingle along his arm when their hands met. The rush of heat caught him by surprise.

"I'm sure he keeps you on your toes." He released her hand. "I'm Reed Malloy. Are you and Kyle new in town?"

She nodded. "We moved here from Virginia. I'm opening a business"—she pointed to the sign over a tiny shop that read ALLY'S ATTIC—"and Kyle and I are staying with my uncle. Maybe you know him. Archer Stone."

"Yeah, I know Archer. Sheriff Graystoke's deputy. I didn't know the town's bachelor had family."

"I think we're his only family. I know he's all we have. He was my mother's brother."

Was. Reed didn't bother to ask more. He was well

acquainted with family that was here and then gone in the blink of an eye.

"Come on, Kyle. Time to get back to work." She set down her son and kept his hand firmly in hers as she started toward the shop.

Reed moved along beside them. "What sort of business is Ally's Attic?"

"It's a consignment shop. People can bring in things they have that still work but they have no room or use for. They can set a price, or let me set what I think is a fair price. I get a percentage of each item I sell. It's also a swap shop. For a fee, I can arrange for folks to trade something they have for something they want in my shop."

They stepped inside, and Reed looked around at the neat shelves, the clever presentations of items already listed for sale or trade.

Ally pointed. "Like that piano in the window display. Clara McEvoy brought it in yesterday. Her husband and son-in-law delivered it, saying she was glad to be rid of it. No one's touched it since her daughter grew up and moved away. Just this morning, even though we don't officially open until Saturday, a woman knocked on the door and left her card with a promise to be back after school today to pay me. Besides teaching here at the school, she wants to teach music in her home, and this piano is the answer to her prayers. She wanted to lock in the sale before anybody else even had a chance to see it."

"Looks like you're doing the folks in town a service, while making money doing it."

She smiled. "That's the plan. I certainly hope so. I really need this to work out for us."

Us.

Reed cleared his throat. "So, is your husband helping?"

"I don't have a—"

Kyle tugged on his mother's leg. "I'm hungry."

Reed looked from the little boy to his mother. If he'd heard correctly, she'd been about to say she didn't have a husband. For some reason he didn't want to probe too deeply, that comment had his heart lifting.

Ally glanced at the clock on the wall. "Oh, honey, I'm sorry. I got so busy, I forgot all about lunch. Come on. I'll fix some peanut butter and jelly sandwiches."

Before she could catch his hand, Reed blurted, "I'm thinking about lunch, too. Have you eaten at D and B's Diner?"

The minute the words were out of his mouth, he regretted them. Apparently his mouth was working ahead of his brain. Or what little brain he had at the moment.

Ally shook her head. "We haven't had time to visit any of the businesses here in town yet. We've been too busy cleaning and stocking the store. It's easier and a lot cheaper to just catch a snack here."

He noted her flush of embarrassment. "Well then, it's time you met the town newspaper."

At her arched brow he explained, "Dot and Barb. The twin sisters who own D and B's. They know everything that happens around Glacier Ridge almost as soon as it happens, and they're more than happy to share the news with their eager customers. In fact, just as many folks come in for the gossip as for their famous sandwiches, pot roast, and pie."

Though she was laughing, she shook her head. "Thanks for the invitation, but I can't…"

"My treat." He stared pointedly at Kyle. "Besides, it saves you from having to fix lunch. You can save the peanut butter and jelly for tomorrow."

Kyle looked up. "Do they have grilled cheese?"

Reed nodded. "In fact, it's one of my favorites."

"Oh, boy." He turned pleading eyes toward his mother. "Please, Mama."

She sighed. "All right." She caught his hand and trailed Reed from the shop.

As they started along the sidewalk, she added, "You had me at not having to fix lunch."

Reed grinned. "And here I thought it was my charm."

CHAPTER TWO

When Reed stepped inside the diner alongside Ally and Kyle, he was greeted by Dot Parker, who gave one of her famous throaty wolf whistles.

"Well, now, don't you look just as handsome as ever, Reed Malloy. Where've you been keeping yourself?"

"I'm spending a lot of time up in the hills with the herd."

"Ranchers. If it isn't spring calving, it's summer grazing, or fall roundup. Then, just as you catch your breath, the seasons start all over again."

Dot, her white hair pulled back in a bun, a polka-dot handkerchief pinned to the pocket of her pink dress, turned to give Ally a long, slow appraisal. "I'm not surprised Reed discovered our newest citizen of Glacier Ridge. This cowboy just seems to be a magnet for every pretty woman in Montana."

"Dot, this is Ally Shaw. And this is her son, Kyle."

"Hey, pretty Ally. And you, little guy, are as sweet-looking as your mama. I was hoping I'd get to meet you soon."

"Ally is opening a shop called Ally's Attic."

"I already heard all about it. And all about you," Dot added to Ally. "I hear you're staying with your uncle, Archer Stone. Hard to believe that cranky bachelor would put up with a niece and her young son."

"Not for long. As soon as I can clean the upper rooms of my shop, Kyle and I will be living there." Ally noted the way everyone in the diner was hanging on her every word.

"Come on. I'll show you to your table." Dot led the way, keeping up a running commentary as she did.

Reed threaded his way slowly among the diners, stopping to greet and chat with most of the regulars. All of them had a smile and a handshake for one of the area's favorite cowboys.

Over her shoulder Dot called, "Folks can't wait for your grand opening on Saturday. They're dying to see all the stuff their neighbors are willing to part with. I don't know how much of it you'll be able to sell, but I'm betting your shop will be full of nosy neighbors eager to see everybody else's rejects."

Dot stopped at a table in the corner of the little restaurant.

"I never think of them as rejects," Ally said sweetly. "One man's junk is another man's treasure. In fact, before coming up with the name Ally's Attic, I'd intended to call my shop Junk-to-Treasure, but I was afraid any reference to junk could turn buyers off."

"Yeah. It's catchy," Dot said with a laugh. "But I like the name you finally decided on better."

"Hey there, handsome cowboy." Dot's twin sister, Barb, looked through the kitchen pass-through where she was working the grill. Instead of the polka dots favored by her sister, she wore pink overalls with a pink checked shirt, the sleeves rolled above her elbows, her hair tied back with a pink bandana. "The specials today are my famous grilled three-cheese on sourdough and fresh apple pie."

"You just told me what I'm having." Reed winked at her as he held a chair for Ally.

Kyle scrambled up on the opposite chair and was kneeling to reach the table.

"Kyle, too. Right?" Reed winked at the boy. "He said the only thing he wants is grilled cheese."

"Then this is your lucky day, Kyle." Dot was smiling broadly as she handed him a coloring book and a box of crayons. "Would you like a high chair?"

The little boy looked horrified. "Those are for babies. I'm almost five."

"Oh. Sorry. What was I thinking?" Dot chuckled as she turned to Ally. "How about you? Want the special sandwich, or something more substantial?"

"I guess I'll have the same as Reed and Kyle. My son will also have a glass of milk, and I'll have a cup of tea."

"You got it." Dot turned to Reed. "Coffee for you, or the usual?"

"The usual." Reed glanced at Kyle, busy coloring. "And you'd better bring a spare glass. Once a certain someone sees it, he'll want to share."

Dot walked away, returning minutes later with small bowls of coleslaw, Ally's tea, and Kyle's milk.

When she was gone, Reed looked across the table. "I told you Dot and Barb don't miss much. If you asked, they could probably tell you where you last lived, for how long, and why you decided to settle in Glacier Ridge."

She smiled. "They're hardly secrets. I lived in Virginia."

"With Kyle's father?"

"Rick is..." She swallowed and tried again. "Rick was a Marine."

Reed saw the glint of military dog tags at Kyle's throat.

Seeing the direction of his gaze, she nodded. "His third tour in Afghanistan ended...suddenly." She shot a quick look at her son, pleased that he was absorbed in the coloring book. "I want Kyle to wear those in honor of the father he doesn't remember."

"I'm sorry."

She nodded and fell silent as Dot began passing around plates of grilled cheese sandwiches, pickles, and thick steak fries.

When she set a tall, frosty chocolate milk shake in front of Reed, Kyle looked up, his eyes behind the glasses suddenly as big as saucers.

Before he could even ask his mother, Reed was pouring some in the empty glass Dot provided.

"I don't think your mom will mind, as long as you drink your milk, too."

The boy struggled to slurp up the milk shake through a straw and finally gave up, using a spoon instead.

Ally laughed as she wiped at his chocolate mustache. "Now try a little of your sandwich."

Taking her own advice, she tasted hers, then looked at Reed. "This is really good."

"Yeah. Dot and Barb have had a lifetime to get it right." He nibbled a fry. "What did you do in Virginia?"

"I worked for a security firm."

"That sounds like a big deal."

She smiled. "I was just one insignificant worker bee in a huge hive. And when Rick..." She gave a shrug. "I realized I wanted something..." She shook her head, searching for the words. "Something not so big and impersonal. Kyle has been in day care since he was born. With all that's happened, I just want to make a satisfying life for him. I'm hoping living near my only family member, in the comfort of a small town, will make a difference."

Seeing that Kyle was now listening, Reed turned his attention to the boy. "So. What do you think of D and B's grilled cheese?"

"It's good." The boy drained the last of his shake. "But not as good as this." He turned to his mother. "Can I have some more?"

"Let's see if you still want some after you drink that glass of milk."

The boy picked it up and started drinking. But by the time it was half empty, he set it aside. "My tummy's full."

"That's a good thing. There's always tomorrow."

"Can I have more milk shake then?"

She was chuckling. "We'll see."

Reed winked at the little boy. "When mothers say that, it means I hope by tomorrow he forgets all about it."

Kyle looked at his mother. "Is Reed right?"

Now she was laughing out loud. "I'm not about to share all my mom secrets with you. And you"—she turned to Reed—"are old enough to know better."

"Yes, ma'am." He winked again at Kyle. "We'll talk later. I know a lot of mom secrets."

The little boy covered his mouth and giggled.

When their plates were empty, Dot walked over and cleared the table. "Ready for that pie?"

Reed and Ally nodded.

Dot picked up Kyle's plate. "I know most little boys don't care much for pie. How about some cherry gelatin?"

"Okay, I guess." He glanced at his mother. "Will I like it, or is it just something that's 'posed to be good for me?"

That had the adults laughing.

Ally was still grinning. "Why don't we wait and see what you think?"

Minutes later, as she and Reed dug into apple pie with a dollop of vanilla ice cream, Kyle tentatively tasted his gelatin topped with a spoonful of whipped cream.

He looked up, smiling broadly. "This is good."

"Well, then." Ally bit back the smile that threatened. "I guess I won't bother trying to tell you it's good for you."

"'Cause you'd be teasing, huh, Mama?"

She gave a shrug of her shoulders and shared a knowing smile with Reed.

When Dot slid the bill on the table, Reed placed some money on top of it and handed it to her.

"How was everything?"

"Best grilled cheese ever." He lowered his voice. "You realize you're sworn to secrecy. Yancy can never know I said that."

The two shared a laugh before Dot turned to Ally and Kyle. "I hope we'll see you here again. Don't be strangers."

"Thanks, Dot. We'll be back."

"And Barb and I will make it over to your shop on grand opening day. Like everybody else in town, we're dying to see what our neighbors have been hoarding for years and are now willing to part with."

"Maybe you have a few things of your own you'd like me to sell or trade."

Dot's brow lifted. "You could be right. There's this fancy little chest my aunt gave me when I was just a girl. She called it a handkerchief chest, and Barb and I have used it for jewelry through the years. But the drawers are too small for anything but a few pieces of jewelry, and it's more suited to a little girl than the two of us. It's just taking up space in a spare bedroom. I think I'll see if Barb is ready to let it go."

"You could make some little girl in Glacier Ridge really happy next Christmas."

At Ally's words, Dot gave a nod of her head. "I think you just said the magic words."

As Reed and Ally and Kyle walked to the door, Dot was already in the kitchen area, her head bent close to her twin sister.

Reed held the door and trailed Ally and Kyle back to her shop.

As they walked, Ally turned to him. "Who is Yancy?"

"Our ranch cook."

"You have a cook?"

"And a butler, and a maid, and..." Seeing the look on her face, he burst into laughter. "Just kidding. But Yancy Martin has been our cook for a lifetime. He's considered one of the family."

Once inside, he gave a last look around before stepping back toward the door. "I think you may be on to something here. If Dot's excited, she'll have every one of her customers sharing that excitement. You'd better prepare for a run on sales when you hold your grand opening."

As he started to push open the door, Ally put a hand over his. "Thank you for lunch, Reed. And a huge thank you for catching Kyle before any harm came to him."

"You're welcome." He looked beyond her to where the little boy was busy running a toy truck along a strip of plastic highway through a plastic town. "Bye, Kyle. See you."

The boy looked over and shoved his glasses up the bridge of his nose. "Yeah. See you. I liked the milk shake. I even liked the...gela..."

"Gelatin," Ally prompted.

"Yeah." He returned his attention to his toys.

Reed was grinning. "You might want to keep this door locked until your grand opening. Or at least keep any Super Kid capes out of sight when your back is turned."

"I like the way you think." Her smile was bright enough to light up the room. "Thanks again."

Reed paused outside as Ally turned the lock in the door, ensuring that Kyle wouldn't wander away again. He watched as she began tackling the contents of a fresh box of items for her store before he sauntered down the sidewalk.

What had started out to be a dull day had turned into something quite different than he'd anticipated. Because of Ally and Kyle Shaw.

"Hey, sonny boy." Great One looked over his shoulder when Reed walked into the clinic. Both Agnes and the two doctors, Leonard Cross and his niece, Anita Cross, were laughing at something the old man had been telling them.

"Did you find his heart?" Reed called as he strolled over.

"Ha." Nelson LaRou gave a shake of his head. "See the disrespect I get from this generation?"

"They love you. We all do." Old Dr. Cross turned to Reed. "We not only found your great-grandfather's heart, but we've decided that it's healthier than mine too."

"Exactly what I predicted. When do you want to see me again?" Great One addressed the question to both doctors, since they worked as a team.

"I think six months." Dr. Anita glanced at her uncle for confirmation, and he nodded in agreement.

"Thanks, Docs." Reed took hold of Nelson's arm as they started toward the exit.

Once in the truck, Reed headed out of town before turning onto the interstate.

Nelson stretched out his legs and turned to study his great-grandson. "Did you tip a longneck or two at the Pig Sty?"

Reed shook his head. "I never got that far."

As quickly as possible, he told Nelson about his horror at seeing a little boy dashing into the street and how they found his mother racing along the sidewalk, looking absolutely terrified when she'd discovered her four-year-old missing from her shop.

"What sort of shop?"

"It's a consignment shop she's calling Ally's Attic. She takes the things folks no longer want or need and sells them for a commission or offers them in trade for something of equal value."

"Sounds like a clever girl."

"Yeah. She seems really smart and ambitious."

"I take it she's pretty."

"What makes you think so?"

The old man shrugged. "It's the tone of your voice when you talked about her. And the way your face lit up. So, when do you plan on seeing her again?"

"Who says I will?"

"I'd put money on it, sonny boy."

Reed broke into laughter. "You think you're so smart, Great One."

"Smart enough to know my great-grandson." He paused a beat. "Did you have lunch?"

"Yeah. I took Ally and Kyle to D and B's Diner."

Nelson chuckled. "I'm proud of you. You don't let any grass grow under your feet."

"Yeah." Just thinking about Ally Shaw had Reed putting on his sunglasses, hoping to hide the gleam in his eye. "Just a chip off the old block. I had a good teacher."

"That you did, sonny boy. That you did. I was quite the ladies' man in my day. That is, until I met my Madeline. After that, it was all over. No woman could even come close."

He closed his eyes and nodded off with a smile on his face.

Watching him, Reed grinned.

This day had turned out a whole lot better than he'd expected.

And all because of a daring, freckled super kid in glasses.

And his gorgeous mom.

CHAPTER THREE

I'm tired, Mama."

At Kyle's words, Ally paused in her walk along the sidewalk to glance at her son. As he flopped down on a patch of hot concrete, her heart went out to him. The day had been long, and he'd been so good. Well, except for that lapse when he'd run into the street in his cape, thinking he was invincible. Thank heavens for the kindness of Reed Malloy.

Reed Malloy. He'd been sneaking into her thoughts a lot today. When she'd seen a tall, darkly handsome cowboy striding toward her, holding firmly to her son, her heart had done a funny little dance. A reaction to fear, she told herself. Still, she couldn't help being impressed by the way Dot Parker and her sister had acted like fangirls over him at lunch. Or the way everyone in the diner had greeted him like a long-lost friend.

Not to mention the easy way he had with Kyle.

In his young life there hadn't been any men who would go out of their way for a busy, curious four-year-old.

"Can you carry me, Mama?"

Ally sighed. Between her shoulder bag stuffed with Kyle's toys and the bag of groceries in her arms, there was no way she could lift him.

Still, the look on his face nearly broke her heart.

She knelt down. "Climb on my back and I'll be your trusty steed." It was a game she and her son often played.

He eagerly did as she said, wrapping his chubby arms around her neck.

"Now hang on tight, honey." She wobbled to her feet, struggling to balance the additional weight before getting her bearings. She continued on toward her uncle's house.

"Can I have another milk shake tonight?"

"Afraid not. We're eating healthy. But I'll think about it tomorrow."

"Reed said when moms say that, it means they hope their kids forget about it."

"Reed should keep some thoughts to himself."

"Maybe we'll see Reed tomorrow and he'll share his milk shake again."

"Maybe." And wouldn't that be lovely? It occurred to Ally that running into Reed Malloy had been the bright spot of her very long and challenging day.

As she started up the walk to her uncle's house, she sighed. "It doesn't look like anybody's home yet."

"Maybe Uncle Archer will be at work." Her son's tone sounded hopeful, and she thought again how difficult it had to be for Kyle, coming to a brand-new place and being made to feel that he was somehow in the way.

If only Archer would cut her son a little slack. Ever since they'd arrived here in Glacier Ridge, her uncle had let her know that he didn't want to see any of Kyle's antics, or hear him whine, or have to deal with him in any way.

Invisible.

That was the term Archer had used. *Just make sure the kid is invisible when I'm around.*

Though she'd been the one to initiate a renewal of family relations after a lifetime of separation, Archer had seemed to be on board with it. At least in their earlier exchange of letters.

Now, after only weeks here in Glacier Ridge, she could feel the tension building within her uncle.

She hoped by the end of another week she could have the upper floor of the shop cleaned out, so she and Kyle could have their own private apartment.

Maybe then, once Archer had his space to himself, he would relax, and they could become the family she yearned for.

Family.

It meant everything to Ally. She wanted, more than anything, for Kyle to be part of a loving family.

On the porch she knelt down and waited for Kyle to climb off her back. Setting aside the purse and bag, she fitted her key in the lock. Before she could turn it, the door swung open.

Inside, she could hear the sounds of Kenny Rogers's mellow voice crooning about his lady pouring from Archer's main-floor bedroom. Her uncle seemed stuck on music from the eighties. And all of it sad love songs with haunting melodies and lyrics about broken hearts.

"Looks like your uncle's home, honey." She picked up her burden and started toward the kitchen, with Kyle trailing behind.

At her words, he seemed to have a meltdown. "I'm hot, Mama."

"I know. I am, too. If you'd like, take off your sweaty shirt and I'll get you a clean one."

As she walked through the house, she turned on lights and opened windows, hoping to chase the gloom. No wonder the rooms were hot and stuffy. Because her uncle worked long hours, the house was always closed up.

She couldn't fault Archer for his taste. It was a bachelor's house, with dark walls, heavy, oversize furniture, and scarred wooden floors. The kitchen had a metal table and four chairs, out-of-date appliances that, thankfully, worked, and cupboards and drawers with a few missing handles and pulls.

But he'd permitted her and a very active four-year-old to move in and disrupt his comfortable existence, and for that she would be forever grateful.

After setting Kyle up in a corner of the kitchen with his trucks, she searched through a basket of clean clothes atop the dryer until she found a T-shirt. Sorting and folding their laundry would have to wait until after they ate.

She opened the grocery bag and began cutting fresh chicken into strips, along with peppers, zucchini, broccoli, and cauliflower.

Soon the kitchen was filled with the wonderful fragrance of stir-fry.

Down the hall the music abruptly ended. Minutes later Archer's voice could be heard swearing a blue streak. He stormed into the kitchen, hair rumpled, eyes heavy-lidded, and Ally realized he'd been sleeping through the din.

"Hi." She looked up with a smile. "How was your—"

He held up Kyle's damp, dirty shirt. In his other hand was the chain containing Rick's dog tags. "What did I tell you about leaving stuff lying around?"

Kyle hurried over to stand beside his mother.

"Don't hide behind your mother's skirts, you little—"

Ally held up a hand. "This is my fault. I told him—"

"Don't you dare defend that kid."

"Archer, he's only four..."

"When I was his age, your mother was sixteen. She was tough as nails. Unlike you, she didn't make excuses for me. She expected me to be as tough as her."

"She'd just lost her mother..."

"Yeah, we'd both lost our mother. I may have been only four, but my big sister was old enough to boss me around and pretend she was in charge. She had no right. She wasn't my mother."

The barely controlled fury in Archer's tone shocked Ally.

"I know it was hard. You were both just kids."

"One of us was a kid. The other was a slut."

"Archer, that's my mother. Please..."

"Yeah, well, the more she tried to boss me, the more I showed her I was my own boss. When she finally left Glacier Ridge, I never even said good-bye. Just good riddance."

Ally knew that Archer's relationship with her mother, his older sister, had ended badly and that the two had never spoken again. But now, as the two remaining survivors, Ally had convinced herself that she and Archer would be able to put aside the past and forge a new and loving relationship. But each day under his roof was proving to be harder than the day before. Did he see his sister every time he looked at her? Could that be the reason for his deep-seated anger?

Archer smugly pointed to the drop of blood on the floor at his feet as proof of his righteousness. "Thanks to your kid's carelessness, I stepped on the edge of this piece of metal and cut myself." He turned the full power of his fury on Kyle. "And all because you can't pick up after yourself, boy." He hurled the shirt and dog tags at Kyle, missing him by mere inches. "Next time you forget, you won't get them back. I'll lock them in my room, and they'll be mine."

"They're mine." In a rare display of bravado, the little boy's eyes flashed behind the glasses. "They were my daddy's."

"You keep them where they belong or you don't see them again. They'll be mine forever. You understand?"

"Yes." Kyle's lower lip quivered as he snatched up his father's dog tags and clutched them to his chest.

"And don't you dare cry like a girl."

Archer turned his furious gaze on Ally. "As for you, I expect the kid's mother to handle a few simple rules. And the first one is this: pick up after yourselves."

"I'll remember." Ally nodded toward the stove, hoping to soften his temper. "Would you like some supper? I made chicken stir-fry." She turned toward the cupboard. "I'll get some plates."

Archer crossed the room and lifted the lid on a pot of cooked rice, and then on the skillet of chicken and vegetables. "This looks disgusting."

"Oh. Sorry. I didn't know you don't like stir-fry."

"Never tasted it. If it isn't plain and simple, I'm not interested. I like to see what I'm eating. I can't stomach mush." He turned away. "You two can eat that slop. I'm heading over to Clay's Pig Sty for some real food."

When Ally looked over to make a comment, the doorway was empty. Her uncle had already stormed away. Minutes later she heard the front door slam.

Knowing she and Kyle were alone, she let out a deep sigh.

After setting the table, she turned. "Go wash up, honey, and we'll eat."

The little boy slunk out of the room.

When he returned, the tight, pinched look of fear was wiped from his sweet face. With Archer gone, he was his sunny little self, with no thought to the earlier ugly scene.

He climbed up onto a chair and dug into his dinner.

"I like chicken stir-fry, Mama."

"Me too." She watched as he ate the vegetables without complaint. From the time he was a toddler, she'd made sure to introduce him to a variety of foods and flavors. He was more familiar with fruits and vegetables than he was with sweets.

"More milk?"

He nodded, and she filled his glass.

He drank before wiping the back of his hand across his milk mustache. "When I'm big, I'm going to drink a chocolate milk shake every day."

"You might want to think about one a week."

"Why?"

"I'm not sure it's healthy to have one every day."

He thought about it a moment. "Is it healthy to eat bananas every day?"

"I don't think it would hurt."

"Then why not milk shakes?"

"That's a good question." She laughed. "I wish I had a good answer. But I just think that much ice cream every day might not be good for you."

"But if it is"—he finished the last of his stir-fry—"then could I have one every day?"

Ally sighed. Why did kids seem to fixate on the very things parents would rather forget? She gave a shake of her head. "I wish Reed Malloy had never introduced you to D and B's chocolate milk shakes."

"I'm glad he did. Reed's nice."

"Yes, he is."

"Nicer than Uncle Archer."

Ally held her silence.

"Think we'll see Reed tomorrow?"

"I guess we'll just have to wait and see." Ally pushed away from the table and set the kettle on the stove.

"I'm done, Mama. Can I play with my trucks?"

"Yes. But just until I finish my tea. Then you and I are heading upstairs. We've both had a long day."

"Are you going to read the rest of the story you started yesterday?"

"If I can stay awake long enough."

"That's what you said yesterday."

She ruffled his hair. "I know. But you were asleep before me."

"I'll stay awake tonight."

"We'll see."

"Reed said that means—"

She burst into laughter. "I know what Reed said. Now I'm really going to make him pay for revealing a mom secret."

Kyle was grinning as he returned to his trucks in the corner of the kitchen.

As Ally poured boiling water into her cup, she studied her son, so innocent, so willing to put aside that angry scene and play, as though it had never happened.

She stared out the window at the growing darkness. Here in Montana, far from the bustling city she'd always called home, everything seemed so different. So much open space. And the night sky. Without all the neon, it seemed bigger. Closer. The moon and stars so bright, so defined, she felt as though she could reach out and touch them.

That ought to give her comfort, but the truth was, all this space and lack of people frightened her.

When she'd left her former life behind, severing ties with

the people she'd worked with, the neighbors she'd known for a lifetime, she'd expected to feel alone and lonely. And at times, she did. But she hadn't expected to feel so alienated from everything that was familiar and comfortable.

She couldn't complain. For the most part, she'd been quickly embraced by the good people in Glacier Ridge.

All except her uncle.

It seemed odd that her only living relative would be the one to make her feel like an intruder.

He had every right, she reminded herself. He'd carved out a comfortable life for himself.

He was a respected deputy in the sheriff's department. He had buddies to hang out with at the local saloon. And his neighbors had known him since he was a boy.

If he seemed set in his ways, that was his right.

She and Kyle needed to get out of his way as quickly as possible.

She walked away and returned with the laundry basket, quickly sorting and folding their clothes. She set Archer's things in a neat pile atop the dryer and picked up the rest. "Okay, buddy. Time to take a bath and get ready for bed. Let's go."

As she trailed her little boy up the stairs, she came to a decision. Once the grand opening was out of the way, she would put as much energy as possible into cleaning out the upper floor of her shop. She wasn't going to wait another week. She would move in within days, even if it meant doing without a few necessities for a while.

That way, Archer would have his old way of life back. And she and Kyle could move on and make a new life.

One, she hoped, that would be satisfying and would give them both a sense of peace going forward.

CHAPTER FOUR

Be still, my heart."

Dot Parker, wearing a red polka-dot dress with a red lace handkerchief pinned to the breast pocket, stood in the middle of the crowd milling about Ally's Attic and began fanning herself with a printed menu of the items for sale. "All three handsome Malloy brothers in the same room. This is almost more than this old body can take."

"Hey, Dot." Matt brushed a kiss over her cheek, while his wife, Vanessa, gave her a hug.

Luke and Ingrid continued holding hands as they both greeted her warmly.

"Where's Barb?" Reed asked.

"Somebody has to watch the diner. I promised her I'd only stay an hour or so, just long enough to check out all the bargains. Then I'll go back and relieve her so she can get here before the grand opening is over."

Reed looked around. "This may be the most citizens

of Glacier Creek I've ever seen in one place, except for church."

Dot chuckled. "That's what I just told Ally."

"Where is the owner?" Ingrid looked around. "I can't wait to meet her."

"She went that way." Dot pointed toward a crowd gathered around a collection of antique dinnerware set atop a lace-covered table. In the center, turned away from them, was a trim redhead wearing an emerald-green sundress.

"Oh, Luke." Ingrid started inching toward the display. "We could use a set of good dishes. Let's take a look."

As they drifted away, Reed rolled his eyes. "I never thought I'd see the day my wild-and-crazy brother would waste time looking at dishes."

Dot patted his arm. "Don't be too hard on him, Reed, honey. One day it may happen to you."

"Not a chance." Reed began a slow circle of the room, intrigued by the variety of items Ally had managed to accumulate. Every shelf, cupboard, and display surface was filled. Yet every item was displayed with great taste.

She'd set out a variety of musical instruments on a raised platform, resembling a stage. The piano, now sporting a fringed shawl and a SOLD sign, was surrounded by an assortment of guitars, banjos, and a violin. There were three different electronic keyboards, a drum set, and a dented trumpet. A half dozen ranchers and their children were examining the various instruments. The most popular seemed to be drums and guitars.

Spotting Kyle's carrot top in a corner of the shop, laughing with half a dozen boys and girls who were playing with an assortment of toys, Reed paused.

"Hey, Kyle."

The little boy jumped up, holding a cast-iron soldier that

was probably new a hundred years ago. "You came. I told Mama you'd be here."

Reed looked around. "This is a lot of stuff for your mom to keep track of. How does she do it?"

Kyle shrugged. "I guess she likes being busy. She told me to stay here and she'd be back." He scanned the sea of heads that towered over him. "I don't see her. She's wearing a green dress."

"I guess that shouldn't be too hard to spot." Reed nodded toward the cluster of children. "Are you in charge of selling to them?"

Kyle's eyes widened. "Am I 'posed to?"

Reed winked. "I was teasing. I'm sure your mom is doing enough selling today for both of you."

As he started away, Kyle caught his arm. "When everybody leaves, you think we could share a milk shake?"

Reed's smile grew as he leaned down to whisper, "It's a date. But only if it's chocolate. And only if I can have a grilled cheese to go with it."

Kyle put a hand over his mouth to hide his giggles.

Reed moved among the crowd, stopping to admire a collection of farm implements before he spotted a display case filled with electronic gadgets.

"I figured that would get your attention, bro." Matt was grinning as he walked up beside him. "Since you're the family tech gadget guy."

"Why would somebody sell a drone?"

"Look around you. Why would somebody sell any of this stuff?"

Reed shrugged. "I can see stuff that's been outgrown by a family. But this drone looks brand new."

"How about the farm implements?" Matt indicated the collection.

"Probably from one of the ranchers being foreclosed."

"I hadn't thought of that." Matt moved away to study the collection more closely.

Within minutes he was joined by Frank and Grace.

"Hey, cowboy. You thinking of buying?" Ally sidled up beside Reed.

"Yeah. I love gadgets. I never dreamed you'd have something like this for sale."

"I was told by the teen who brought it in that after a collision with his family ranch house, the barn, and a couple of cows, his father said he could sell it or it would wind up in the trash can."

Reed joined in her laughter before giving her a long, probing look. "Your cheeks are as red as your hair."

"I'm sure that's a combination of relief and nerves. Relief that people showed up. Nerves because I hope some of them came to buy and not just to look."

"I don't think you need to worry. Look at this crowd. They're happy, and they're checking out every display."

She laid a hand on his arm. "Thanks so much for coming. I wish I could stay and chat, but I have to get back to work."

He nodded, enjoying the quick flash of heat from her touch. He continued to watch as she made her way across the room, pausing every few steps to answer questions and share a laugh with her customers. Despite the casual look of her tousled hair, that ankle-skimming dress gave her a city chic that set her apart from everyone else in the room.

A short time later, as she dashed back and forth between her cash register and customers, Dot stepped behind the counter and gently pushed her away. "I'll handle the sales. You go and mingle."

"Oh, Dot, I should have hired someone. It never occurred to me that I'd have so many people show up."

"Don't you worry about a thing, honey. Ringing up sales is what I do best. Now go sell that stuff."

With a laugh Ally stepped away from the counter and walked up to a group of ranchers examining her display of tools.

Within the next hour there was a line of paying customers forming at the single register.

Ally stepped behind a second counter to say, "If anyone is paying cash, I can handle it here. Credit cards will have to wait for Dot."

The line split, becoming two, and before long had thinned to a manageable number for Dot to handle alone.

She whispered to Ally that it was time for her to relieve her sister, or Barb would have her head.

Ally gave the woman a hard hug. "You're my lifesaver, Dot. Thank you so much."

"My pleasure, honey. I'll tell Barb to keep an eye on the crowd when she gets here. Besides handling the grill, my sister knows a thing or two about a smokin' cash register."

The two women shared a laugh before Dot headed out the door and back to her diner.

Minutes later her twin sister rushed inside the shop and made a slow circle around the room, studying with interest the variety of items for sale and the clever way they were displayed.

She pulled Ally aside. "Dot's been bragging on you, honey, and I have to say I thought she was exaggerating. Now I see you're every bit as talented as she said. This business is just a grand addition to our town. It's exactly what's needed, and nobody thought of it until you came along."

Ally's cheeks turned a deeper shade of red at her praise. "Thank you so much, Barb. You'll never know what it means to me to hear you say that."

"It comes from the heart, honey." She leaned closer to whisper, "Dot told me you got swamped. If it happens again, give me a nod and I'll step behind the counter and lend a hand."

"You and Dot are my angels of mercy. Thank you."

As Ally moved among the crowds of people, her heart was lighter than it had been all day. The good people of Glacier Ridge were not only supporting her in her fledgling solo effort, but they were even stepping in to lend a hand so she wouldn't feel overwhelmed.

Ally handed the rancher a receipt. "Thanks, Will. I hope your daughter enjoys playing her new keyboard."

"She's been begging for piano lessons since second grade, but the thought of buying a piano and hauling it out to our ranch just wasn't something I'd consider. The minute she spotted that keyboard, I figured it was something we could manage." He watched as his oldest son loaded the instrument into the back of their truck parked outside at the curb. "You just made all her wishes come true."

Ally was beaming as the lanky rancher tipped his hat to her before walking out the door.

A teenage girl, who'd been standing in the middle of the room watching Ally deal with the latest sale, approached, holding the hand of a teenage boy.

The girl, sporting bright orange spiked hair and a tie-dyed T-shirt over wide-legged pants straight out of the sixties, cleared her throat. "I saw the way Dot and Barb gave you a hand."

Ally dimpled. "They were my lifesavers."

"You look like you need some help. And I really need a job. My name is Gemma York. And this is..." She drew the boy beside her. He had shaggy hair that brushed the collar of a faded plaid shirt. His denims had more holes than Swiss cheese. "...Jeremy Clancy."

"It's nice to meet you, Gemma and Jeremy." Ally turned away from the cash register to concentrate on the girl. "Do you have any experience in retail?"

Gemma shook her head, sending orange spikes dancing across her forehead. "But I really want to have a place of my own someday."

"What would you sell?"

"Vintage clothing."

Ally allowed herself to study the girl's outfit. "Like that?"

Gemma nodded.

"Is there a market for it in Glacier Ridge?"

Gemma shrugged and glanced shyly at her boyfriend. "It's all I like to wear. I bet there are others who'd like my stuff, too."

Ally paused for a long moment, and the girl nervously gripped her hands together.

Seeing her nerves, Ally gave her a smile. "I do need help. But I'm not able to pay anybody yet." She handed the girl a pen and paper. "Leave your name and a number where I can reach you. When I earn enough to hire someone, I'll call you."

Gemma's smile came quickly. "You will? Thanks. Um…" She flushed. "I don't have a number. But if you don't mind, I'll just stop by every once in a while."

Before Ally could say a word, the girl caught Jeremy's hand, and the two walked out the door.

Ally watched them go before glancing at the clock on the wall. She'd run two hours over the original time she'd listed for her grand opening. But it had been time well spent.

She looked up at the sound of laughter and spotted Kyle and Reed together in a corner of the room, their heads bent close as they studied a thick book of instructions.

"…camera would have been here…" Reed turned the

page before touching an index finger to the drone. "But it's missing. I guess that's why someone decided not to keep it."

"But it could fly?" Kyle's eyes were wide with excitement.

"We'll just have to wait and see. I've been thinking about ordering one of these. But a bigger one that has about ten times the power and visibility of this one."

"What's visi...?"

"Visibility. The means how far the camera can film. How much it can see and record."

Ally paused beside them. "You're thinking of ordering a toy?"

Reed's grin was as wide as her son's. "It may be a toy to you, but think of the possibilities for a rancher using a drone."

"You mean to scare the cows?"

He got to his feet. "You ought to see the look on your face. I know they're marketed as toys, but what a way for a rancher to keep an eye on his property, his herds, even his wranglers. Right now we have to take up our plane every few weeks to get a bird's-eye view of our ranch. With a drone, we could cover thousands of acres in half the time."

She was shaking her head. "Boys and their toys."

Reed nudged an elbow in Kyle's ribs. "My grandfather likes to say the only difference between men and boys is the price of their toys."

Though he was certain Kyle didn't have any idea what that meant, he was rewarded by the boy's wide grin.

"Reed said he'd share his milk shake with me if you'd go with us to the diner. Can we, Mama?"

She looked from her son to Reed. "Are you bribing a little boy?"

"Yeah." He winked. "I figured he'd be easier than his mother."

"Can you two wait until I check out my register and make out a bank deposit? I don't want to leave all this money lying around overnight."

"And then we'll go to the diner?" Kyle turned pleading eyes toward Ally.

"Yes. Then we'll go to the diner. And you can have some more of that really healthy milk shake."

She was laughing as she made her way across the room and began sorting through the receipts, all the while making notations on a legal pad.

Within the hour she'd written up a bank receipt and added it to the bag containing cash and credit card slips, all neatly tallied in her ledger.

On the way to D & B's Diner, she deposited it in the overnight drop box at the bank.

Her heart was light. She'd made a profit on her first day. She'd gotten to know two neighbors who'd stepped in to lend a hand when she'd felt overwhelmed. And she'd already found a girl eager to work.

Maybe, just maybe, her dreams weren't so foolish after all.

CHAPTER FIVE

That was good." Kyle walked between his mother and Reed as they stepped out of the diner.

"What did you like better?" Reed tucked his hands in his back pockets. "The fried chicken and mashed potatoes or the chocolate milk shake?"

"They were all good. But I liked the chocolate milk shake best."

"No surprise." Reed looked over the boy's head to Ally. "And you?"

"The food was great. But the comments from so many of the customers about Ally's Attic just made my day." Her voice lowered with feeling. "Hearing them say how much they like my shop was food for the soul."

"Yeah. I'd say your grand opening was a huge success."

Ally looked up at the streetlights glowing softly in the gathering dusk. "You'll never know how scared I was that nobody would show up."

Kyle tugged on his mother's hand. "I'm tired. Can you carry me?"

Before she could respond, Reed dropped to his knees. "Here, little buddy. Climb on my back. I'll give you a ride home."

"Oh, boy, Mama. Just like you always do." The little boy was grinning from ear to ear as he settled himself on Reed's broad back and wrapped his arms around Reed's neck.

As they walked past the now-darkened businesses of the town, Ally sighed. "This is what I like best about being in Glacier Ridge."

"Saturday nights?"

She shook her head. "Walking home. I never did that in the city. I drove everywhere. To the store. To day care."

"Did you drive here from Virginia?"

She shook her head, her voice lowering. "I sold my car and my house. Along with everything I could live without." She gave a shaky laugh to cover what she'd just revealed. "I decided I was making a clean break from the past. Besides, it made flying here easier if I lightened our load."

Reed looked at her with interest. "I guess we can all afford to simplify." He paused a moment before saying, "We can't do much walking on the ranch. Most of it requires a lot of driving. Of course, some of it is on all-terrain vehicles or on horseback. Or in my brother, Luke's, case, on his Harley. There are a lot of wide-open spaces between home and our herds."

She looked over at him. "It must have been fun growing up on a ranch."

"If you consider mucking stalls, branding bawling calves, and babysitting ornery cows fun."

She laughed. "You should hear your voice, Reed. Even

while you're trying to complain, there's just something in your tone that tells me you love it."

He winked. "I do. I wouldn't trade places with anyone in the world."

"You're so lucky." She caught sight of her son, his head bobbing slightly before lowering his face to Reed's shoulder. "My poor, brave baby. He put in such a long day. I could see him trying to fight sleep while he was slurping that milk shake, but now he just can't fight it anymore."

Reed chuckled. "I thought he'd gone awfully quiet. Is he out completely?"

Ally nodded. "I could take him if he's getting heavy."

"Are you kidding? He doesn't even weigh as much as a sack of grain." He gave Ally a lingering look that had the color flooding her cheeks. "Neither does his mother."

"Don't be fooled by my size. I'm stronger than I look."

"You don't have to remind me. I saw the way you handled that mob of people today." He held her gaze. "It was pretty impressive."

Again she flushed, and this time she managed to look away, avoiding Reed's eyes, until they started up the walk to her uncle's house.

They paused on the front porch, and Ally dug into her pocket for the key.

Before she could use it, the door was flung open, and Archer Stone stood in the doorway. He reeked of smoke and whiskey.

When he caught sight of Reed, his mouth turned into a scowl. "Malloy. What are you doing here?"

"Giving your nephew a ride home."

"He can't walk?"

"He's just a little kid who's put in a long day." Reed smiled at Ally while directing his words at Archer. "You missed the big event in town. You should have been at your niece's grand opening."

"Some of us have to work for a living."

Reed chose to ignore the underlying anger in Archer's tone. "Speaking of work, Ally's business is going to be a smashing success, if the crowds today were any indication."

"And if those crowds fade away?" Archer glared at Ally. "I hope you have more staying power than your mother did. The minute life got too tough around these parts, she turned tail and ran as far and as fast as she could, grabbing on to the first guy who offered her a ride out. And she never looked back."

Ally recoiled as though she'd been slapped before trying to cover it by reaching for Kyle. "I'll take him up to bed now."

Reed stepped back a pace. "You're as tired as he is. You lead the way and I'll carry him to his bed."

Archer barred the way. "In case you've forgotten, Malloy, this is my house. I don't want you here."

Reed met his narrowed gaze. "And your reason is . . . ?"

"I don't need a reason to bar someone from my own house. But how about this? My niece is a single mother. Being a lawman, I happen to know that makes her a target for certain types of men. And I don't want you sniffing around."

Seeing Ally's cheeks redden as her eyes registered her shock at his vicious words, Reed stepped closer, causing Archer to step back. "I'll remember that. But right now, I'm more concerned with getting this little guy to his bed." He turned to allow Ally to precede him. "Lead the way and I'll follow."

Ally walked past her uncle and started up the stairs with Reed trailing behind. When they reached the bedroom, Ally opened the door, revealing two twin beds. Pausing beside one, Ally reached up and took Kyle from Reed's shoulders.

The boy was so sound asleep he barely stirred.

She slipped off his glasses and set them on the night table. After removing his shoes and socks, she shrugged him out of his jeans and shirt and tucked him under the blankets wearing only his underwear.

She pressed a kiss to his cheek and wiped strands of russet hair from his forehead before straightening.

"Thank you, Reed. For dinner, and for carrying Kyle home." She held out her hand.

When he took it in his big palm, she added softly, "I'm sorry about that scene downstairs."

"You have nothing to apologize for. Archer has always been prickly. And especially around my family. He's made it clear he resents my family's success, even though it came with a lot of hard work that continues every day."

"Prickly." Ally latched on to the single word. "That's a good term. He's...prickly around us, too. But I think there are a lot of reasons. He disapproved of my mother, and he disapproves of me, as well. That goes without saying. But he also resents having us intrude on his privacy. I'm hoping once we're on our own, my uncle will be willing to put aside his anger and accept us as family. That's why I'm determined to turn the upper rooms of my business into our own apartment as soon as I can get them cleaned and find enough furniture to set up housekeeping."

"I know a lot of ranchers looking for extra work. I could make a few phone calls and have at least the cleaning done in a day or two."

"You could?" For a moment an eager, hopeful light came into her eyes. Then she shook her head. "Thanks for the offer. But I don't want to pay for work I can do myself."

"I understand." He recognized her need to feel independent and admired her sense of pride. "But if you hit any snags, just let me know."

Her smile was quick. "Thank you. I'll walk you to the door."

"No need." He put a hand on her arm, absorbing a quick sizzle of heat. "You've put in a long day. The last thing you need is another scene downstairs."

Ally looked up just as he looked down. For the space of a heartbeat their gazes met and held.

Reed lowered his head.

Ally froze.

Just then Kyle sighed in his sleep and turned on his side.

They gave a guilty start and moved apart, the moment shattered.

Reluctantly Reed turned away and stepped through the doorway before turning toward her. "Good night, Ally. I'll see myself out."

He descended the stairs and glanced around, expecting to find Archer waiting for him.

Through the open door he caught a whiff of smoke. As he stepped out onto the front porch, he saw Archer leaning against the porch rail, the gleaming red tip of a cigar in his hand.

"You took your sweet time upstairs."

"Helping Ally get Kyle to bed."

"That better be all you were doing. As for Ally, she doesn't need your help. She's been doing it all on her own since the kid was born." A sly look came into his eyes. "Or maybe she hasn't told you yet. His father was military. Never around. Too busy to even bother making it legal, if you know what I mean." His eyes narrowed on Reed. "And don't try to tell me you give a rat's . . . a care in the world about that kid.

I know what you're up to, Malloy. From what I know about you Malloys, you've got every woman in this town fawning over you. But that's not enough for you, is it? I guess you're more like your old man than I realized. He thought he was better'n the rest of us and could have any woman he set his sights on. Even some other guy's woman."

The mention of his father had Reed's eyes flashing fire before he carefully banked his temper.

As Reed started down the steps, Archer called after him, "Just remember what I said. I won't have you sniffing around my niece, Malloy. She's off-limits to the likes of you."

The thought of a satisfying, knock-down, drag-out fight had Reed's blood heating. But just as quickly he swallowed his anger, knowing that a mean-tempered bully like Archer could easily retaliate by hurting the two upstairs, who would have no way of protecting themselves.

It took all his willpower to simply walk away.

Reed drove through the darkened town, past Clay's Pig Sty, past D & B's Diner, the barbershop and spa, the medical clinic, before turning onto the interstate.

His mind wasn't on his driving. He kept turning over and over the anger in Archer Stone.

Through the years Archer had made no secret of his jealousy over the Malloys' success, without ever once conceding the fact that it took the entire Malloy family working twenty-four hours every day just to keep a ranch of that size operating. But it was easier for some men to hate the success of others in order to overlook their own failures.

Archer's painful childhood was well known around Glacier Ridge. His mother died after a lingering illness in a distant hospital in Helena, leaving a sixteen-year-old daughter and a four-year-old son. Their father, forced to work on ranches around the area to pay his enormous medical debts, left the two alone for long stretches of time to fend for themselves. The girl left town as soon as she was able, latching on to a cowboy who was just passing through and leaving Archer behind. After that, Archer was forced to accompany his father, drifting from ranch to ranch, before landing a solid job in law enforcement.

Archer seemed to relish his position as deputy to the chief. It got him a pass if he happened to drink too much at the Pig Sty or bullied an opponent in a poker game. With that badge pinned to his shirt, Archer Stone was a man to be reckoned with. Sheriff Eugene Graystoke was a fair and honorable man and had probably never heard as much as a whisper about his deputy's off-duty behavior over the years. Especially since it didn't seem to impact Archer's work.

Grandpop Frank used to say he wouldn't judge another man's behavior unless he first walked in his shoes.

Remembering those words, Reed struggled to put aside his anger at Archer Stone by concentrating on Archer's niece.

Just thinking about Ally Shaw had the smile returning to Reed's face. She was almost too pretty to believe, with that spill of red hair, that porcelain skin, and the parade of freckles across her nose.

Maybe that's what had first caught his attention. But it was her determination to make a life for herself and her little boy that had him looking beyond her beauty.

What made a young woman sell her car and furniture and buy a building in a town she'd never seen? The answer came immediately. She'd left a good job, a comfortable, familiar part of the country to risk everything for the sake of her son's future.

There was just something about little Kyle. Those big, oversize glasses that gave him the look of a wise, old owl. The red hair and freckled face. That big, easy grin that melted the heart. For a four-year-old he was pretty fearless. And the kid was smart. At an age when most children couldn't even read, he'd listened to the directions in the drone's manual and was able to put his finger on the exact spot where the camera would go, if the camera hadn't been missing. Unless Reed was badly mistaken, the kid would probably be able to master flying that drone in half the time it would take most grown-ups.

As his ranch came into view in the distance, Reed was deep in thought.

There was no doubt that Archer had attempted to sully his niece's reputation by deliberately spilling the secret that she and Kyle's father hadn't married.

That fact meant nothing to Reed. What he saw when he looked at her was a heroic mother who was determined to make a fresh start and build a better way of life for herself and her son.

Each little fact he learned simply added another layer of admiration.

As taken as he was by the freckle-faced super kid in the owlish glasses, he was, if possible, even more taken with the super kid's mother.

CHAPTER SIX

Frank Malloy looked up from the far side of the kitchen, where he and Grace were enjoying their morning coffee with Great One. He grinned at his grandson, Reed, just stepping in from the mudroom, accompanied by Burke. "You're up early, sonny boy. You already finished with the barn chores?"

"Yeah." Reed helped himself to a frosty glass of freshly squeezed orange juice from a tray on the counter, gulping down half before crossing the room.

Burke chose coffee, hot and strong, and stood aside, cupping his hands around the mug.

Reed smiled at Grace. "Did you buy anything at the grand opening yesterday?"

Frank stared pointedly at his wife. "Your grandmother bought out half the store."

Reed arched a brow. "You bought other people's hand-me-downs?"

She merely smiled. "That just shows how little you know about things. I prefer to think of them as treasures."

Frank nodded toward a piece of pottery on the counter. "You call that thing a treasure?"

Gracie's smile grew. "That *thing* happens to be a hundred-year-old gravy boat that perfectly matches the set of dishes I inherited from my grandmother."

"And what about that ugly piece of furniture you badgered me into hauling home in the truck?"

"It's a hope chest. I had one like it as a girl. Somewhere between Connecticut and Hollywood and here in Montana"—she sent a knowing look at her father—"someone or something caused it to go missing."

Great One shrugged. "I couldn't imagine what you'd want with a hope chest in the middle of the wilderness."

"And so you took it upon yourself to sell it along with all the furnishings in one of our homes."

A slow smile spread across the old man's features. "Hope chests are for those still hoping, Gracie girl. If you recall, you boldly told your mother and me you'd found the man of your dreams, and you were never coming back to us."

Frank draped an arm around Grace's shoulder and drew her close to press a kiss to her cheek. "And I thank heaven for it every day."

Reed chuckled. There was no doubt his grandparents were still very much in love. "What else did you buy, Gram Gracie?"

"Well, let me see. There's that silver bowl that Nessa admired. I believe I'll surprise her with it on her birthday. And the four little miniatures depicting the four seasons; that caught Ingrid's eye. And—"

"Breakfast is ready. Get it while it's hot."

At Yancy's announcement, they drifted toward the big trestle table while Grace continued her litany of purchases.

As they took their seats, Frank looked across the table at

his grandson. "If your grandmother's shopping experience was any indication, I'd say Ally's Attic is a big success. She has to be very happy with her first day."

Reed nodded, just as Matt and Vanessa, Luke and Ingrid, Ingrid's little sister, Lily, and Ingrid's ranch foreman, Mick Hinckley, stepped in from the mudroom and gathered around the table.

"Just in time," Great One remarked. "Though I'm not surprised. You always seem to make it here just as the morning chores are finished and the meal is about to start."

"We plan it that way, Great One." Luke winked at his wife. "But Matt and I really intended to lend a hand with mucking the stalls." He stared at their youngest brother. "Looks like someone got a head start on the morning."

Reed forked an omelet onto his plate before passing the platter to Matt. "I thought I'd head to town after breakfast and give Ally a hand."

"With her shop?" Matt nudged his wife. "Are you giving up ranching for business in town?"

Vanessa looked beyond her husband to smile at Reed. "Be sure to tell her how much we all love her new place."

"I will. But I'm not helping with the shop. I thought I'd give her a hand cleaning the upper floor of the building so she and her son can live there."

"Where are they living right now?" Grace asked.

"At her uncle Archer's place."

Luke's smile faded. "Archer Stone is her uncle?"

Reed nodded.

"Poor thing." Luke shared a look with the others as he held the platter for his wife. "I'm surprised he'd open his home to anyone."

Reed kept his tone deliberately bland. "From what I saw last night, I'd say he's already regretting the invitation."

Frank Malloy paused with his fork halfway to his mouth. "What did you see?"

Reed shrugged. "His usual nasty temper. Ally's convinced that he's temperamental only because she and her son are intruding on his bachelor lifestyle. She admitted that she really wants to move out so her uncle can have his privacy back and then they'll be one big happy family."

Luke was frowning. "Archer doesn't need an excuse to be nasty. His temper has been growing worse every year. A lot of the regulars at Clay's Pig Sty have mentioned his drinking. He's always liked his liquor, but lately it's started taking a toll."

Reed set down his coffee. "He'd had plenty to drink last night. Maybe that's what loosened his tongue. He made it clear he has no love for our family." He glanced at the others. "Anybody know why?"

Frank cleared his throat. "When Archer and Patrick were boys, they were friends. At least we all thought so. But after Patrick and Bernie married, that friendship became strained." He glanced at his wife. "We figured it was just that Patrick had no time for his old pals. With the thousand and one ranch chores, and then the arrival of you three boys"— he looked around at Matt, Luke, and Reed—"Patrick didn't have the time he once had for his friends. Besides, he had everything he wanted right here. There just was no need for him to go to town to hang out with his old buddies."

Grace nodded. "I agree. Old friendships are often strained once one or the other no longer has the same goals or common interest."

Reed set aside his empty cup. "Great breakfast, Yancy." He glanced at the others. "Anybody interested in going to Glacier Ridge and lending a hand cleaning the upper floor of Ally's Attic?"

Frank chuckled. "From the lack of enthusiasm, I'd say you're on your own, sonny boy."

Reed joined in the laughter as he sauntered from the kitchen and paused in the mudroom to retrieve his hat from a hook by the door.

"Just remember, sonny boy," Frank called out. "You've got a herd depending on you and a big, fat contract that could make or break your future."

"I haven't forgotten, Grandpop. I'll be up in the hills tomorrow at dawn."

A short time later Reed's truck was moving along the ribbon of driveway toward the highway that led to town.

Like most businesses in town, the door to Ally's Attic was unlocked and the OPEN sign displayed.

Reed took his time studying the building Ally had bought. Though old and faded, it was sturdy enough. He seemed to remember seeing a roofing contractor working here no more than two or three years ago, when old Hampton Major owned it. After Hampton's death, his out-of-town family was desperate to sell, and the building had fallen into disrepair. Still, with a coat of fresh paint it could be a welcoming place. He had no doubt painting it would be one of Ally's priorities, as soon as she earned enough.

He hoped Ally had been able to buy it at a fair-market price.

Inside, a neatly typed card on the counter informed customers to ring the bell for service.

Hearing voices coming from the upper floor, Reed climbed the stairs.

A mound of broken and discarded furniture stood in one corner of the room. A sofa that had probably been new when his grandparents were young. A bookcase with warped shelving and cracked glass panels. An old-fashioned child's wooden high chair.

The window coverings had been removed, allowing sunlight to filter through the layer of dirt and grime on the windows. Two stuffed garbage bags attested to the fact that the floors had been swept clean.

Ally was on her knees in the far corner of the big room, scrubbing the scuffed hardwood floors to a high shine.

Reed stood a moment, enjoying the way she looked. Faded skinny jeans that hugged her backside like a second skin. And a damned fine backside it was. A denim shirt, sleeves rolled above her elbows, shirttails tied at her midriff, emphasizing small, perfect breasts. Copper hair pulled back in a ponytail, with damp wisps falling soft and loose.

Kyle was the first to spot Reed. He came out of a second room hauling some sort of antique pull-toy that *clack-clack*ed with each movement.

When he saw the tall cowboy in the doorway, his face lit with excitement. "Hey, Reed. Look what I found."

At her son's words, Ally sat back on her heels, eyes wide, cheeks bright pink as she turned to stare at Reed.

"Looks like fun." Reed dropped to his knees to examine the toy. "What is it?"

The boy shrugged. "I don't know. I never saw one like this before. Mom said I could play with it while she cleans our 'partment."

"It looks to be hand-carved. I bet a rancher made this out of a block of wood for one of his kids."

"Mom said she'll sell it when I'm through playing with it."

Reed stood and turned to Ally. "From the looks of things, you must have started before dawn."

Ally smiled as she got wearily to her feet, pressing a hand to the small of her back. "It was still dark outside. The minute I heard my uncle leave for work, I got ready for the day."

Reed glanced at the old-fashioned light fixture on the ceiling. "I'm glad to know the lights work."

She nodded. "So far, everything works just fine. I checked the lights, the heat, and flushed the toilet and ran water in the sink and tub, just to be certain. When I bought the building, the agent assured me that the family selling it would be responsible to see to it that everything was in good working order. But he warned me that it would need a good cleaning." She gave a wry smile. "He wasn't kidding."

Reed picked up the garbage bags. "I'll toss these in the back of my truck and then I'll be back to give you a hand with the rest."

Her smile brightened. "Thanks. What about your ranch chores?"

"Like you," he called over his shoulder, "I got an early start."

Within minutes he returned. "How about all this junk? Want me to toss it in my truck?"

She laughed. "You forget. I'm in the junk business. Or as I like to call it, hidden treasures."

He joined in the laughter. "Sorry. What was I thinking?" He studied the ugly old sofa. "Do you really think someone will buy this?"

She arched a brow. "Trust me. In my business, there's a perfect someone for every person's discards." She began removing the cushions. "Let's get it downstairs, and I'll figure out how best to display it."

He glanced at the broken sections of bookshelves. "Don't tell me you hope to sell this, too?"

She shrugged. "I think it's beyond help. But any of those old glass panels that aren't broken will appeal to someone refinishing something similar."

"Okay." He picked up an armload of cushions and hauled them down the stairs before returning to wrestle the sofa down to the shop.

When all the furniture had been disposed of, he climbed the stairs to find Ally just putting the finishing touches on the wood floor that was as shiny as brand-new.

He looked around. "What's next?"

Ally led the way into the first of two bedrooms. In the smaller room she had a wooden bed frame already assembled. With Reed's help she lifted a box spring and mattress atop the frame and began dressing the bed with a simple blue plaid quilt and blue pillow covers etched with a horse and rider.

"I picked those out myself," Kyle said proudly. "They were in a box of stuff."

"A box someone brought here overnight and left on my doorstep," Ally explained. "I guess some folks didn't get the word that this is a resale shop, and they thought I'm now the local junkyard."

"You mean all this stuff was free?"

"That's right. And it doesn't get any better than free."

"Do you like my bed?" Kyle asked.

"I do. You have good taste. Like your mother. You like horses?"

"Uh-huh." The little boy flopped backward on the bed, giggling as he bounced. "I like looking at them."

"Did you ever ride one?"

The little boy sat up, shoving his glasses up the bridge of his nose. "No. But Mom said one day I can. They look really big." He peered at Reed. "Do you have a horse?"

"I do. In fact, we have lots of horses on our ranch. If you'd like, I'll take you there one day and you can ride one."

"Wow." The little boy turned to his mother with shining eyes. "Can I, Mama?"

"We'll see."

The minute the words were out of her mouth, she caught Reed and Kyle looking at each other with matching grins.

"What'd I tell you?" Reed winked at the boy. "It's what moms say every time they don't want to commit."

At Reed's words she shot him a mock hairy-eyeball. "And what did I tell you about giving away mom secrets?"

Reed put an arm around Kyle's shoulders and steered him out of the room. "Come on, partner. This is where we get busy. What do you say you and I start cleaning windows?"

The two were sharing a conspiratorial chuckle as they snatched up window cleaner, rags, and a roll of paper towels before heading toward the front room.

"I'm hungry, Mama." Kyle stood across the room, watching Reed and Ally wrestle a small wood table through the doorway and into the kitchen.

Ally wiped a hand across her forehead. "I brought some supplies. I'll make peanut butter and jelly sandwiches in a few minutes."

"Don't bother." Reed set four straight-backed wooden chairs around the table. "Kyle and I will walk down to the diner and pick up something."

Seeing the light that came into her son's eyes, she put her hands on her hips. "Would that something happen to include a chocolate milk shake?"

Reed turned to Kyle. "What do you think, little partner? Can you handle it?"

Kyle was already dancing toward the stairs.

"I guess I got my answer." Reed winked. "What'll it be? A burger with all the trimmings or something lean and healthy?"

"A juicy burger sounds heavenly." Ally put a hand over her heart. "I'm in need of protein."

"Me too. We'll be back soon."

He ambled out of the kitchen, and she paused to watch him leave before taking a breath and digging into yet another box of hand-me-down items that had been left on the doorstep.

As she pulled out some colorful chair cushions and matching place mats, she whispered a prayer of thanks for the good ranchers who had decided to use her shop as a place to dispose of unwanted household goods. This anonymous donor hadn't left a name or a price for the items, leaving Ally a clear signal that they were the result of spring cleaning and not considered good enough for resale.

She sighed as she studied the bright, cheery additions to the aged kitchen. They were certainly good enough for her.

Beggars can't be choosers.

She wasn't reduced to begging. Not by a long shot. She'd had a successful career, a car with all the bells and whistles she'd bought to haul Kyle back and forth to day care, and a house that her mother had left her with no mortgage or debt. She'd been given a generous severance package when she'd left her company and a guarantee from her supervisor that she could have her old job back if things didn't work out. She'd liquidated everything and banked all her savings to see to Kyle's future. If her little business couldn't earn enough to pay the bills, she could always get a job and put Kyle back into day care. Still, she hoped and prayed she wouldn't have to make that decision, or she'd be right back where she started, except with severely limited career choices so far from a bustling city.

Unable to sit still, she picked up a rag and started viciously scrubbing the brown stains that discolored the ancient sink. While she worked, she thought again about her decision to reconnect with her uncle. At the time, she'd convinced herself that it was important to give Kyle the gift of family. But there had been another motive as well. Her timetable for leaving Virginia had been rushed by the behavior of one of her fellow employees, who'd become not only aggressive but also intolerable. Because of him, she'd gambled that a simple life in her mother's hometown seemed a better alternative than the life she and Kyle were leading. She'd already been making plans to relocate, but one man's determination to morph from business friend to something more had accelerated her timetable.

Now, seeing how angry and annoyed Archer was, she was more determined than ever that the move to this little apartment would make a difference in their relationship.

Archer would come around once she and Kyle were out of his house. Out of his hair. He'd had a lifetime to become set in his ways. He obviously enjoyed his bachelor existence and was now forced to put up with two strangers crowding his space. It didn't matter that they were blood relations. She could see how a woman and child would cramp his style. Moving out of his space would put a smile on his face and love in his heart.

It had to. She'd risked everything for a gamble that she desperately needed to win.

When the sink sparkled, she walked into the bathroom and turned her energy loose on the ancient tub and toilet, both bearing the rust stains of years of neglect.

"Hello, the house."

At Reed's shout, Ally tossed yet another cleaning rag into

a brimming bucket of rags and hurried to the kitchen, where Reed and Kyle were depositing armloads of bags and carry-out containers.

Ally's laughter bubbled up. "What army are you planning on feeding?"

Kyle's eyes were as big as saucers. "Wait'll you see, Mama."

Reed set out paper plates and napkins and plastic knives, forks, and spoons.

At Ally's arched brow, he grinned. "Courtesy of Barb and Dot. They asked if you had any dishes, and I told them I hadn't seen any."

"I'll get around to some eventually."

"Until then"—he held up a bag filled to the brim with disposable tableware—"they sent you enough for a month or more."

"Bless them."

She watched as he opened the first of several containers to reveal thick, juicy burgers. One container was loaded with enough fries for several meals. A plastic tub held salad fixings, along with half a dozen lidded containers of dressing.

As they settled around the table, Ally gave a deep sigh. "Just looking at all this makes me realize how hungry I am."

Reed pointed to the clock on the wall. "You realize it's closer to supper time than lunch time?"

Ally gasped. "Where did the day go?"

Reed gave her an admiring look. "You've put in a full one."

"Look, Mama." Kyle held up a cardboard cup holder with three extra-tall containers. "Reed ordered giant-sized milk shakes."

"For our giant-sized appetites." Reed and the boy shared knowing smiles.

For long minutes nobody spoke as they dug into their

food. When at last Ally found her voice, she was practically purring. "Oh, this all tastes like heaven."

Reed sipped his drink. "Kyle said you didn't take time for breakfast."

She looked across the table at her son. "Didn't I make you toast and peanut butter?"

The little boy nodded. "And a cup of hot chocolate. And you put a plate of cheese and fruit in the fridge for lunch, but you didn't eat any, Mama."

She shrugged. "I was in a hurry to get started. My mind wasn't on food."

Reed looked around. "Your hard work paid off. This is a really great place to live. And one good thing about living here, you'll never be late for work."

Ally sat back with a laugh, feeling refreshed and renewed. "Now it's time to tackle the other bedroom."

"I'll give you a hand." Reed shoved away from the table and started boxing up the leftovers. "Does the refrigerator work?"

She nodded and took the containers from his hand to set them on the refrigerator shelves. "There's an old stove and oven that work, too."

Reed glanced around. "No microwave?"

She shook her head. "Too modern for this place, I guess. But I have all the necessities."

Together they walked to the second bedroom and lifted the box spring and mattress onto an old wooden frame that had been carefully polished. While Reed threaded a pair of white curtains on a small metal rod, Ally dressed the bed in simple white sheets and a white quilt. For color she added two mismatched red and blue pillows.

Reed leaned a hip against the windowsill. "You've got a real flair for making a plain room feel homey."

She flushed. "I don't have much to work with."

"That's just it." He trailed her along the hallway to the small living room, where Kyle was busy playing with the now-empty box, turning it into a fort. "My grandmother and my sisters-in-law all commented on how smart your displays were yesterday. I'm betting my grandmother bought more than she'd planned to, just because everything looked so special." He shook his head. "The music stage, with all those instruments. The tables filled with lace cloth and fancy dishes. And the farm implements all around that bale of hay. Really clever."

Her cheeks turned even brighter pink. "I'm glad people noticed. I gave it a lot of thought."

Kyle looked up from his fort. "Can we sleep here, Mama?"

She gave a shake of her head. "I wish we could. But all our clothes and personal things are at Archer's house. And I'm too tired to think about packing them up tonight. We'll spend tonight at Uncle Archer's and then haul the rest of our things over in the morning."

"My truck's out front. If you're finished here, I'll drive you back."

"Thank you. I'll take you up on your offer." With a sigh she stretched her arms over her head. "I think I'm going to hurt tomorrow in places I've never hurt before."

"You got a lot done." To keep from staring at the way her shirt stretched tautly across her breasts, Reed looked around at the sparkling apartment. "And it shows."

Ally walked through the apartment, turning off lights before calling to her son. "Time to go, Kyle. Your fort will be here waiting for you tomorrow."

The little boy trailed Reed down the stairs and out to the street, where the lights were already coming on along Main Street.

As they moved along the streets to Archer's house, Kyle kept up a running commentary about Dot and Barb and how much fun he had at their diner.

"Dot let me stand on a stool at the cash register and showed me how to ring up a sale. She said I should learn how, so I can help you run your business. And Barb took me in the kitchen and showed me where she makes the best milk shakes in the world. And she said when I get bigger, she'll let me try to make one myself."

"You did all that in one visit?"

"We had to wait a long time, 'cause Dot said she always makes special stuff for Reed." He turned to their driver. "Doesn't she, Reed?"

"She does. And has since I was no bigger than you."

"You were little like me?"

Reed chuckled. "Once upon a time."

"That's how all my books start. Were you little like me, too, Mama?"

"I was." She glanced over his head to smile at Reed. "Once upon a time."

The three shared a laugh.

As they pulled up to Archer's house, Ally noted the house in darkness. "Looks like my uncle is still at work."

At her words, Kyle visibly sighed with relief.

Reed turned off the engine and circled the truck to open the passenger door.

On the porch, Ally dug in her pocket for the key and unlocked the door before switching on the interior light.

Kyle raced inside. "Where are my trucks, Mama?"

"Up in your room. I wanted to be sure we didn't leave anything lying around. You know what Uncle Archer said."

"Okay. 'Night, Reed."

"Good night, Kyle."

Ally held the door. "Would you like to come in?"

Reed removed his hat, shoving a hand through his hair. "I don't think it would be wise." He waited a beat before saying, "I wish I could give you a hand again tomorrow hauling all your belongings over to the apartment, but I need to head up to the hills where my herd is grazing. I've been away from them too long."

Ally put a hand on his arm. "Please don't apologize. You've already done so much. I never would have had the apartment ready so quickly without your help today. Thank you, Reed. For everything."

He closed a hand over her shoulder, drawing her slightly nearer. "You're welcome. I enjoyed the hard work. And the company wasn't so bad, either."

That brought the smile back to her eyes. "Well..." She started to turn away.

His fingers tightened at her shoulder. "I don't know how long I'll be up on the ridge, but when I get back, I'd like to stop by." Seeing her eyes widen, he added, "Just to see how your apartment looks with everything in place."

She dimpled. "You're always welcome, Reed. And I know Kyle will be thrilled to see you."

"Thanks." He leaned close and touched his mouth to hers.

It was intended as the merest brush of mouth to mouth, but the moment they came together, the sudden flare of heat changed everything.

The hat slipped from Reed's hand and drifted unnoticed to their feet. His fingers were tangled in her hair, though he couldn't recall how they got there.

Her hands fisted in the front of his shirt, and he was enveloped in the most amazing sensations.

She smelled of lemon and furniture polish. And she tasted as sweet as the wildflowers that grew in the high country.

He absorbed a quick sexual tug, so deep, so unexpected, his head swam.

In some part of his brain he recognized the slam of a car door, but his mind was already clouded by erotic images that had him pressing her back against the door and taking the kiss deeper.

Her little purr of pleasure encouraged him to linger over her lips. He could feel himself sinking deeper into a pool of deep, dark temptation.

"You son of a..."

Archer's fierce oath was a dose of ice water that had them lifting their heads and breaking contact.

CHAPTER SEVEN

At the wave of pure fury, Ally stepped back, as though poised to run.

Archer Stone barreled up the walkway and grabbed a fistful of Reed's shirt. "What part of my warning didn't you understand? Now I'm going to have to teach you a lesson, Malloy."

Reed's work-roughened fingers closed around Archer's wrist and squeezed like a steel vise until the deputy swore and yanked his hand free.

Rubbing his bruised wrist, he shot Reed a hate-filled look. "I ordered you to stay off my property, Malloy. Now I'm going to spell things out. You come near me or mine again, I'll arrest you. You hear me?"

"You figuring on hiding behind that badge, Archer?"

The man's eyes were flat. "I won't need a badge next time. I find you here, I'll shoot first and ask questions later."

Ignoring him, Reed turned to Ally. "I'm sorry for this."

"I'm not. It just reinforces my decision to move out as soon as possible. Now the decision has been made for me."

Archer spun toward her. "What do you mean...?"

Before her uncle could finish, she reached out a hand to Reed. "Could you wait just a minute while I get Kyle? I'd like you to drive us both back to the shop."

"What about your things?"

She shot a glance at her uncle's face, twisted in a look of absolute fury. "We don't need things. As long as we're somewhere safe and comfortable, we'll be fine."

She turned away. Minutes later she and Kyle stepped out onto the porch. While holding firmly to Kyle, still clutching his trucks, she turned to Archer. "I'm sorry this ended so badly. Thank you for the use of your house. If you don't mind, I'll come by tomorrow and pick up the rest of our things."

He swore. "Why am I not surprised that you're leaving with a man you hardly know? You're just like your ma. I guess some things never change."

Though her eyes filled, she lifted her chin. "Reed Malloy spent the day making it possible for us to have the space we need, in order for you to have your privacy back. You ought to be thanking him."

Archer's face twisted into an insulting sneer. "I'm sure you'll find a way to thank him for both of us. It's the way of women like you."

Without another word Ally spun on her heel, lifting Kyle tightly to her chest, and followed Reed toward his truck, with Archer spewing a string of fierce oaths at their backs.

As soon as they were buckled in, Reed put the truck in gear and pulled away. In the rearview mirror he saw the silhouette of Archer still standing in the glare of the porch light, still raising his fist to them.

"I'm sorry my presence caused all this."

Ally glanced toward her son in the backseat, quietly moving a toy truck across the window. She kept her voice low enough that Kyle wouldn't overhear. "It wasn't you. It was the alcohol."

"Maybe. But drunk or sober, Archer has the right to order me off his property, and I have no right to interfere with such an order."

"I understand. I'm just glad now I have a place of my own."

"A place without your clothes or even the simplest things, like a toothbrush, a pair of pajamas for Kyle."

"We're fine without any of those things. All we need is to be together, and safe."

Reed pulled over to the curb. "Why don't you let me take you to my ranch for the night? My family could come up with everything you and Kyle need to be comfortable."

She gave a quick but firm shake of her head. "We're almost home. And we'll be fine as soon as we get upstairs."

"How do you know Archer won't follow you here?"

"We're out of his hair. I really believe his anger is related to the fact that he lost his sense of privacy when he opened his home to us. We need our own space and he needs his. Please, Reed. Just take us back to our apartment."

Reluctantly Reed continued driving.

As they pulled up to the shop, Ally unbuckled her son and took his hand before leading him to the door.

Reed stepped up beside them. "I'll see you safely upstairs."

Ally shook her head. "We're fine now. We need to do this on our own. Thank you again, Reed."

He paused, understanding her need to take charge of their situation but feeling a need to see to her safety. "Take my cell phone number. If you need anything at all, just call me."

She plugged his number into her phone, then gave him hers.

He held the door. "I'll wait until you lock up down here and I see a light go on upstairs."

She gave him a grateful smile as she led Kyle inside and locked the door. Kyle turned and waved before the two disappeared.

A minute later Reed saw the light go on upstairs, and Ally stepped to the window to wave to him.

Once in the truck, Reed sat a moment before pulling away.

He hated leaving Ally and Kyle alone like this. But it had to be better for both of them than spending another night under Archer's roof, when he was in such a temper. Still, Reed had no doubt his family would have made Ally and Kyle feel welcome.

His family. He'd been letting them carry the bulk of his work while he'd been distracted here in town. He was glad now he'd taken the day to help Ally with that apartment, even though it had been precious time he'd lost with his herd.

It was good that Ally was able to be on her own. Apparently she'd had plenty of experience. He understood her hunger for family, but he wondered if putting distance between herself and her uncle would have the desired effect of eventually bringing them together.

There was so much anger simmering inside Archer Stone, it could easily explode, causing a rift wider and deeper than the one between Archer and Ally's mother all those years ago. That chasm had never been bridged.

He sincerely hoped Ally and Kyle hadn't come all this way on a doomed mission.

* * *

Burke climbed the hill and paused beside Reed, looking out over his herd spread below him.

"Why the frown? I figured you'd be happy with such a healthy herd."

Reed pulled himself out of the dark thoughts that were plaguing him. Thoughts of Ally and Kyle facing Archer's fury this morning when they returned for their clothes. He cursed the often absent cell phone service that plagued them this high in the hills.

Nothing to be done about it. He'd neglected his obligations long enough. The herd, the ranch, the demanding chores were dependent on him. As was his family. He had a contract to live up to. A healthy herd to deliver.

He forced a smile. "They're even better than I'd hoped. I really think Leone Industries will be so pleased with the results of this experiment, they'll want to expand the contract."

"Like you said, son, organic beef is the future."

Reed nodded. "It's a risk. A herd of this size, with no antibiotics to ward off disease, could become a disaster if they were to come into contact with a virus." He pointed to the new fencing he'd built to segregate this herd from the others, while he dealt with the dozens of things that could go wrong with raising a completely organic herd of cattle.

"Like you asked, son, I have the wranglers weigh at least a dozen of the herd once a week, along with a dozen from the open-range herds, just to be certain they're gaining weight at the same rate." Burke shook his head. "I have to admit I was the first to doubt they could weigh the same without the use of any hormones. But so far, they're equal."

Reed and Burke walked down the hill and made their way through the cattle milling about, pausing every so often to run a hand over a sleek hide or to look into clear eyes, searching for any sign of a less-than-healthy animal.

Hours later, after taking blood samples that would be sent to a lab in town and feeling satisfied with what he'd seen, Reed slipped off his hat and wiped the sweat from his forehead. "So far, so good, Burke. Now, if we can bring this herd through roundup without incident, Leone will boast of buying the ultimate organic beef."

"And charge their customers double," the old foreman said with a chuckle.

"They'll have to, if the cost of raising these million-dollar babies is any indication."

Burke nodded. "That fence alone cost you a pretty penny. Then there are the lab fees, the need to hire extra wranglers to guard this gold mine and weigh them weekly."

"Not to mention protecting them from predators. But there's no choice. When I signed this contract with Leone, I knew I was betting the future of our ranch on these babies."

"Your family is proud of you, son."

"It's too soon for that." Reed clapped a hand on Burke's shoulder. "You know what Great One likes to say. Don't count your money until it's in the bank."

Burke chuckled. "Leave it to your great-grandfather to throw water on your fireworks."

Reed grinned. "It's called 'keeping it real.'"

"Well, I don't know about you, but I'm real hot and sweaty and starving. You ready to head on up to the range shack?"

In answer Reed pulled himself into the saddle. "More than. I want a long swim in the creek, a change of clothes, and whatever Yancy sent up with us for supper."

"Now you're talkin', son." Burke mounted and turned his horse toward the distant meadow, with Reed's horse moving along beside.

* * *

"This is something I never get tired of." Reed leaned his back against his saddle and lifted a blackened coffeepot from the fire to top off Burke's cup and then his own.

The old cowboy nodded. "Give me a cool evening, supper over an open fire, and that view of the sun setting over the hills, and I'm already gone to heaven."

They sat in companionable silence for long minutes, enjoying the whisper of the breeze in the trees and the distant lowing of cattle.

After a string of nights in the range shack, they'd opted to spend their last night in bedrolls under the stars.

"It's been a good week, son."

"Yeah." Reed stretched his long legs toward the fire.

Burke looked over. "I figured you were having such a good time in town with the pretty shopkeeper, you might need a nudge to get your head back in the game."

"My head's always in the game." He shot Burke a look. "But you're right about one thing. That shopkeeper is pretty."

"Miss Grace said she has a son."

"Kyle. He's four."

"His daddy?"

"Gone. One too many tours of military duty."

Burke gave a hiss of breath. "That's a tough thing for a young woman and boy."

"Yeah. She came west hoping to give her son a sense of family. That's why she moved in with Archer."

"How's that working out?"

Reed gave a slight shake of his head. "About how you'd expect with Archer Stone." He took a long drink of coffee before asking, "What's his history with our family?"

The old man gave a shrug of his shoulders. "It's like your grandparents said. He used to be your pa's friend. I thought they were thick as thieves. Then they weren't."

"Do you remember anything in particular that could have driven a wedge between them?"

Burke stared down into his coffee. "It was too long ago, son. The only ones who know for certain are the ones involved, and Archer's the only one left of them. But if I had to guess, I'd say jealousy played a part."

"I know he resents our success. But it's nothing new. Our ranch wasn't exactly failing all those years ago when he and my dad were friends."

Burke shrugged and held his silence.

Reed tossed aside the last of his coffee before linking his hands behind his head and settling deeper into his bedroll.

Burke rubbed his shoulder. "You'd be wise to hit the trail early in the morning if you hope to get those blood samples to the lab. Rain's coming."

"How'd you hear?"

"I listened to my body. These old bones know before those TV weather people."

The two shared a chuckle.

"Did your bones say if the rain would be here tonight?"

"I think we'll be dry until morning."

"Good." Reed pulled his hat over his face and closed his eyes. "Night, Burke."

"Night, son." The old man continued watching the ribbons of color fade as clouds scudded across the moon.

Burke had always been a man of few words. But, despite the years, his memories of Reed's parents were as clear as yesterday. Patrick was the firstborn of Frank and Grace. The crown prince and heir apparent to the Malloy dynasty. And he'd lived up to all their expectations. He worked hard, played harder, and lived life on a fast track. Bernadette Doyle had been the prettiest girl in Glacier Ridge. There were plenty of young hotshots falling all over themselves to get her attention. But once she'd fallen for Patrick Malloy, it was all over. She had eyes for only him.

They'd been too young, but there was no stopping them. When most young people were thinking about prom and high school graduation, they were married. When their friends left for college, they were busy raising the first of their three sons.

They never looked back. Never regretted their impulsive behavior. They were the happiest, most loving couple he'd ever known. If anything, their love rivaled that of Frank and Grace.

And then they were gone. Killed on a snow-covered road, coming back from a night on the town. And the Malloy family had been forever changed by that one terrible moment that would be, in Burke's mind, forever frozen in time.

He set aside his empty mug and settled himself comfortably into his bedroll, drifting back in his mind to relive all the pain and chaos of that one terrible night.

Great One's fancy car a twisted heap of metal up against a tree alongside the snow-covered road. A half dozen vehicles pulled into a semicircle around the scene of the accident. The sheriff, taking notes and snapping photos. His deputy, Archer, who'd been the first one to arrive, sitting dazedly in the snow. A couple of nearby wranglers who'd ridden their horses over to see if they could save any lives. Ranchers in the area who'd seen the fireball and driven their trucks to the site. Frank and Grace, in a state of shock. Colin, who'd been working out in the barn, furious that the bloody bodies hadn't been covered while the investigation continued. Yancy holding on to Great One, who stood in the falling snow, filming the scene like the famous director he was, to keep from allowing his emotions to take over. And Burke himself, alone in the bitter cold, standing to one side, feeling the pain of all of them, while his own heart shattered beyond repair.

Later, as the family struggled to explain to three little boys what had happened, it was Burke who'd dredged up the terrible words to relay the news that their parents were gone.

He gave a last glance at the young man asleep nearby. Reed had been nine years old. And now, all these years later, that singular moment in time had left an indelible mark on his soul. The bright, bold, fearless boy had become an even bolder man, as if, by facing such a daunting challenge so early in life, he'd built an invisible armor against any further attack. As if he dared the world to try crossing his path again. His loss had given him a laser focus on his goals. And every setback had made him even more determined. His work had become his life. Yet that same fearless, workaholic cowboy had a secret, compassionate side. Burke had seen it time and again. Reed Malloy had a tender spot in his heart for anyone or anything beaten down by life.

To Burke's way of thinking, a young woman and her son standing against the world would be a magnet for Reed.

The fact that the woman was a pretty little thing, and the kid a fatherless boy, just made the attraction even stronger.

CHAPTER EIGHT

That supper was worth coming home to." Reed, freshly shaven, his hair in need of a trim, sat back with a smile and looked around the big trestle table. The entire family had gathered for their traditional Saturday evening meal.

Great One sipped his martini. "How's that fancy organic herd coming along?"

"So far, they're exceeding expectations." Reed knocked a fist on the wooden table for luck. "Let's just hope they come through late summer without a problem."

"There are a lot of weeks between now and roundup." Frank eyed his grandson. "Did you ask Burke to stay with the herd?"

"It was his idea. I thought we had enough wranglers for the job, but he said he'd hang around, just in case."

Matt closed a hand over his wife's, so their fingers were twined, a note of affection that wasn't lost on the others.

"Burke knows how much this herd means to you and the rest of us. I think it's become his challenge as much as yours."

"Yeah." Reed nodded. "Besides, while the weather is gentle, he admitted he'd rather be up in the hills than anywhere else."

"I'm with Burke." Luke brushed a wisp of hair from Ingrid's cheek and allowed his hand to linger a moment. "Maybe you and I ought to take a break from house-building this week and ride up into the hills."

Ingrid's smile grew.

Lily's eyes lit with excitement. "Can I come along?"

"You bet. You can bring your camera, Li'l Bit. Maybe we'll even catch a glimpse of Gram Gracie's herd of mustangs."

Lily turned to Grace. "Want to come along, Gram Gracie? We could make it one of your photographic safaris."

Grace gave the little girl a warm smile. "I'd love to, but I promised Frankie some time with him. And you need time with Luke and Ingrid, as well. But I don't see why you and I couldn't head on up to the hills in the coming weeks and spend some time hunting for my mustangs."

"Oh, boy. I can't wait. Two whole trips to the hills." Lily turned to her sister. "Can I go pack?"

Ingrid was laughing as the girl made a mad dash from the room. "You realize our little trip will just whet her appetite for your next safari. She'll pester you until you set a date."

Grace merely smiled. "I know she will. But I was being serious. I'm thinking I need to use this fabulous weather to its best advantage. Soon now, Lily and I will make time for our next photo safari."

"Good." Luke's smile was positively wicked. "And while you and Lily are off playing in the hills"—he shot a heated look at Ingrid—"we'll put our alone time to some good use, too. We'll owe you big-time, Gram Gracie."

While the others laughed, Reed pushed away from the table.

Frank looked up. "Where're you going, sonny boy?"

"Too much love and honeymooning around here for me. I think I'll head into town. Anybody interested in going along?"

Matt, whispering something to his wife, looked over. "Sorry. We've got plans. And they don't include going to town."

Reed gave a mock shudder. "I'd rather you didn't share anything more." He looked toward Luke and Ingrid. "You two?"

Two heads shook in unison.

Luke grinned. "But you might run into Colin. He and Dr. Anita were planning a cozy dinner for two."

"Sounds like they're getting serious."

Grace sighed. "I certainly hope so."

As Reed started toward the mudroom, Great One called, "You planning on seeing your pretty little shop owner?"

Reed plucked a denim jacket from a hook by the door and kept his tone impersonal. "I may run into her in town."

"You're bound to if you stop by her shop."

Great One's comments had everyone around the table grinning.

As Reed sauntered out to his truck, Matt slapped a bill on the table. "Ten dollars says he sees the redhead within ten minutes of hitting town."

Luke shook his head. "That's a no-brainer. But twenty says it'll take him less than five minutes. And when we ask him to confirm it, he'll deny everything."

That had everyone chuckling as the truck's tires spewed gravel before rolling along the driveway that led to the interstate.

* * *

Reed parked his truck in an empty spot along Main Street and sprinted to Ally's Attic.

After his week in the hills, he was impressed by the changes already in place. She'd painted a bright red arch around the door and had filled two giant urns with bright red petunias, tall spikes, and trailing ivy, giving the entrance a festive look. It would be impossible to walk past without pausing to admire the view. And once a person paused, they would be drawn in by the clever displays in the windows.

One window appealed to ranchers, with a bale of straw and an assortment of tools artfully arranged, along with a battered Stetson and a pair of well-worn work gloves.

The other window appealed to young families just starting out, with a faded sofa sporting colorful pillows, an antique dresser painted neon turquoise with glittering silver hardware. A stuffed bobcat had been arranged on the dresser top, alongside an oval mirror trimmed with horseshoes.

All were things that had outlived their usefulness in various ranches and homes around the area. Yet in Ally's hands, they'd become clever and attractive treasures to someone. The entire display had Reed grinning.

Inside he found Ally showing a rancher and his family a display of farm implements. On the other side of the room, Gemma York, wearing a fringed hippie-style vest and torn denims, was busy showing the rancher's teenage son how to play chords on a guitar, while a girl of nine or ten was plinking the keys of an electronic keyboard.

In a corner of the room Kyle was busy running plastic ranch trucks along a vinyl highway that he'd turned into a steep hill by draping one end over the edge of a coffee table. When he caught sight of Reed, he let the trucks fall and raced across the room and into his arms.

"Where've you been?"

Reed scooped him up and wondered at the lightness in his heart. "Up in the hills with my cattle."

"I'm glad you're back."

"Me too."

Kyle shouted, "Look, Mama. Reed's here."

Reed nodded toward Ally, who acknowledged his presence with a quick smile.

As Reed set the little boy on his feet, he called, "See? You were wrong, Mama. Uncle Archer didn't scare Reed away."

She flushed clear to her toes before returning her attention to her customers.

Kyle had no idea he'd caused his mother any embarrassment. "Want to see my trucks?"

"Sure." Reed had to tear his gaze from Ally. She was wearing an ankle-skimming skirt in pale green, with a simple white shirt and white sandals. Her hair fell in soft waves to her shoulders. He trailed Kyle to the space where he'd been playing and knelt down.

"Want to race?"

"Why not?" Reed waited to see which vehicle the boy would pick.

After Kyle chose a silver cattle-hauler, Reed picked up a shiny blue pickup.

"We start here." Kyle set his cattle-hauler at the top of the hill.

Reed set his pickup beside Kyle's.

"These are the rules. Remember now." Kyle's eyes behind the big glasses were fixed on Reed like a teacher giving a lecture. "When I say go, give your truck a push. Okay?"

Reed was grinning. "I think I can remember that much."

"Go."

Reed touched a finger to his vehicle a second after Kyle

set his own truck in motion. The two toys raced down the vinyl strip and landed at the end inches apart, with Kyle's landing first.

"I won!" The little boy's fists pumped in the air.

"Good going, little buddy."

Kyle beamed with pleasure. "Want to go again?"

"Well, yeah. You always want to give the loser a second chance."

They raced again and again, with Kyle winning three out of four races, thanks to Reed's intentionally late starts. At least that was all he would admit to. The fact that he was distracted by the sight of Ally shouldn't have had any bearing on his ability to win.

Across the room they heard the sound of laughter and voices all talking at once as the family weighed the pros and cons of the purchases they were considering.

Ally accepted a credit card from the woman, who was delighted at their family's successful shopping venture.

"Thanks for your help, Gemma," the boy called as he picked up the guitar.

"You're welcome." Gemma waved and smiled.

The man hauled several farm implements outside to his truck, while his children followed, high-fiving each other before struggling to carry their musical instruments.

When they were gone, Ally walked over to where Gemma was standing. "I didn't know you could play the guitar."

The girl flushed. "I can't really play. Just a few chords Jeremy taught me."

"Those few chords just made a sale. So thanks." Ally considered for a moment before saying, "I really like the way you stepped in, Gemma."

The girl shrugged. "Selling's fun. It's what I want to

do. Especially vintage clothing. I love wearing stuff I know other people wore."

"Where do you find them?"

"Mostly in the trash."

Ally bit back a smile. "What would you call your shop, if you had one?"

Gemma gave a shake of her head. "I don't know. I guess my dreams haven't gone that far yet."

Ally thought a moment. "There's a little back room I'm not using. With a few clothes racks and some shelves, you could store a lot of clothes."

The girl's eyes went wide. "I don't have any money to pay you rent."

Ally nodded solemnly. "I understand. But you could always earn the rent by working for me and selling your vintage clothes on the side." She tapped a foot while she mulled. "You could call your little space...Gemma's Closet. It sort of goes with Ally's Attic."

Now Gemma's eyes filled. "Are you being serious?"

Ally shrugged. "Why not? I need some help, and you need to start your own business. It could be good for both of us."

Gemma grabbed Ally in a bear hug. "Oh. Thank you. Thank you. You won't regret this."

Ally hugged her back. "Just one thing. I'll need the names of some references."

Gemma flushed and stepped back, holding herself stiffly. "I've never worked anyplace. Except some babysitting."

"That'll do." Ally pointed to a pad of paper on the counter. "Give me the names and phone numbers of people you've babysat for, and as soon as I check them out tonight, you can get started."

Gemma's smile faded as she began writing on the paper.

They all looked up when Jeremy opened the door. Before he could step inside, Gemma darted toward him. "Gotta go. I'll see you tomorrow."

"Thanks, Gemma. And thanks again for help with that last sale."

Gemma was already steering her boyfriend out the door. "Let's go, Jeremy."

With a nod toward Ally and Reed, the boy took her hand and the two stepped out, letting the door close.

Ally watched Gemma sprint away, with Jeremy following.

When she turned back, Reed shot her a grin. "You're not afraid she'll scare off more customers than she'll draw?"

Ally laughed. "I know she looks"—she shrugged—"different. But there's something sweet about her. I like her. Besides, she's persistent. And I admire that."

Reed tucked a strand of hair behind her ear. "Because she reminds you of you."

Ally flushed before turning the OPEN sign around on the glass door, indicating that her shop was now closed for the day.

Reed bent to help Kyle pick up the cars. "Did you two have dinner?"

Kyle answered for both of them. "We got macaroni and cheese at D and B's and ate it upstairs in our 'partment."

"Sounds good. Did you have dessert?"

Kyle shook his head. "We didn't have time. Mama said we had to eat fast 'cause there were customers waiting."

"Then it's a good thing you decided to hire some help."

Ally sighed. "After that big rush at the grand opening, I learned my lesson. I'd have been swamped without Dot and Barb's help. I hope Gemma works out."

"So do I." Reed tucked his hands in his back pockets.

"Now that you're closed for the day, how about going for ice cream."

"At D and B's?" Kyle was already heading for the door.

"Have you tried I's Cream yet?"

Both Kyle and Ally shook their heads.

He grinned. "I can see that you both need to get out around town more often. Ivy has the best ice cream in Montana. Come on."

They danced out the door and headed up the sidewalk until they came to a glittering little shop with festive colored lights and paper lanterns in the windows.

Inside, they studied the dozens of varieties of ice cream being offered before making their choices. Outside, they settled themselves on wooden stools made of tree stumps arranged around a smooth tree-stump table.

Kyle was busy licking a purple-and-green confection.

Reed arched a brow. "How's your Spotted Lizard ice cream?"

"Good." He eyed Reed's double-dipped cone. "What's yours?"

"Jolly Holly. Red berries and mint." Reed turned to Ally. "And yours?"

"It's called the Kitchen Sink." She grinned. "It has everything. Nuts. Cookie chunks. Candy pieces. Bits of marshmallow."

"You're one brave soul." Reed winked at Kyle. "Your mom's the first one I've ever met willing to try that."

When they were finished, Ally went inside and returned with a handful of wet towels to wash away all traces of ice cream from Kyle's hands and face.

She was just tossing the towels in a waste bin cleverly made to look like a tree trunk when she heard Reed say, "Gram Gracie said I might run into the two of you in town."

He turned to include Ally in the introductions. "Ally Shaw and Kyle, this is my uncle, Colin Malloy, and Dr. Anita Cross."

"Hello." Ally offered a handshake. "It's nice to meet you."

"I saw your new shop." Anita was smiling. "It looks fascinating. I can't wait to find some time away from the clinic to stop by and browse."

"Come by any time. And once we're settled, I'm hoping to bring Kyle to the clinic for a well visit."

"We'd love to see him." Anita stooped down, so she was eye level with the little boy. "How old are you, Kyle?"

"I'm almost five."

"Do you like picture puzzles?"

His eyes went wide. "Uh-huh."

"Good. We have a table with several puzzles in our waiting room. And a prize for the first patient to complete one."

"Oh, boy." He turned to his mother. "Can we go there now?"

"Not tonight. But soon."

Anita stood and winked at Ally, who was looking amazed at his reaction. "Call Agnes, our assistant, whenever you'd like to set up a time."

"I certainly will." Ally arched a brow. "Do you have children, Anita?"

"Not yet." She cast a sideways glance at Colin. "Why do you ask?"

"Because you're a genius at reading them."

"All part of my training."

Ally shook her head. "Some things can't be taught."

Colin caught Anita's hand. "See? I'm not the only one who thinks that." He turned to the others. "She's got a special way with people. All people. And it's a gift."

Reed clapped a hand on his uncle's shoulder. "I'd say you're a lucky man."

Colin beamed before nodding toward the ice cream shop. "Time for that fancy dessert I promised you."

"Try the Kitchen Sink," Ally said. "It was amazing."

"Thanks." Anita laughed. "Now I don't have to agonize over all those choices."

After calling good night, they parted.

Reed turned back to see his uncle and the doctor arm in arm as they entered I's Cream Shop.

He and Ally walked along the streets, with Kyle between them, pausing occasionally to call out to someone they knew or to peer into the windows of shops along the way.

"Are you all settled into your apartment now?"

Ally looked down at Kyle's smiling face. "We are. And we've found a nice rhythm to the days. While I work, Kyle has his own corner of the room where he can play. We're able to eat our meals upstairs together most days, thanks to the bell on the counter. Whenever I hear it, I know there's a customer downstairs. And then, in midafternoon, Gemma comes in and I get to take Kyle upstairs for some quiet time. It's just so nice having precious time together."

"And your uncle? Has he come by to see the place?"

Her smile faltered. "Not yet. But soon, I hope."

"Is he cool to the fact that you've moved out?"

"I'm not sure how he feels." She thought a moment before saying, "But I think, now that he realizes we're really gone, he's grateful to have his privacy back. I'm hoping the next step in our relationship is peace and, in time, friendship."

"Sounds ambitious, but good. I know it's something you want. I hope it's something Archer wants, too." He paused when they came to a crosswalk and, without thinking, he picked up Kyle before catching Ally's hand when it was clear to cross.

When they reached the other side, he set Kyle on his feet, then continued holding Ally's hand until they came to her shop.

"I like what you did with the entrance."

Ally studied it with a critical eye. "Thanks. It certainly helps. As soon as I see more profit, I intend to paint the entire building. But for now, the bright entrance helps me forget how dingy the rest of the building looks."

Kyle danced up to the door and waited while Ally fished out her key. "Can Reed come upstairs and see my pictures?"

Ally looked over. "If you have plans...?"

"No plans, except to see the two of you." He held the door as they stepped inside. "I'd like to see your pictures, Kyle."

The little boy raced up the stairs ahead of them.

Ally turned to lock the door and gave out a little hiss of surprise as a figure loomed in the doorway.

A man's hand pushed against the door, shoving it inward.

"I'm sorry. I'm closed for the..." Ally's words died in her throat. Her face registered a mixture of shock and surprise. "Glen? What in the world are you doing in Montana?"

The man, dressed in a rumpled suit and tie, looked beyond her to where Reed stood and shot him a dismissive look. "I came here to see you."

Ally's tone shifted from suspicion to anger. "But how could you find me? I didn't tell anyone at work where I would be."

"My specialty is security. Remember?" He reached out a hand. "Why don't you send the cowboy away and we can talk?"

She shrank back, away from his touch.

Seeing her reaction, Reed stepped in front of her. "Reed Malloy." He stuck out his hand, forcing the man to accept his handshake. "And you are...?"

"Glen Lloyd." The man shook hands before folding his arms across his chest. "Ally and I worked together in Virginia. We go back a ways."

"The lady doesn't seem thrilled to see you."

Glen's hands suddenly fisted at his sides. "What's that to you?" A sly look came into his eyes. He turned to Ally. "And you tried to paint yourself as that independent, I-can-go-it-alone chick. I'll give you this. You had me fooled. And now you've already found some poor hick in this backwater town to be your champion."

Ally sounded weary. "Go back to Virginia, Glen. If our supervisor knew you'd broken through security to find me, she'd have your job."

His eyes narrowed. "Are you threatening to report me?"

Ally shook her head. "It doesn't have to come to that if you just leave." She opened the door and stood her ground until he walked outside.

Even then, she remained at the door, watching him walk away as she hugged her arms about herself, as though holding herself together by a thread.

CHAPTER NINE

Ally remained at the door until she saw Glen Lloyd settle into a nearby car and drive away. When she turned, Reed was silently watching her.

"You deserve an explanation, Reed."

"Only if you want to talk about him."

"I want to tell you." She took a deep breath. "Glen was a coworker in Virginia. Other than a photograph of Rick and Kyle on my desk, I made it a point to keep my private life private in the workplace. But Glen noticed my lack of a wedding ring and started asking questions. I told him my personal information was off-limits." She crossed her arms over her chest. "When word came that Rick hadn't made it home from his last assignment..." She sighed. "Glen started coming on to me, saying now more than ever I needed a good guy in my life. A responsible, dependable guy. There was something...off about him. Something almost...creepy. The more I evaded, the more he pushed, saying he wanted 'to comfort' me." Her eyes narrowed. "When I made the decision to move, I deliberately made certain Glen was kept out of the loop. I left without a word to him. It never occurred to me that he would break company rules and sneak a look at my personnel file."

"Was Glen your reason for leaving Virginia?"

"No." She gave a vehement shake of her head. "I certainly wouldn't uproot myself and my son over him. I came here hoping to connect with family."

"Now that Glen's found you, do you feel threatened?"

She thought about it before looking toward the door. "I'm not sure how I feel. I'm still trying to process the fact that he went to so much trouble to find me. In Virginia I thought of him as annoying, but harmless."

"Montana is a long way from Virginia. Any guy who would come this far shouldn't be considered harmless." Reed paused before adding, "I think you need to have a chat with Sheriff Graystoke."

She blinked. "Isn't he my uncle's boss?"

Reed nodded.

"I don't want to do anything that could cause more friction between my uncle and me."

"I guess you need to decide which is more important, your shaky relationship with Archer or your concern about a coworker who invaded your private files and followed you all the way from Virginia."

Ally stood tapping a finger on her arm, a sure sign that her mind was working overtime. "I suppose, in the morning, I might..."

"Reeeed." Kyle's voice carried from above the stairs. "You coming up?"

"I'll be right there, little buddy." Reed turned to Ally. "You were saying?"

She shook her head. "I'll sleep on it and hold off making a decision about talking to the sheriff until morning."

"That's your call." He indicated the stairs. "Mind if I go up and see Kyle's pictures?"

Without a word she led the way.

Kyle was standing impatiently in the doorway of his room. "Come on, Reed."

Ally turned toward the kitchen. "You go ahead. I'll make some coffee. That is, unless you want to leave. Maybe, after Glen..." She looked away. "Maybe now you'd rather leave."

"I have all the time in the world."

His words had her visibly relaxing.

When Reed stepped inside the room, the little boy pointed to the framed pictures hanging over his bed. "I drew them, and Mama put these..." He paused, searching for the right word.

"Frames. Your mom framed them?"

"Yes. And let me paint the frames red and blue, like my pillows."

"Hey. These are good." Reed moved closer to study the crude drawings of a red-haired boy in glasses wearing a cowboy hat and sitting astride a black horse, like the horse on his pillow. A second picture was of a boy and man standing in a meadow of green grass and bright flowers, staring at the sky, while above them hovered a drone being operated by the boy.

"That's me." Kyle pointed to the boy on the horse. "And that's you and me with the toy in Mama's shop."

Reed ruffled Kyle's hair. "Are you sure you're only four?"

"I told you. I'm almost five."

"I forgot. This looks awfully professional, even for a kid who's almost five."

The little boy was beaming under such rare and unexpected praise. "Mama, wait till you hear what Reed..."

He ran toward the kitchen, with Reed trailing behind.

Archer's voice filled the room. "That coffee smells good. Were you expecting...?" The deputy's voice trailed off when he caught sight of Reed coming out of Kyle's room.

His friendly tone turned to a furious snarl. "I get it now. So I was right. This is why you were in such a hurry to move out of my house and into a place of your own."

Kyle's eyes went wide before he ducked behind Reed.

Reed stepped farther into the room. "Hi, Archer."

The man ignored him.

Ally filled a cup with coffee and held it out to her uncle. "Here's your—"

"Don't play nice with me. Now that you've got your own little love nest, it's party central."

"Archer, it's not what you think..."

He shoved her hand away, sending hot coffee sloshing over the rim of the cup. At the top of the stairs he pivoted. "A word of warning, Malloy. You think you're such a hotshot. That entrance downstairs should have a revolving door. If Ally's anything like my sister, you'll just be one of many."

His booted feet beat a steady tattoo down the stairs. Moments later the door slammed.

Without a word Ally set the cup aside and dropped to her knees, mopping up the puddle of coffee on the floor.

Kyle crept out from behind Reed and walked over to his mother. "Why was Uncle Archer so mad, Mama?"

She brushed at her eyes before managing a weak smile. "I guess he didn't like my coffee."

"That wasn't nice. He was mean to you." He patted her

shoulder before climbing up to kneel on one of the kitchen chairs to sip the chocolate milk Ally had already set out for him.

Ally rinsed the rag at the sink before filling two cups with coffee and setting them on the table and sinking onto a chair. Instead of meeting Reed's gaze, she lowered her head and stared hard at the table.

The presence of the little boy had Reed fighting to bank his temper before crossing the room to sit across from Ally.

Kyle watched him take a sip. "Do you like Mama's coffee?"

Reed managed a smile. "It's perfect. Hot and strong, just the way I like it."

"Reed likes my pictures, too. Don't you, Reed?"

"Yeah, little buddy. You're an artist."

Kyle downed his milk in a few swallows and climbed down from the chair. "Can I go get my pj's on?"

Ally roused herself. "Need some help?"

"I can do it." He turned to Reed. "When I'm ready for bed, will you come and say good night?"

"You bet. Just give me a holler."

When they were alone, Reed reached across the table to take Ally's hand in his. "I'm sorry about my timing. I seem to be always in the way at the very time your uncle decides to show up."

She pulled her hand free and shoved away from the table, her eyes narrowing to little points of flame. "Don't you dare apologize for my uncle's bad behavior."

"Hey." He rounded the table and caught her by the shoulders.

Embarrassed, she tried to push away, but he held on firmly. He could feel the little tremors rocketing through her, proof that she was fighting a war of emotions.

"You have a right to your feelings."

"No. I'm not feeling..." She surprised him by bursting into tears.

Once started, she allowed the tears to flow until the front of his shirt was damp.

When she was done, he handed her a handkerchief. She wiped her eyes and blew her nose, and knotted the handkerchief into a ball that she gripped in one fisted hand.

"Feeling better?"

She looked away. "I feel stupid. I never cry."

He put a hand under her chin, forcing her to meet his eyes. "Hey, Red. Talk to me."

Her head came up sharply. Despite her anguish, a small smile curved her lips. "Red?"

"Sorry. I can't help it. Every time I see that hair, I think of a red flag just teasing me to charge in and"— without realizing it, his voice lowered to a whisper— "devour you."

His fingers plunged into a tangle of hair and a fierce look came into his eyes before he lowered his face to hers.

She remained perfectly still as his mouth covered hers in a kiss so hot, so hungry, it rocked them both back on their heels. There was nothing sweet or gentle about the kiss. It was filled with so many emotions. Anger. Anguish. All flash and fire that had them both reacting as though burned.

He lifted his head to stare down into her eyes and felt a wave of such tenderness. He found himself wanting, more than anything, to make her feel cherished. Protected.

He lingered over the kiss, allowing her to sink slowly, deeply, into the passion. He drank in the sweet taste of her and ran his big, work-roughened hands over skin that was as smooth as cream.

When he felt her gradually responding to his tender touch, he stepped back, his hands framing her face.

A hint of moisture glistened on her lashes, and he felt again the need to comfort. To protect.

This time, when he lowered his head and his mouth moved over hers, taking, demanding, she brought her arms around his neck and offered more.

"Do you know how long I've thought about kissing you?" He spoke the words inside her mouth as he took the kiss deeper.

He changed the angle of the kiss and dragged her roughly against him, needing to feel her in every part of his body. Her breasts were flattened against his chest. Her thighs pressed to his. Her mouth on his, opening to him, eager, avid.

His hands moved along her sides until his thumbs encountered the fullness of her breasts.

When she drew back, he brought his hands to her shoulders to calm, to soothe. "You feel so good in my arms."

She drew in a long, shuddering breath. "Reed, you don't know anything about me."

"This is all I need to know." His hands weren't gentle as he dragged her close and pressed her back against the kitchen counter until their bodies were fused. The quick sexual tug was so compelling, dragging him down, down, until he was drowning in the taste of her, the feel of her, warm and willing in his arms.

He heard her sigh as her arms came around his waist, and he was lost. Lost in a kiss that spoke of hunger, and need, and a desperate desire to take and give until they were both sated.

He plunged his hands into her hair while he ran hot, wet kisses across her forehead, her cheek, her jaw, before returning to her lips. The most compelling lips he'd ever tasted. He wanted, more than anything in this world, to fill himself with her. And he knew, though it was nothing more than a few kisses, he could easily cross a line.

His heart was pounding in his chest, his lungs straining.

"Mama. Reeeed."

The sound of Kyle's little voice calling from his bedroom was a dash of frigid water on two overheated bodies. It was probably the only thing that could have brought Reed to his senses.

Two heads came up.

Twin sighs filled the air as they struggled to respond.

Ally was the first to find her voice. "We'll be right there, honey."

She put a hand to Reed's chest, as though to steady herself.

"I'd say Kyle's timing is as bad as mine. Or as good," Reed murmured against her temple.

"I think it's a good thing." Her voice was shaky, revealing nerves.

When she was composed, she turned away and started from the kitchen, with Reed following. He paused in the doorway of the little boy's bedroom while Ally walked to the side of his bed and settled herself on the edge of the mattress.

"I brushed my teeth."

"You're such a good boy."

He looked over at the man standing in the doorway. "Want to hear my prayers?"

"Sure." Reed walked in and paused at the foot of the bed.

Kyle folded his hands and said solemnly, "Bless my mama. And bless my daddy in heaven. And bless Uncle Archer, so he learns to like us." He looked shyly toward the tall man who filled his line of vision. "And bless Reed and keep him safe. Amen."

Ally pressed a kiss to her son's mouth. "Those were fine prayers. Good night, honey."

"Night, Mama."

Reed reached under the covers and pinched Kyle's big toe. "Good night, little buddy. Thanks for those prayers."

"You're welcome. Night, Reed."

Ally turned off the light and left the door slightly ajar, so that light from the hallway filtered into the boy's bedroom.

She and Reed descended the stairs in silence.

When they reached the lower level, she said, "You should go now."

"I know." Instead of turning toward the door, he paused to look at her. "I don't like knowing you and Kyle are alone here."

"Reed, I've been alone for most of my life."

"I understand. But tonight is different."

She put her hands on her hips. "In what way?"

"Your uncle left in a huff. You've had a taste of his temper."

"He's gone now. That hot temper will cool."

"I hope so. But there's also your coworker who drove a thousand miles to find you without your permission. Now that he knows where you are, who's to say he won't come back?"

"Glen isn't dangerous. He's just..." She shook her head. "He's impulsive. He's annoying. But I honestly don't believe he'd hurt me."

"I wonder how many women have said those words and lived to regret them." He paused before adding, "I'd feel better if you'd let me stay."

His words had her going very still before she sighed. "I can't let you stay here, Reed. That little scene in the kitchen

.ought to be enough to tell both of us that we need some space."

"All right then. There's another choice."

At her arched brow he decided to say his piece. "You could consider coming home with me. You and Kyle would be surrounded by my family."

A ghost of a smile curved her lips. "Knowing how my uncle feels about you and your family, that sort of thing would certainly guarantee that he and I would never reconcile."

Reed thought about it before nodding. "I get that you're between a rock and a hard place. Still, I'm not comfortable leaving you and Kyle alone here."

"If there's any trouble, I'll call you."

He shrugged. "That's not enough. I live an hour away." He indicated her cell phone. "Will you agree to put the sheriff's number on speed dial?"

"All right."

As he dictated the number, she programmed it into her phone.

"You promise you'll call him if you feel threatened in any way?"

"Promise."

"And call me, as well?"

"I will, Reed."

"Okay." He turned toward the door, then turned back and drew her close. Against her temple he murmured, "I could sleep down here. Didn't I see an old bedroom set over in one corner?"

"You did. And I'm telling you again. You can't stay. We both know where that will lead."

"But..."

"Nice try." She brushed a quick kiss over his lips before stepping back. "Good night, Reed."

His smile was quick and dangerous. "You're a tough woman, Red."

"Yes, I am. And don't you forget it."

He let himself out and waited until he saw her turn the key in the lock. With a lift of his hand he sauntered toward his truck.

As he drove away, he watched the lights in the shop go out and a light in the upper bedroom go on.

They could be upstairs together right now. Kyle was asleep. They could...

Bad idea.

Still, he was worried about her.

Though he tried to tell himself he had the noblest of intentions, the truth was, he was no longer sure of anything.

He definitely wanted to ensure that she and Kyle were safe. But there was no denying he wanted her.

And had, he realized, since the first time he'd seen her.

Reed was sleeping so soundly, the phone on his bedside table rang three times before it penetrated the thick layer of fog.

He was barely aware of what he was doing as he snatched it up, hoping to silence the noise.

"Yeah?"

"Reed."

The sound of his name in that breathy voice had him instantly alert and swinging his legs to the edge of the bed. "Ally. What...?"

"I heard glass breaking downstairs and I—"

The line went dead.

He swore as he pulled on denims, boots, shirt and made a mad dash down the stairs and out to his truck.

While he gunned the engine and tore along the highway, he called the sheriff's phone. Getting the lawman's message center, he drove like a madman, grateful there was no traffic on the interstate.

By the time he rolled into town and raced along Main Street, his adrenaline was pumping at a furious rate. He grabbed his rifle, jumped out of his truck, and ran toward Ally's shop. When he saw the shattered glass of the big display window and noted the front door standing open, his heart nearly stopped.

Inside, Ally, barefoot and wearing a knee-length cotton kimono, her hair in wild disarray, was talking with Sheriff Eugene Graystoke.

Just seeing the sheriff there was enough to have relief surging through Reed.

"Malloy?" The sheriff turned to him with a questioning look.

Reed stepped past him to put a hand on Ally's arm. "You all right?"

"I'm fine."

"Kyle?"

She shook her head. "Sleeping."

He let out a long, slow breath before turning to the sheriff. "I tried phoning you, but you didn't answer."

"When Ms. Shaw called, I headed over. Any other calls went to my message center. What are you doing here, Reed?"

"Ally called me."

"So, you two are friends?" The sheriff looked from one to the other.

Reed didn't bother to respond. "Did you see who did this? Was anybody hanging around when you got here?"

Sheriff Graystoke shook his head. "The street was empty. No vehicles. I made a visual check of the rest of the building and found no further damage, other than the big front window."

Reed looked at the damage. Shards of glass cluttered the pretty display and spilled over to litter the floor.

The sheriff cleared his throat. "I've asked Miss Shaw for the names of anybody who might have a grudge against her, or who may want to make mischief."

"Mischief?" Reed's tone was incredulous.

Eugene pointed. "If someone wanted to break in, they would have forced the door. Instead, they chose a display window. And it doesn't appear to be premeditated, but rather something done on the spur of the moment."

"Why do you say that?" Reed studied the display, trying to see it through the eyes of a lawman.

"They used a tan brick." Eugene pointed to where it sat amid the rubble. "There's a pile of them just down the street, where Gert and Teddy Gleason are adding some fancy columns to their spa building. I'm thinking that your intruder was hot under the collar, and seeing the bricks gave him the idea to vent some anger."

Reed turned to Ally. "Did you give him Glen's name?"

The sheriff answered for her. "Glen Lloyd. Former co-worker who lives in Virginia."

To Ally he said, "You happen to have a picture of this guy?"

She thought a minute. "His photo will be in the company manual. I can bring it up on my computer and send it to your phone or computer."

Eugene nodded. "Perfect. Once I get it, I'll send it out to law enforcement agencies around the area. If he's on the run, we'll find him."

"And if he's still in the area?" Reed asked.

Eugene shrugged. "Glacier Ridge is a small town. He should be easy enough to spot if he's still here."

Reed looked at Ally. "What about your soon-to-be new employee? Did you check her references?"

"An employee?" The sheriff took out his notebook. "Who would that be?"

"Her name is Gemma York."

Eugene frowned. "I know her. Dropped out of school. Hangs with a boy..." He thought a minute. "Jeremy Clancy. She was involved in a theft of some money from a family where she was babysitting. The family refused to prosecute, but I've always had my suspicion about those two. The last I heard, her mother threw her out of the house and she and the boy were sleeping in his truck."

Ally had a hand to her mouth to cover her gasp of surprise. "Oh, poor Gemma."

Eugene's frown grew. "Don't be too quick to pity her. Poor Gemma, as you call her, could be the one who caused this damage."

"She wouldn't do that." Ally pointed to the back room. "I suggested that she could work for me and in return she could set up her own little business in there, rent free."

"Business?"

"Vintage clothing."

Eugene frowned as he continued writing in his notebook. "Did you at least think to ask for references before hiring her?"

"I did. But there were no names on the sheet of paper she gave me."

"Uh-huh." The sheriff nodded.

"While we're talking about suspects..." Reed looked over at Ally. "Did you tell the sheriff about Archer's visit earlier tonight? He was furious when he left."

The sheriff's head came up sharply. "My deputy? Why would he be visiting you, Ms. Shaw?"

"Archer is my uncle."

Surprise showed in the sheriff's eyes. "As far as I knew, he had no kin except an older sister. Dee."

"Dee was my mother. When I came to town, I lived with him for a few weeks, until I was able to move into the upper apartment of this building."

"Well, I'll be." He shook his head. "Everybody's been talking about the new business in town. I wonder why Archer never mentioned you two were related."

Ally flushed. "He never forgave my mother for leaving. And he...doesn't approve of me. I'd rather you not mention any of this to him. It will only add to his anger."

Eugene gave her a long, slow appraisal. "Archer may be my deputy, but he's not above the law. If he paid a call on you and left in a temper, he'd better have a very good alibi about where he was when this went down."

Ally bit her lip. "Maybe...I could save you confronting him until"—she took a deep breath—"we take a look at the footage from my security camera."

Reed's head swiveled, and he started grinning.

Ally started talking faster to cover her embarrassment. "I didn't want to spend money on expensive equipment for this shop, but I did manage to jerry-rig a camera I took from a toy drone."

Eugene Graystoke shook his head from side to side while a smile creased his face. "A security camera in Glacier Ridge? That's a first. Who'd have thought?"

Ally swallowed. "While living in Virginia, I worked in security. It just seemed the most natural thing to do when I opened my shop here. I mounted the camera over the front door. Since it was meant for a toy, I don't know if it's capable of capturing anyone beyond the door all the way to the display window, but I can take a look at the video on my computer."

The sheriff was rubbing his hands together. "Now you're talking, Ms. Shaw. Would you mind turning it over to me?"

"I'd be happy to. Would you like the information sent to your phone or your office computer?"

"Both. How I love technology." He jotted down his office computer information and handed it to her. "I'll head to my office now and review the footage when I get it. Then I'll be in contact."

"Thank you, Sheriff."

"In the meantime, you'll need to get that window boarded up and see that all your doors are secure."

"I will."

He turned to Reed. "I'd like to talk to you outside."

Reed trailed the sheriff out the door.

The lawman didn't waste time on small talk. "You and the lady more than friends?"

"Not yet. But if I had my way, that would change."

"I see." Eugene thought a moment. "I heard from Barb and Dot that she has a son."

"Kyle. Four. Or, as he likes to say, almost five."

A hint of a smile touched Eugene's lips. "Yeah, I get that. I have three kids of my own. I'll tell you, Reed. I don't like the looks of this. There was real anger in that damage. I tried to keep it on the down-low and call it mischief. But it has the look of someone in a fit of fury."

"You don't think she's safe here."

The lawman shrugged. "The lady is a smart cookie. And careful. That camera was a stroke of genius. But I'm not sure that's enough to protect a mother and child from someone bent on doing harm."

"I asked her to come to the ranch. She refused. And I can't blame her. She has a business here, and a place she's turning into a home for her and her son."

"If she can't stay at your place, how about you staying here, at least for the night?"

Reed nodded. "I'd be happy to. The lady ... not so much."

Eugene looked him in the eye. "You might want to be a little more persuasive. If it comes down to saving her money or her life, I hope she makes the right choice."

The two shook hands before the sheriff sauntered off.

CHAPTER TEN

Reed rummaged through the back of his truck and returned to Ally's shop with some sheets of plywood and a tool belt. Because there was often a repair of one kind or another needed at the range shacks up in the hills, he was prepared for emergencies.

After clearing the window of all the broken glass, he neatly hammered the wood into place around the window frame.

Inside, Ally was busy sweeping up the debris and dumping it into a trash can.

When she finished, she turned toward the stairs. "Come on. I'll make some coffee."

Before she could walk away, he came up behind her and put his arms around her, drawing her back against him. "Slow down. Take a minute to breathe."

"I'm afraid to."

"Why?" He murmured the word against her ear.

She gave a long, drawn-out sigh. "If I let myself think, I'll turn into a blubbering baby."

"Hey." He turned her into his arms and gathered her close.

"Oh, Reed. When I heard that sound..." Her body trembled with a series of shudders. "I was terrified."

Though she fought, the tears she'd been holding at bay won. Once started, they flowed like a river.

At last she drew in a deep breath. "This is the second time tonight I got your shirt wet with my tears."

"I'm not complaining."

"I am. I feel like such a coward."

"You?" He held her a little away and stared into her eyes. "Red, you're the bravest woman I know."

She dragged in another breath before pushing free of his arms. "Come on. After waking you and dragging you all this way, the least I can do is give you coffee."

She took his hand and led him up the stairs. Once there, she paused. "First, I need to check on Kyle."

"You go ahead."

The minute she was gone, he filled the coffeemaker and plugged it in before rummaging through the refrigerator. A short time later, when she returned carrying her laptop and wearing shorts and a denim shirt she'd tossed on in haste, she looked around with surprise. "Wow. You work fast."

The table was set with paper plates, cups, and saucers. Coffee was perking, and Reed was turning scrambled eggs onto two plates.

"So do you." He gave her an admiring look. "Great legs, Red."

She didn't bother to respond as she quickly set up her computer.

Reed filled two cups and handed her one before standing behind her to view the video over her shoulder.

They watched several minutes of cars parking and people walking past the shop. There were long stretches of empty film, as dusk settled and the space directly in front of the shop went blank except for an occasional passerby. They saw themselves leave and later return. They watched Gemma and Jeremy leave hand in hand, saw Glen arrive and leave, followed by Archer's arrival and departure. Reed watched himself walk from the shop. Then darkness filled the video for what seemed an endless amount of time. Suddenly a shadowy figure could be seen approaching, then stepping just out of camera range. Moments later the camera shook violently.

"That's the moment of impact," Ally announced.

"Can you play it again?"

She did, playing it over and over. But the shadowy image was so blurred, and just enough out of range of the camera, it was impossible to detect whether it was a man or woman, or even a large animal.

"Can you enhance that?" Reed asked.

Ally shook her head. "With the right equipment, I could. That was something I routinely did in my job. But here, without expensive high-tech backup, I'm afraid this is all I have. A blur of movement, and then that crash."

Reed pointed to the way the figure approached the door, then ducked back. "It looks as though the intruder caught sight of the camera."

She nodded. "It's easy enough to spot. I didn't try to camouflage it."

"Still, not everybody would be expecting surveillance in a place like Glacier Ridge." He put a hand on her shoulder and squeezed.

She closed a hand over his, her gaze still fixed on her computer screen.

He set a plate of toast and scrambled eggs next to her laptop. "Here. Eat."

She smiled. "Thanks." But instead of eating, she kept replaying the video.

"How's Kyle?"

She looked up, distracted. "Sleeping like a baby."

"Sheriff Graystoke likes my idea."

"What idea?"

"Of having you and Kyle stay at the ranch."

She moved her computer aside and simply stared at him. "I have a business to run."

"I agree. But after work, you have a life to live. Spend your nights with my family at the ranch."

"Reed, you can't just move two strangers, a woman and her child, into your family's home and expect them to welcome us with open arms."

"That's exactly what they'll do. You're not strangers. They saw both of you at the open house."

When she opened her mouth to argue, he pointed to her untouched food. "Eat."

She took several bites of egg and swallowed.

He reached across the table and picked up her toast, slathering it with strawberry jam before handing it back to her.

She tasted, smiled, and proceeded to eat everything on her plate before reaching for her coffee. "That was really good. Thank you."

"You're welcome. Now, about spending your nights at my place..."

She held up a hand. "I'll think about it."

"There's that mom secret code again, which means you don't want to make a decision."

She couldn't help laughing. "I should be so mad at you for clueing Kyle in on mom secrets."

"Say yes."

"What would I be agreeing to?"

"Spending your nights with the most amazing, crazy, fun family you'll ever meet."

She rolled her eyes. "Don't try to oversell this, Reed."

"Okay. You want honesty? They're nosy and opinionated and overbearing. And I love every one of them."

At her wrinkled brow he added, "Come on. You'll enjoy yourself. And Kyle will love it. I'll have him roping and riding and becoming a natural-born cowboy in no time."

"Every city boy's dream." She gave a long, deep sigh. "Why do I think you're not going to let up until I give in?"

"You're starting to know me too well. Say yes."

She took another drink of coffee and sat back, brooding, before she looked over at him. "I'll think about—"

"Yes or no?"

From between gritted teeth she muttered, "I guess I'm willing to give it a try. But not tonight. I'm not willing to wake Kyle from a sound sleep."

"Then I guess I'll just have to stay here the rest of the night."

She shot him a look. "Fine. You saw that old bedroom set downstairs. I don't have any sheets for the bed, or even a spare pillow, but you're welcome to it."

He grinned and picked up his empty plate before setting it in the sink. As he started toward the stairs, he said in an exaggerated drawl, "Don't you worry, little missy. You're talking to a cowboy here. I'm used to sleeping in the wild with nothing more than a saddle for a pillow and a rifle by my side."

At the top of the stairs he paused and turned. "If you start to feel scared or lonesome, you know where to find me."

She tossed a wet dishrag at him, missing his head by inches.

He continued down the stairs, chuckling all the way.

Ally sat at the kitchen table reading the email sent by the sheriff, acknowledging receipt of the surveillance video, and asking several questions. After answering them via email, she played the video again, staring intently at the computer screen.

Reed was right about one thing. Whoever had approached the door had spotted that little camera and backed off quickly. That fact could point to Glen, since he'd spent years in the security business. But then, she reasoned, her uncle would have had plenty of experience with security, as well, while working in law enforcement.

And what about Gemma? These days, most young people expected to find cameras pointed at them everywhere they turned. There had been plenty of time for Gemma to spot the unsophisticated security Ally had rigged over the door.

Ally drummed her fingers on the table, thinking about what Sheriff Graystoke had revealed about Gemma. She really liked the girl. There was something edgy and determined about her that touched Ally in a special way. Still, she couldn't deny Gemma's reluctance to offer up any references. It could be because she was ashamed of being accused of stealing. Or it could be because she was actually guilty of the theft. But would Gemma resort to destruction of the shop to deter Ally from learning the truth? Was this frightening damage done merely as a distraction?

There were too many questions whirling around in her mind. Questions without answers. With a sigh Ally carried her laptop to her bedroom and set it on her dresser before undressing and pulling on the little sleep slip she wore to bed.

Too keyed up to close her eyes, she lay very still, trying to sort out her thoughts.

Though she would never admit this to Reed, she was relieved that he'd insisted on staying. Just knowing he was downstairs gave her a feeling of safety. Whoever broke her window could decide to return and attempt more destruction. But at least she wouldn't have to face her attacker alone.

Alone. That word had defined her life for so long. She and Kyle alone against the world. And now, suddenly, there was someone else.

Reed wanted her to spend her nights at his ranch. The thought brought a smile to her lips. She tried to imagine herself and Kyle on a ranch. They would be two fish out of water.

Still, Kyle would be in little boy heaven. He'd always loved horses. Tractors. But always, in the city, they'd been toys, and life on a ranch merely a daydream. What would he do with a real horse? A real tractor? How would he fit into real ranch life?

Real. Reed Malloy was the real thing. A cowboy. A man's man. Maybe that was why her son was so drawn to him. For all his young life, her sweet boy had been denied the attention of a man.

She rolled to her side and punched her pillow. The same could be said for her. Ever since she'd first met Reed Malloy, she'd been fighting an almost overpowering attraction. It would be so easy to give in and just let things happen. But the timing was all wrong. She needed to get her life in order before allowing anyone else in. A man like Reed Malloy would be a definite distraction. He was already messing with her mind.

She rolled to her other side and pulled the sheet over her

head just as she heard a loud thump coming from downstairs.

The intruder had come back, bent on even more destruction. And now Reed was in the line of fire.

She was out of bed, heart pounding, cell phone in hand, as she raced headlong down the stairs and careened into a wall of solid muscle with enough force to leave her stunned. She felt as if she'd just slammed into a wall of concrete.

"Hey now." Reed's voice whispered in her ear.

His arms came around her just in time to keep her from falling.

"I heard…" She held on and found she could barely breathe. Sucking in air she tried again. "I thought …"

Her face was pressed to his naked chest. He was, she realized, barefoot, his jeans unsnapped and low on his hips. She couldn't decide if she was breathless from the dregs of her own fear or from the feel of all those glorious muscles wrapped around her.

"Sorry." He ran a hand down her hair in an attempt to soothe. "I was moving some furniture to free up a recliner I'd spotted. I didn't mean to wake you."

At his touch she went very still as she was forced to absorb the most amazing sizzle of heat along her spine. A sizzle that had her nerves jumping.

Sensing her unease, he closed his big hands over the tops of her arms and held her a little away. Now, as he studied her, a wide smile curved his lips. "Why, Red, is this what you were wearing under that robe thing?"

"The robe thing is called a kimono."

"Whatever." His smile grew as he studied the little wisp of nude silk barely skimming her from torso to hips. "I do like your choice of night wear, ma'am."

Seeing her flush, he couldn't help himself. His fingers teased the spaghetti straps at her shoulders, sending a series of shivers along her spine.

"I wonder. If I were to do this..." He moved one tiny strap off the shoulder, causing it to slip down her arm. The bit of silk at her torso slid dangerously low, revealing the swell of her breast visible beneath the fabric.

She saw the wolfish look that came into his eyes.

"And then, if I were to do this..." He bent his head to run hot, wet kisses down her throat.

Her heart nearly stopped, and for a moment she could do nothing more than shudder as he moved his mouth across her shoulder, dropping kisses in the sensitive hollow between her throat and neck.

"Reed..."

"Shhh. Don't stop me now. I'm just getting started. Just relax."

"Relax?" She tried to laugh, but the sound turned into a sigh of pure pleasure.

"I love your skin." He licked the soft, rounded flesh made more pronounced by the lowered strap.

She gave a gasp and had to fight an almost overwhelming desire to offer him more.

"Now if I just..." His words were a mere whisper as he moved his mouth to take the second strap in his teeth.

Oh, dear heaven. She was drowning in sensations, and about to go under.

Before he could dislodge the strap, she slapped both hands against his chest and pushed free.

"Don't, Reed. I...don't want this."

Though his breathing was ragged, he stood perfectly still, his eyes steady on hers. "That's not what I heard your body saying."

Again he gave that dangerous smile that had the power to melt her bones like hot wax.

"Then read my lips." She resolutely turned away from him. "I'm going upstairs. Alone."

As she fled up the steps, she prayed her rubbery legs wouldn't fail her.

All the way up, as she held herself as stiffly as possible, she could feel his gaze burning holes in her back.

With her heart slamming against her ribs, she sought the sanctuary of her bedroom.

Once there, she sank down on the edge of the mattress and buried her face in her hands, marveling that she'd found the strength to resist.

She'd wanted what he was offering. With every fiber of her being she'd wanted him. But she no longer trusted herself to know whether what she wanted was what would be the best thing for her and her son. She'd taken what she wanted before, and it had been all wrong. Getting burned once was all it took to make her more afraid than ever of playing with fire.

Reed Malloy seemed to be a good, honest man. He'd certainly come rushing to her rescue the moment she called. But her judgment had proved wrong before. And for that, she'd paid a dear price. For now, for as long as necessary, she had no intention of putting her trust in a man. Any man. Because now there was an even more important element in her life than her own wants and needs. She and Kyle were a package deal. What her son didn't need in his young life was a mother who kept repeating the same mistakes. What Kyle needed most from his mother was honesty, integrity, stability. And if that meant she would have to stand alone against the world, so be it.

* * *

Reed settled himself into the lumpy recliner he'd hauled across the floor.

Ally Shaw was a puzzle. There was no doubt in his mind that she'd been as aroused as he. And then, without warning, she'd fled up the stairs like a heifer with a pack of wolves at her heels.

It was obvious the lady had been badly hurt and was still carrying the scars.

A fatherless son wasn't the only casualty Rick left behind. Her Marine had apparently shied away from commitment, as well. Or, Reed thought, maybe he was reading this all wrong.

He folded his hands behind his head and thought about those terrible days shortly after the loss of his parents. He'd been surrounded by so many loving, caring family members. His brothers, his uncle, his grandparents, Great One, Burke. Yancy. They'd kept him so busy around the ranch he'd barely had time to think. And yet, in the quiet of the night, he'd grieved as only a boy can grieve the loss of the most important people in his life. And despite the circle of loving, caring family, he'd had moments of terrible fear. Fear of losing all of his family as he'd lost his parents. Fear of dying young. Death was no longer an abstract thought. Death had become a reality for him.

So how did a kid like Kyle deal with his loss?

Did he wake in the night, fearing the loss of the most important person in his young life—his mother? Did he think about his own death? Did he worry that everything safe and secure could be taken from him in an instant?

And what about Ally?

From what Reed could see, she was an amazing, selfless mother who, though struggling with her own loss, was working overtime to make a new life for her son and herself.

What sort of courage did it take to move halfway across the country in order to connect with the only family she had left? A family member who would rather push her away than welcome her home?

Ally seemed to have more in common with Gemma York, the strange little misfit, than with her own uncle. But then, the more Reed thought about it, the more it seemed to make perfect sense. Gemma was searching for her place in this world. A rebel, looking to forge her own future.

Reed smiled in the darkness. Ally was more than a puzzle. She was a gorgeous, smart, fascinating woman who was wounded and working hard to hide her scars. A woman with all that baggage would prove to be a real challenge to any man who wanted more than a casual relationship. Not that he knew what he wanted. For now, he'd settle for getting to know both Ally and Kyle better. And maybe earning their trust. And making them laugh. And easing their burdens a bit.

A rumble of laughter bubbled up from his chest. Who was he kidding?

All of that may be true, but not the whole truth. If he were being honest with himself, he'd have to admit that Ally Shaw had him tangled up in knots. Instead of spending every minute he could spare with the very special herd that would determine the future of his family ranch, here he was, miles from home, trying to sleep on a lumpy chaise and wishing he could be upstairs in her bed, making mad, passionate love.

But the lady in question was a tough cookie, and it looked as though she would need plenty of careful persuasion.

He smiled and rolled to his side.

There was nothing he liked better than a challenge.

CHAPTER ELEVEN

Ally woke with a start. A glance at the clock told her she'd overslept. No surprise. After last night's incident, she'd tossed and turned for what seemed like hours before falling into a restless sleep.

She showered quickly and dressed before stepping into Kyle's bedroom. The bed had been neatly made; the room picked up. There were no clothes or toys on the floor. Puzzled, she made her way to the kitchen, where Reed and Kyle were at the table, eating and laughing quietly together.

Kyle's smile lit up his entire face. "Look, Mama. Reed said he was too tired to drive all the way back to his ranch, so he slept downstairs last night. And he made pancakes."

Ally's eyes went wide. "Pancakes? You made pancakes?"

Reed shot a glance at Kyle. "Now, why do you suppose she's so surprised?"

"'Cause nobody ever makes breakfast for Mama. Except

once, when I made corn flakes. But I spilled the milk all over the table."

"Little boys are allowed to spill milk once in a while." Reed indicated a place at the table. "Sit. I'll get your pancakes."

Ally sat down, noting her son's damp hair and clean clothes. "You took a shower all by yourself?"

Kyle shook his head. "Reed turned on the water and made sure it wasn't too hot first. And he said we had to be quiet and let you sleep while we made the bed and cleaned up my room."

"I don't know what to say, except to ask, who are you and what have you done with my real son? You know. The one who spills the milk and leaves things on the floor for his uncle to step on?"

Kyle put a hand over his mouth and giggled before turning to Reed at the stove. "Uncle Archer got really mad at me when I left my daddy's dog tags on the floor at his house, and he stepped on them in his bare feet."

"Did he cut himself?"

"Uh-huh. And he said if I ever leave them lying around again he'll keep them." As he spoke, the little boy touched a hand to the metal tags hanging on a chain around his neck and tucked beneath his shirt. "But he can't keep them. They're mine."

"I'm sure you'll see they're always in a safe place from now on." Reed flipped pancakes onto a plate before turning from the stove.

Ally stared at the stack of pancakes and the cup of steaming coffee Reed placed in front of her.

When her jaw dropped, he winked. "No need to thank me. Just eat."

She didn't need coaxing as she dug into her breakfast.

When the plate was empty, she sat back, sipping coffee. "That was wonderful. Thank you."

"You're welcome."

She looked up at the sound of hammering coming from downstairs. "What's...?"

"That's Thorny. Darnell Thornton. He and his employee, Ethan, are handymen. I phoned him first thing this morning and gave him the dimensions of the glass you needed replaced. I told him it had to be done before you opened for business today." Reed pushed away from the table. "I'll go down and see if they need a hand. Then I have to head out. I've got a herd of cattle waiting for me up in the hills."

Kyle climbed from his chair. "Can I go down with Reed?"

"We'll all go." Ally set aside her cup. "I want to meet these handymen. I'm sure I'll have need of them again sometime."

She followed Reed and her son, who danced ahead.

"Hey, Reed." One of the two men looked over from his perch on a ladder, where he was busy sealing the inner rim of glass.

A second man stood outside, doing the same, before stepping into the shop.

"You made good time."

The handyman chuckled. "You told me to have this done before nine or you'd have my hide."

"I did. Thorny. Ethan." Reed nodded toward the second man. "This is Ally Shaw and her son, Kyle."

"Kyle. Ms. Shaw." Thorny handed a business card to Ally. "Anything you need done, Ms. Shaw, you just call."

"Thank you, Darnell. And you can call me Ally."

"Sure thing, Ally. And everybody in town calls me Thorny."

Reed winked. "Now that you're in good hands, I'll say good-bye."

"Bye, Reed." Kyle impulsively wrapped his hands around Reed's leg. "You coming back tonight?"

Reed looked down at the boy. "That depends on your mama."

Ally stood back, watching her son before looking up into Reed's face. "Thank you again." She lowered her voice, grateful for the noise of the workmen as they began retrieving their tools. "For staying the night. For getting this window replaced so quickly. For making breakfast. That was an unexpected treat. I seem to owe you for a lot of favors."

"You're welcome. And you don't owe me a thing." He tugged on a lock of her hair and watched as Kyle ran off to pick up some blocks of wood the handyman was about to toss in a bin.

Reed kept his tone to a whisper. "Did you give any thought to spending your nights at my ranch?"

She looked away quickly. "You'll never know how grateful I am for your offer, Reed. For everything you've done for me. But I need to be here."

He tucked his hands in his back pockets to keep from reaching out to her. "I was pretty sure that would be your answer. You're a very independent lady, Red. I wish I could be here for you and Kyle, but it's time I headed back to my herd in the hills for a few days. If you need anything at all, call me."

He waved at Kyle, who waved back before returning his attention to his wood, which had now become his latest toys.

"I will," Ally said.

"Promise?"

"I'll call if I need anything at all."

"Good. Just remember that there's often no cell phone service in the hills. Just keep the sheriff on speed dial."

And then he was gone, sauntering down the street to his truck.

Thorny, satisfied with the repairs, handed Ally a bill and left.

Ally turned the little OPEN sign around, indicating she was open for business.

As she began tidying up the shop, it seemed unusually empty without Reed.

Without Reed.

What a strange choice of words.

She glanced at the old recliner where he'd spent the night. The thought of lying there with him sent an unexpected shaft of heat through her, catching her completely by surprise.

Reed Malloy seemed to have a talent for surprising her.

After last night she thought she could label him as just a lecherous cowboy. This morning he'd turned everything upside down by being not only a perfect gentleman, but also a thoughtful, caring one at that. And now, just as quickly as he'd raced into her life, he was gone.

What was she going to do about him?

She straightened her shoulders and picked up a broom and dustpan. It was time to turn off her disquieting thoughts and get to work. Work had always been her salvation. There had been a time when she'd been able to lose herself in confidential security videos for her employer. That was guaranteed to take her mind off her own troubles.

Now she was here in tiny Glacier Ridge, turning someone's well-used items into someone else's treasures and hoping to earn enough to pay her bills.

These two career choices couldn't be more different. But both were challenging. And for now, for today, she was grateful for the chance to lose herself in satisfying work.

* * *

Ally rang up a sale and waved good-bye to the rancher and his wife as she idly answered the phone. Hearing the sheriff's voice, she tensed.

"Yes, Sheriff?"

"Just wanted to let you know that so far there's been no sign of your coworker, Glen Lloyd. I've sent his photo to law enforcement agencies in this area and asked to be notified if and when they spot him."

"Thank you."

"Archer showed up for his morning shift as usual and said he spent a couple of hours at Clay's Pig Sty before heading home to bed. I checked his alibi with Clay, who agreed that Archer was there at the time he claims."

"I'm glad."

"You are? Why?"

She sighed at the wave of relief that rushed through her upon learning her uncle had an alibi. "Because the last thing I want is to add any more layers of trouble to an already heavy family situation."

"I see." The sheriff paused. "After viewing your security video, I drove around and found Gemma York and Jeremy Clancy sleeping in his truck. They swore they drove to a safe place to park for the night after leaving your shop, and never left. Since there's nobody who can verify their alibi, I've told them they're still prime suspects." He paused. "You might want to think twice about allowing that girl back in your shop."

"Thank you, Sheriff. I'll give it careful thought. But for now, I'm inclined to give her a chance."

His tone grew stern. "I can't tell you how to run your business, Ms. Shaw. But I'd advise you to lock up your valuables when those two are around."

"I appreciate your suggestion."

Ally hung up the phone and glanced at the clock. It was well past noon. With the sheriff's words ringing in her mind, she emptied the cash register and tucked the money in her pocket before setting the sign announcing that anyone seeking help could ring the bell. Then she called to Kyle and led him up the stairs for a lunch break.

It saddened her that a single act of violence was already having a ripple effect on her. Until now, she'd never given a thought to anyone in this serene little town stealing her hard-earned money while she was on a break. But, she reasoned, if someone was willing to throw a brick through her window, they would be just as willing to break into her cash register while her back was turned.

Even small towns, she reasoned, had their share of trouble.

"Hey, Gemma." Kyle's shout had Ally looking up from the ancient dresser she was cleaning of an accumulation of years of neglect. One side of it was already gleaming with fresh polish.

"Hey, little man." This day Gemma was wearing a long, Mandarin-style gown slit up both sides, revealing a pair of shocking pink tights underneath. On her feet were badly scuffed hiking boots. She had tucked several chopsticks in her orange spiky hair, giving her head the look of a creature from outer space.

"Hey, Ally." Gemma walked up beside her and lowered her voice so Kyle wouldn't overhear. "The sheriff had a lot of questions for me about the vandalism here. I want you to know I'm sorry that happened, and to know absolutely it wasn't me."

"Thank you." Ally set aside her cleaning supplies. "He told me about a theft you were accused of. Is that why you didn't want to give me any references?"

Gemma swallowed, then seemed to come to a decision. "You deserve to know. I was babysitting for Mrs. Rider's little Carly. She's five. She's a sweet kid. And Mrs. Rider was starting a new job in town and said if I worked out, she'd pay me to be there five days a week after Carly got home from kindergarten. I really wanted that job." She sighed. "About an hour after I got there, Mrs. Rider's nephew Cory stopped by." She wrinkled her nose. "I never had any use for Cory Rider. He was always making fun of the way I looked. I think he did it to impress the kids he was hanging with. Anyway, he said he was going to wait for his aunt to come home. I didn't pay much attention to him. I was busy playing with Carly and her new dollhouse. He went off to the kitchen, and later, I saw him coming out of the back room. I asked what he was doing, and he said he'd used the bathroom. Then he said he wasn't going to wait any longer for his aunt. When Mrs. Rider came home, I was busy feeding Carly. I remember I made her mac and cheese. The next thing I knew, Mrs. Rider came flying out of her bedroom to say I'd stolen fifty dollars from her keepsake box on top of her dresser. She called the sheriff, and he came right over. I told both of them I'd never even gone near her bedroom. I told them to ask Carly. I'd never left her alone. And I told the sheriff to search my backpack. Then I remembered Cory and told her maybe he'd stolen it." Gemma looked up to meet Ally's narrowed gaze. "That's when Mrs. Rider told the sheriff to forget about the whole thing. She didn't want to press charges. I figured she knew her nephew couldn't be trusted but didn't want to admit it to the sheriff. But the way Sheriff Graystoke was looking at me, I knew he still thought I was the one who did it."

"That has to hurt, knowing people think you're a thief."

Gemma's eyes widened in surprise before tears welled up

and she turned away. "After that, nobody would trust me to babysit their kids."

"What did your family say?"

The girl bent down to pick up a shard of glass that had been overlooked. She tossed it into a wastebasket and kept her back to Ally. "My dad's dead. He was sick a long time. After that, my ma sold our ranch and moved to town so she could work."

"And you quit school."

"I...didn't need school anyway, so now I'm with Jeremy. He gets me."

"He doesn't tease you about the way you dress."

The girl shook her head. "He likes the way I look."

Ally kept her tone deliberately bland. "So do I."

Gemma whirled. "You...do?"

Ally smiled. "Yeah. You have a unique look, Gemma. And you manage to pull it all together."

For the first time, a smile touched the girl's lips. "Thanks."

"I still need help here. So, if you're willing, my offer stands. You can work for me."

"You'd trust me here with your stuff?"

"Yes. Unless you do something to make me think otherwise."

"And your cash register?"

Ally nodded. "It goes with the territory. If I'm not here, you'll be handling the customers and their payments."

Gemma took a deep breath and stared at the back room. "And my vintage clothes?"

"If you'd like to turn the back room into Gemma's Closet, be my guest. We'll agree on a fee that is fair. Instead of paying it, you can earn it by working here. Anything you earn from the sale of your clothing, plus what you earn for working for me over that set amount is yours to keep." She stuck out her hand. "Deal?"

Gemma nodded. "Oh, yeah. Deal."

They shook hands.

Gemma turned toward the door. "I need to tell Jeremy. I'll be right back."

She raced out the door and was seen flying down the sidewalk. Half an hour later she rode up alongside Jeremy in his battered truck, and the two of them began hauling plastic bags into the shop and toward the back room.

Ally pointed to a clutter of badly damaged items that she'd planned on discarding. "If there's anything there you can use to display your clothes, feel free to help yourselves."

Several hours later Gemma caught Ally's hand. "Come see what we've done so far."

Gemma and Jeremy had fashioned hanging racks for some of the clothes out of wooden clothes poles with rope strung between them. Swinging from the rope were tie-dyed shirts, caftans, wide-legged pants, fringed vests, velvet coats. There were even a few pair of hot pants. They'd taken an old chest that was lacking drawers and used the top to display dozens of colorful scarves and vintage jewelry. A scarred wooden sideboard displayed hobo bags, belts, and an assortment of boots and shoes.

The effect was charming.

"Oh, Gemma." Ally looked around the back room filled with clothes from bygone days. "You really have a knack for this."

The girl beamed. "Thanks. So does Jeremy. He's the one who came up with the idea of the sideboard."

"The two of you make a good team." Ally turned away. "Now I need to take Kyle upstairs for some mom time. I'll come back later."

"Don't worry about the shop."

Jeremy looked disappointed. "How late will you be working?"

"As long as Ally needs me." Gemma caught his hand. "Remember, Ally said I could set this up as long as it doesn't keep me from taking care of her business first."

"Okay." The boy leaned close to press a kiss to her cheek. "I'll leave you to it. It's going to be good."

"Yeah." Gemma hurried from the back room and into the shop just as a customer stepped inside.

When Ally hesitated on the stairway, Gemma called, "You go ahead. I've got this."

Ally gave a wave of her hand and continued up the stairs for a much-needed break from the business.

It had been a long day. But a good one.

She'd settle for good anytime.

CHAPTER TWELVE

Reed finished drawing blood from a heifer and labeling the vial before depositing it in a cooler.

Burke ambled over, leading his mount, to take the cooler from his hand. "Luke's heading up here and said he'll take this to the lab when he leaves."

"Good." Reed slapped his hat against his leg before wiping his brow. "I don't know about you, but I'm starving."

"We don't have to cook. Yancy's sending supplies with Luke."

"Even better." Reed caught the reins of his horse and followed Burke as they threaded their way among the cattle milling about.

After unsaddling their horses, he and Burke turned them loose in a small corral before heading toward the range shack.

Luke stepped out of the cabin and handed each of them a frosty longneck.

Reed's grin widened before he tipped up his beer and took a long swallow. "I like your timing, bro."

Luke nodded toward the herd. "All healthy?"

"So far. Of course, as Burke likes to remind me, a lot can happen between now and roundup."

"You've brought them this far. What's another few weeks?"

The two brothers shared a smile, while Burke drank his beer in silence.

"What did Yancy send us for supper?"

"A couple of things. Steaks and twice-baked potatoes and a big pot of chili. Your choice."

Reed turned to Burke, and the two men grinned.

Reed spoke for both of them. "After the day we put in, we could eat those steaks raw."

"Sorry." Luke pointed to a fire pit where wood and kindling had been neatly piled. "I like mine cooked. So you two will have to wait until I cook them over the fire."

Reed drained his beer. "Perfect. That gives me enough time to wash up in the creek." He turned to Burke. "You coming?"

"I'll be along, son." The old cowboy helped himself to a second longneck. "But first I intend to just sit here and let the day go by."

Reed stepped inside the range shack to retrieve clean clothes before ambling down to the stream for a long, lazy swim.

"You make a mean steak, Luke." Reed set aside his empty plate before leaning his back against a log and stretching his long legs toward the fire.

"Wish I could take credit. It's all Yancy, and whatever he decides to pack up."

"That man knows what a wrangler wants after a long day with the herd." Burke splashed whiskey into his coffee.

Luke glanced toward his brother. "With all you've got

riding on this herd, I'd have thought you'd be spending all your time up here. After all, this is your bread and butter, and possibly the future of our ranch. But lately, I think Burke's been here more than you."

Reed met his steady look. "You got something to say?"

Luke nodded. "Seems to me you've been spending a lot of time in Glacier Ridge. Rumor has it you're soft on the owner of that consignment shop."

"You been hanging around Dot and Barb?"

Luke shrugged. "Where else would I get good gossip? So? Are you falling for the newcomer?"

"Her name is Ally Shaw."

"Yeah. Ally. And she has a kid."

"Kyle. He's almost five."

"You mean he's four."

Reed couldn't help grinning. "Yeah. But he prefers to say he's almost five. It makes him feel older."

Luke chuckled. "That's like Ingrid's sister, Lily. She'd much rather say she's almost ten. Of course, some days I think she's nine going on nineteen."

The three men shared a laugh.

Luke sobered. "Is this...thing with Ally Shaw serious?"

Reed frowned. "We barely know each other."

"That's not what I asked." He studied his brother. "When I woke up from my accident on the cliff and saw Ingrid looking down at me, I didn't even know her name. But it hit me like stampeding herd that I was sure as hell going to get to know everything I could about her before I left."

"Yeah. Well." Reed winked at Burke. "That's what happens to a guy with a concussion. You probably saw two Ingrids swimming in your line of vision."

"As a matter of fact, I did. And both of them took my breath away."

Reed held up a hand. "Enough. I just had a really great supper. Please don't spoil it with all that gooey love stuff."

Luke turned to Burke with a dangerous grin. "You hear him? Know what I think?" Without waiting for a response, he added, "I think my little brother has already fallen off his own private cliff. And though he's trying hard to deny it, he's already up to his neck in gooey love stuff."

The old cowboy gave a hoot.

Seeing that Reed wasn't going to take the bait, Luke got to his feet. "Okay. Time for me to head home. I'll get those blood samples to the lab in town tomorrow."

"Thanks." Reed stood up.

"And maybe, while I'm in town, I'll stop by Ally's Attic and pay a call on the owner. Anything you'd like me to tell her?"

Reed punched his brother's shoulder. "Don't bother. Whatever I have to say, I'll tell her myself."

"I just bet you will." Luke lifted a hand. "Night, Burke. Take care of Mr. Tough Guy here. We wouldn't want him to start singing silly love songs to the coyotes."

He was still laughing at his little joke as he climbed into the ranch truck and put it in gear.

When the lights of the vehicle disappeared, Reed strolled back to the campfire. "You going to sleep out here or in the cabin?"

Burke roused himself from his musings. "Probably out here."

"Me too." Reed walked to the range shack and returned with their sleeping bags.

Tossing one to Burke, he spread the other by the side of the fire before heading back inside. He stepped out a few minutes later with two longnecks and handed one to Burke before sitting down and stretching out his legs.

"A shooting star," Burke called, pointing to the western sky.

"Yeah. I see it."

"I remember how excited you boys used to get whenever I'd point one out. You'd scrunch your eyes shut and make a wish." The old man was grinning when he turned to Reed. "You too old for that now?"

"Hell, no. I'll do whatever it takes to make my wishes happen."

"So, if you were to make a wish right now, what would it be?"

Reed tipped up his bottle and took a long pull before saying, "That my herd makes it to roundup without any problems."

Burke kept his gaze steady. "I don't think that'd be your first wish, son."

"What makes you think that?"

"Because"—he chose his words carefully—"it took you a couple of beats to come up with it. What was your first thought?"

Reed stared up into the sky. "That Ally and Kyle stay safe."

The old man's brow shot up. "You think they're in trouble?"

Reed settled himself more comfortably before he began talking. For the next half hour, while Burke listened, Reed spilled everything he could about Ally, her son, the incident at the shop, her relationship with Archer Stone, her co-worker, Gemma.

When at last he finished, he set aside his empty bottle and gave a slow shake of his head. "I can't believe I just told you all this. I guess by now your ear's been chewed clear off."

"I don't mind a bit, son." The old man merely grinned. "Seems like you had a heap of information filling you up, and you needed some place to spill it. And you know your secrets are safe with me."

"Yeah. Thanks. I appreciate it, Burke. What I appreciate even more is that you don't bother offering me a lot of empty advice."

"I'm happy to oblige."

Reed rolled to his side and put his hat over his face. A short time later his breathing was slow and easy, alerting Burke that he was asleep.

The old cowboy made his way to the cabin and returned with a mug of coffee. While he sipped, he watched the night sky with its endless display of big orange moon and glittering stars.

This was the first time he could ever recall hearing Reed talk about a woman. Always before it had been the ranch, the family, the herds.

There had been plenty of pretty girls to turn that boy's head. Hell, all three of the Malloy brothers had the women of Glacier Ridge, from sixteen to sixty, making eyes at them. And Reed, like his brothers, had sampled plenty of honey being offered. But until now, he'd never heard Reed express anything personal about a female.

Tonight it was all about Ally Shaw and her son.

There had been a look on Reed's face and a change in his voice when he spoke of them.

This sounded serious, at least on Reed's part.

But what about the lady in question? From what Reed had said, Ally had some serious, messy issues to deal with. Her son's father. A coworker stalking her. An uncle bearing a grudge from his past.

That was a lot for one lone woman to shoulder.

Burke watched another shooting star dance across the sky and found himself automatically making a wish.

Reed and his brothers were special to Burke. They were like his own. Matt and Luke were now happily married, and their futures looked bright. He wanted that same happiness for Reed. But the old man had lived long enough to know that not all wishes came true.

"That was close. Good shooting, Reed." Burke knelt beside the dead cougar.

Reed and Burke had been riding the perimeter of the herd when they'd seen a streak of color as the cougar leapt from its perch to attack a lone cow separated from the herd.

Reed dropped to the ground and studied the predator. "This is the first one I've seen in more than a year."

Burke looked it over carefully. "Full-grown male. Probably far from his usual hunting ground. Drawn here by the herd."

Reed returned his rifle to the boot beside his saddle. "He couldn't resist an easy target. We'll have to call up more wranglers. Just until roundup time. If there's one cougar in the area, there could be more."

Burke nodded. "I'll see to it. I'll have Fleming dispose of this while Finley heads over to the big herd on the south ridge to choose more wranglers."

"Good." Reed pulled himself into the saddle and came to a decision. If he needed to be here another day or a week, or even more, so be it. The safety of the herd took precedence over comfort. "I'll circle around and make sure the herd's secure."

"Well, look who's back." Yancy looked up from the stove as Reed and Burke trudged into the mudroom.

The two took their time, hanging their hats on hooks by the door before kicking off filthy jackets and boots and turning toward the big sink to scrub hands and faces.

As they stepped into the kitchen, Grace and Frank, seated across the room with Great One and Colin, broke into wide smiles.

"You're both looking like wild men," Grace called.

"Or maybe mountain goats," Frank added with a wink.

"I feel like an old goat." Burke accepted a mug of coffee from Yancy.

Reed saluted his grandparents and great-grandfather. "It's been raining for two days and nights. I think the sky opened up last night. Burke said he thought he spotted cats and dogs falling. Before I do anything else, I'm heading upstairs to wash away the sea of mud I've had to eat along the trail."

"Good." Great One was grinning like a fool. "And then you can taste the special meal Yancy's prepared. He promised me it will put any Hollywood restaurant to shame."

"From Yancy's lips...," came a voice from the doorway. "That's why we're here. To sample Yancy's finest."

They looked over to see Matt and Vanessa, trailed by Luke and Ingrid, and her sister, Lily, as well as their ranch foreman, Mick.

Reed paused in the doorway. "I'm not surprised to see all of you. Mention a special meal, and everyone shows up hungry. But I wouldn't care if Yancy served rattlesnake. Raw. After two weeks up in those hills, I'm ready for anything."

He waved at the family before hurrying away.

The others chuckled among themselves as they began filing into the room.

"How bad was it, Burke?" Frank turned to their foreman.

"Let's see. We woke in the night to find the roof in the range shack leaking and had to fix it before we got drowned. It rained so hard we were up to our knees in muck while tending the herd. Reed shot a cougar before it could take down one of his precious cows. Oh, and we ran out of food three days ago and had to resort to eating jerky and that canned stuff they call stew that's stored in the cabin for emergencies. Reed and I decided it's made with skunk meat."

He drained his coffee and turned away. "Like Reed, I need a long, hot shower. If I'm running late, go ahead and start without me."

When he was gone, the others gathered around and helped themselves from a tray of drinks and appetizers Yancy had placed on a low coffee table in front of the fireplace.

Frank turned to his wife. "All our chicks are back in the nest, Gracie girl."

She nodded. "It's a good feeling, isn't it?"

The two held hands while their family gathered around to await Yancy's feast.

"Well, sonny boy." Frank looked over when Reed stepped into the kitchen. "You clean up real good."

"Thanks. I try." Reed snagged a longneck from a tray and joined the rest of his family gathered around the fireplace.

His sister-in-law, Nessa, touched a hand to his smooth chin. "You're right, Matt. This is your brother, and not some itinerant cowboy fresh from the hills."

"Not too fresh." Reed pressed a kiss to her cheek. "You wouldn't have wanted to get this close to me before that shower."

"Oh, I don't know about that." Luke drew an arm around his wife's waist. "Ingrid hugs me even when I come in from the fields."

"That's because you're still in the throes of newlywed bliss, bro." Reed punched his brother's shoulder. "We'll see if you can brag the same way years from now."

Luke returned his good-natured punch. "When a guy's

got it, he's got it. And even when I'm old and gray, she'll be greeting me with those hugs and kisses." He turned to his grandparents. "Just ask Grandpop and Gram Gracie. Those two still have the spark."

"You're right about that." Reed winked at his grandmother. "As for me, I'm just happy to be wearing dry clothes. For the last couple of days Burke and I have been drenched from morning to night, and everything, including our boots, was soggy."

Luke deadpanned, "Ah, the romantic life of a rancher that writers have glorified for years."

The others joined in his laughter.

The minute Burke stepped into the room, Yancy announced, "About time. I guess it took you longer than Reed to shower off all that mud." He looked the foreman up and down. "But at least you look more human than mountain goat now."

Grinning, Burke snagged a longneck from the tray just as Yancy announced, "Supper's ready."

The teasing and laughter continued as they gathered around the table. Frank held Grace's hand as he escorted her to her usual place beside him.

Yancy circled the table, passing platters loaded with thick slices of prime rib, potatoes au gratin, and asparagus picked fresh from the garden.

As always, Great One took one taste before turning to Yancy with a beatific smile. "Perfection, Yancy. Absolute perfection."

The cook was beaming. "Thanks, Great One. I was hoping it measured up to your memory of Hollywood's best."

"It doesn't measure up, Yancy. It surpasses. I don't know how you do it, but you always manage to surprise and please me."

With a smile that rivaled the sun, the cook retrieved a basket of freshly baked rolls and began passing them.

While the conversation swirled around, both Reed and Burke ate in silence.

Finally, after his last bite of prime rib, Reed looked over. "If anybody here ever starts to forget just how great a cook Yancy is, I suggest we condemn them to time in the hills eating canned stew."

There was a roar of laughter from the others, while Yancy merely grinned.

"The trouble is," Burke added, "the hours are so long, and the work so draining, we're never sure if we're eating something out of a can or old shoe leather."

Reed nudged Nessa. "That's what I was doing wrong. I should have forgotten about those cans in the cabin and settled for a few slices of Burke's old boot."

When the laughter faded, the cook said, "If you think supper was good this far, wait until you taste the dessert Lily and I made just for Miss Grace."

At that Grace's head came up. "For me? What is it?"

Yancy shared a look with the little girl before shaking his head. "We're going to make you wait. But we both know you'll be pleased."

"Oh, what terrible teases you two are." Grace turned to her husband and batted her lashes like a teen. "Did they happen to share their secret with you?"

He shook his head. "They know me too well. If I knew, you'd find a way to get that secret out of me. You always do, Gracie girl." He looked around at the others. "My girl has always been my weakness."

"Really?" Luke gave an exaggerated shrug. "We never noticed."

That had them all grinning.

Colin shoved away from the table. "I'm skipping dessert. I got a text from Anita. There's a lull at the clinic, and we're going to grab a drink at Clay's Pig Sty before the next rush."

At his mention of Dr. Anita Cross, looks were exchanged around the table. Despite his tight-lipped refusal to discuss his personal life, the family was convinced that their relationship had gone far beyond attraction.

Grace touched a hand to Colin's. "Give Anita my love."

He squeezed her hand. "Thanks, Ma. I will."

When Colin was gone, Frank indicated the door. "I think we should take that surprise dessert in the other room. What do you say?"

Grace shot him an adoring smile. "I like the way you think, Frankie."

Her husband scraped back his chair and helped her to her feet. The two led the others from the kitchen to the great room, where a cozy fire had been set. Despite the heat of the day, the evenings were always comfortably cool, chilled by the breeze blowing down from the highlands.

As they gathered around, Great One in his favorite overstuffed chair, the others on sofas and chairs arranged for easy conversation, Yancy pushed a trolley filled with a carafe of coffee, mugs, brandy, and assorted plates and forks for the dessert.

He beckoned Lily over, and the two of them, whispering like conspirators, stepped back into the kitchen.

Grace watched with avid interest. It was well known to the entire family that Grace Malloy had a sweet tooth and liked nothing better than to indulge it.

Yancy and Lily stepped into the room carrying a footed cake plate on which rested the tallest cake any of them had ever seen.

Luke winked at his wife. "Pretty fancy. Have the two of you entered some sort of TV cake contest?"

Lily covered her mouth and giggled, while Yancy explained, "This is a seven-layer strawberry cream torte. Lily and I picked the berries ourselves and made up this recipe as we went along."

He cut into the giant torte and began arranging slices on plates while Lily scooped strawberry-vanilla ice cream on top of each slice.

Grace was given the first slice.

She lifted a bite to her mouth, chewed, swallowed, gave a deep sigh of pleasure, and then looked around before giving a thumbs-up. "Oh, wait until you taste this. It just melts in my mouth."

"Okay. Time's up." Matt nudged his wife before signaling to Lily and Yancy. "Stop the torture and pass that around so we can taste it for ourselves."

For the next few minutes there was silence as the dessert was handed out and everyone began devouring it. Then the room was filled with the *ooh*s and *ah*s of murmured pleasure.

Even Great One, who preferred his coffee and brandy after dinner to anything sweet, was persuaded to give it a try. After several bites, he looked over at Yancy. "My man, if you ever decide to leave Montana, you, along with your able assistant, Lily, could make a fortune baking this decadent splendor in the Hollywood hills."

"Not on your life." The cook winked at Lily, who was too busy eating to say a word. "My assistant is really my intern. It's my intention to train Lily to one day be my replacement."

"It'll never happen." Luke helped himself to a second piece. "First of all, you're not replaceable. And second, Lily has already told us she wants to follow Gram Gracie into a career in photography. You'll have to find another intern for your cooking and baking business."

Grace and the little girl shared a knowing smile. "Speaking of which, we need to make time for another photographic safari before the summer is over."

"Better wait until this rain lets up," Reed muttered.

"That's true." Grace looked over at her grandson. "Seeing the way you and Burke looked when you got home earlier, I intend to give those hills plenty of time to dry out before I tackle them."

"Now, Reed." Frank set aside his empty plate and picked up a cup of coffee. "Tell us about how your special herd is faring."

It was all the encouragement Reed needed to talk about his favorite subject. Now that he'd had his fill of dinner and dessert, he was feeling replete and content. For the next hour they discussed the weight of the cattle, the health, the feed, and even the amount of range grass being devoured.

From Reed's tone of controlled excitement, they could see the depth of his devotion to this project. Over the years, his enthusiasm for the future of their ranch hadn't dimmed but had, in fact, grown even stronger.

"I'm glad the herd is thriving, son."

Frank drained his coffee and turned to his wife. "Ready to go upstairs, Gracie girl?"

She nodded. "

Reed got to his feet. "I'm not ready to turn in yet. Think I'll head into town. Anybody care to join me?"

One by one the others around the room shook their heads.

Reed gave them all a lazy grin. "Okay. I guess there are no takers. I'll see you in the morning."

Minutes later they heard the truck door slam and watched

the headlights play across the windows before disappearing along the driveway.

Frank turned to Burke. "You'd think, after all that time in the hills, he'd be eager for his own bed. Unless, of course, there's a stronger magnet in Glacier Ridge."

When Burke simply sipped his coffee, Frank plowed ahead, hoping to get the old man to open up. "I'm thinking you're the logical one to ask, since you just spent the last two weeks with Reed. You think Ally Shaw is his reason for heading into town tonight?"

The old man grinned. "You have to ask?"

"No." Frank shot a look at his wife. "But we're more than a little curious about just how much she means to him."

Burke studied the toe of his boot before looking up at the faces watching him. "I figure Reed would have answered that if you'd asked him."

Luke drew an arm around Ingrid. "No need to ask. Our boy's hooked. Only a pretty woman would have a cowboy heading to town at this time of evening. Especially when he hasn't slept in his own bed in weeks."

The others were nodding and smiling as they got to their feet and began calling their good nights before making their way upstairs.

When they were alone, Great One turned to Burke. "You've spent a lifetime knowing everyone's secrets around this place and keeping them to yourself. I wouldn't expect you to change now. But I'm willing to bet you already know a hell of a lot more about Reed than you're letting on."

The two men shared a smile, and Great One held up the bottle of brandy.

Burke shook his head. "I'm already on overload. Time for me to hit the sack."

As Burke walked away, Nelson LaRou helped himself to

a splash of brandy and sat staring at the dying flames of the fire. If he were a younger man, he'd have taken Reed up on his offer to head to town, if only to watch the reunion of his grandson and the pretty shopkeeper. But since he was stuck here on the ranch, he'd have to rely on his storyteller's imagination and see it in his mind's eye.

A lonely single mother and a cowboy fresh off the range. That would be enough to cause quite a display of fireworks.

He'd bet good money that Luke was right. Reed was already hooked. He only hoped the lady in question shared his great-grandson's passion.

Because Reed was the youngest, Nelson had a special fondness in his heart for him. When the lads were younger, he'd watched Reed fight for his place among his older siblings. He'd always admired the boy's tenacity. And now, as Reed had grown from boy to man, he displayed a quiet strength, a steely determination, to reach his goals and achieve his heart's desire.

Reed had worked tirelessly since his early teens. No one put in more hours with the herds than Reed. And now, finally, this year could be the one that would reward him for all his hard work.

Nelson sighed. It wasn't the right time for a dedicated rancher to be distracted by a pretty woman. But then, he thought, was there ever a right time? Love was such a fickle mistress. She could come creeping up when it was least expected.

And wasn't that both terrible and wonderful at the same time?

CHAPTER THIRTEEN

Reed!" Kyle jumped up from his spot in the corner of the shop and raced headlong across the room to fly into Reed's arms. "Where've you been? Me and Mama missed you."

Reed scooped him up and swung him around before setting him on his feet. "I missed you, too, little buddy." He looked over to where Ally was standing with two older women. "I missed you both."

Ally lifted a hand in greeting, while continuing to describe the age of the dining table and matching chairs formerly owned by a minister and his wife from a nearby town. "They were reluctant to let go of it, because it had formerly been owned by Reverend Tupper's mother, but their new parsonage is too small to accommodate it, and they agreed it was time to let it go."

Reed stood perfectly still, letting the sound of her voice wash over him. He'd missed it. Had missed her. And everything about her, including that sultry voice.

Kyle tugged on his arm. "Want to play with my trucks?"

"Sure. Why not?"

As they crossed the room, Gemma stepped through the doorway, now decorated with strands of beads that fell from a peace sign on which she'd hand-lettered the words GEMMA'S CLOSET in neon colors.

Gemma was dressed in wide-legged pants and an exotic tunic in hot pink. Her hair was the same shade of pink spikes, and dangling from one ear were a plastic moon and stars that brushed her shoulder. The other ear sported a silver snake that followed the curve of her lobe, its tongue poking out from between strands of hair at her temple.

"Interesting look." Reed pointed to the sign. "This is new."

She smiled. "Jeremy found it in a trash can outside a recycle center in Maysfield."

"That's a long way from Glacier Ridge."

She nodded. "He went there to look for a job."

When two teenage girls walked in and headed toward the back room, Gemma turned away, calling, "Got to get to work. Talk to you later."

"Yeah." He watched her walk away before kneeling beside Kyle. "What are we playing?"

"Mama got these new toys in a bundle yesterday." He held up some ancient cast-iron trucks that appeared to date back to the nineteen hundreds.

"Wow." Reed picked up one and began to examine it closely. "This is a beauty."

"It is?" The little boy studied the one in his hand. "But they're all the same color. Want to race?"

Before Reed could answer, the women buying the dining room set walked out the door and Ally hurried over.

Reed got to his feet and stared at her for long moments without saying a word.

She was dressed in a pale yellow sundress with a rounded neckline and fluttery short sleeves. The skirt fell to just above her ankles. She wore white sandals that showed off pretty pink polish on her bare toes.

Because he knew Kyle was watching, he whipped his hat from his head and said, "You look...pretty." Inwardly he groaned at such bland words. But words failed him. The truth was, she took his breath away. Just seeing her, he would have gladly devoured her on the spot if they were alone.

She stood twisting her hands together and smiling up into his face. "And you're all tanned from the sun."

"Life in the hills." He nodded toward the door. "So, did you make a sale?"

"Yes. They said they'll have someone come by tomorrow with a truck to pick up their purchases." She glanced at her son, looking from one to the other. "You were gone a long time."

"I hadn't expected to stay that long, but the herd needed me. I'm sorry I didn't call or text, but service rarely works up in the high country."

"That's all right. I was..." She smiled at her son. "We were both fine."

"No...trouble?" He didn't want to ask more in front of Kyle.

She shook her head, sending a cloud of red hair dancing about her cheeks. "No trouble. Did you eat?"

"Yeah. Yancy had a special supper ready. How about you and Kyle?"

She nodded.

He watched as the two girls who'd been shopping in the back room walked toward the door carrying bulging plastic bags. "Looks like Gemma's business is picking up."

"She's developing a following."

When Gemma held the door and the girls left, Ally called, "You can turn the sign around, Gemma. We're closing early."

"Great." Gemma did as she was told and waved a hand at the truck parked across the street.

Within minutes Jeremy stepped inside and called a greeting before taking the girl's hand.

"Bye," they called in unison before skipping away toward the truck.

Reed watched them go before turning to Ally. "So, things are working out between you and Gemma?"

"She's perfect. She agreed to get here around noon each day, so Kyle and I can go upstairs for some family time. And she stays until closing."

She indicated the upstairs. "Want to go up for coffee?"

"Maybe later. Why don't we take advantage of the great weather and walk around town?"

Kyle's eyes went wide. "Maybe we could walk to D and B's for a chocolate milk shake, or I's Cream?"

Reed's smile grew. "I don't see why not."

"Oh, boy." The little boy was quick to put away his trucks and hurry to the door.

As Reed trailed Ally out the door and waited while she locked up, he was grinning. "That didn't take any persuading at all."

Ally dropped the key in her pocket and took Reed's outstretched hand. "When it comes to sweets, Kyle is the first in line."

As they made their way along Main Street, they greeted friends and neighbors out for a stroll. After the fourth such greeting, Reed turned to Ally. "You've managed to make a lot of new friends."

She nodded. "It still amazes me. I've met more people

since moving here than I ever knew in all the years I lived
in the city. I used to get in my car, drop Kyle at day care,
and go to work. At the end of the day, it was the same. Once
home, I never went out because most of my fellow workers
were single. There was no place in that life for a mother with
a young son. Now"—she lifted a hand to indicate the parade
of people passing by—"Kyle and I feel free to visit D and
B's Diner, or stop by I's for ice cream, or walk to the school-
yard and play on the swings and slides."

As they passed the sheriff's office, Eugene Graystoke
poked his head out the door. "Hey, Reed. Glad to see you."

The two shook hands.

"I was up in the hills with my herd."

"That's what I heard." The sheriff darted a glance at Kyle,
up ahead, his nose pressed to the glass of the hardware store.

Knowing he couldn't be overheard by the boy, he said,
"I'm sure Ms. Shaw told you there's been no sign of Glen
Lloyd, either here in Montana or in Virginia. But since her
former boss said Glen took his vacation leave, and then extended it to a leave of absence, they don't know if or when
to expect him back. That means he could be anywhere." He
turned to Ally. "Have you heard anything more since that
email?"

Reed's head swiveled. "Email?"

Ally flushed. "There were a number of them. They came
while you were in the hills. They started off friendly enough.
Glen said he was thinking about me and hoped I was thinking about him. Then he suggested several meetings. And
finally, they became long, ugly rants saying I was a heartless
tease, and he was going to teach me a lesson."

"Did you answer?"

"Of course not. But I passed them along to Sheriff
Graystoke before deleting them without giving a reply."

The sheriff held up a hand before Reed could say a thing. "For the record, they're all in my file, with a copy to the state police special unit. And Ms. Shaw knows that if she gets any more emails from this guy, I'll do the same." He turned to her. "So our guy's gone silent?"

She nodded. "Not a word. Maybe he's finally given up. There hasn't been a single incident since the front window was smashed."

Eugene Graystoke looked thoughtful. "We'll hope that no news is good news. But I can't stress enough that you need to stay vigilant."

"I will. Thank you, Sheriff."

"Good. Now you'd better keep an eye on that little guy."

Ally and Reed walked away and caught up with Kyle, who was now peering into the windows of the barbershop. Putting him between them, they each took one of his hands as they crossed the street and headed toward I's Cream Shop.

Later, as darkness settled over the town, they made their way through the nearly empty street and paused to allow several vehicles to pass. As a stream of trucks drove by, the wail of a man loving a woman could be heard in one of them.

Reed held tightly to Kyle's hand. His other arm was around Ally's waist. He leaned close to whisper in her ear, "Now there's a song for the ages."

For the space of a heartbeat they stared into each other's eyes, until Kyle tugged on Reed's hand.

They crossed the street and headed toward Ally's shop.

She dug out her key and unlocked the door.

As she did, Reed looked up. "Is that a new security camera?"

She nodded. "The other one didn't offer enough range. I'm hoping to buy a couple more as my profits increase."

"That's a good thing."

She paused. "Want to come in for coffee?"

"Sure. I'd like that."

He followed her inside and trailed Kyle up the stairs to the apartment.

Once there, he looked around at the bright, homey touches that had been added to the tiny sitting room. Framed pictures of Kyle as a baby. Photos of Ally and Kyle riding a merry-go-round and eating cotton candy. Splashing in a pool. And laughing. Always laughing.

"This looks really good."

Kyle beamed. "Mama let me help pick out the ones I like best. She said they make her happy."

Reed walked closer. "They should. They're happy memories."

"Want to see some more?"

"Sure thing. Where are they?"

"I'll get them." When Kyle hurried off to his room, Reed stepped closer to study the photos more clearly. "No pictures of Kyle with his dad?"

"Rick's military assignments kept him out of the country most of the time."

"But when he came home..." Reed shrugged. "I guess, if I had a son like Kyle, I'd be snapping photographs of us together all the time."

Before Ally could respond, Kyle was back, carrying a pile of pictures in his arms.

"Look." He dropped them on the sofa and began spreading them out. "Here's me and Mama at her work when I was just little. She let me do stuff on her computer."

"Wow. Look at you. Working like your mom."

"Yeah." The little boy's smile was as wide as a mile. "And here's me and Mama jumping in a pile of leaves." He pointed. "That's me."

"All I see is a pile of leaves."

"There's my hair. See?"

Reed chuckled. "It's hard to see where your red hair starts and the red leaves end."

Kyle turned to Ally with a look of astonishment. "That's just what you said, Mama."

"Great minds." She started toward the kitchen. "While you two are looking at old pictures, I'll start the coffee."

Reed watched her walk away, admiring the way the long skirt hugged her bottom. When he realized Kyle was watching him, he dragged his attention back to the pile of photographs. Though there were more than a dozen, not one, he noted, had a trace of Kyle's father. Odd, he thought. Rick may have been gone for long periods of time while on assignment for the military, but his return should have triggered some picture-taking moments between father and son.

"Coffee's ready."

At Ally's call, Reed helped Kyle gather up the photographs and carry them to the boy's room, where he deposited them in a big box in the bottom drawer of his dresser. Then the two of them walked to the kitchen.

The table held two cups of steaming coffee and a glass of milk, along with a plate of brownies.

"Me and Mama baked these today while Gemma was working downstairs."

"You baked them?" Reed helped himself to one and took a big bite before humming with pleasure. "I've always had a weakness for brownies. Are you sure you baked these? They're really good."

Kyle was beaming. "I helped, didn't I, Mama?"

"Yes, you did." She passed the plate to him before taking one for herself. "Actually, we made two batches. I gave the other one to Gemma to take with her."

"So, no regrets with your decision to hire her?"

"None. She's a natural at selling."

"Natural?" Reed grinned. "I doubt that word would ever be used to describe Gemma. She's the most unnatural teenager I've ever seen."

"I know she looks different. But more and more young people are discovering her place. And I've noticed that once my customers overlook her odd way of dressing, they're attracted to her, as well. She's sweet and pleasant, and she really knows how to sell."

Kyle yawned loudly, and Ally glanced over. "Ready to get into your pj's?"

"Not yet." He was staring at Reed.

Seeing it, Reed caught the boy's hand. "Come on, little buddy. Why don't I lend a hand?"

"Okay." Kyle was off his chair and racing toward his bedroom with Reed following behind.

A short time later, amid lots of laughter, Kyle called, "Mama, I'm ready for bed. Want to hear my prayers?"

She walked into the room to see Kyle already under the covers and Reed sitting on the edge of the bed, just putting away one of her son's storybooks.

"Look, Mama. Reed read *Goodnight Moon* to me. I said it was a baby book, but he said those are the best. And I really liked it."

"I see." She settled herself on the opposite side of his bed. "Then I guess you won't need another story tonight."

"Uh-uh." He struggled to keep his eyes open.

Minutes later, after whispering his prayers, he called, "Night, Mama. Night, Reed."

"Good night, little buddy. Or should I say good night, moon?"

Kyle was already fast asleep.

* * *

When they were back in the kitchen, Ally turned to Reed with an arched brow. "Okay. How did you do that?"

"Do what?"

"That magic you worked on my son. I expected to find him scheming a way to stay up for just another hour. Instead, I find him already in bed and practically asleep."

Reed shrugged. "No magic. I watched while he brushed his teeth and got into his pajamas. I snagged a book out of the pile by his bed and started to read."

"He never lets me read any of his baby books."

Another shrug. "Yeah. He told me it was a baby book. And I told him those were my favorites. After that, he settled down and went into his zone."

"His zone."

"His 'My-eyes-are-so-heavy-I-can't-keep-them-open-another-minute' zone."

Ally shook her head. "In case you haven't noticed, at the kitchen table my son was staring at you with a hunger in his eyes that I've never seen before. As though you were that plate of brownies and he wanted to devour you."

"Yeah. I noticed." Reed's smile was quick and dangerous. He reached out and drew her close. "I wish his mother would look at me that way."

She put a hand to his chest to hold him a little away. "And inflate that giant ego of yours, cowboy?"

"Aw. Come on. Just enough to let me know I was missed. At least a little."

Her voice lowered. She avoided his eyes. "You were."

"What was that? Could you say it louder?"

"You were. Missed."

He lifted her chin, forcing her to look at him. "That wasn't so hard, was it?"

"A painful admission. So..." She flushed slightly. "Your turn. Did you miss me, too?"

"Way more than I wanted to. I was up there to do a job, and a certain red-haired witch kept getting in my head, messing with my mind." His tone deepened. "All the time I was up in the hills, I kept worrying that you were just a dream. Tonight, on the way to town, I started thinking I'd show up in Glacier Ridge and find this old building still empty, and you and Kyle were figments of my imagination."

"That's some imagination you have, cowboy."

He lowered his face to press his mouth to the hair at her temple. "Oh, lady, you have no idea the things I've imagined."

His hands tightened at her waist and he pulled her against him.

When she lifted her head to protest, he cut off her words with a kiss that rocked them both back on their heels.

She came up for air. "Reed..."

"Shh." He kissed her again, lingering over her mouth. "Oh, baby, how I needed this."

He slid his hands along her arms and lifted them to his neck. When she didn't pull away, he moved his open palms down her arms, down her back, drawing her even closer. And then, while his mouth moved over hers, taking her on a slow, sensual ride, his hands trailed her sides until they encountered the swell of her breasts. His thumbs found her nipples already hard through the fabric of her dress.

He swallowed her little gasp of surprise. When she stiffened and tried to pull away, his kiss gentled, as did his touch, until she sighed and relaxed in his arms.

She drew in a long, deep breath. "You should probably go."

"Yeah." He nuzzled the corner of her eye, her cheek,

before lowering his mouth to the sensitive hollow of her neck. "Or I could stay."

She involuntarily shuddered at the press of his lips to her tender flesh. "That's not a good—"

"Have mercy. Think of that long drive back to my ranch." His hands were roaming again, finding all kinds of interesting places to touch. To tease. Until he had her, and himself, thoroughly aroused.

"I'm not ready..."

"I am. Red, I'm so hot, I'm practically going up in flames."

"I know. I am, too. But I'm just not ready for..." She put a hand to his chest and backed up a step. "I need some space. I can't think when you're this close."

"Neither can I. But we don't need to think. Why can't we just go with our feelings?"

With her chest heaving, she took another step back, and then another. "I did that once." Her eyes misted and she blinked furiously. "And I learned a very important lesson. There are always consequences to acting on our feelings without thinking."

The sight of her fighting tears was a splash of ice water.

He gathered her close and pressed his forehead to hers. "Sorry. I know better. But you're killing me, Red."

In response she merely held on and dragged in deep, calming breaths while he did the same.

When the trembling passion had cooled enough, Reed touched a hand to her cheek in an achingly sweet gesture. "You know I want you. That isn't going to change. But I'm glad you had the brain tonight. I guess one of us needed to be sensible."

She managed a weak smile. "You don't make it easy."

"Good. I'd hate to think this was one-sided." He plucked

his hat from the table. "Since I can't stay the night, I'd better leave while I can still walk."

"I'll go downstairs with you." She led the way and opened the door to the shop.

In the doorway he turned and gathered her close. Against her ear he whispered, "Whenever you find it in your heart to let me in, I'll be waiting. Good night, Ally."

He brushed a kiss over her cheek.

She surprised him by drawing him close and giving him a hard, hungry kiss before stepping back.

He shook his head while keeping his eyes steady on hers. "I've never been a patient man. Like I said. You're killing me, Red."

Without a backward glance he strode away.

As he did, he had the strangest sensation that he was being watched. Not just by Ally, but by another pair of eyes.

He made a slow turn. There seemed to be no one around, but the feeling persisted.

He heard the door to the shop close. Heard the lock being thrown.

Still feeling prickly, he climbed into his truck and drove away.

Ally turned the key and stood very still, watching as the taillights on Reed's truck receded along Main Street.

Turning away, she switched off the lights as she climbed the stairs.

In her apartment she paused in front of the framed photographs she'd arranged on the wall.

She wasn't surprised that Reed had noticed the absence of Rick in all the pictures. Reed noticed so many things that others might overlook. Since she'd first met him, he displayed a rare sensitivity that she found endearing.

Endearing. What an odd term to describe a tall, handsome, rugged cowboy. But Reed Malloy was so much more than that. He was so natural and easy with Kyle. He never seemed self-conscious when he played with her son. Or when he read him a story. He didn't appear to be like so many men who tried to amuse a child just to impress someone. Reed made her little boy laugh in a way she'd never seen before. And wasn't he the same with her? Natural and easy. Though they were doing ordinary things, like having a sandwich at D & B's Diner, or ice cream at I's, the fact that she and Kyle were doing them with Reed made them feel like special events. With Reed, everything was more fun. Even the most mundane, everyday things she'd always taken for granted.

She wished with all her heart she could invite him to stay. It hurt to send him away. But she had to guard her son. Herself. She touched a hand to her chest. Her heart. More than anything she needed to protect herself from making a rash decision that could do more damage.

Hadn't there already been enough? She was a mother. No matter how overwhelmed she might feel, she needed to be calm and disciplined and sensible. Kyle deserved it. She deserved it.

She thought about her own mother. Strangers probably thought Dee Stone was one tough cookie. After all, as Archer had said, his sister left home at sixteen with the first cowboy who offered her a ride out of town, and never looked back. But if Dee's life as a girl in Glacier Ridge had been difficult, her life afterward had become a nightmare. When her cowboy left her in Oklahoma, she'd had neither a job nor a place to stay. The owner of an all-night diner had taken pity on the girl and offered her a job flipping burgers by day, washing dishes by night, and allowed her to sleep in a back room until she saved enough for a room in town. She'd made her way across the country doing the jobs nobody else wanted, and an encounter with a handsome, smooth-talking real estate salesman in Maryland convinced her she'd found her happy ending.

Six months later the salesman was gone, and so was all the money she'd saved up to buy her dream home. But she'd been left with something unexpected. A daughter. Ally smiled at the memory. She'd grown up without a father, but she'd had the best mother in the world. The two of them had faced life head-on, and her mother had faced her impending death the same way. With courage and grit. And she'd left her only child with happy memories, a strength of will, and a hunger for family.

That hunger had made Ally vulnerable. But she couldn't blame Rick for her own weakness. He'd made it clear that he was already wedded to the military life. There was no room for the demands of a family.

She turned off the lights as she passed from the tiny living room to the kitchen. She paused to check on Kyle before making her way to her own bedroom. Once there, she undressed and opened the window, allowing the curtains to flutter inward on a fresh breeze.

It would be unbearably humid in Virginia, but here in Montana, with the air blowing down from the hills, it was as cool and clean as a mountain stream. She breathed deeply before settling herself in bed. Leaning toward the night table, she turned off the light and lay in the darkness.

Thoughts of Reed had her smiling. There was just something about him. He made her feel she'd made the right choice moving clear across the country. Even though her connection to her uncle had been largely unsuccessful, so far, she could feel some of her doubts and insecurities slipping away when she was with Reed. He made her believe in herself. Believe that she could make this town her forever home. And make this little business successful enough to provide a life for herself and her son. When she was with Reed, she truly felt she could trust him.

Trust. It wasn't something she would ever again give lightly. She'd trusted one man with her heart, and he'd trampled it. Still, Reed seemed different. Better. But she knew it would take more than just a feeling before she would trust fully. She knew, too, that she was older, and hopefully wiser. But did wisdom really come with age? And how would she know, really know, without risking more pain? That wasn't something she would allow herself to think about.

Instead, she thought about how she felt in Reed's arms. Oh, the man knew how to make a woman feel special. He had all the right moves. Which could mean only that he'd had plenty of experience.

She lay perfectly still, reliving each heart-stopping kiss. Each whispered word. Each mind-numbing touch of those work-roughened hands. How she wished she could simply give in to the passion and enjoy what he was offering.

She was just beginning to doze when she heard something. A light thud, as though something had fallen off a dresser onto the floor.

Her eyes snapped open and she was surprised to see a flickering light beside her bed.

A light?

She sat up and tried to make sense of what she was seeing.

Fire. A flame that had already caught the edge of her sheet and was now snaking along the foot of the bed.

In one quick motion she was out of her bed and snatching up her cell phone. She pressed speed dial as she raced head-long toward Kyle's room.

When she heard a distorted voice, she shouted, "There's a fire at Ally's Attic. Hurry. Fire!"

CHAPTER FOURTEEN

Reed was nearly home, though it wasn't at all where he wanted to be. He'd spent the long ride with the windows wide open, hoping the chilly night air would help clear his mind. It wasn't working. All he could think of was Ally. All he could taste was her. All he could see was the way she'd looked in that unguarded moment when she'd blinked back tears.

He didn't need to know the details to know she'd been hurt. He hated that fact, but he couldn't undo what had already been done. All he could do going forward was to be patient and to understand that she needed to work things out in her own time.

For him, this was all uncharted territory. Ally may be a beautiful, funny, talented woman, but he'd known plenty of other women who fit that description. Ally had something else. Something unique. She was ambitious. Fearless and driven to make her own way. But she was also a mother. That would make her doubly cautious, in order to keep her son safe from the pain of her past. And that meant that he had to respect whatever boundaries she set.

He swore and slapped a flat palm on the steering wheel. His damnable sense of honor was becoming a liability. This wasn't how he'd seen himself spending the night.

When his phone rang, he glanced at the caller ID and a smile touched his mouth. She was calling to say she'd changed her mind.

"Yeah? Ally?"

He could hear her voice, high-pitched, distorted, yelling something he couldn't understand.

"Ally? What's ... ?"

He caught one word before the line went dead.

Fire.

With screeching tires he braked and spun the wheel, turning the speeding truck in the opposite direction. With one hand he dialed Eugene Graystoke's number while he floored the accelerator and drove like a madman toward town.

"Sheriff's office." Eugene's voice sounded sleep-roughened.

"There's a fire at Ally's Attic. She and her son live upstairs."

"I'm on it." With those words, the line went dead.

Reed wasn't much for prayer, but in his mind he was already storming heaven to keep two very special people safe.

"Kyle."

Smoke had Ally coughing furiously as she raced into her son's room.

She was forced to disentangle the little boy from his bed linens before hauling him into her arms and heading for the stairs.

Every downward step felt like a mile-long hiking trail, while behind her she could hear the crackle of flames as they fed on draperies and rugs and bed linens, growing hotter and higher with every minute.

Though Kyle stirred, she could tell he was befuddled and not completely awake yet.

Once down, she fumbled with the locked door, ready to kick a bare foot through the glass if it didn't open. After several frantic moments the door gave and she made a dash out into the cool night air. From inside she could hear the smoke alarms going off one by one as the fire gained strength.

Within minutes she looked up at the sound of a police siren drawing near.

Sheriff Graystoke was out of his SUV and racing toward her.

He put an arm around her shoulders. "Reed called me. Is he here?"

"No." She felt her legs trembling and wondered how much longer she could stand while holding Kyle to her chest.

"Where is he?"

"I don't know. I dialed the first number my finger found in the dark. My only concern was getting Kyle out safely."

"I notified the fire department volunteers. Do you know how the fire started? The stove? A cigarette?"

"No. No. I heard something drop. I guess it came through the open window."

"It? What do you mean?"

"It seemed to be a torch of some kind that landed beside my bed."

Eugene Graystoke was staring at her as if she'd gone mad. "Are you saying you were firebombed?"

Ally tried to wrap her mind around something so alien to her. "I don't…"

There was a terrible sound of screeching brakes. Reed's voice cut through the night. "Thank heaven you're both safe."

Ally looked up to see Reed racing toward them.

Eugene's face was as dark as a thundercloud. "Ms. Shaw just said the fire was started by a torch through an upper window."

"A torch?" Reed was rocked back on his heels.

A single fire truck drove up, horn blasting, as cars and trucks began filling the street. Vehicle doors slammed. Men began milling about, hooking up hoses, shouting orders. A truck pulled up alongside the sheriff's vehicle, and Gemma and Jeremy rushed over to Ally.

Gemma was pale as a ghost. "Are you okay?"

Before Ally could respond, the sheriff caught Gemma's arm and rounded on her and Jeremy. "What are the two of you doing here?"

Jeremy swallowed twice before he was able to say, "We heard the fire siren and followed the truck."

"Where were you?" Eugene's eyes were narrowed in suspicion.

"We were sleeping in Jeremy's truck." Gemma's hand snuck into the boy's.

"We were parked over behind the jail, Sheriff." Jeremy flushed. "We figured it'd be a safe, quiet place to spend the night."

Gemma's chin lifted. "You don't think we did this, do you?"

"I don't know what to think. All I know is, until I've conducted a thorough investigation, everyone's a suspect."

The sheriff turned to Ally. "Our fire force is made up of all volunteers. Right now, I need to join them and lend a hand."

His head swiveled back to Gemma and Jeremy. "This

isn't over. I want to talk to both of you later." With that terse statement, he strode away.

Reed took one look at Ally's bare feet and night slip, and Kyle in his thin pajamas, his chubby arms hugging her neck with a death grip.

"Here." He took the boy from her arms and led her toward his truck.

"But the sheriff…"

"Eugene will want to talk to you later. Right now he'll be with the others, helping put out the fire." He opened the passenger door and eased Ally inside before setting Kyle on her lap.

At once Ally hugged the shivering little boy close.

Gemma spoke to her through the open window. "Ally, I hope you believe Jeremy and I were asleep when this happened."

Ally reached a hand to the girl. "I believe you, Gemma. And the sheriff will, too, when he has time to get past this." She looked beyond Gemma to Jeremy, standing behind with his hand on the girl's shoulder. "You two need to get some sleep now. Tomorrow is soon enough to deal with all this."

"Is the entire building burning?" Gemma asked softly.

Ally shrugged. "I don't know. All I know is we were lucky to get out alive. I know you're worried about your merchandise. Right now, I have no answers."

Gemma nodded. "We'll come back tomorrow and see if we can do anything to help."

Ally watched as the two teens climbed into Jeremy's rusting truck and drove slowly away.

Reed removed a blanket from the backseat and wrapped it around mother and son. Then he walked to the driver's side to slide in beside them before gathering them into his arms.

Ally's teeth were chattering. "I can't stop shaking."

"Shock. It's a normal reaction when you realize what just happened and how much worse it could have been. Just hold on and breathe."

Kyle looked over at Reed. "What happened? Why are we out here?"

"There's a fire in your building, little buddy."

The boy touched a hand to his mother's cheek. "Is our 'partment going to burn down?"

His question had Ally's heart contracting painfully. She pressed her mouth to his cheek. "I hope not. The firemen are up there now, trying to put it out."

"If it burns, will we have to go back to Uncle Archer's?"

Ally sucked in a breath. The fear and sorrow in Kyle's voice matched the emotions swamping her. Everything she'd worked so hard to achieve was gone. Their situation was even worse than before. Now they were left with nothing.

"I don't know, honey." Her voice trembled, signaling that she was close to breaking down under the weight of all that had happened in such a short span. "I just don't know."

"I do." Reed tightened his grasp, holding them firmly in the circle of his arms. "The two of you are coming home with me."

"Like this?" Ally indicated their nightclothes.

"Like this." Reed tugged the blanket up to their chins.

"Maybe..." Ally swallowed back her unshed tears and tried again. "Maybe they'll get the fire out fast enough to salvage some of our things."

"It doesn't matter. If you're able to save some things, or if everything is ruined, you're still coming home with me." Though he kept his tone soft, there was a thread of steel beneath each word. "Until we find out who's behind this, I'm never leaving you two alone again."

* * *

When a tap sounded on the truck window, Reed lowered it.

Eugene's face was grim. "The fire's out. Some of the volunteers will remain, to make sure there are no hot spots. The rest are headed back to their homes and ranches. It'll be daylight soon, and they have their own chores to see to."

"Thank you, Sheriff." Ally glanced toward the soot-darkened windows of the upper floor. "Was there much damage?"

"Enough. Between the fire and the amount of water needed to put it out, there's not much salvageable upstairs. Not too much damage on the main level. That's mostly smoke and water damage." He sucked in a breath. "We think we found the original torch near your bed, though it was badly burned to a charred mess. I'll send it to the state lab for testing."

Archer Stone stepped up beside the sheriff, his face and clothing soot-darkened.

He pinned Ally with a look. "What's this Eugene tells me about a stalker?"

Ally gave a sigh. "A man I worked with in Virginia."

"A lover?"

She gave an involuntary shiver. "A coworker. Nothing more."

"Nothing more?" His face twisted into a sneer. "That's a lot of anger from a guy who got nothing but work from you."

"Anything more was in his own mind."

When Archer opened up his mouth to say something, Reed deliberately interrupted to spare Ally any more verbal sparring with her uncle. "Eugene, I'd like to take Ally and Kyle back to my ranch. I can bring Ally back later today to talk with you, if that's all right with you."

The sheriff nodded. "I agree, Reed. The upper rooms aren't habitable, and probably won't be for some time. What these two need right now is a couple of hours to rest and some hot food in a place where they can feel safe and comfortable."

Archer's furious tone betrayed his anger. "What the hell's the matter with you, Eugene? What gives Malloy the right to interfere? These two are my kin."

The sheriff turned to his deputy with an arched look. "Which you didn't even admit to until I heard it from them."

At the sheriff's words Archer's voice went up a notch, along with his temper. "If they're going to stay anywhere, it ought to be with me. That's what folks will say. It's only right and proper."

The sheriff looked more amused than annoyed. "Since when did you worry about things being right and proper, Archer?"

"But the Malloys…"

"The Malloys are good, decent folks. I'm sure they'll make your niece and great-nephew feel right at home."

Archer's eyes blazed. "You're forgetting. This is an active investigation. It would be a lot easier if they were staying with a man of the law."

"Easier? What could be easier than having Frank and Ms. Grace pamper these two and soothe some frayed nerves? What could be easier than having Reed drive your niece to my office?" The sheriff turned to Ally. "Going through something like this can be an emotionally exhausting event, Ms. Shaw. I'm sorry you and your son had to deal with this. For now, I think you should go with Reed and try to get some rest. Late afternoon is soon enough for you to come back to town. We'll have a good long talk, and you can tell me everything you remember about the events leading up to the fire."

"Thank you, Sheriff." Ally turned to her uncle. "And thank you, too, Archer, for helping the firemen, and for offering us shelter." She reached for his hand, closing it between both of hers. "I really appreciate all you've done. I think, for now, I'll do as the sheriff suggests and let Reed take us to his ranch. But if your offer still stands in the days to come, I'd be happy to accept your hospitality."

Some of the fire seemed to go out of Archer's eyes, though his tone remained layered with anger and sarcasm. "I guess we'll just have to see. Maybe once you get used to the comfort of the big, fancy Malloy ranch, you'll forget all about us common folks." He pulled his hand free and took a step back.

Reed turned on the ignition and put the truck in gear. As they started along Main Street, he watched the sheriff and his deputy recede in the rearview mirror. When he looked over at Ally, she had closed her eyes and kept her face pressed to the top of Kyle's head. The little boy, seated between them, had fallen fast asleep.

As the truck ate up the miles to his ranch, Reed found himself wondering if Archer's anger was the sort of righteous indignation any man would feel on behalf of a beloved family member who'd been threatened with danger or if that anger could have actually been the trigger that initiated both the torch and the fire.

Reed knew that the prime suspect remained Glen Lloyd. The man had already proven to be unstable, having driven halfway across the country to find a woman who had done nothing more than share his workspace. From all appearances, he was an angry, sullen man. And he'd emailed her since then. The fact that this strange, angry man was in hiding, and appeared to be in no hurry to return to work, added up to a man with evil intent.

Still, his initial contact with Ally had been some time ago. What had he been waiting for? What could have triggered this hideous act tonight?

Whether this firebomb had been tossed by Glen Lloyd, or Ally's uncle, or a complete stranger, the fact remained that she and Kyle were in real and present danger. A broken window could be construed as a threat or malicious mischief. But a firebomb was no idle threat. If not for Ally's quick thinking, she and Kyle could have perished in their beds.

The thought left Reed shaken to his core.

He had no intention of leaving them alone again until this mystery was resolved and their safety was assured.

Dawn light crept slowly across the sky, bringing with it the most glorious sunrise. Ribbons of pink wove their way around the hills, illuminating the dark outline of herds that seemed to fill every meadow in the higher regions.

Ally kept her arms around her sleeping son, whose head rested on her shoulder. "Will we be at your ranch soon?"

Reed turned to her with a smile. "We've been on Malloy land for the past half hour."

"Half an hour?" She turned for a better look at the green fields that seemed to stretch all the way to the horizon. "How much land does your family own?"

He shrugged. "A couple thousand acres, give or take a few."

"Thousand..." She shook her head, unable to process such a figure.

When the house came into view, she fell silent as she studied the graceful, three-story structure made of wood and natural stone. Though its size could have been imposing, it appeared instead to be both solid and homey, with a wide covered porch that ran the length of the building. Beyond were several towering barns and outbuildings. In the distance, past hayfields, she could make out the dark outlines of yet more cattle. And could hear the sound of their lowing through the closed windows of the truck.

As Reed drove along the gravel driveway, Ally's head swiveled as she tried to take it all in.

He pulled up behind a line of several trucks. "Looks like everybody's already here. Not surprised. Any mealtime brings a crowd."

Reed stepped down and circled around to open the passenger door. He helped Ally out, then reached in and unbuckled Kyle's seat belt before lifting the little boy into his arms.

Kyle stirred and rubbed his eyes. "Where are we?"

"At my family's ranch." Seeing the way Ally carefully drew the blanket about herself, he put an arm around her to lend his support.

They climbed the porch steps and walked through the mudroom before stepping into the kitchen. Inside, the chorus of voices suddenly fell silent.

"Well now. What's this?" Frank Malloy took in the sight of his grandson holding a little boy at his shoulder, one arm around the waist of the young woman they'd met at her shop's grand opening. She was wrapped from head to toe in a blanket.

"There was a fire in town last night, and I've asked Ally and her son, Kyle, to stay with us until they can sort through the damage."

His grandmother was on her feet and hurrying across the room with her arms outstretched. "Welcome to our ranch, Ally. Kyle. I'm sorry you're here for such a sad reason, but I'm glad the two of you weren't hurt in the fire." She looked down at Ally's bare toes peeking out from beneath the blanket. "It had to be frightening to evacuate in the middle of the night."

"It was."

"I'm sure you were forced to leave with nothing but the clothes on your backs."

Ally flushed and nodded.

Seeing her discomfort, Vanessa crossed the room. "Hi, Ally. I'm Nessa Malloy, Matt's wife. We met at your store."

"Of course. I remember you." Ally smiled as recognition dawned.

"Come with me." Nessa took Ally's hand. "I'm sure we can find something of mine that will fit you, after you've had a chance to shower away all the smoke and soot."

"I don't want to be any trouble."

"Don't be silly."

Ally turned to Reed. "Kyle…"

"Will go with me." Reed gave her a gentle smile. "I think the two of us need a shower, too."

"All right."

"Wait. I'm coming, too." As Nessa led her away, Ingrid jumped up to follow them. "What Nessa doesn't have, I'm sure I can provide."

A short time later the three women descended the stairs, all wearing matching smiles.

Ally was dressed in a pair of slender denims, a pale green cotton shirt, and calfskin boots. Her tangled hair had been brushed long and loose.

The sight of Kyle kneeling at a coffee table, his red hair damp from a shower, wearing a pair of faded denims and a T-shirt in lemon yellow, had her smiling.

"Wherever did you find something to fit?"

Kyle pointed to a pretty little dark-haired girl kneeling beside him. "Lily said they don't fit her anymore, so I can keep them."

"That's very kind. Who is your new friend?"

"Mama, this is Lily. She's Ingrid's sister."

"Hello, Lily." Ally crossed the room to shake the girl's hand. "Thank you for the loan of your clothes."

"You're welcome. But Kyle can keep them. They're too small for me now."

"Mama, this is Colin. He's Reed's uncle."

"Colin." Ally offered her hand to the man who bore an amazing resemblance to his nephew. "We met at I's Cream Shop in town. You were with Dr. Anita Cross."

"Ma'am. I remember." His smile, so like Reed's, was dazzling. "Actually, I'm uncle to not only Reed, but also to Luke and Matt."

"And young enough to be their brother."

That brought another smile from this tall, handsome man.

"Mama, the man at the stove is Yancy." It was clear to all of them that the little boy was enjoying the fact that he'd already met everyone. "Yancy does all the cooking here."

"Yancy." Ally extended her hand, and the cook removed an oven mitt before shaking hands.

"Mama, this is Burke." Kyle stretched his neck to see the face of the tall, rangy cowboy. "He's the ranch foreman. And that's Mick. He's Ingrid's foreman."

Ally shook hands with each man.

"And this is Great One."

Ally arched a brow. "Did I hear my son say Great One?"

"That you did." In his best Hollywood director's voice Nelson explained. "I'm great-grandfather to Matt, Luke, and Reed, and when they were much younger, they decided I should be called Great One. I consider it a perfect fit."

Ally couldn't help chuckling. "Well then, hello, Great One." She offered a handshake. "It's lovely to meet you."

"And you, my dear." He indicated Kyle. "You have a very bright little boy."

"Thank you. I can't get over the fact that he already knows all your names."

Reed winked. "We told him there would be a test later to see if he was paying attention."

That had everyone grinning.

Great One leaned forward. "Reed has been bringing us up to date. I hope your building hasn't suffered irreparable damage. When the family returned from your grand opening, they were all singing your praises. They had high hopes for your new business."

"So did I." She clasped her hands together. "Now I guess I'll just have to wait and see what the sheriff reports when I go to town later today."

"We'll all hold a good thought." Grace pointed to a tray of cups and glasses on the countertop. "We have coffee, juice, milk, and tea. Please help yourself."

Noting that Kyle already had half a glass of foaming orange juice when he returned to his coloring, Ally helped herself to hot tea.

From across the room Yancy said, "Breakfast is ready."

The others got to their feet and made their way around the big table.

Reed held a chair for Ally and sat beside her, while Lily took Kyle's hand and led him to the place between her and Great One at the far end of the table.

Ally and Kyle watched in silence as platter after platter of scrambled eggs, sausage and bacon, and light-as-air pancakes were passed, as well as a basket of toast and biscuits still warm from the oven.

In the middle of the table stood a pot of wild strawberry jam, as well as several pitchers of maple syrup that were quickly passed from hand to hand.

Great One took a bite of pancake before touching his

thumb and index finger to his lips. "Yancy, my man. I believe you've outdone yourself."

In an aside, Lily whispered, "Great One always says that."

"He does?" Kyle's eyes got big. "Why?"

Lily shrugged. "I guess 'cause he just loves Yancy's cooking."

Kyle tasted the pancake. Around a mouthful he said, "Mama, wait till you taste this. It's almost as good as Reed's."

That had everyone staring at Reed, who never missed a beat before saying, "That's what years of watching the master chef will get you."

Yancy paused in midstride to turn from the stove. "You made pancakes?"

"Yeah."

Luke added, "At Ally's place?"

Reed looked at the faces around the table. "What are you all looking at? It's not as though it's my first time cooking. We all take turns up at the range shacks."

"Yeah." Luke nudged his wife. "After a night of babysitting cattle in the cold mountain air. What's your excuse for making breakfast at Ally's, bro?"

Reed's grin was quick and dangerous. "I put in a tough night of babysitting a lumpy recliner. A recliner, I might add, that Ally actually believes can bring good money from some poor fool."

Matt managed a straight face. "You're telling us you slept downstairs in Ally's shop on a lumpy recliner?"

From the end of the table, Great One intoned, "That's his story and he's sticking to it."

The entire family burst into laughter, while Ally's face flamed.

"Hey now." Reed caught her hand under the table and squeezed. "There are children present."

They turned to Kyle and Lily, who sat, heads bent, whispering.

At the sudden silence, they both looked up.

"What?" Lily asked. "What did we miss?"

Grace reached over to pat her hand. "It's nothing, darlin'. It looks like you two are getting acquainted."

Kyle nodded. "Lily's going to teach me how to ride a horse."

Across the table, Ally's jaw dropped. "Just like that? You think you're going to climb up on a horse and ride?"

"Lily says everybody on a ranch rides horses like kids ride bikes in the city."

"Or Harleys." Ingrid batted her lashes at Luke.

"Well, some of us do." He pressed a kiss to her cheek before turning to the children. "But Lily's right. If you're going to be on a ranch, Kyle, you may as well learn how to ride a horse."

"Is that okay, Mama?"

Ally took in a long, slow breath. "I'll think about it."

Reed winked at Kyle. "We already know what that means."

Ally punched his shoulder before she realized everyone was watching. To Grace she said, "Your grandson has been revealing to my son all kinds of mom secrets."

"Which are not so secret." Reed grinned at Kyle. "Such as, 'I'll think about it' really means 'I don't want to say yes, so I'll put you off until you forget the question.'"

Luke shared a knowing smile with Lily. "What did I tell you? It isn't only your big sister who pulls those pranks. Kyle's mom does the same thing."

Ingrid patted Ally's hand. "A word of warning. These

Malloy men are very irreverent about sacred secrets of adults."

"That's because they still think of themselves as bad boys," Nessa added.

Matt wrapped both arms around her and pulled her close for a kiss to her neck. "And you're glad of it."

She laughed and nodded before saying to Grace, "He's right. I'm very glad he remains one of your bad boys."

The others shared her laughter.

As Yancy began clearing the table, the adults sat back, sipping hot coffee.

Lily turned to her sister. "Is it all right if Kyle and I go out to the barn? He wants to see the animals."

"As long as you both understand the rules. Kyle can't attempt to ride unless he gets his mother's permission and has an adult present. And you, young lady, are not to allow him to get too close to old Bunny. That mare has a mean streak, which is worse now that she's ailing."

"I won't. Promise."

Ingrid nodded. "It's all right with me." She turned to Ally? "And you?"

Ally smiled at Kyle. "Go ahead. I know you're dying to see the animals. Stay close to Lily, honey."

The two caught hands and fairly danced out the door.

When they were gone, Frank glanced at Reed before turning his attention to Ally. "Now about this fire..."

For the next hour, she and Reed filled them in on all that had been going on in her life.

"Where do you go from here?" Frank drained his mug and smiled his thanks at Yancy, who moved around the table refilling cups.

Ally sighed. "I haven't had time to think it all through yet."

"Will you repair the building and continue with your business?"

She nodded. "I don't see that I have a choice. I sank a great deal of money into this. The building and contents are insured. There should be enough to make repairs. But until the authorities find Glen, I won't feel safe there."

"Nor should you." Grace exchanged a look with her husband before saying, "We'd love to have you and Kyle stay here with us while you go forward with the repairs."

"That's so generous of you, Grace." Ally looked around the table. "Of all of you. But I need to be in town, to direct the repairs and to run my business."

"I can understand that." Frank held up a hand. "We can loan you a spare truck. I know it's a long drive, but it's late summer, and the roads are clear. But the more important issue is your safety. Now that you've suffered two acts of violence, I can't imagine you sleeping above your business."

"But it could be weeks before they find Glen. He's already been hiding out, without a trace."

Frank nodded. "That's true. This guy seems clever about staying out of sight. He also seems like a coward who chooses to do his deeds under cover of darkness, against a woman and child."

"My uncle Archer has invited me to stay with him in town."

"I understand you stayed with your uncle when you first arrived in town. You have to know that he spends considerable time on the job. That means you and Kyle could be alone, especially on those nights when Archer pulls all-night duty." Frank could see Ally mulling his words. "I doubt a coward who targets a woman and child would try anything here at a ranch filled with so many people. So I urge you, if not for your sake, then for Kyle's, to consider staying with our family until this issue is resolved."

When Ally fell silent, Reed looked around at his family before touching a hand to her shoulder. "Is it settled, then? Are you willing to stay here, at least for now?"

Ally took in a deep breath. "Thank you. All of you for your generous offer." She turned to Reed. "Yes. At least for now, we're more than grateful to be here."

Reed impulsively leaned close to brush a kiss over her cheek.

While around the table nobody spoke, Luke said what the others were thinking. "Well, that's a relief. From that fierce look in my brother's eyes, I was afraid if you said no, Reed might have to resort to locking you in a room and throwing away the key."

After hearing Ally's narrative of the danger, and the tension they were all feeling, the family's laughter was a welcome release.

Still smiling, Grace happened to look at her grandson.

Though Reed laughed with the others, there was indeed a look in his eye. A fierce protectiveness that told her, more than words, just how much this young woman and her son had come to mean to him.

She'd seen that same look before. In her son, Patrick, whenever he'd looked at his beloved Bernie.

The apple didn't fall far, she thought. Though there had been girls who'd vied for the attention of her youngest grandson from the time he'd been a teen, none had ever sparked such a look before. This time was different. This young woman was different.

Grace turned to Frank, and the two exchanged a look they'd perfected over a lifetime. A look that spoke volumes, though they said not a word.

CHAPTER FIFTEEN

Reed led Ally up the stairs, where they followed a hallway until he stopped outside a door. "This will be Kyle's room while you're here."

He opened the door and stood aside, allowing Ally to precede him.

She noted a sturdy brown quilt and the brown-and-white-checked throw across the foot of the big bed. There were shelves holding an assortment of books and games and a flat-screen TV standing atop a chest. An open door across the room revealed an attached bathroom.

She turned to Reed. "Kyle's room? This is bigger than our entire apartment. It's certainly big enough for both of us."

"No need to share. The second guest room is next door."

He led the way and opened a door to reveal a king-size bed covered in a white down quilt. To one side was a desk and chair, and in a little alcove stood an overstuffed glider and footstool, and beside it a table and lamp that invited a

chance to curl up with a good book, or perhaps to simply enjoy the spectacular view out the floor-to-ceiling window that
overlooked the hills in the distance.

"Oh, Reed." Ally covered her mouth to hide her gasp of
surprise. "This is . . ." She shook her head when words failed
her.

"Yeah. I know it's primitive. But hey, this is Montana,
after all."

She joined his laughter.

He touched a hand to her cheek. "It's good to hear you
laugh again."

When she lifted her head in surprise, she caught a look in
his eye that had her heart racing. "You make it easy to laugh,
Reed."

"Right now, I don't feel like laughing. I feel like . . . this."
He lowered his mouth to hers.

The flare of heat was sudden and intense, catching her by
complete surprise.

He backed her up until they bumped the open door.
Against her mouth he whispered, "We could always close
this and take advantage of our time alone."

"With your entire family just downstairs I should be completely turned off. Instead, you make it sound a little too
tempting."

"I'm glad to know you're as tempted as I am." He
dragged her close, kissing her with an urgency that had her
heart racing overtime.

When he was holding her like this, kissing her like this,
she had an almost overpowering desire to forget all her good
intentions and just go with her feelings. "Oh, Reed." She
wrapped her arms around his neck, giving herself up to the
pleasure he was offering.

"You taste like maple syrup, Red. Something I could never

resist." He took the kiss deeper and drew her firmly against him until she could feel him in every pore of her body.

Why did he have to be so good at this? How was she supposed to be sensible when everything about this man screamed pleasure and passion? When every touch was calculated to make her want more? And she did. She wanted so much more than just his kisses.

"Let's just shut this door and tune out the rest of the world." Reed continued kissing her while with one hand he reached behind her to the doorknob.

"Hey, Mama. Guess what me and Lily did."

At the sound of Kyle's voice, the two stepped apart with equal parts guilt and frustration.

Dragging in several gulps of air, Ally managed to say in her perfect mother-as-teacher voice, "Lily and I."

"Yeah." Kyle took the last two steps up the stairway in a single leap and dashed up beside them. "What are you two doing?"

"Reed was showing me where we'd sleep."

"Oh. Me and Lily . . . Lily and I fed the horses carrots. She said there's a bin of carrots in the barn that we can use as treats whenever we're out there."

"That's nice." Ally took a step away from Reed, hoping to clear her head. As she did, she saw the way he continued staring at her in that way he had, guaranteed to heat her blood even from a distance. "Want to see your room?"

"Can I see it later? Lily wants to show me Yancy's vegeble garden."

She shared a smile with Reed at her son's pronunciation. "It's vegetable."

"That's what I said. Yancy's vegeble garden. Can I?"

Ally nodded. "Yes. As long as it's all right with Yancy."

"He's going with us. He said we're going to pick all kinds

of fresh stuff for supper tonight. And then he's going to let me and Lily...Lily and me help him cook it."

"Oh. That sounds like fun."

"I know. Want to come with us? I bet Yancy would teach you how to cook his vegebles, too."

Ally shook her head. "I'd like that. But I'd better not. I think it's time for me to get ready to go to town."

"Can I stay here with Lily and Yancy?"

"I'll have to check with Yancy first."

"Okay. I'll be out in the garden. I hope they didn't go without me." He flung the words over his shoulder as he raced headlong down the stairs.

A minute later they heard the back door slam.

"Looks like somebody found himself a new best friend."

Ally nodded.

"Now..." Reed took hold of her hand. "Where were we?"

Ally pulled away. "Not a chance, cowboy. Now that I've had time to think, I realize that wasn't such a good idea."

"That's what I was afraid of."

She smiled. "Besides, it's time I went to town and had that talk with the sheriff."

"I'll go with you."

"You have a ranch to run. Cows to tend. And whatever else you do around here. I'm sure there are probably a hundred more important things for you to do than drive me to town."

He ran a hand down her hair. "Since you won't let me take up where we left off..." He gave a wry smile. "I'll use whatever excuse is handy to spend as much time as I can with you, Red. We'll go to town together."

"Look, Mama." As Ally studied the neat rows of Yancy's garden, Kyle used a little shovel to dig around green fernlike stalks. Minutes later he held up a carrot with the sort of pride expected if he'd been holding a gold nugget. "They grow in the dirt, and Yancy says all we have to do is dig them up and wash them." The little boy carefully set his treasure in a basket half filled with vegetables.

"Yes. I see." Ally looked around as her son and Lily moved on to another row and began to dig. "Yancy, this is magical."

He straightened and walked over, peeling off his garden gloves as he did. "I guess growing things is a lot like magic. We dig and hoe and cultivate, and pray Mother Nature will smile on us and present us with this bounty of food."

Like Yancy's kitchen, his garden had been very carefully laid out to be both efficient and pleasing to the eye. There were tomato plants in wire cages to keep them from drooping under the weight of the green tomatoes slowly ripening in the sun. There were rows of lettuce, carrots; green, red, and yellow peppers. Snap peas and beans curled upward around rows of twine anchored between posts. Lining the far side of the garden were strawberry plants nestled in straw, and tall raspberry plants heavy with fruit. Offering shade nearby were apple, cherry, and pear trees.

"This garden isn't the only magic. What you do with the things you grow is amazing."

The man flushed with obvious pleasure. "I found my life's calling here on the Malloy ranch. They give me the freedom to do exactly as I please."

"And why not? It benefits everyone."

"It benefits me, most of all." He adjusted the brim of his hat. "Before coming here, I had no life to speak of. Since being here, I've found everything I dreamed of, and more. They're the family I always hoped for."

Family. His words touched her deeply.

"Yancy. Look."

Lily's excited cry had him turning away. "What's up?"

"Look at the size of this turnip. It's the biggest one yet, and Kyle was the one to dig it up."

"Wow, Kyle. Way to go." Yancy turned to Ally. "Care to join in our little dig?"

She shook her head. "I have to go to town to talk to the sheriff. I came by to get Kyle."

"Would it be all right if he stayed here?" He gave her a gentle smile. "I know he's new to all this, but it would be a shame to take him away now. I think he's having the time of his life."

She looked over at the smile on her son's face. A smile that stretched from ear to ear. "You don't mind?"

"Mind? Ally, I intend to turn those two into my little students. By the time you get back, we'll have harvested a ton of food, and they'll learn how to prepare it all into a royal feast."

"It sounds like a lot more fun than what's awaiting me in town." She squeezed his hand. "Thank you, Yancy."

She walked with him to where Kyle and Lily were filling up their basket. She knelt down beside her son. "Would you like to stay here while I go to town?"

"Oh, yes. Can I stay, Yancy?"

At the cook's nod of assent, Kyle turned to the next row before calling, "Thanks, Yancy. Bye, Mama."

She shared a look with Yancy. "You were right. I would have had a hard time prying him away from this."

As she walked toward the house, she listened to the sound of her son's laughter. It was the sweetest sound in the world, and her heart grew lighter with every step.

"Ms. Shaw." Eugene Graystoke indicated the chairs across from his desk. "I hope you and your son will be able to put last night's incident behind you and move on."

"Thank you, Sheriff." Ally sat, with Reed beside her. "When I left Kyle at the Malloy ranch, he seemed to be having the time of his life digging up carrots and turnips in Yancy's garden."

"That's the amazing thing about kids." The sheriff set aside a stack of papers from his desk to a side cabinet. "Sometimes a little distraction is all it takes to get them to move away from trauma. But I'm sure you know that something like last night's fire could sneak up into his mind when you least expect it. He may suffer from bad dreams for a while."

She nodded. "I intend to keep a close eye on him."

"Good." He steepled his hands atop his desk, an indication that he wanted to get down to the business at hand. "For now, I'll have to accept the word of the two teenagers. My deputy saw their truck parked near the jail at around the time you phoned, Reed. But that doesn't mean they're off the hook." His eyes narrowed. "I'm still not ready to trust either of them. As for that charred bit of torch we recovered from your bedroom, the state lab will need some time to run tests on it. They're also checking every one of the emails Glen Lloyd sent you. So far, there's been no trace of him. I think he may be employing a disguise. The state police will try to enhance his picture with a few different looks, from facial hair to glasses, to see if that brings any response from the public."

"You think he's nearby, Eugene?"

Reed's question had the sheriff nodding. "In fact, most stalkers have a compulsion to watch their intended victims. That's why I've asked Archer to talk to every building owner here in town to see if they've rented out a room to a stranger in the past few weeks."

Reed's eyes narrowed. "You think this guy will strike again?"

"I do. I believe his first act against Ms. Shaw was a broken window. His second was much more violent. A fire that could have caused death. His emails went from an invitation to get together to an angry tirade accusing her of thinking she was too good for the likes of him. This follows a typical stalker's love-hate pattern."

Eugene turned to Ally. "From my research on stalkers, I've learned that his behavior at work was also a pattern. It's no wonder you didn't realize what was happening. This man went from being attracted to you to deciding that you needed his protection when Kyle's father died. He saw himself as your savior and protector, and probably convinced himself that it was only a matter of time before he would break down any barriers you'd set up between them. But when you not only rejected his advances but also moved far away, his obsession took over his life. First he used up his vacation time to persuade you to come back with him. Now he's taken a leave of absence. Our state police experts believe he's crossed a line, and now, for him, there's no turning back."

Seeing the stunned look on Ally's face, Reed took her hand and held it between both of his.

The sheriff stood. "I'm sorry, Ms. Shaw. I know this is a lot to process. I honestly believe we'll catch this guy soon. But until we do, I'd like you to promise me you'll never be alone."

"What about my apartment? My business?"

"They're not worth your life. Why not hire someone to remodel your apartment and close up the business until we have Glen Lloyd in custody?"

"That business is my only source of income." She sighed as she considered his words. "I'll need some time to think all this through. As much as I want to get on with my life, I have to admit that this has me really frightened. Not just for myself, but for my son. And I hate that this man, who meant nothing whatever to me, is now controlling my life."

Eugene walked around his desk to put a hand on her shoulder. "Your anger is understandable, Ms. Shaw. As a lawman, and as your neighbor, I share that anger. But I do believe we'll find this guy soon and put an end to all your trouble."

"Oh, I hope so." She gave him a tremulous smile. "Is it all right if Reed and I go up to my apartment now and take a look at the damage?"

"Go ahead. We've finished with our investigation. Just don't let yourself get too upset by the damage you see. Remember that it can all be repaired in time."

Ally walked around the tiny apartment, moving from the small great room to the kitchen, and then to her bedroom, where the blaze had destroyed everything. What hadn't been consumed by fire had been forever ruined by the force of so much water from the fire hoses.

Kyle's drawings. The framed photos that they'd hung over the sagging sofa. All the little mementoes of their lives lay in tatters. And all because of a madman who was determined to control her life.

Seeing the tears that welled up in her eyes, Reed put an arm around her waist and drew her close. "Remember what the chief said. It can all be repaired in time."

"Time." Ally sighed, resting her head on his shoulder, feeling weary beyond belief. "I remember my mother telling me that everything happens for a reason. She was talking about her own life and the difficult choices she'd made that led her to our final days together. By then, she'd been at peace. She said she'd learned that she was where she wanted to be, with the only one who mattered, because she'd learned to be patient with herself." Ally looked up at Reed. "Maybe I'm supposed to learn patience. With myself. With my son. With the world around me."

"That's probably the lesson we should all learn in this life." He turned her in his arms and kissed her gently. "We need to get out of here." He caught her hand and led her down the stairs.

They stared around at the once pretty showroom. Now much of the contents lay water-soaked. The room reeked of smoke.

At a knock on the door they looked up to see Gemma and Jeremy.

Ally waved them inside.

Their disheartened looks mirrored the sadness Ally was feeling.

Gemma looked around. "Hey, where's Kyle? I was hoping to see his happy little face."

"He wanted to stay at Reed's place. He's found a new friend, and he seems to be having a grand time."

"I'm glad." Gemma touched a hand to the lumpy sofa now waterlogged and still dripping. "Can any of this be cleaned?"

Ally shrugged. "I don't know. Think about all the good people who brought their old treasures here, hoping to earn some money. Now everything's ruined."

Hearing the tremor in Ally's voice, Reed drew her close and pulled out his cell phone. "Want me to call Thorny and see when he can start on the repairs?"

Ally nodded.

Gemma took Jeremy's hand and the two of them walked to the back room. Ally trailed behind, dreading what she would see. Everything had been flooded by the fire hoses and lay in soggy heaps.

Gemma turned in Jeremy's arms and began silently weeping.

Ally's heart went out to the girl. She was so young to have had so many things go wrong in her life.

Reed stepped into the back room. "Thorny said he's been through this kind of fire damage before. He knows the steps that need to be taken, both for the authorities and for the insurance company. He can assess the damage and start repair within a couple of days." He turned to Jeremy. "You find a job yet?"

Jeremy shook his head. "I've been looking everywhere. But..."

"Thorny would like to hire you."

"He would?" The boy looked thunderstruck.

"He said he'll need all the help he can get. And, Gemma, if you're willing, Thorny would like you to begin to catalog for the insurance company all the items that can't be cleaned up for resale. They'll send a representative out to double-check them, and they'll make a settlement to every one of the families who've left items here."

"Oh, Reed." Ally gave a sigh of relief. "That's such good news."

"Yeah." He caught her hand before turning to the teens. "We need to get out of this gloom."

The four of them stepped out of the building and into the sunshine.

Reed shook Jeremy's hand. "Keep an eye out for Thorny's truck. When he gets here, you and Gemma can sign on for the cleanup crew. And until he pays you"— he reached into his pocket and withdrew some bills—"this should be enough to get a room somewhere and a couple of meals."

The two teenagers were speechless.

It was Gemma who finally found her voice. "That isn't necessary. You don't need to do this."

"I want to. You'll be better workers if you've got a decent place to sleep and enough food to give you energy."

As the two walked to Jeremy's truck, Ally touched a hand to Reed's cheek. "That was sweet and generous."

He gave her a devilish grin. "Just don't go around sharing that news. I wouldn't want to ruin my reputation as a tough guy."

"Your secret's safe with me."

He caught her hand. "Even though it's against my nature as a guy, I know you need to shop for clothes for you and Kyle. So I'm about to introduce you to Glacier Ridge's one-stop shopping." He pointed to the neat store with bright red-and-white awnings over the windows and a sign that read: ANYTHING GOES. "Trudy Evans owns the shop, and her motto is, if you can't find it at her place, you don't need it."

Ally's smile slowly returned. "And you're going to go inside with me and actually shop?"

"I am. But I should warn you. An hour is just about my limit. I see it as my duty as a guy to grumble and complain after an hour of nonstop shopping."

She laughed aloud. "Reed Malloy, I accept your guy challenge. Let's do this."

CHAPTER SIXTEEN

Pretty, dark-haired Trudy Evans, owner of Anything Goes, nodded toward a half dozen handled bags resting on the counter. "I think that's everything, Reed. These are Ally's clothes, and these bags are the things she picked out for Kyle."

"Thanks." He handed her a credit card and signed the receipt before tucking away his wallet.

Ally stepped out of the back room that served as a dressing room wearing a simple white gauzy shirt with the sleeves rolled to her elbows and new denims tucked into a pair of brown Western boots.

Reed's smile grew. "Now you look like a permanent resident of Montana."

"Thanks." Ally shared a smile with Trudy. "Actually, these were Trudy's idea. I was going to go for sandals, but she said boots would be more practical."

"Not to mention more expensive," Trudy said with a laugh. "Sorry. That's the business side of me."

"Don't apologize. You did good work, Trudy." Reed collected the bags and started toward the door.

"Wait," Ally called to his back. "I have to pay for this."

"It's all taken care of." Trudy nodded toward Reed.

"No." Ally stopped in her tracks. "That wasn't part of the deal. These are my responsibility."

"We'll settle up later. Right now, I'm about to get cranky if we don't stash these things in the truck and head on over to Clay's Pig Sty for a beer and a sandwich."

When Ally seemed about to argue, Trudy winked at her. "It's a pattern with guys. After an hour or so, they get really antsy if we don't treat them to some kind of manly reward for being good sports about shopping. In this town, nothing beats a longneck and a pulled-pork sandwich at Clay's Pig Sty."

Ally gave a toss of her head before giving out a throaty laugh. "Why not? I've been dying to see what the inside of the Pig Sty looks like."

Trudy called, "Have fun. And prepare to be surprised." She came around the counter and gave Ally a hug. "And again, I'm really sorry about the damage that fire did to your place. The whole town is hoping your business is up and running again soon. We all love having a new place to shop."

"Thanks, Trudy." Ally floated away, wondering at the lightness around her heart.

Reed caught her hand and gave her a long, measured look. "What's with that glow?"

"In all my years living in the city, I never felt the sort of easy acceptance I've been experiencing since coming to Glacier Ridge. The people here are just so warm and loving."

"You want loving?" He stowed the bags and turned, catching her hand as they began walking along the sidewalk.

"Baby, just say the word, and we can ditch the town and people, find a secluded spot, and I'd be more than happy to show you just how warm and loving a guy from this small town can be."

"Why am I not surprised by your offer?" She punched his shoulder. "You're such a guy."

Ally and Reed stepped inside the door of Clay's Pig Sty to the smell of onions on the grill and the wailing of Willie warning mamas about the perils of cowboys.

"Hey, Reed," came a voice from behind the grill. "It's been a while. You been up in the hills with that pricey herd of yours?"

"Yeah." Reed had to shout to be heard above the din. "Hi, Clay. Say hello to Ally Shaw."

"Hey, Ally. You the owner of that new business in town?"

"Yes, I am." She nodded vigorously, knowing he couldn't hear her.

"Heard you had a fire. Shame there was so much damage. You going to give the town another chance?"

Another nod of her head.

The man, with sweat rolling down his face in little rivers, shouted, "Good for you, little lady. The special today is—"

Every voice at the bar joined in to shout, "—pulled-pork sandwiches and spicy sweet potato fries."

That was followed by a roar of laughter.

"But that's just the special," Clay added. "For our newcomer, I should say we're also serving stuffed pork chops, grilled pork loin strips over rice, and pork wedges with tomato and vinaigrette salad."

"I'll have the pulled-pork sandwich," Ally shouted.

"Make that two. And two longnecks." Reed caught her arm and steered her through the maze of tables filled with rowdy wranglers and ranchers until they reached a quiet booth in the corner.

As they sat, Ally looked around. "It's so clean."

"That's every visitor's first impression."

"And why not? You have to admit, the name Pig Sty brings a certain image to mind."

He grinned. "Yeah. Poor Clay's been living with that for all his years in business."

Clay himself walked to their booth to set down two long-necks. The smiling owner was wearing a plaid shirt and suspenders holding up his faded jeans.

"Nice to finally meet you, Ally. My wife was at your grand opening, but I had to work that day. Thanks to you, I had one of my best days ever. You brought a lot of hungry and thirsty folks to town."

"I'm glad I was able to help. Did your wife find anything she liked at my shop?"

His smile widened. "Your question ought to be, what didn't she like? I figure, from her level of enthusiasm, I'll be wading through a whole lot of stuff in the next couple of months while she spends our money."

"Good for me."

He nodded. "Yep. And good for our town. Your sandwiches are coming right up."

Minutes later he returned with fork-tender pulled-pork sandwiches on home-baked sourdough bread, along with bowls of coleslaw and a big plate of fries for sharing.

After one bite, Ally closed her eyes and gave a hum of appreciation. "Oh, this is heavenly."

Reed had to laugh. "Admit it. You're surprised."

She joined in the laughter. "I am. This isn't at all what I expected from a place called the Pig Sty."

"It happens every time Clay has a visitor new to town."

Ally eyed Reed over the rim of her longneck. "Why did those guys refer to your herd as pricey?"

"I'm raising an experimental herd of sorts." He sipped his beer. "Matt was able to persuade an Italian firm to take a chance on Malloy Angus cattle that are free of any hint of antibiotics or hormones. If they meet all the test requirements, they can be labeled as such and sold for much more than ordinary beef in the finest restaurants around the world."

"That sounds simple enough." She studied him. "But I doubt it's that easy to do, or everyone would be doing it."

"True enough. I've been experimenting with this type of herd since I was a teen. Along the way I learned some powerful lessons."

"Like what?"

He grew thoughtful. "The first couple of years, I didn't realize that my herd would have to be segregated from the rest, and without the benefit of antibiotics they ended up getting diseases they had no defense against." He smiled, remembering. "Then I learned something else. A segregated herd can be a defenseless herd, unless I want to pay more wranglers just to patrol the area. One year, I lost nearly three times more calves than the normal number we lose in spring, due to predators that figured out they could slip in and out of the herd after dark without getting caught."

"Ouch."

"Yeah. I'll say." He nodded. "I lost more money than I could ever have earned in those early years. An expensive lesson, and one I could afford only because my family absorbed the cost. The average rancher can't afford to do what I'm doing. I'm just grateful my family has been patient and willing to keep paying out without ever seeing a cent of profit, while I worked it all out."

"So, are you seeing a profit now?"

He gave a snort of derisive laughter. "I'll tell you after roundup."

She leaned forward, eyes wide. "Is there a real roundup like the kind I see in old Westerns?"

"Why, yes, ma'am," he drawled. "Along about this time every year. You can feel free to join us if you've a mind to. We need all the hands we can get."

Chuckling, she reached for a sweet potato fry. "I know you're teasing me, but I'd really love to see it."

"I'd like that, too. In fact, if you'd like, you can be a part of it." He closed his hand on hers. "I've got a lot riding on this season. I want to prove to myself, and more important, my family, that this isn't some silly pie-in-the-sky idea. I need this herd to pay off big-time."

She nodded toward all the men at the bar. "How do they know about this?"

He grinned. "Half the town knows, since most of them moonlight as wranglers at our spread when they aren't needed at their own. Ranching is a tough way to make a living."

"Then why do so many keep on ranching?"

He shrugged. "Most of us grew up on ranches. It's what our fathers and grandfathers did. It's what we love."

"And yet, so many ranches are failing."

"Yeah. Ranchers have to live with crazy weather, disease of their cattle, predators, many of which are protected species, and enormous debt. But ranching's in our blood, and we can't seem to leave for another way of life. Maybe we like knowing we have at least a little control over our own destiny. When things work out, it can be really soul-satisfying."

"In charge of our own destiny." Ally looked suitably impressed. "I like that."

"Yeah." He shot her a look of admiration. "I figured that would appeal to an independent soul like you."

"It's what I'm striving for." She flushed. "Not quite succeeding yet, but I just can't seem to give up on the dream."

He squeezed her hand. "Good. Keep that finish line in sight. It's worth the race."

Ally and Reed stepped out of Clay's and headed along the sidewalk of Main Street. The town was alive with ranchers shopping for supplies and equipment and workers on their lunch hour, out for a stroll.

With every few steps they paused to call a greeting or to exchange small talk. Most of the folks in town wanted to talk about the fire and, hopefully, to glean a bit of gossip from their newest business owner.

Ally's standard response quickly became, "The sheriff is still investigating the source of the fire."

As they walked away from yet another round of conversation, Reed took her hand. "You're getting real good at this."

"At what?" She slanted him a look.

"Don't play cute, Red. You've figured out how to evade like a regular detective."

"Why, thank you." She managed a smile. "I think I'm handling this rather well."

"Yes, you are." He brushed a kiss over her cheek and she looked startled.

"Reed, people can see us."

"Really?" He looked around, then caught her by the shoulders and leaned in to kiss her soundly.

When he lifted his head, he wore a very satisfied smile as he muttered, "There now. That will give them something to talk about."

He took her hand. "That kiss reminded me how much I enjoy dessert. Time for a stop at D and B's Diner."

Inside, Reed kept Ally's hand in his as he led the way between the tables to the little old-fashioned counter.

Dot Parker, a pencil tucked behind her ear, wearing her favorite polka-dot dress and a crisp white apron, hurried over. "Reed Malloy, it's about time you brought our Ally to town." She turned to Ally. "We heard all about the fire, and the fact that you and Kyle went with Reed to his place. The sheriff tells us he's investigating. Now that you're here, you can tell us the rest."

Dot's sister, Barb, looked up from behind the pass-through, where she was working the grill. "Word around town is the fire started with a torch through your window. I can't think of anybody in this town nasty enough to do such a thing. So, honey, who's got it in for you?"

Ally shook her head. "The sheriff suspects a coworker of mine from Virginia."

"I hope I get my hands on him before Eugene does." Dot placed two glasses of water in front of them.

At Ally's questioning look, she frowned. "The sheriff might have to play by the rules, but not me. I'd like to take a torch to this fellow's backside."

Reed was grinning. "I'd really like to see that, Dot."

She glowered at him. "You think I'm kidding. If I get my hands on that guy..."

"Take their order," her sister bellowed.

"I know what Reed's in here for. A chocolate shake, right, Reed?"

He nodded.

She turned to Ally. "Hot tea and fresh apple pie?"

"That sounds heavenly."

Dot took a moment to shoot her sister a smug look before starting on their order.

Minutes later, as they enjoyed their desserts, Dot stood

in front of them, eager for any hint of gossip. "So, this coworker of yours, Ally. Is he good-looking?"

She turned to Reed. "You met him. What do you think?"

Reed shrugged. "Not my type."

Dot poked a finger in his chest. "Just stick to the question."

"Pretty average looking. The sheriff is preparing some flyers to pass around town. Eugene thinks he's hiding in plain sight, maybe using some sort of disguise."

Intrigued, Barb came out of the kitchen to stand beside her sister. "You mean we've got a real detective case going on in our town?"

Reed nodded. "And the sheriff intends to enlist everybody's help in solving it."

The twin sisters exchanged excited looks.

"Thanks for the dessert. I really needed my chocolate shake fix." Reed placed his money on the counter and caught Ally's hand before heading toward the door.

Once outside he said, "Okay. We've put an ad in the newspaper." At her blank look he explained, "Telling Dot and Barb is like telling the entire town. They couldn't wait for us to leave so they can start spreading the word. By this time tomorrow, every person in this town, and every rancher for a hundred miles around, will be on the lookout for any stranger who could be your firebomber."

He adjusted his Stetson and shot her a satisfied grin. "Time to head on home, little missy. Our work here is done."

Ally stepped into the kitchen to find Yancy lifting something from the oven.

"Good morning, Yancy."

He looked over. "Morning, Ally. You feel as rested as you look?"

She nodded. "Five nights here and the minute I climb into bed, I'm asleep. It must be something in the air."

"It could have to do with the chores you've been doing since you got here."

She grinned. "Speaking of which..." She looked toward the back door. "Is everybody in the barn?"

"If you mean Reed, yeah."

She flushed before heading toward the mudroom. "I'll just give him a hand with the mucking." She slipped her feet into tall rubber boots and picked up a pair of worn leather work gloves before striding purposefully toward the barn.

Inside she could hear the teasing, laughing voices of Matt, Luke, and Reed as they forked wet hay and dung into a wagon.

"Hey." Reed's head came up the minute he caught sight of Ally in the doorway. "You here to work?"

"Absolutely." She helped herself to a pitchfork from a hook along the wall.

When she stepped into the stall beside him, he drew her close for a quick kiss. Against her mouth he said, "You don't belong out here, lady. Why don't you help Yancy in the kitchen instead?"

"I'd rather be here. He's not as pretty as you are." With a laugh she lifted a forkful of hay, tossing it into the wagon.

Reed stood back to watch. "For a city girl, you learn real fast."

"It's the least I can do to thank you for our room and board."

He leaned close, aware that his brothers were listening. "I can think of a much nicer way to thank me."

"I just bet you can." She tossed her head and bent to her work.

* * *

"And after me and Lily"—Kyle saw his mother open her mouth to correct him and quickly said, "Lily and I helped pick all those vegebles from Yancy's garden, we came in here and he let us help cook them. Yancy says I'm a really good cook. Oh, and me and Lily...Lily and I were allowed to go to the barn after our cooking lesson so we could see the puppies." Out of breath after eagerly reciting his entire afternoon's activities, Kyle turned big eyes on his mother while the rest of the family unwound before supper with drinks and appetizers.

Great One sipped his martini while Grace and the women enjoyed iced tea. Frank and his grandsons were drinking longnecks and were soon joined by Colin, Burke, and Mick, coming in from a long day in the hills.

"Sounds like you had quite a day." Ally turned to Lily. "Now what's this about puppies?"

"Luke's dog, Molly, had six." Lily piled a wedge of cheese atop a cracker and handed it to Kyle, who was staring at her with a look of pure adoration. "Want to go see them?"

"Maybe after supper would be better," Grace suggested. "I don't think Yancy would be too happy to have us trooping out to the barn when his meal is almost ready to be served."

Lily started across the room. "Can we help serve tonight, Yancy?"

Kyle stuffed the entire cracker into his mouth before rushing after Lily.

Reed leaned close to Ally to whisper, "Looks like someone has a crush."

Ally smiled. "I was just thinking the same thing. But it's really sweet. Kyle has never had a sister, or a best friend."

"Dinner's ready."

All through the meal Ally watched and listened as Kyle and Lily recited the latest activities. She couldn't recall ever seeing her son so happy. In truth, she couldn't recall ever feeling this relaxed and happy either.

Nessa and Ingrid seemed eager to share not only their clothes and any accessories she needed but their stories of how they'd come to meet and fall in love with Matt and Luke, as well. It helped to know that both women had faced their own dangers and had formed a special bond with this warm and loving family.

Family. These good people were so much more than she'd ever imagined a family could be.

"Kyle and I baked these," Lily declared as she handed Great One a basket of steaming biscuits.

He dutifully took a bite and gave the two children the benefit of his warm smile. "You'd better watch your back, Yancy. These two will soon want your job."

As they finished their meal, Kyle and Lily bent close to whisper before Lily asked aloud, "Can we show you the puppies now?"

"I love surprises." Grace stood and took Frank's arm, leading the rest of the family from the table and out the back door to the barn.

Luke had built a small enclosure for the big dog and her puppies, so they couldn't wander.

The brown lab's tail began wagging the minute the family surrounded her and her pups. And when Lily and Kyle knelt and began picking up the wriggling puppies, Molly licked each one as if giving her blessing.

"This one's my favorite," Kyle declared, holding up a tiny ball of fluff.

"Why? He's the runt of the litter," Luke said with a laugh.

"What does runt mean?" Kyle snuggled the pup to his chest.

"He's the smallest. The others will soon walk all over him."

"Not Toughie," the little boy declared.

"Toughie?" Luke bit back the laughter. "How'd you come up with that name?"

"'Cause he doesn't stop until he gets to his mama." Kyle walked over to his mother. "Want to hold Toughie?"

Ally couldn't resist cooing at the sweet little bundle of fur. "Oh, aren't you just the cutest thing." She pressed her face into the softness and was rewarded with wet doggie kisses.

"Careful." Reed leaned close to whisper, "Just remember that cuddly little pup will soon be bigger than its mama. And right now you'd need a bed three times bigger than the one Kyle uses if you were to take Toughie home with you."

She gave him an indignant look. "I have no intention of taking him home with me. But that doesn't mean I can't enjoy holding a puppy."

"That's what they all say. But those cute and cuddly puppies have a way of sucking you in."

Around the pen, the others joined in the laughter.

Ally studied Molly and her pups. "I swear that dog is smiling."

Reed crossed to the dog and knelt to scratch behind her ears. "She's happy for the company. And probably glad to have some relief from those hungry babies."

"I don't know. She's keeping a very careful watch over every one of them."

"That's what mamas do." Grace handed a pup over to Lily, who placed it beside its mother.

The older woman caught her husband's arm. "It's time we got back. I know you men want to discuss this year's roundup."

By the time the family entered the great room, a cozy fire burned on the hearth.

While Yancy pushed a cart laden with coffee and mugs and a crystal decanter of Great One's favorite liquor, the children could be heard talking in hushed tones in the other room.

Minutes later they passed around bowls of strawberry shortcake, mounded with fresh berries and whipped cream, amid a chorus of approving voices.

"We picked the berries," Kyle said proudly.

"And Yancy showed us how to bake shortcake. It's like a biscuit, but sweeter." Lily turned to the cook. "Isn't that right, Yancy?"

"Indeed it is. And the two of you are excellent students." After passing around coffee, he helped himself to a dessert and settled into his favorite chair by the fire, where Great One was enjoying an after-dinner brandy.

"I've been thinking..." Nessa looked around the room.

"Uh-oh." Matt chuckled. "Whenever my beautiful wife says those three words, I know it will cost me money."

She gave him a playful punch on the arm. "While the men are planning their roundup, why don't we girls plan a day in town?"

Ingrid looked over with interest. "What would we do?"

Nessa arched a brow. "I was thinking of a visit to Gert and Teddy Gleason's spa."

Grace was already shaking her head. "I'm planning on leaving on a camera safari soon. It would be a waste for me to visit a spa and then traipse up to the wilderness."

"But that's the perfect time to visit the spa." Nessa's eyes widened. "Don't you see? Before you begin your Spartan existence, you should fortify yourself with as much pampering as you can get. And then when you come back from that safari, you'll want additional pampering."

Reed glanced beyond his sister-in-law to his brother, Matt. "So this is the sort of thinking you have to deal with, bro?"

Matt spread his hands. "What can I say? I'm so blinded by love, I'm beginning to see the logic in the craziest things, and even agree with Nessa's version of truth."

Reed looked around at the others in the room and gave a shake of his head. "Poor Matt. Looks like he joined the cult and drank the Kool-Aid."

While the others roared with laughter, Matt leaned close to his wife and kissed her cheek. "Let my little brother make his lame jokes, sweetheart. Once upon a time, I was just like him. Ignorant and unaware of just how much of life I was missing."

"You got that right, bro." Luke took Ingrid's hand in his and lifted it to his mouth. "One of these days it'll be our little brother's turn to get shot by Cupid's arrow."

While Reed merely grinned, Ally looked around. Watching Reed's brothers and their wives interact, her heart did a funny little dip.

Love, it would seem, was alive and well in the Malloy household. It was almost enough to make her a believer.

Almost.

Frank drained his coffee before standing and helping Grace to her feet. Hand in hand, they called out their good night before climbing the stairs.

Nessa blew them a kiss. "If you'd like to stay home, you could spend an entire day surrounded by beautiful ladies."

"One beautiful lady is all I need." Frank put an arm around his wife's waist.

As the others began drifting off to their rooms, Ally looked to where Lily and Kyle were lying in front of the fireplace. Minutes ago they'd been whispering. Now, both children were sound asleep.

She turned to Ingrid. "I guess there won't be any bedtime stories tonight."

Ingrid smiled and motioned to Luke, who crossed the room and lifted the little girl in his arms. Ingrid waved to the others as she trailed Luke up the stairs.

Reed walked over and picked up Kyle. The little boy barely stirred as he twined his chubby arms around Reed's neck. For a moment Ally stood perfectly still, feeling a jolt at the sight of her little boy in the arms of this big, strong cowboy. They looked so right together, so comfortable, she was forced to blink back tears.

With Ally leading the way, Reed carried the sleeping boy up the stairs and into his room. He stood back while Ally removed Kyle's clothes, which bore the stains of her son's earlier garden chores and kitchen adventures: grass stains, flour smudges, gravy spills. Tossing them in a hamper, she put on the new pajamas she'd purchased at Anything Goes. Then she pulled up the bedcovers and bent to brush kisses over his forehead and cheek.

When she stepped out of the room and walked to her own door, Reed followed.

At the doorway she turned to say good night.

Before she could say a word, he gathered her close and, without a word, kissed her with a hunger that caught her by surprise.

"Reed…"

"Shh." He moved his mouth over hers, tasting, feasting. Inside her mouth he whispered, "I've been thinking about this for hours."

"And here I thought you were lost in Yancy's heavenly dinner."

"It didn't even come close to this." He gathered her against him and ran hot, wet kisses across her forehead, down her temple, across her cheek. "Now this is heaven." He took the kiss deeper. "I wish you and I could ride up into the hills alone tonight."

She lifted her head. "The hills where wild animals lurk?"

He chuckled against her throat, sending heat spiraling along her spine. "I'd keep you safe, even if it meant throwing myself in their path."

She sighed and wrapped her arms around his neck. "I believe you would."

"Know it. I'd never let anything hurt you." His mouth returned to hers and he took her on a long, slow ride of pleasure.

Know it.

The words played through her mind as she gave herself up to his kisses.

He backed her up until they bumped into the wall of her room. And still he continued raining kisses over her upturned face.

He framed her face with his big hands and stared down into her eyes. "Listen."

She gave a puzzled look. "I don't hear anything."

"Exactly." His smile was quick and dangerous. "The household's asleep. There's just us, here in your room, with that big, empty bed."

"I can't..."

He cut off her words with a passionate kiss that had her head spinning. "Never say never, Red."

"But I..."

He wrapped her in his arms and kissed her until heat rose up, threatening to choke them. And still he continued kissing her, while his big, work-worn hands moved over her, touching her at will. Her body responded, her breasts tingling from his touch, while a feeling like a fist tightened deep inside. She was stunned by a raging hunger that ached to be fed. Taking her silence for acceptance, he reached for the buttons of her shirt, all the while keeping his eyes firmly fixed on hers. As he slid the fabric from her shoulders, he dipped his head to trail kisses down her throat, and lower, to the soft swell of her breast. As his mouth closed around one erect nipple, she suddenly gasped and pushed free of his arms.

He lifted a tangle of hair from her cheek, then kept his hand there, stroking gently. "I know you have issues. I know you've been hurt. But you have to know I'm not him. I'd never hurt you, Ally."

She took in a long, slow breath. "I believe you, Reed. I do trust you. But what about me? How can I trust myself, when I've made so many mistakes in the past?"

His hand stopped its movement. "You're not talking about your stalker now, are you?"

When she didn't speak, he kept his eyes on hers. "This is about Kyle's father."

She looked away, avoiding his eyes.

He gathered her close and pressed his mouth to a tangle of hair at her temple. "If you can't share it with me, I don't know how to help you. But know this. We've all made mistakes in our past. And we grow, and learn, and make better decisions as we move on."

"I hope that's so. But until I can trust myself..." She gently pushed him away.

He moaned. "Do you have any idea what you're doing to me, Red?"

"I'm sorry. I don't mean to."

"I know." He gave her one of his heart-melting smiles.

"We've still got all night." He nodded toward the bed. "We could just lie down over there and talk things out."

Despite the turmoil inside her mind, she burst into laughter. "Nice try." She stood on tiptoe and brushed a quick kiss over his mouth. "Now go."

"Can't blame a guy for trying." He started toward the door, then stopped, dragged her close, and kissed her until they were both breathless. "Just remember. If you change your mind, if you'd like to unburden yourself, or if you need someone to rub your back in the night, I'm right next door." He turned away. "Night, Red. Sleep tight."

He strode resolutely out the door without a backward glance.

CHAPTER SEVENTEEN

Ally awoke to the sound of men's voices below. It took a moment to remember that she was safe at the Malloy ranch. Safe. Such a lovely, reassuring word. With each day here the feeling of safety grew.

She showered and dressed in her new denims and a pretty mint green tee. When she checked Kyle's room, it was empty, the bed rumpled from his attempt to straighten the covers. She smiled, thinking how sweet it was that he'd made the effort. He was such a good boy. And he filled her life with quiet joy.

Downstairs, the family had gathered around the conversation area of the kitchen, discussing plans for the day.

When Ally stepped into the big room, they looked up and called out greetings.

"Morning, Ally." Matt and Nessa were standing off to one side, talking in low tones.

"Good morning."

"Hey, Ally." Ingrid turned from Luke to point to the back door. "Don't worry about Kyle. He just ran off to the barn with Lily. They wanted to check on Molly and her puppies. They'll be back in time for breakfast."

"Thanks."

She turned to find Reed beside her, holding out a glass of freshly squeezed orange juice. "Thank you."

"You're welcome." He gave her a probing look. "I hope your night was better than mine."

"You had a rough night?"

He touched his palm to her cheek. "Couldn't sleep."

She experienced the warmth that always accompanied his touch. "Sorry."

"You should be, since you're the reason for my lack of sleep." He gave her a smoldering look. "I wish we could spend the day together."

"At the spa?"

"We could leave that to the others, and I'd find us a private spot to talk ... and stuff."

"It's the 'and stuff' that could be a problem."

"Think of it as a pleasurable challenge." He leaned close to murmur in her ear, "Of course, that could be said of you. I'm finding you a pleasurable challenge. And a daunting one."

"Same goes, cowboy." She stepped away from him when Kyle and Lily charged into the kitchen to report on the puppies.

While the children breathlessly described the silly antics of the dogs, Ally could feel Reed's steady gaze on her. When she looked over, he winked, and she felt the quick sexual tug.

What was she going to do about him? Reed Malloy was too sexy for his own good. And if she didn't guard her heart, she could find herself in over her head.

Too late. She already was.

* * *

Within the hour the family had enjoyed a raucous meal, and the men were now getting ready to tackle dozens of ranch chores while the women prepared for a trek to town for a day at the spa.

Frank and his Gracie were standing quietly, arms about each other, faces close.

Matt and Nessa were embracing.

Luke and Ingrid were locked in a passionate kiss.

Reed turned to where Ally stood, flanked by Kyle and Lily.

He crossed the space that separated them and tousled Lily's hair before kneeling to hug Kyle. "Looks like you and Yancy and Great One will be in charge of all the manly chores around here for a few hours."

"We will?" Kyle brightened. "Like what?"

Standing, he picked up the boy and held him in his arms before turning to Ally. "For one thing, I'll expect you two to watch out for each other while your moms are gone to town."

"Okay."

"And you and Lily will have to look out for Molly and the puppies."

"We will."

Reed reached out his other arm and drew Ally close. "Your only job is to enjoy your girly day. You've earned it."

She lifted her head. "Thanks."

Before she realized what he intended, he lowered his face and kissed her.

Kyle giggled. "Reed. You're kissing my mama."

"Yeah." Reed set him on his feet. "I hope you don't mind, little buddy."

"Uh-uh." The boy looked from Reed to his mother.

"Well, then. In that case..." He straightened and gathered her close, kissing her again. A hard, lingering kiss that left her head spinning. "Just so you don't forget about me the minute I'm out of sight."

When he released her and took a step back, she brought her hand to her throat in a gesture of surprise. "As if I could. Especially after that."

"Good. That's what I intended. And when you get back, we're going to talk...and things." He winked before sauntering toward the idling truck where Burke sat waiting.

Kyle caught his mother's hand. "Reed hugged me."

"That's wonderful." She watched the truck start up a dirt trail that circled the barns, sending up a cloud of dust.

"That's 'cause he likes me."

When she knelt to gather him close, he touched a hand to his mother's cheek. "He likes you, too."

"It was just a little kiss good-bye."

"Uh-huh. 'Cause he likes you." He pushed free of her arms. "Me and Lily are going back to the barn to see the puppies."

She didn't even bother to correct his grammar. She was too busy dealing with her heart. A racing heart that was doing the strangest dance inside her chest.

"All right, girls." Nessa had appointed herself leader of their day's activities. "Yancy graciously invited Lily and Kyle to have a cookie-baking lesson while we head to town."

"We may have to nominate that man for sainthood," Ingrid muttered in an aside.

"Oh, I don't know." Grace looked out the window where the two children and Yancy were kneeling in the grass, surrounded by frolicking puppies. "It's hard to tell who's having more fun."

The women gathered around her and watched the scene with murmured words of approval.

Grace's eyes were crinkled with pleasure. "It's such a joy to watch children and puppies. I'm sure Yancy is enjoying them as much as Frankie and I are. I've so missed having little ones around."

Her father looked up from his favorite chair.

"Have fun with your girls, Grace Anne."

"You know I will."

Once in the truck, Nessa drove while the others relaxed and settled in for the long drive to Glacier Ridge.

After Nessa parked the truck along Main Street, she turned to the others. "We have some free time before we hit the spa. I called ahead and reserved chairs for pedicures at one o'clock."

"That gives us enough time to shop at Anything Goes." Grace led the way toward the pretty little shop with its red-and-white-striped awning.

Inside, owner Trudy Evans looked delighted to see them. "Ladies. What a lovely surprise."

Grace hugged her. "We're having ourselves a girly day. Shopping. A visit to Gert and Teddy's spa. And probably tea and pie at D and B's before we head home."

"Oh, what fun, Miss Grace." Trudy looked around at the lovely young women rummaging through the merchandise. She sighed. "You're so lucky to have girls in your life. There's nothing like it."

"Don't I know it?" Grace laughed. "For years I was surrounded by all that testosterone. And now I feel so blessed to have these wonderful young ladies around me." She lowered her voice. "They keep me young."

Trudy put a hand on the older woman's shoulder. "Miss

Grace, you don't need anybody else for that. You and your Frank are the youngest old-timers in this town."

"Why thank you, dear." Grace's eyes danced with laughter. "Help them find some fabulous things."

"I'm happy to." Trudy walked away, and the three young women were soon off to the back room to try on their choices.

More than an hour later the countertop was littered with piles of clothing. T-shirts. Shorts. Pretty sandals. Assorted lacy undergarments.

As Trudy began placing their choices in handled bags, the young women held out their credit cards.

Trudy shook her head. "Sorry. I'm told your money's no good here."

They looked at one another with matching frowns as she explained, "I had a call early this morning from Frank Malloy. He said he'd have my hide if I allowed anyone except him to pay for whatever you chose. So put away your cards, ladies. When Frank Malloy uses that tone with me, I know he means business."

Grace burst into laughter. "That old softie. And all the while he was teasing me about wasting an entire day on girly things."

They called out their good-byes to Trudy as they carried their purchases to the truck.

Nessa checked her watch. "Time to head over to the spa." As they crossed the street, they caught sight of Dr. Anita Cross heading straight toward them.

"Right on time," Nessa called.

When the others turned to her with looks of surprise, she explained, "I called Anita to see if she had time to join us for a pedicure."

"And I told Nessa I'd make time," Anita added with a laugh.

She hugged Grace and then each of the young women. When she hugged Ally, she said, "I'm still waiting for that well visit with Kyle."

"I know. Soon, I hope. But things—"

Anita silenced her with a finger to her lips. "I know. You've been a little busy since the fire. It's all anybody talks about here in town. I'm so relieved that you and Kyle escaped without a scratch. But what makes it all so awful is the fact that it was a personal attack. Not to mention the damage to your business."

"Sheriff Graystoke believes he'll have the person in custody soon. As for my business, Thorny assures me he'll have things up and running as soon as he can make all the repairs."

"I'm so glad." Anita drew an arm around Ally's waist as their party stepped inside the spa.

Gert and Teddy Gleason were both standing behind the glass-topped desk, eager to greet their little party.

Teddy looked up from his ledgers with a wide smile. He wore a black smock that buttoned across one shoulder. Though he'd begun this business as a barbershop, he'd quickly realized what the town really wanted. Now his simple barbershop had been turned into a lovely spa.

"Miss Grace. Ladies." His wife, Gert, tall, model-thin, her hair tied back in a bun, was wearing a pink smock over yoga pants. "We have all our chairs ready so that you can have a lovely visit while you get your pedicures."

Grace stared around admiringly. "The chairs aren't out here?"

"This area is for our stylists." Gert nodded toward three young women, all in pink smocks, busy cutting hair. One other employee was giving a manicure. "We keep our pedicure chairs in here." Gert opened a door to admit them to a charming room with soft music playing, and in one corner, a fountain spilling water. Five chairs were arranged in a circle. Five young women in pink smocks greeted them and led them to their places, before filling the basins with warm water.

As Grace settled herself in the leather recliner, a young woman touched a button and the chair began gently vibrating along her back. A second button activated the recliner's many positions.

"Oh my." Grace laughed like a girl as she slid off her shoes and placed her feet in the warm, scented water before settling in to relax.

A man in a black smock stepped in from a back room and moved among them holding out a tray on which rested chilled bottles of fizzy water.

"All the comforts of Chicago," Nessa called as she plucked a bottle, and the others laughed at her remark.

"I was just thinking this is one of the few things I miss about Boston," Anita chimed in as she helped herself to water. "And now I won't ever have to miss it again. Boston has come to Glacier Ridge, Montana."

"And to think I've been missing all this comfort." Grace turned to Ally, who had gone ashen as she accepted a bottle of water from the tray. "You look pale, dear. Is anything wrong?"

Ally shook her head, wishing she could shake off the feeling of dread that unexpectedly gripped her. "I don't know. I just feel..." What did she feel? She couldn't explain. But there was such a feeling of unease holding her in its grip, she was worried she was about to become physically ill.

Anita smiled. "Colin tells me you're from Virginia."

Ally nodded before sinking back against the cushions, fighting a distinctly light-headed feeling.

Around her, the young women were recounting stories of their lives before coming to Montana.

While the others enjoyed sharing fun anecdotes about themselves, Ally, though struggling to smile and nod, fell silent.

While their feet were sanded, scraped, and buffed, Ally saw the door handle of the back room turn. The door was opened slightly, as though someone was peering around while remaining hidden. The door suddenly closed with a resounding click.

Ally felt a momentary chill, despite the warmth of the room, as the thought exploded in her mind.

The employee with the tray. Though she hadn't been paying attention, there had been something about him.

Glen? In disguise?

Ally reached for her cell phone and listened in frustration to the message before saying quickly, "It's Ally Shaw. I just saw Glen. In the spa."

Before anyone could react, she lifted her feet from the water and struggled to slide them into her sandals.

The girl in the pink smock touched a hand to Ally's leg. "I haven't done your polish yet."

"There's no time." Ally turned to the others. "That man. The one with the tray. It's him. The stalker who firebombed my building."

While they watched in stunned silence, she raced out the back door, wearing one sandal and leaving the other behind in her haste.

CHAPTER EIGHTEEN

Ally tore open the back door of the spa and stepped out into a patch of concrete that held trash cans and recycling bins. Fearing that Glen could be hiding behind one of them, she looked around carefully before starting forward. She'd taken no more than a few steps before an arm locked around her neck, halting her in midstride.

Glen's voice, next to her ear, was low with fury. "Looking for me?"

Before she could utter a word, she was yanked off her feet and dragged through another doorway. Once inside a room, she was slammed roughly against a wall. With no way to protect herself, her head hit so hard she saw stars swimming before her eyes. Her knees buckled, and she felt herself sinking to the floor. When she looked over, Glen was watching her through narrowed eyes. Light glinted off the blade of a knife in his hand.

Though she wanted to scream, she struggled to keep her

tone soft, afraid of fueling his already seething anger. "Why are you doing this, Glen?"

"You need to ask why? You two-timing bitch. Did you think I wouldn't see you with that cowboy?"

"I don't know what you—"

He slapped her hard enough to have her head snapping to one side. He slashed out with the knife, catching the sleeve of her T-shirt and slicing the tender flesh of her upper arm.

When he grabbed her by the neck of her shirt to pull her savagely to her feet, she could hear the fabric tearing.

"Just so you know how fine this weapon is, I've worked on the blade until it's razor-sharp. Sharp enough to slit your pretty throat in one clean slice. Are you ready to die?"

"Why, Glen? Why are you—"

"Shut your mouth." He pressed the tip of the blade to her throat, drawing blood. "You and I don't belong here in Hicksville. If we're smart enough to work for a top security firm, we're too good for this backwater town. At least one of us is. But now you've lowered yourself to their level. Just look at the stupid fools who run this so-called spa. All I had to do was tell them I needed a place to stay and they allowed me to sleep in this storage room." He nodded toward the cot on the far side of the room. "What they didn't know was that I'd already broken in here before I asked for a job and knew this window offered a clear view of the front door of your shop. I had the best seat in town." He gave a shrill laugh, so alien with his deep voice. A laugh that reminded Ally of a madman.

His laughter died as abruptly as it started. "After I smashed your front window and ruined that pretty little display, I thought you'd learned your lesson. You sent the cowboy away. And you were reading my emails. Even though you didn't answer me, I could tell you were definitely interested."

Ally thought about the thick file of those emails in the sheriff's office. Emails that declared his love, before becoming more and more demanding. "If what you said in those emails is true, why did you firebomb my apartment, knowing it would hurt me and my little boy?"

"Because you let the cowboy back into your life. And don't you dare try to deny it." He slapped her again, hard enough to have her crying out in pain. "I saw the two of you in the doorway. All wrapped around each other like lovers." His voice lowered with fury. "When Rick died, I made it clear I would take care of you. But you decided I wasn't good enough. You ignored me. And then you left me. Left me without a word." He smiled, and his smile was more frightening than his frown had been. "You thought you were so smart. But I'm smarter. Finding you was easy. I had enough security clearance to go through your files without anyone being the wiser. So now I've found you. And I've come to a decision. That precious brat that you claim to love so much could have had a safe home with me, if you'd gone along with my plans. Now, since you think you're too good for me, the kid will grow up without anyone. I intend to make him an orphan. And it's all your fault. I want you to think about that when you're dying. You chose some Montana cowboy over me, and it cost your kid his only parent."

As he lifted the knife, Ally held out her hands to him. "Please, Glen, think about what you're doing. The sheriff won't stop hunting until he finds you. And if you kill me, you'll spend the rest of your life in prison. But if you walk away, right now, I promise I won't press charges against you."

"Liar! You're doing it again. Lying to me like I'm some kind of brainless idiot." He stepped back as though the touch of her suddenly repelled him. "Your whole life has been one big, stupid lie." He raised the knife until the tip of the blade was aimed straight for her heart. "And now you have to pay."

Reed was leaving Will's Feed Supply when he passed the ranch truck parked outside Anything Goes. When his cell phone rang, he decided to let it go to message. He was feeling too mellow. The sight of all those fancy handled bags tossed on the front seat had him grinning. A day with other females was exactly what Ally needed after all the chaos in her life.

When his cell phone continued to ring, he plucked it out of his shirt pocket and checked the caller. His smile grew and he glanced over at the spa. Leave it to Ally to want to share her good time with him.

"Hey, Red."

The sound of her voice had him hitting the brakes. Without even bothering to park, he was out of the truck and running as fast as he could.

In the spa, in those initial moments after Ally shouted and made a run from the room, there was complete confusion while the others struggled to process what had just happened. It was Grace who pressed the sheriff's number to report what they'd just witnessed.

As the truth dawned, the women rallied, ignoring fresh polish dripping from their toenails, struggling to slide wet feet into shoes that resisted.

By the time Sheriff Eugene Graystoke came rushing into the room, they had already made a mad dash for the back door.

Nessa tore it open, only to see nobody around.

"All right now," Eugene shouted above the voices. "Everybody calm down and tell me what transpired here."

Grace described Ally's ashen features after accepting a bottle of water from a male employee and her frantic race to catch him.

"And none of you thought to stop her?"

Grace was indignant. "There was no time, Eugene. She screamed into her cell phone and shouted to us that the man in the smock was the one who'd firebombed her shop. Then she was just gone." Grace snapped her fingers. "Just like that. Now we have to find her before that awful man has time to hurt her."

"You ladies stay here. I'll get that basta—that stalker," he amended for Grace's sake. "He can't get far." The sheriff dashed around a corner of the building and paused to look both ways.

Seeing neither Ally nor a stranger, he was forced to absorb a sudden prickle of dread. A dangerous stalker had been working under their very noses and now was gone without a trace.

And Ally Shaw with him.

After hearing Grace's call, he'd already alerted his deputy and had put out a call to the authorities in nearby towns. Now he stepped back into the salon and gathered Gert and Teddy and their employees around the cluster of terrified women.

The sheriff held out a flyer. "This look like the guy working for you?"

Teddy shrugged. "Could be. But his hair is blond, and he has a mustache. And he called himself Gerald Lodge."

"But this is the guy?"

Teddy looked at his wife for confirmation. After studying the picture for a few moments, they both gave tentative nods.

"Do you know where he's been staying?"

"Here." Teddy pointed to a small supply room at the far

end of the building. "He said he was homeless, and since we have a cot and washroom in there, we said he could stay until he could save enough to rent a room somewhere."

"You all stay here. And stay together." With a look of steely determination, his gun in hand, Eugene started in the direction they'd indicated.

Ally faced her attacker and swallowed back the knot of fear that threatened to choke her. Her life no longer mattered. All her thoughts were centered on Kyle. He was so young. So innocent. He didn't deserve any of this.

An orphan. The word struck pure terror in her heart. Before his fifth birthday, he was without a father and was now about to lose his mother.

"Don't do this, Glen." Her voice grew strong. "It's evil."

"You're the one who's evil, slut."

As he grabbed a handful of her hair and was about to plunge the knife, the door was kicked open and Reed stormed across the room, grabbing Glen's arm and twisting it behind him.

With his other arm around Glen's neck, Reed looked beyond him to Ally. "You all right?"

She was too overcome to speak. She simply nodded as she began to sink to her knees.

Reed shoved Glen aside to go to her aid.

The door was kicked in again, slamming against the wall with such force the sound reverberated through the entire building, causing it to shudder.

While Reed gathered Ally close, Glen spun around and found himself facing Archer Stone, with fire in his eyes, holding a gun aimed at his head. "Drop the knife, creep."

When Glen hesitated, Archer's voice resonated like thunder. "This badge I'm wearing says I have to give you a chance to surrender before I use deadly force. But I'm going to tell you true, you sick bastard. Once my temper's up, nobody has a chance to cool it. There's nothing I like better than a good knock-down, drag-out fight with somebody who makes me mad. So I hope to hell you resist."

When Glen looked around for a chance to escape, Archer holstered his gun and smiled. "You've just made my day, you scumbag."

With all the force of a vicious animal, Archer charged Glen, twisting his wrist until the bones snapped and the knife fell to the floor with a clatter.

Instead of simply subduing Glen, Archer held him upright with one hand while beating a fist into his face again and again.

"The woman you threatened is my kin. And I want you to stay alive long enough for me to beat you senseless, you miserable coward. That'll teach you to stalk someone in this town. And then I'm hoping you at least raise one of your arms, so I have an excuse to blow your miserable head off."

Seeing the blaze of unleashed fury in the deputy's eyes, Glen struggled to back away. The more he struggled, the more Archer's temper grew, until it was a raging fire sweeping through every fiber of his being, completely taking over his control.

Seeing it, Ally caught Reed's arm. "You have to stop Archer. Please stop him. He's going to kill him."

Hearing her, Archer's eyes narrowed. "It's what scum like this deserves. Or are you forgetting? Minutes ago he was going to kill you."

"But Reed is here now. And you're here. You've both saved me. Please, Archer, don't do this. You're a man of the law."

"Yes, I am. And the law says I can use reasonable force

if a lawbreaker is resisting." He landed a punch in Glen's midsection that sent him bouncing backward against the wall.

As Glen pushed himself forward, Archer hit him again, driving him backward with such force he fell facedown on the floor.

Archer hauled him to his feet, and Glen screamed an obscenity before trying to butt his head into Archer's midsection.

Archer reached for his gun. "That's more like it. Looks like you're resisting arrest, scumbag."

Reed caught Archer's arm, twisting it viciously. "Stop now, Archer. You're out of control."

At that very moment Sheriff Graystoke came running into the room and skidded to a halt.

"All right, you two." For long moments he studied the scene before he strode forward, stepping between his deputy and Reed.

To Reed he ordered, "Back off."

Reed did as he asked. When he turned to Ally, the look of horror on her face had him reaching for her, but she sidestepped away.

Eugene studied the bloodied, battered man in Archer's grasp. "Now, Archer, you back off, too."

"He's resisting arrest." Archer's finger hovered over the trigger.

"I said back off. I want him alive." In the silence that followed, Eugene's voice was firm. "I know your blood's hot and your temper's on a short leash right now, but you need to get control of it or it'll get you into big trouble. You can't afford to lose control, Archer. I'm telling you to holster your weapon and stand down. Now."

Archer was breathing hard, sweat pouring down his face, nearly blinding him. His free hand fisted and unfisted at his side as he fought to control the fury still racing through his system.

When at last he released his hold, Glen wobbled and slid to the floor, where he lay limp and bloody.

After several minutes, Archer holstered his gun before stepping around the sheriff. With a snarl of rage he twisted a fist in the front of Glen's shirt, hauling him to his feet. With as much force as possible he twisted Glen's hands behind his back and cuffed him.

Eugene took in the scene of carnage, noting the blood streaming down Glen's battered face, and then at Ally, whose rigid pose was in sharp contrast to the look of absolute horror on her face.

Despite the sheriff's warning, the women burst into the room and formed a protective circle around Ally, whose ashen features said more than any words.

"Ally...?" Before Grace could ask more, Ally put up a hand to stop her.

Her T-shirt was torn, and blood spilled from the knife wound to her arm. But it was the look in her eyes that had them worried.

Her voice was little more than a whisper. "I'm alive. We're both alive. And that's enough."

The women surged forward and surrounded her in a group hug, while Archer announced, "This sniveling little coward was holding a knife and telling her he was going to make her son an orphan."

Again, Ally flinched at the word.

Seeing it, Dr. Anita Cross stepped forward while Grace gathered her close and held her. "Sheriff, would it be all right if we took Ally to the clinic?"

Eugene nodded. "I'm grateful you're here, Dr. Cross. See to her."

Anita calmly took one of Ally's arms and began steering her toward the door.

Ally pushed free of the helping hand to turn back and say to the sheriff, "I have no doubt Glen intended to kill me. I could see the madness in his eyes and hear it in his voice. If Reed hadn't arrived in time..."

She swallowed and tried again. "And then my uncle. If not for the two of them, I would be dead now."

Archer stood a little taller. Reed watched Ally with a look of grave concern.

"But..." Ally struggled to find the words. The brutality of the encounter between her uncle and Glen had left her shaken to her core. Still, it was Archer's job. She had no doubt that, except for the timely arrival of Reed and Archer, she would have died at Glen's hand.

"But?" Eugene pushed her to continue.

She gave a shake of her head. "It's nothing. I guess I'm too emotional to think clearly." She held out a hand to Reed, and he took it, twining his fingers with hers.

Eugene Graystoke cleared his throat. "Well, now. I guess you're the hero of the hour, Archer. How did you get here so fast?"

The deputy kept a firm grasp on his prisoner. "I got your call about the stalker at the spa. I wasn't sure, but just as I was pulling up I thought I saw someone dash into this room, so I just followed my instincts and, sure enough, there he was, that scumbag."

Eugene gave a nod of approval. "Go ahead and take him over to the jail. I'll be along when I finish here."

Everyone fell silent as the deputy hauled Glen Lloyd from the building. As he and Archer brushed past Ally, she remained as still as a statue, refusing to show any emotion.

Ally felt her limbs go weak and fought to remain

standing. She was feeling suddenly light-headed. "You were right, Sheriff. He was hiding in plain sight. And able to know exactly what I was doing and when. Would you like me to make a statement?"

Eugene shot a knowing look at Reed. "I think for a little while, you need to feel quiet and safe." He glanced at Grace. At her nod of approval, he added, "After you're checked out by Dr. Cross at the clinic, why don't you go home and let the Malloy family feed you and let you rest? Then later this evening, if you're feeling up to it, I'd like to come by and we'll have ourselves a little talk."

Ally nodded, too overwhelmed to do more than allow Reed and the women to lead her out to Reed's truck.

From the windows of the nearby businesses, faces peered out, watching the parade of women with interest.

Once they settled her inside the vehicle, Reed drove to the clinic.

Once there, he and the women waited while Anita disinfected the knife wound and carefully stitched it. After applying a dressing, she handed Ally two pills.

At Ally's questioning look, she said, "Something to quiet your nerves and help you sleep."

Ally set them aside with a shake of her head. "Thank you, Anita. I really appreciate all you've done. But I need to be clear-headed when I see Kyle."

"Then take them later. At bedtime."

"All right." Ally forced a thin smile. "Thank you."

The two women walked together along the spotless hallway of the clinic until they joined the others in the waiting room. There, after bidding good-bye, Ally allowed herself to be led to Reed's truck for the drive home.

Along the way, Ally fell silent.

The silence was broken only by the quiet hum of the

truck's engine, which managed to weave a kind of magic. Or maybe it was the magic of Reed's tender care that brought Ally such a sense of calm.

By the time they arrived at the ranch, Ally felt her fears beginning to evaporate, knowing the man who wanted to bring harm to her and her son was now safely behind bars.

As she stepped from the truck, the women parked behind and gathered around her.

She took in a deep, calming breath. "I didn't realize how tense I've been since all this began. It's only now, feeling this amazing sense of freedom, that I see how deeply all this has affected me. I was in a prison of sorts. Never knowing when my stalker would strike again. But now..." A tentative smile started, then spread. "Thank you all for being here for me."

Reed draped an arm around her shoulders as they moved together toward the porch.

The door opened and Lily and Kyle burst onto the top step, their smiles brighter than the sun, their eyes wide with excitement.

Kyle dashed up to his mother and flung his arms around her waist. "We baked cookies. Wait till you see them. Yancy showed us how to make shapes. Puppies and horses and kittens. And..."

Out of breath, he paused while Lily finished for him. "And we got to make colored frosting, too. Kyle made a brown puppy, and I made a pink kitten."

"Oh, and we made yellow chicks," Kyle added.

Ally knelt down and gathered her son into her arms, pressing her face to his hair, breathing him in. For several minutes she remained that way, fighting the rush of tears that threatened. Finally, after several deep breaths, she stood, her smile firmly in place. "I'm so glad you had such a special day with Yancy."

"Did you have a special day, too, Mama?"

She bent to brush a kiss over her son's upturned face. "A very special day, my sweet boy." She caught his hand. "Let's go inside. I want to hear everything you did."

"We petted the horses. And Yancy allowed me to sit in the saddle. And Reed, he said he'll have me riding like a cowboy in no time. And…"

As the others trailed Ally and Kyle up the steps, they shared knowing glances. Despite the terror of this day, Ally was able to smile and interact with her son. How could they do any less?

CHAPTER NINETEEN

Eugene Graystoke wiped his boots on a mat and hung his hat on a peg by the back door before stepping into the Malloy kitchen.

An inviting carafe of coffee and mugs sat atop the counter, along with cream and sugar and a plate of cookies. All trace of the earlier meal had been removed from the spotless kitchen.

Reed greeted him. "Ally will be down soon. She went upstairs with Kyle. She said she wanted to read to him and just lie with him awhile."

The sheriff nodded. "I expect that will do them both good."

He looked over when Ally stepped through the doorway. She'd showered and changed into clean denims and a yellow cotton shirt.

"Sheriff. I'm sorry you had to make the long drive out here tonight."

"I didn't mind, Ms. Shaw. It's my job."

"Well, I appreciate it. And please. Call me Ally."

He smiled. "You look better than you did this afternoon, Ally."

"I feel much better."

He indicated the kitchen chairs. "Why don't we sit, and you can fill in some of the details I may have missed."

She nodded.

Reed discreetly left the room. From the great room came the hum of quiet conversation. Both Ally and Eugene knew the others had gathered there in order to give them both their privacy.

The sheriff took out his ever-present notebook. "Why don't you begin at the beginning, from the time you first met Glen Lloyd."

She did as he asked, explaining how the office was set up, how each security expert was assigned a partner, and how easily she and Glen had fallen into a rhythm of work.

"It must be easy in such a close environment to get to know each other in a more personal way."

She nodded. "I'm sure for most of the teams, that's so. And they often socialize after work, which only adds to that personal bond. But in my case, because I had a son spending all his waking hours in day care, I never went along on any of the after-hours activities."

"Did Glen mention it?"

"Often. He resented the fact that I was always too busy to socialize."

"He took it personally?"

"He did. But once I explained about my son, and Kyle's father doing another tour in Afghanistan, he seemed to back off. But then, when I received the news that Rick had been killed, he became"—she shrugged—"a little too concerned about me. I found myself becoming abrupt with him in an effort to hold him at arm's length."

"Did he express anger?"

"Some. But it was guarded anger. More like concern that he cloaked in questions about my finances, my family. I considered them too personal to reveal. And then, when I decided to leave and try to reconnect with my mother's family here in Montana, I deliberately kept that news from anyone at work." She gave a deep sigh. "It never occurred to me that Glen would go into my personnel file."

The sheriff paused in his writing to look up. "Did he admit to anything when he confronted you today?"

Ally gave him a tremulous smile. "Glen admitted that he'd carefully planned most of what happened, from breaking into my file, to finding me in Glacier Ridge. Once here, after he realized I still wasn't interested, the stalking became more intense. Before asking Gert and Teddy for a job, he broke into their storage room to assure himself that it offered him a clear view of my shop. That night he broke the display window happened when he flew into a rage after seeing—" She flushed before saying, "After seeing me kiss Reed."

"So you and Reed were romantically involved by then?"

She shrugged. "I didn't know what we were. Maybe I still don't know what we are. Attracted, of course. But we haven't taken it beyond that. And right after that incident with the smashed window, Reed went up in the hills to oversee his herd. Glen thought he'd frightened me enough to send Reed away, and that made him think he could win me over with those emails I showed you."

The sheriff nodded. "Emails that gradually changed from declarations of love, to demanding your submission, to downright fury."

Ally sighed. "Then Reed returned, and Glen saw us…"

Again she paused and swallowed before forcing herself to go on. "Glen saw the two of us in a passionate embrace. That seemed to push him over the edge, and he decided that he had to kill me."

The sheriff took his time topping off his coffee. "Now about the final confrontation with Glen. I'd like to ask you about your uncle."

He saw her flinch and look away.

"Ally, it's no secret that Archer has a vicious temper. It's gotten him in some trouble through the years. Nothing serious, that I know of. But I'd like you to tell me what you witnessed."

"I thought..." She shuddered. "I honestly feared Archer was going to kill Glen."

"Did Glen resist arrest?"

She looked over. "Sheriff, I'm not sure any more just what I saw. At the time, I was so relieved to see both Reed and my uncle come storming into that room, I believe my brain just closed down. I have no doubt I was minutes away from being killed. And I don't want to sound ungrateful, but..."

When she hesitated, he prodded. "Just say what you're thinking, Ally."

She took in a deep breath. "I've never seen that depth of violence before."

"Are you talking about Glen or Archer?"

"Archer. It frightened me as much as Glen's threat to kill me. But worse than that, it left me with a sick feeling."

The sheriff reached a hand across the table and covered hers. Despite the heat of the kitchen, her flesh was cold and clammy.

"You should know that Archer's temper is legendary around these parts."

Ally nodded. "Reed tasted that temper. Archer claimed he

was just trying to protect his niece, but it frightened me then and it frightens me now."

"Archer and I had a long talk back at my office. He admitted that his temper got out of control, but added that it was because he felt so protective of you. And since it's a family matter, I'm willing to overlook it this time. Other than today, I've never seen him cross the line. And if Glen resisted arrest, Archer's actions may have been justified." He cleared his throat. "When I got back to the jail, Archer wanted to interrogate Glen. I thought he was too close to the issues, so I requested a state expert. Glen has admitted stalking you. And his testimony so far corroborates what you've told me. He thought he had a chance of winning your heart, if he could get you alone. Especially after Reed went back to his herd, and Glen thought you'd sent him away. But when Reed showed up on the night of the fire, Glen witnessed the two of you saying good night, and it set off the violent reaction that led to the firebombing." He squeezed her hand. "Glen's computer is being tested by the state police lab. With his confession, and the computer evidence to back up those emails, there's a good chance he'll do a pretty long stretch in prison. Hopefully, long enough to get help for his mental illness."

Ally sighed. "I can't tell you how relieved I feel."

"I understand. I feel the same way. As the long-time lawman of this county, I considered that firebomb, which I believe the court will consider attempted murder, to be a personal smear on our town's good name."

He scraped back his chair. "Knowing the Malloy family as I do, I'm sure they're itching to get in here and talk to you. I hope you don't mind if I poke my head in the other room and let them know we're finished here."

Ally smiled. "I understand."

He pulled open the door, and the family nearly fell into the room, proof that they'd been listening at the door.

Eugene stared at the old man struggling to look dignified. "Nelson, I hope I spoke loud enough for you."

Great One gave him a wicked smile. "Not quite. But I caught enough of the words to know that evil man won't be around to bother Ally anymore."

The sheriff smiled and nodded at the others. "Thanks for the coffee, Yancy. Ms. Grace. Ladies. I'll be on my way now. And, Reed, I'll want to interview you about this later."

He turned and winked at Ally before sauntering out to the mudroom to retrieve his hat.

Minutes later they heard the sound of his engine and watched the headlights flash across the windows as he drove away.

Grace took a seat beside Ally and caught her hand. "Just so you know, we're all here for you."

Ally said softly, "I'm just so grateful to all of you for being here."

Grace got to her feet. "I think it's time we all turned in. It has been a very long day."

"It has." Nessa looked around the circle of family. "And as director of female operations around here, we'll need to plan another girly day, just to finish what we started."

They all managed to smile before bidding good night and starting for the stairway.

Reed kept Ally's hand in his as they climbed the stairs. She walked past her door, choosing instead to pause outside her son's bedroom.

"I need to be with Kyle tonight. I hope you understand."

"I do." He brushed a soft kiss over her lips before watching her step inside and closing the door.

She sank down beside Kyle in bed and gathered him ever

so gently into her arms, breathing in the wonderful little-boy smell of him. She thought about the struggles of the past years and whispered a prayer of thanks for this wonderful gift in her life.

This day, she had almost been taken out of Kyle's life forever. Her beautiful little boy would have grown up without knowing how much she loved him. As she listened to his heartbeat, she fell asleep secure in the knowledge that she'd been given a second chance.

Ally awoke and lay for long, silent moments, before glancing at the clock on the nightstand.

It was barely past midnight, and she was wide awake.

She slipped out of Kyle's bed and made her way out the door and down the stairs, hoping to find her way in the dark to the kitchen.

As she approached, she could see a light under the closed door. Pushing it open, she spotted Great One seated at the table, a glass of whiskey in his hand.

"Can't sleep, either?"

He nodded. "Still thinking about all that's happened today. And you?"

She filled a kettle with water and set it on the stove before turning to him. "I'm in a funny mood. Relieved, but not really ... settled." She managed a shy smile.

"Grace Anne tells me you were positively heroic when you spotted your stalker and ran after him."

She was shaking her head in denial. "That wasn't heroic. It was desperation. I'm the farthest thing from a hero you've ever known."

"What would you call yourself, Ally?"

She looked away, avoiding his eyes. "A liar. A cheat. A coward."

"Now why do you say that, girl?"

When she didn't answer, he put a hand on hers to stop her from turning away.

She looked over and saw the compassion in his eyes. "Why do I feel I can tell you, and you won't judge me?"

"Because I won't. I'm an _old_ man, Ally. There are no surprises left. I've heard and seen everything this life has to offer."

When the kettle whistled, she filled her cup and returned to the table, taking the seat across from him.

Nelson again put a hand over hers. "It has to be difficult to raise a child alone. But lots of women do, and you've proven yourself to be very courageous."

"That's not courage. It's all an act. I go to sleep every night afraid. And every morning I go into my act, pretending that I know what I'm doing and where I'm going."

He gave her a gentle smile. "My dear, you're talking to Nelson LaRou, Hollywood's greatest director. Haven't you heard? I'm the expert on weaving fantasy. I also happen to have an excellent eye for actors. I can spot the real ones and the phonies in a single glance. You're not very good at playacting. What you feel for your son is no act."

"I didn't say—"

He shook his head. "What you did today was real. You faced a man determined to kill you, and your only thought was your little boy. Your love for him is real." He gave her a gentle smile. "And though you may not know it yet, what you're feeling for my grandson, Reed, and he for you, is real. That's no act."

"I don't deserve a man like Reed."

"Why would you say such a thing?"

"Reed is the most decent, honest man I've ever met.

There's a natural goodness in him that just shines." She took a sip of tea to soothe the ache in her throat. "He doesn't need to be saddled with a single mother who's made every mistake in the book."

"Isn't that for him to say?"

She sat back with a stunned look. "Why are you so quick to defend me? Are you saying you wouldn't care if your grandson loved a woman like me?"

"A woman like you?" He paused, gathering his thoughts. "Let me tell you a little story. There was this loudmouthed, flamboyant young dandy who had the world's biggest ego. And he met the most stunning, elegant, refined woman, a product of Eastern finishing schools, her parents so wealthy they could have bought her a king or a prince for a husband. But once she met the egotistical show-off, she set her sights on him. And he was so smitten, he'd have gladly given up his dreams of fame and fortune in Hollywood if she would but say the word."

"You?"

He laughed, a deep, rich rumble that began in his throat and bubbled up and out of his mouth. "Madeline Sawyer Lawton, the most sought-after debutante in Connecticut, defied her family and gave me her heart. Not to mention our beloved daughter, Grace Anne."

Before Ally could say a word, he held up a hand. "And there's more. Our daughter, Grace Anne, the delight of both our lives, was also the product of Eastern boarding schools, and not only old money but piles of new Hollywood money. When she came west for a photographic assignment in her senior year at university, she fell madly in love with a handsome rancher. The loudmouth director forbid her to marry a lowly, backwoods cowboy, which only made her more determined than ever to have him. And Madeline knew at once that her daughter, so like her mother, had found the great love of her life."

Ally's eyes were wide. "Ms. Grace and her Frankie."

"So now you've heard two love stories in a single night. Neither man deserved the fabulous woman who put love above everything. I'm betting my grandson doesn't deserve a special woman like you, either. But if the two of you are meant to be, love will triumph. That's just the way of it, my girl."

"And you would give your blessing to such a thing?"

"Who am I to even consider giving a blessing? I'm just an over-the-hill Hollywood director who knows something about acting and real life. Believe me, real life is a lot tougher than playing let's-pretend. But infinitely more rewarding." He pushed himself to his feet and turned away. Over his shoulder he called, "Ally, girl, don't put labels on yourself. Just follow your heart."

"But how can I trust my heart when my heart was wrong before?"

"Wrong?" He put his hand on the doorknob and paused, turning to fix her with a look. "The choices you made gave you that little boy. How could you possibly find anything wrong in that?"

He walked away, leaving Ally alone at the table, mulling all that she'd been through on this amazing, heart-stopping day.

She'd been given back her life. She was now free to raise her son in a place she was learning to call home. And best of all, she'd just been persuaded that she had the right to love and be loved by a good man.

Who would have thought a famous Hollywood director, a master of manipulating people to believe the unbelievable, could point out the truth so clearly?

CHAPTER TWENTY

Ally awoke feeling a surge of anticipation she hadn't experienced in a long time. The fact that she was free of Glen's stalking had finally sunk in. And her frank talk with Nelson—Great One, she mentally corrected—had left her feeling better about herself than she had in a very long time.

After a long shower, she walked to her son's room, to find it empty, his clothes stuffed into a hamper leaving one sleeve sticking out. The bed was crudely made up, and she could see his efforts paying off. Each morning her little boy was getting better at his chores. And so was she, she promised herself. Each day they would both get better, and stronger, and more self-confident.

When she walked into the kitchen, she found Frank and Burke drinking coffee and engaged in an animated conversation with Grace and Nelson.

Frank hurried over to put an arm around her shoulders. "How are you feeling this morning, Ally?"

She shot a glance at the children to be certain they weren't listening. They were busy whispering behind their hands like two conspirators. "I feel so relieved to have it behind me."

She took in a deep breath, prepared to answer questions. Instead, he surprised her by handing her a glass of freshly squeezed orange juice and saying, "I'm sure you need some time to take in all that's happened to you. I hope you'll take things a day at a time."

"Thank you. I'll try." She looked around. "Is Reed in the barn?"

"He went with Colin up to the herd. He said he'd try to be back by tomorrow."

Ally struggled to hide her disappointment.

Lily and Kyle tugged on Grace's hand.

"Ask her, Gram Gracie," Lily said in a stage whisper that could be heard clear across the room.

Ally turned. "Ask me what?"

Grace drew the two children into the circle of her arms, clearly enjoying their attention. "Lily has been begging me to take her on one of my camera safaris. And, of course, we'd both like Kyle to come along."

The little boy was nearly bouncing off the walls in excitement. "Please, Mama. Say yes. Pleeease. I picked up all my clothes this morning and made my bed. And I'll do whatever you want me to, if you'll say I can go with them. Pleeease."

Ally was already shaking her head in refusal. "Don't you think he's a little young to go into the hills? There are all kinds of wild animals and..."

Frank laid a hand on her arm. "I agree he's young. But I took my grandsons along when they were his age, and Lily really wants her new best friend with her."

New best friend. The words sent Kyle into a little spin that had his glasses slipping down the bridge of his nose.

"It'll give Lily a chance to share with Kyle all she's learned about hiking and photographing mustangs."

Before Ally could protest, Frank held up a hand. "I promised Gracie that Burke and I would go along. I'll make Kyle my special buddy. I'll shadow him every step he takes. He'll never be out of my sight, Ally, I promise."

"And," Grace added, "Lily gave Kyle one of her old cameras, and we've been working with him. He's already proving to be a very smart student. I think he shows promise as a natural photographer."

"And we'll get to sleep in sleeping bags under the stars." Kyle was wiggling like a puppy. "And sit around a campfire every night while we eat."

Ally swallowed back her protest when she looked at her little boy, staring at her with such pleading in his eyes. "Well, a campfire and a sleeping bag. I guess that's every little boy's dream. How can I refuse? I guess..." She sighed. "I guess this is something you really want."

"See, Lily." Kyle was jumping up and racing over to hug his mother. "She didn't say she'd think about it."

The whole family burst into laughter.

Ally wrapped her arms around her son and peered over his head. "When are you planning this...camera safari, Gram Gracie?"

"Today."

Her smile faded as her arms tightened on her son. "So soon?"

Grace pointed to the window. "The weather for the next three days promises to be nearly perfect. With autumn closing in, we have to take advantage of it while we can."

Ally took in a deep breath, considering the changes that

were happening so rapidly she could barely keep up. Yesterday she'd feared her son would grow up alone. Today he was being offered the promise of time with so many good people who cared about him.

Kyle stepped back and tipped up his face to watch her. "Please, Mama. I really, really want to go with Lily and Burke and Gram Gracie and Grandpop Frank."

Frank walked over to take his wife's hand. "Considering all you've been through, you could use some quiet time. And maybe you could go to town and assess the progress being made on your building."

Ally couldn't help chuckling. "You've thought of every argument, haven't you?" She turned to her son with a grin. "I guess you'll be joining Lily on a grand adventure."

"Oh, boy!" Lily grabbed Kyle's hand, and the two of them danced around the room.

Grace walked over to hug Ally. "I know you'll worry. It's the most natural thing in the world. But it really will be a grand adventure for Kyle. And with any luck, we'll bring back photos of wild mustangs."

Ally thought about the many magnificent photos that lined the walls of nearly every room in this house and couldn't help putting a hand to her throat as she thought about seeing such mystical creatures in the wild. "Oh, Gram Gracie. This is so generous of you. I know this is something Kyle will never forget."

"Nor will I. You have no idea how much I enjoy the company of these two young ones." The older woman gave a girlish laugh as she turned to the children. "Time to pack our things. We're heading up to the hills."

Kyle and Lily dashed up the stairs, and the others had to hurry to catch up.

Within the hour they'd loaded a truck with their backpacks, Grace's photographic equipment, and enough of Yancy's food to feed half the town.

As they drove away, Ally stood waving until the truck disappeared over a ridge.

When she turned, Nelson was leaning on his cane and watching her from the porch. "He'll be fine."

"I know." She made her way to his side. "But I can't help feeling shaky about this."

"This is a big step for both of you."

"Yes." She bit her lip to keep it from quivering.

He drew her close, and she reflexively rested her head on his shoulder. "I didn't think it would be so hard to let him go."

"Letting go is always painful. But it's the way of things. Birds push their young from the nest, not to be cruel, but to teach them to fly. And parents put their little ones on big yellow buses and send them off to school, so they can soar."

"That's not quite the same as allowing my four-year-old to go into the wilderness. Still…" She kissed his cheek. "Thank you."

"For what?"

She smiled through her tears. "For being so wise. For being you."

Nessa came racing into the kitchen, looking flushed and out of breath, her hair damp from the shower. "I just had a text from Matt. He's asked me to meet him up in the hills to see how the house is shaping up."

Ingrid looked equally excited. "Luke sent Mick ahead to pick me up and drive me to my ranch. Luke will meet us there on his Harley. And with Lily gone, we'll get to spend a few days there, before heading back here. We've been neglecting my place, and it's time to see to chores."

Nelson, seated in his favorite chair, turned to Ingrid.

"Seems like that's been happening a lot lately. What have you decided about your ranch?"

Ingrid shook her head. "My neighbor, Bull Hammond, has made an offer to buy me out." She explained to Ally, "When Luke and I met, I was running my father's ranch and struggling to keep it going. Now that Luke and I are married, and living here while building our own spread, my closest neighbor wants to absorb my family land into his."

She stared out the window at the distant hills. "Still, it's Lily's heritage, too. And I have to be certain it's the right thing to do before I sign off on our dream."

Ally caught her hand. "I guess I'm not the only one learning to let go."

At the sound of a truck's horn, Ingrid hurried from the room, calling, "Here's Mick. I can't wait for Luke to get to my place."

Yancy looked up from the stove, where a big pot of soup was simmering. "What time do we have to be in town, Great One?"

Nelson glanced at his watch. "We'd better go." He lumbered to his feet and slipped on a cashmere sport coat before adjusting a silk ascot at his throat. "Time for me to look like a proper Hollywood icon."

Yancy turned to Ally. "Great One and I have an appointment in town that will last for a couple of hours."

"A marathon showing of some of my greatest films," Nelson put in.

"Oh, what fun. I bet the citizens of Glacier Ridge love having a celebrity living among them."

Nelson gave a slight bow of his head. "And I'm happy to play that role in all its glory. I always give them as much time as they require for questions and answers and autographs after the movies play."

"Which means," Yancy added, "we won't be home for supper. But I've made soup, and there are all the fixings for chicken and steak fajitas for supper."

"Thank you, Yancy." Ally dimpled. "I'm sure I won't go hungry."

A short time later she followed them out to the porch to wave good-bye before walking back into the house. The silence of the rooms seemed oddly out of place after so much activity.

She smiled, thinking of the excitement she'd sensed in both Nessa and Ingrid, knowing their men would soon be with them.

She thought of Reed in the hills. Though she wished she could see him, she understood his responsibility to the herd.

As Ally descended the stairs, she recognized the sound of an approaching vehicle.

Hurrying to the back door, she watched as a dusty ranch truck, with Reed driving, pulled into the barn.

Without giving a thought to what she was doing, she raced out the door and ran all the way to the barn before pausing in the open doorway.

Reed was just stepping down from the driver's side. The sight of him took Ally's breath away.

When he spotted her, he paused for the merest second. "I decided I needed to see you more than I needed to check on my herd."

He stood where he was, studying her through narrowed eyes as she walked closer. He slipped off his hat, shaking the dust from it against his leg.

"I'm glad. I needed to see you, too." She took a step closer, until they were mere inches apart. "It's done." She lifted a hand to his cheek. "It's over. Really over now. And I can get on with my life."

He closed a hand over her wrist while his gaze moved slowly over her upturned face.

His voice lowered with feeling. "I want you, Red."

"And I want you." She lifted herself on tiptoe to brush her mouth over his.

For a moment he went completely still. "You do?"

"More than I wanted to."

"Good." He nuzzled her cheek, her temple, before claiming her lips. "I'd hate to think I was the only one feeling this terrible need."

"Oh, Reed." Her arms encircled his neck and she dove into the kiss with a hunger that caught them both by surprise. "I'm so glad you're here."

His arms tightened around her, dragging her so close, she could feel his heartbeat inside her own chest. A heart that was thundering like a herd of mustangs.

He shot her a quick, sexy grin. "If I'd known you were going to greet me like this, I'd have never left."

He kissed her again, savoring the clean, fresh taste of her. "Where is everybody?"

"Kyle and Lily have gone on a photographic safari with your grandparents and Burke. Nessa's meeting Matt at their new house site. Ingrid and Mick are meeting Luke at her ranch. And Yancy drove Great One to town for a movie marathon." She glanced around. "Where's your uncle?"

"Colin's meeting Anita at his cabin. Whenever she can get away from the clinic, that's become their sanctuary from the world." He gave a short laugh. "They think nobody knows."

He framed her face with his hands. "So, it's just you and me?"

"Uh-huh." She drew his head down and poured herself into a kiss that rocked him back on his heels.

Against her mouth he whispered, "I hope you mean what that kiss is saying."

"I do."

His head came up sharply, and he studied her with sudden interest. "I'm dusty and sweaty and I smell like a trail bum."

"You smell like a man. A man I've missed more than I would have ever believed. And if you don't kiss me right this minute, my poor heart is going to explode."

Sudden awareness sparked in his eyes. "We wouldn't want that, would we?"

With a muttered oath he backed her against the door of a stall and kissed her until they were both struggling for breath.

Against her temple he whispered, "Okay, woman. Who are you, and what've you done with the ice princess I left a few days ago?"

"Her ice melted. And so did her heart."

With a growl more animal than human, he dragged her close and kissed her, while his big hands moved over her, kneading her flesh, pressing her to the length of him.

She returned kiss for kiss, touch for touch, nearly crawling inside his skin, unable to get enough of him.

Coming up for air, he caught the hem of her T-shirt and stripped it over her head. For the space of a heartbeat he simply stared at the silk-and-lace bra that revealed more than it covered. Then he reached behind her and unhooked it.

As it fell away, Ally felt the heat of his gaze. If looks could scorch, she was quickly burning to ash.

He leaned close to run nibbling kisses down her throat, then lower, over the soft swell of her breast before taking one already erect nipple into his mouth.

The heat was inside her now. Melting her bones like hot wax. Causing her blood to flow like molten lava. A pulse began throbbing deep inside, to her very core.

She couldn't stop the little moan of pleasure that only seemed to inflame him more.

He dragged her close and kissed her like a man starved for the taste of her. His hands were in her hair, drawing her head back as he kissed her until they were both struggling for air. And still it wasn't enough. Their breath was coming hard and fast as they moved ever closer to the madness that was taking over their last thread of control.

She wanted him to take her now, quickly, to satisfy the desperate need building inside her.

Her voice, when she could manage a word over the fire raging inside her, trembled. "Now, Reed."

Ally tugged his shirt aside with such force, buttons popped. Then she ran her hands over his muscled torso and gave a little hum of pure pleasure.

"Careful, Red. You're about to send me over the edge."

"That's my intention."

Instead, he took a step back, as though fighting for control. "Not yet, babe. Not when I've waited so long for this. For you." He reached for the snaps of her jeans just as she reached for his. When her fingers fumbled, he helped her until their clothes lay in a heap at their feet.

His mouth covered hers in a slow, deep kiss. Without warning his fingers found her, hot and wet, and he took her on a wild, quick roller coaster, up and over, all the while watching her eyes as they went wide with shock and surprise, before her body shuddered.

"Reed…"

He gave her no time to recover as he dragged her close and kissed with such passion it had them both gasping for air.

"Wait." Ally put a hand to his chest her breathing ragged.

He pressed his forehead to hers as he struggled for breath. "Red, if you're about to tell me no again, I'll die."

"No. I mean...I don't want you to stop."

He gave a short, ragged laugh. "You just saved my life. You jump-started my heart. Feel it." He pressed her hand to his chest. "I was about to go into cardiac arrest."

Her breath was coming hard and fast. "You're not the only one. After what you just gave me, I need a minute."

"And I need you." He dragged her into his arms and kissed her with such hunger, she melted into him.

His hands moved over her at will now, touching her everywhere, lighting fires wherever he touched. And she responded by doing the same, until they were so hot their skin was slick with sheen. And still they teased and tormented until the need became too great.

"Sorry, Red. I can't wait a minute longer." He lifted her off her feet.

She wrapped her legs around him, her greedy mouth on his, arms clinging fiercely to his neck as she opened herself completely to him.

Blind with need, he thrust into her, driving her against the door of the stall.

"Ally. Ally." Her name was torn from his lips.

"Reed, I...Oh, I missed you. Reed..."

Hearts pounding, lungs straining, they took each other with all the force of a raging stampede, climbing, climbing, until they began a sudden free fall.

And reached a heart-stopping, shuddering climax.

CHAPTER TWENTY-ONE

For the longest time they remained locked together, bodies fused, hearts pumping furiously.

Reed's face was buried in her neck, his hot breath tickling her flesh as their breathing gradually eased and their heartbeats returned to normal.

Reed was the first to move. He lifted a hand to her face. "I think I saw stars."

"Me too. But your face was in each one." She sounded breathless.

"Yeah? How'd I look?"

"Sexy."

"Good." He gave a satisfied grin. "That was really…"

"Amazing."

"Yeah." His smile came. That wonderful rogue smile that always managed to tug at her heart. "So were you, Red. Amazing."

"That was"—she traced the outline of his lower lip—"worth waiting for."

He set her gently on her feet before taking her hand and tugging her down to a bed of straw, using their clothes as a cushion. He drew her into the circle of his arms and ran nibbling kisses over her forehead, her cheek, the tip of her nose.

"Speaking of waiting"—he brushed a long, lingering kiss over her mouth—"the last time I was with you, I was afraid I'd have to wait forever. What caused this sudden change? Was it the fact that Glen is no longer threatening you? Is that what finally melted the ice?"

She shook her head. "Glen was never the problem. He had nothing to do with my unwillingness to make love with you, Reed." She ran a fingertip over his arched brow. "My issues started long before Glen and his threats. Actually, it was your great-grandfather who helped me to see the truth."

"Great One?" He looked at her as if he couldn't believe what she was saying.

As quickly as possible, she told him about her midnight encounter with his great-grandfather. And though it was still painful to admit, she knew it was time to tell him the truth. All of it.

"I met Rick shortly after my mother died. She was the only family I had, and I was living alone in the home I'd shared with her. Rick and I were introduced by mutual friends. He was tall, dark, handsome, and looked really great in his uniform. I knew he was using a tired old line, saying how pretty I was and how much he needed a woman to come home to whenever his latest tour of duty was over. He didn't promise me forever, but he promised me today, and it was enough for a woman who was feeling all alone and, honestly, scared to death of the future."

Reed was listening intently. "Why did you think that made you a liar?"

She shook her head. "I'm trying to be honest with you, and with myself." She took a breath. "In no time we were a couple, at least to our friends. And when I found out I was having a baby, I couldn't wait to tell Rick."

Reed watched her in silence.

"He went ballistic. He said a baby wasn't in his plans, and he had no intention of playing the daddy game. *Playing the daddy game.* Those were his hateful words. And he accused me of planning the pregnancy to trap him." She gripped her hands tightly. "I couldn't believe he thought I would use a baby as a trap. I honestly thought once he held his son in his arms, everything would change. Instead, he let me know Kyle was mine. Only mine. Whenever he was home on leave, he insisted I get a sitter, and we went out alone. He started staying with a friend rather than at my place. And by the time he left for what would turn out to be his last tour, we weren't even together anymore. He told me he'd found a new, young playmate with her own apartment. One who shared his desire to never settle down or burden him with children."

"He actually said that?" Reed's indignation flared like a torch. "Burden him?"

Ally touched a finger to his lips. "It's in the past now. Think how sad it is to know he wasted the last year of his life rejecting his own infant son."

"Does Kyle know any of this?"

She shook her head. "I've done all I can to keep that fact from Kyle. He was too young to even remember his father. If he thinks of Rick in the years to come, he'll know only that he was a war hero who died before he could get to know his only child. Kyle never needs to know more than that."

She moved on, telling Reed in detail about Great One's

reaction when he'd heard her story, as well as his kind words of wisdom.

Caught up in her narrative, Ally sat up, tracing a finger over and over Reed's chest. "For the first time in years I feel free. Free of guilt and fear and, most of all, of being unworthy of love."

"Unworthy?" He sat up. "Ally Shaw, I think you're the most amazing woman I've ever known."

"But I've made a lot of mistakes—"

"Shh." Reed drew her into his arms. Against her temple he murmured, "Right now, the only thing that matters is we're here, alone, with the entire day to ourselves. Let's not waste it on any more sad talk. Not when there are better things to do. Besides, I was so hot, I took you like an animal. Let me make it up to you."

She pressed her mouth to his throat. "I guess I could be persuaded. Especially since we're already naked and lying in the hay."

"That's the great thing about ranches. There are so many places for a guy to take his special girl."

"Am I your special girl?"

"You bet." With great tenderness, he began to show her, in the only way he could, just how special she was to him.

As they lost themselves in the wonder of their fresh, new feelings, Ally could feel her poor heart, for so long battered and bruised, begin to ever so gently heal.

And all because of this thoughtful, caring cowboy, who knew just how to make a woman feel cherished.

"Come on, Red." Reed sat up and caught Ally's hand.

"Where are we going?"

"To the house to shower. I don't know how you've been able to stand me for this long."

She pretended to wrinkle her nose. "I was willing to make a sacrifice for the sake of some really hot sex."

"As I recall, you attacked me before I had time to think how filthy I was."

She laughed. "As I recall, cowboy, you did the noble thing and gave in without a word of protest."

"Anything to please my lady." He grabbed up their clothes.

"Wait." She put a hand on his to stop him. "I'm not about to walk out of this barn naked. I need to dress first."

"Why?" He was grinning. "You think the horses will mind seeing you in your birthday suit?"

"What if somebody drives up?"

"There's nobody home. We're miles from town. It's like being alone in the universe." He took her hand and started toward the house.

Though he strode forward without a care in the world, Ally kept looking around, afraid at any moment someone would drive up and catch them strolling around as naked as the day they were born.

Once in the house, they climbed the stairs.

Ally stopped outside her room. "I'll see you in a little while."

"Okay." He was wearing a wicked grin.

Ally walked to the bathroom and turned on the shower. Moments later, as she stepped under the spray and began to shampoo her hair, she felt arms around her and gave a yelp of surprise before turning to find Reed, laughing.

"What are you doing?"

"The same as you. Showering. I hope you're willing to scrub my back."

"You're crazy."

"That's me. Now come here, woman." He dragged her

into his arms, and the two of them stood under the warm spray, laughing and rubbing soap on each other.

Within minutes the soap was forgotten as, with bodies tingling, hearts suddenly pounding, they came together flesh to flesh in a steamy tangle of arms and legs, while water cascaded over them.

Ally woke from a nap to find Reed lying beside her, watching her.

She stretched. "How did we end up in my bed?"

"Your fault." He kissed the tip of her nose. "You were shampooing my hair. You have the most amazing fingers, by the way. I've never had my hair and scalp massaged by a woman, so I was really into it. And the next thing I knew, we were tumbling into bed."

"We got the pillows wet."

"And the sheets. Don't worry. I'll toss them in the washer later." He gathered her close. "I can't get enough of you."

"I should feel guilty, having so much fun while every-one's away."

"There's that old guilt thing again." He kissed her, long and slow and deep. "When will you accept the fact that we deserve to have fun?" He chuckled. "Hell, we waited long enough."

"You didn't make it easy."

He gave her a steady look. "You mean you were tempted?"

"You know I was. In fact, I think you liked pushing all my buttons and watching me squirm, knowing I was trying to do the sensible thing."

"You do look cute when you squirm, Red. In fact, you look so cute right now, I think I'm going to have to ask for thirds. Or is it fourths?"

She shook her head and struggled to hold back the laugh that bubbled up. "Reed Malloy, you're a glutton."

"Yes, ma'am, I am. Lucky for you."

She wrapped her arms around his neck and pressed her mouth to his. "Mmm, I'm so lucky."

And then there were no words as they took each other on a slow, delicious ride to paradise.

"Come on." Reed caught Ally's hand and together they walked down the stairs. "I've worked up a powerful appetite." He paused to brush a kiss over her lips. "Not just for loving, though I do believe I could live on that alone."

She laughed. "Loving's fine, but you need to feed me."

"I intend to. My last meal was around dawn." In the kitchen he glanced out the window to see the sun casting long shadows on the distant hills. "It's past suppertime, and I need some fuel if we're going to keep on doing what we've been doing all day."

"Are we?" She looked suddenly shy. "Are we going to keep on doing what we've been doing?"

"Red." He cupped her face in his hands and stared into her eyes with a blazing look. "If you don't want to stop my heart, don't even suggest we go back to the old ways of nothing more than a good night kiss."

She stood on tiptoe to brush his mouth with hers. "Trust me, cowboy. Now that I've found out just how good you are"—she wrapped her arms around his waist—"let's hurry and eat and get back to it."

He dug his hands into her hair and kissed her until they were both sighing.

When he finally turned away, he called, "If you get us two longnecks, I'll handle the food."

"You're really going to feed me?"

"Think of it as a reward for some really good loving." He crossed to the stove and turned on the grill.

Soon the kitchen was filled with the wonderful fragrance of chicken and steak grilling on a bed of onions and peppers.

When the fajitas were ready, he filled two plates and turned. "You bring the beer, I'll bring the food."

"Where are we taking this?"

He winked. "I thought, since we have the house to ourselves, we'd take it to my bedroom. That way we get to eat and play all at the same time."

"Very sensible."

They were laughing like two kids let out of school early as they made their way upstairs and into his bedroom.

Once there, he closed the door before turning toward her. "Eat first and then play? Or would you rather play first? Your call."

She was laughing so hard, she could barely get the words out. "Let's get some fuel. Then playtime will be even better."

He shot her a dangerous look. "I like the way you think, Red. Okay. Let's eat. Then we'll move on to the good stuff."

"I'm still really mad at myself for leaving you to deal with that creepy stalker alone."

Reed and Ally lay together in his bed, voices muted after long, lazy hours of loving.

She put a finger over his mouth. "Let it go now. It's over, and Glen won't be bothering me again."

He caught her wrist and pressed a kiss to her palm. "You've had to deal with so much in your life. And always alone."

She shook her head. "Not always. My mom and I were close. Closer than a lot of mothers and daughters. Having lost her own mother at such a young age, she said she was so grateful to have me in her life." Her smile was wistful. "I just wish she'd lived long enough to get to know her grandson."

"He's a great kid." Reed put a hand beneath his head and grinned. "He's really smart. And funny. I see those eyes behind the big glasses and I can almost see the wheels turning in that little brain."

"He's getting to you, isn't he?"

He gave a grunt of agreement. "He got to me the first time I met him, wearing his Super Kid cape and running into the street."

"I was absolutely terrified of you when I saw that scowl. I was really afraid you'd report me for being a bad mother."

"I considered it. Until I met you. Then"—he gathered her close and pressed his lips to a tangle of hair at her temple—"*you* got to me too, Red."

Reed sat up, causing Ally to wake. She yawned, stretched, before sitting up beside him.

He tugged on a lock of her hair. "You were smiling in your sleep."

"Was I? I was having the nicest dream."

"Want to share?"

"We were watching cattle on a grassy hillside. And you were so happy and proud. And you were telling me you'd waited years for this, and now it was all happening."

"What was?"

She shrugged. "I haven't a clue. But you were incredibly happy."

"Maybe we just made love under the stars. That would make me a very happy guy."

"Oh, you." She nudged his arm. "Is that all you can think of?"

"Can you blame me? You made me wait so long, I was one big hunka burning love."

They both laughed at his poor imitation of Elvis.

"Want some coffee?"

"Oh, I'd love some. Come on. I'll make it."

As she started to scramble out of bed, he caught her hand. "Slow down, Red. We've got all the time in the world."

He pulled on his jeans while she slipped into a T-shirt and jeans.

Barefoot, they walked hand in hand down the stairs and headed to the kitchen.

The minute they shoved open the door, they froze.

Nelson was seated at the kitchen table, sipping a brandy.

"Hey, Great One." Reed led Ally inside and closed the door. "How was the movie marathon in Glacier Ridge?"

"A smashing success, sonny boy." If he noticed that Reed and Ally were holding hands, he made no comment about it. "The good citizens kept me there for hours signing their programs. One rancher had an old movie poster he wanted signed. He found it in his father's barn. Can you imagine?"

"You never know what you'll find in those old barns. Sometimes a movie poster. Sometimes a hot city girl."

While Ally blushed, Reed moved easily around the kitchen, filling a coffeemaker with water and ground coffee, turning it on, before taking a seat beside Ally. "You make a lot of folks happy by attending those events, Great One."

"It makes me happy, too." Nelson set down his brandy snifter and stretched out his legs. "My life in Hollywood seems like a lifetime ago."

Reed grinned. "It was."

"But the moment I'm around old movie buffs, it's all so familiar. I can recall how many takes we had to go through before I got exactly what I wanted in that particular scene.

I'm reminded of all the old feuds, the friendships"—he stared directly at Reed and Ally—"the number of love affairs that began on the set."

While Ally's cheeks colored, Reed merely chuckled. "Yeah. As I recall, you've admitted to being the matchmaker to a lot of the stars."

"Just one of my many gifts, sonny boy. I've always been able to spot two people fighting to keep their hands off each other." Nelson gave a satisfied smile as the coffeemaker indicated the brew was ready. "I'll say good night now. Enjoy your late-night après drink."

When he was gone, Reed let out a belly laugh.

Ally arched a brow.

"That sly old dog." Reed chuckled again. "That last dig was Great One's way of letting me know he was on to us."

She thought over the words. "I don't understand. He just told us to enjoy our coffee."

"He told us to enjoy our après drink. Our 'after' drink. And that old man knows exactly what went on before."

He filled two cups with steaming coffee, and the two sat in companionable silence, basking in the afterglow of a day and night of carefree loving, while laughing about Great One's sense of humor.

CHAPTER TWENTY-TWO

It was barely dawn when Reed sat on the edge of the bed, pulling on his boots.

"I wish you didn't have to leave." Ally knelt up behind him and wrapped her arms around his waist, kissing the back of his neck.

He turned and gathered her close. "I'd give anything to stay and keep on doing what we did all yesterday and last night. But the roundup..."

She touched a hand to his mouth to still his words. "I know how important this herd is to your future, Reed. And I'm not complaining. I realize you have to go. I just wish I could do something to help."

"What you gave me is more than I could have hoped for, Red." He stood and helped her up with him, drawing her into his arms. Against her temple he murmured, "And in a few days, when I've brought my herd down from the hills, I hope to heaven we can slip away from the crowd and have another day like yesterday."

"Kyle will be back from his grand adventure, and your family will be eager to spend time with you."

"Kyle has to sleep at some point." He wiggled his brows like a mock villain. "And my rowdy family will have to get in line, woman. You and I have some serious lovin' time to make up."

Her laughter was cut off by his kiss.

For long minutes they clung, until Reed gave a moan of pure misery. "Okay. I'm going to try to walk away, Red. If I make it to the door, I'm not turning around to look at you, or I'll never be able to go."

She stood very still and watched as he strode to the bedroom door and stepped out before closing it.

She listened to the sound of his footsteps as he descended the stairs. Then she hurried to the window to watch as he climbed into his truck. He lowered the window and looked up. Seeing her outlined in the spill of lamplight, he lifted a hand in a salute and drove off in a cloud of dust.

Wrapped in a warm glow, she gathered up her belongings and returned to her own room.

Once in the shower, she let the warm water spill over her, remembering their laughter as they'd shared this space the day before.

As she dressed, she thought about their brief time together. Everything they did, though nothing more than simple, everyday activities, had been so much fun. Because of Reed. He was sexy, funny, and a caring, thoughtful lover. Loving him seemed so easy and natural.

Loving him.

Her fingers paused over a button on her shirt.

Though neither of them had talked about any deep feelings, she knew in her heart she loved him.

She sank down on the edge of the bed and drew in a deep

breath. There. She'd admitted it. No more doubts. No need to second-guess. She loved Reed Malloy.

What she'd done in the past, or what would happen in the future, no longer mattered.

She would simply hug the knowledge to her heart and enjoy the fact that, though she had come to care for the entire Malloy family, she loved Reed in a way she'd never believed possible.

Ally stood on the back porch, hoping for better cell phone service, and spoke with handyman Darnell Thornton. "It sounds as though things are moving along smoothly, Thorny."

"So smoothly, if there aren't any bumps in the road, you should be able to open your shop in less than a week."

"So soon?" She touched a hand to her heart.

"I don't see why not. But it will take longer to repair all the damage to your apartment upstairs. I need to replace just about everything. What wasn't ruined by the fire was so waterlogged from the fire hoses, we need to replace the drywall, the wood flooring, probably the subfloor, and even the stairway."

"But the important thing is the shop." She thought a moment. "I can be there in an hour or so."

"Great. My crew and I will be here working."

They rang off, and Ally floated inside on a cloud.

Finding the kitchen empty, she wandered into the great room, where the blinds had been drawn against the morning sunlight.

Yancy and Nelson were staring, transfixed, at images flashing across a big screen.

Fascinated, Ally remained in the doorway and watched an eerie scene unfold. A snow-covered road. A car, smashed

against a huge, unforgiving tree. And then a close-up of
a man's blood-spattered body behind the wheel, one hand
against the passenger window, as though waving, or trying to
smash the glass. The other hand cradling his face, slumped
over the steering wheel. The camera panned to a woman lying in a snowbank, looking as though she were sleeping.
Her long, dark hair a stark contrast to the whiteness of the
snow. Her hands folded across her waist as though she'd
been posed.

The next scene, jerky and slightly blurred, showed several
vehicles, a mixture of cars and trucks, and a series of tire
tracks in the snow, along with dozens of footprints.

There was sound, as well. Voices cursing. A woman crying. The wail of a distant siren.

She'd heard enough of the death of Reed's parents on a
snow-covered road that she realized what she was seeing.
Though she wanted to look away, she stared transfixed at the
screen until the reel had run its course.

Yancy clicked on a light and caught sight of Ally.

"How long have you been here?"

"A few minutes." She walked over to sit beside Great
One. "You filmed the scene of the accident."

"I did." He nodded. "Filming has always been second nature to me. When we got the call, I picked up my camera and
Yancy drove. I wanted to record everything, so I could look
at it later when my mind wasn't clouded with grief."

"Doesn't it break your heart to watch this?"

"It does. Every time."

"Then why keep looking at it?"

He patted her hand. "Yancy shares my conviction that it
was no accident that took the lives of Patrick and Bernie and
changed this family forever."

Ally sucked in a breath at his remark. "But there's no

other car. Just that tree. Reed said it was a one-car accident, caused by a snowstorm."

"That's what the sheriff and the state police declared when they closed the book on their investigation."

"But all these years later you still believe otherwise?"

"I do." He looked at Yancy, who nodded in agreement. "We do."

"And does your video prove it?"

He looked down at his clenched fist resting on the arm of his chair. "We've studied it a hundred times. A thousand. But it's too blurred to give us a clear image of what we saw."

"And what did you see, Great One?"

"When we first got there, I swear I saw two sets of tire tracks that at one point intersected, as well as skid marks. But within minutes there had been too many vehicles pulling up, and too many feet walking around the scene destroying evidence."

"What did the sheriff say?"

"Eugene believed it was an accident, plain and simple. Patrick and Bernadette had been at Clay's Pig Sty, celebrating their anniversary. The skid was caused when Patrick realized he was sliding into the tree. And the state police who arrived several hours later agreed with his findings." He shook his head. "And the case has been considered closed ever since. The official report is an accident, caused by an unusually heavy snowfall and fueled by alcohol consumption."

"Then why do you keep torturing yourself like this?"

"Because I can't let it go, girl." He pressed a fist to his chest. "I feel it in my heart. In my soul. In my gut. Something happened the night of this crash. Something we haven't yet learned. But I know it's so."

Yancy had listened in silence. Now he added, "This past

year, when we were being held at gunpoint by a crazy cowboy named Lonny Wardell, he told Luke he knew a secret he'd been sworn to keep. A secret about Patrick's death."

Ally's eyes went wide. "Ingrid told me about being terrorized by a wrangler who'd been seeing her mother."

Yancy's voice was low with fury. "Lon Wardell. He grew up around here and worked on most every ranch in the area. He was a drinker and a drifter."

"What did he know?"

"He was shot dead before he could tell us."

She sucked in a breath. "Who shot him?"

"A dozen different rifles. The state police sharpshooters had surrounded him, and when they got their chance, they opened fire."

Ally closed a hand over Nelson's. "Oh, Great One. What a terrible thing to live with." She sighed. "I wish I had the technical equipment I used to work with in Virginia."

At his questioning look, she explained. "I worked in security. My specific job training was enlarging and enhancing security videos to identify the persons caught on camera."

"Is it possible to enhance something as crude and primitive as my old film?"

She nodded. "Possibly. But only with very expensive, high-tech equipment. My firm has such equipment. As do a lot of the tech industries."

Nelson was clearly intrigued.

He clutched her hand. "You know people who could work with my old film?"

Hearing the quivering note of hope in his voice, she swallowed back the lump that had risen in her throat, threatening to choke her. She paused, her mind awhirl with possibilities. "I could phone my former supervisor and see if she would be willing to do this. Not during business hours, of course. But maybe, as a favor to me, she could be persuaded to take up your cause after hours..."

"Do it, girl. Call her. Whatever she wants to be paid for her work, I'm more than willing."

Ally put a hand on his shoulder. "Great One, please understand that she may refuse. I'll do my best to persuade her, as a favor to me. We had a really good working relationship. But I can't make any promises. Everyone in that division works long hours, and they certainly don't relish the idea of doing more of it on their own time."

The old man brightened. "It's worth a try, girl. I'd die a happy man if I could have a definitive answer."

"You realize it may not be what you want to hear."

He nodded.

Ally bent close and kissed his cheek. "I'll call her now, before I leave for town."

"Bless you, girl." Great One squeezed her hand between both of his, before she stood and walked from the room.

Ally found Nelson and Yancy in the kitchen, talking in low tones. Both men looked up hopefully.

She took a seat at the table, facing them. "My former supervisor, Gaylen Webber, has agreed to scan your film." She turned to Great One. "Assuming this is your only copy, are you willing to ship it to her, knowing it could be lost in transit or damaged during the enhancement process?"

When he realized the implications, he took his time before answering. "I hadn't thought of that, but I have to risk it."

An hour later, as Ally prepared to leave for Glacier Ridge, Great One handed her a padded mailer containing his precious film.

She held it in her hands and looked up into his eyes. "Are you sure you're willing to part with this?"

"You know the old saying. Nothing ventured, nothing gained. If I don't risk everything while I have this chance, I'll have to die without ever knowing." He closed his hands over hers. "You've opened a door, girl. I have to walk through it, even if I discover hellfire on the other side."

She walked outside and climbed into the ranch truck Yancy had driven up from the barn. She lifted a hand to the two men standing together on the back porch and watched them in the rearview mirror until they disappeared from sight.

She glanced at her precious cargo, bound for a delivery service in town, and from there to her former office in Virginia.

An old man's deepest-held hopes and fears lay on that strip of film.

Dear heaven. What had she unleashed?

After shipping off the mailer to her former supervisor, Ally crossed the street and headed toward her building.

As she drew near, she glanced at the new roof gleaming in the sunlight. She could hear the sound of power equipment as she opened the front door and stepped inside.

Thorny hurried over. "Hey." He swept a hand. "What do you think?"

She took a moment to look around before smiling. "It looks a lot better than it did the last time I saw it."

She glanced toward the stairway. "Can I go up?"

Thorny held up a hand. "Those stairs were badly damaged. It's safer if you remain down here."

"All right." She took in a breath. Spotting Jeremy on a ladder, Ally asked quietly, "How is he working out?"

"Jeremy's a really good worker. Thanks for recommending him."

"Oh, I'm glad." That news lifted Ally's spirits even higher.

"If we keep on pushing, I think you could open for business within the week. But that would mean a lot of driving for you, since there's no place to sleep here. I can't promise your apartment for at least another week after that. If we're lucky, we may be able to get you back upstairs sooner. But I can't be certain until we get through the next couple of days."

"Don't apologize, Thorny." Ally touched a hand to his arm. "You've already made more progress than I'd anticipated."

"Hey. Ally." Gemma stepped out of the back room and hurried over to hug her boss.

"Gemma. How did Gemma's Closet fare?"

"I had to toss everything. But since it was free to begin with, I just started over. After work, whenever Jeremy isn't too tired, he takes me around to out-of-town yard sales." She turned. "Want to see my new stuff?"

"I'd love to." Ally followed her to the back room and looked around with a smile of appreciation. A clothesline was crowded with fringed jackets and bell-bottom pants. A tabletop displayed hobo purses and beaded evening bags, boots and strappy shoes. A glass display case was filled with vintage jewelry and belts.

"Oh, Gemma. This looks even better than before."

"Thanks. Whenever you're ready to open shop, I'll help you set up your displays, too."

Ally hugged her. "What would I do without you?"

"I'm so thankful to you, Ally. Jeremy and I are both grateful. He finally has a job. He loves working with Thorny.

And he's making enough money that we're able to rent a motel room not far from here on the interstate. It's pretty shabby, but it's better than sleeping in his truck."

"I'm glad." She held the young woman a little away, to study the green-and-blue stripes in her hair and the heavy black eyeliner giving her a cat's-eye look. "Thorny thinks I can open the store within a week. The sooner the better." She put her arm around Gemma's waist as the two walked out of the back room and looked around at the flurry of activity. "We both need to get back to work."

"You've got that right." Gemma squeezed her hand. "I can't wait."

Ally stepped into the sheriff's office and was surprised to find her uncle behind the desk.

"Archer?"

His head came up, and he took his time closing a drawer before crossing his arms over his chest. "You here on business?"

She shook her head. "I came to town to take a look at my building, and I thought I'd talk with the sheriff before I leave."

"He's out at the Taylor ranch. Old man Taylor likes to slap his wife around. From the sounds of it, he went too far this time." He shrugged. "Of course, she's said that before and then refuses to press charges. But this time, she may have had enough."

Ally shuddered.

"If you're worried about your stalker, don't be. His lawyer won the right to have him taken to Helena for incarceration and trial, arguing that travel to this neck of the woods was too far and constituted a violation of his rights." Archer gave a smug smile. "Before that stupid son-of-a—

that miserable lowlife was hauled off, I let him know that, even after he does time, if he ever shows his face in this town again, he won't leave alive."

When she frowned and started to turn away, he came around the desk and closed a hand over her arm. "Sorry. I know that kind of talk upsets you. I realize I've got rough edges. Eugene and I had a talk about it. He said you refused to say anything bad about me, except to say I'd saved your life."

"That's the truth. And I'll be forever grateful, Archer. I told the sheriff I have no doubt Glen would have killed me if you hadn't come to my rescue. But the violence..."

"Being a lawman isn't for the weak. I'm sure it's hard for some to see. Violence comes with the territory. But Sheriff Graystoke said if I wanted to keep my job, I'd have to agree to some retraining."

She turned to look at him. "Retraining?"

He nodded. "The state boys call it"—he rolled his eyes—"sensitivity training. That's for us old-timers who need to learn to be politically correct. Next time a punk resists arrest, instead of breaking his skull, I'll show him my badge and ask him politely to hand over his weapon and raise his hands." A smile tugged at the corner of his mouth. "If he doesn't comply with orders, then I can knock him around until I beat some sense into him."

Seeing her reaction, he grinned. "Just kidding. It was meant as a little joke." He quickly changed the subject. "When are you opening your shop?"

"Next week, if everything goes as planned."

"You and the kid still staying out at the country club? I mean, the Malloy place? Speaking of which...where's Kyle? Isn't he always attached to your hip?"

"He's gone on a camera safari with Frank and Grace."

"Pretty fancy. A camera safari. Is that like a picture-taking trip?"

She nodded.

"Sweet. Already got yourself a babysitter." He gave her a sly look. "Thorny says your apartment suffered the worst damage and won't be ready for a while. Going to be a long drive here and back every day once you open for business." He paused a beat. "You could always stay with me until your apartment's ready."

She blinked in surprise. "You mean it?"

"Yeah. Why not? We're kin."

"It would only be for a week or two."

"That's probably long enough. I prefer my own company. But we can make it work for a week or two."

"Thank you, Archer. That's generous of you. I know how much you value your privacy. You realize Kyle will be with me. But only at night. I'll bring him to work with me during the day."

"Fine. As long as the kid knows his place. No noise. No dropping stuff on the floor. No poking his nose where it doesn't belong. You let him know my bedroom's off-limits."

Ally swallowed. "That's a tall order for a little boy. But I guess he can manage for a week or so. If you don't mind, I'll stop by your place and move some of our things into the upstairs bedroom."

"Suit yourself." Archer turned to grab up the ringing phone on the sheriff's desk.

He put a hand over the speaker. "This is going to take some time."

"All right." *Thank you*, she mouthed before letting herself out of the office.

She grew thoughtful as she made her way back to her shop.

She knew Kyle wouldn't be happy when he learned he had to leave the Malloy ranch. He'd come to feel safe there. Safe and loved. And it would mean leaving his new best friend. That would be tough. He followed Lily around like a devoted puppy.

It was only for a week or two, she reminded herself. Hopefully, by the time Reed returned from the roundup, she and Kyle would be back in their own apartment. The thought of lying with Reed in her bed had her humming a little tune. Maybe she and Kyle would plan a welcome home party, and Reed would ask to stay over. Then she could really welcome him back.

For the rest of the day, while Thorny and his crew finished up last-minute repairs, Ally and Gemma moved among the stacks of furniture and assorted ranch items, deciding how best to display everything.

Gemma positioned a scarred picnic table in one of the big display windows, before opening a faded patio umbrella. Then she rummaged through boxes until she found what she was looking for. A plastic pitcher and six glasses and a tin tray bearing a logo from someone's long-ago trip to Niagara Falls were positioned on one end of the table. She added an old metal coat rack and draped a beach towel on one hook and a slightly used straw hat on another.

She walked outside and stood back to get a better view of the display before turning to Ally, who had followed. "What do you think?"

"Perfect. I'm betting everything in this display will be sold as soon as I'm open for business."

"I've been thinking." Gemma led the way inside and folded a checkered tablecloth and draped it over one end of the picnic table. "You should hold a grand reopening day.

Folks around here are constantly stopping me in the street to ask when you'll be open for business. Everyone's been watching the repairs with real interest. There's been so much buzz about the place. Almost as much as when you opened the first time."

"Really?" Ally chewed her lip, considering. "That grand opening was a lot of work."

"Think about all the ranchers who drive to town on Sunday for church and to pick up supplies."

Ally's eyes lit with the thought. "I suppose I could have some snacks for the customers who come straight from church or the feed store. I wouldn't serve enough to hurt anyone else's business. Just a few nibbles, to whet their appetite for more at the local places. But maybe I could buy some pulled-pork sandwiches from Clay, and have him cut them into bite sizes, to serve on a tray."

Gemma's enthusiasm grew. "And how about brownies and cookie pieces from D and B's and tiny cups of ice cream from I's Cream?"

Ally nodded. "Coffee could be a problem. But I could always buy a case of those little bottles of water."

"Too bad you couldn't have the name of your store on every label."

Ally burst into laughter. "Now you're talking way too much expense for this little business. But I guess I could have some business cards printed up to hand out to everyone."

The two young women moved around the room, discussing how best to show off the items for sale and trying to see each display through the eyes of the ranchers and their families.

By the time the workmen had left for the day, Ally and Gemma had made their plans and agreed to spend the rest of the week making final preparations for their grand reopening. As Ally drove toward the Malloy ranch, her head was spinning with all the ideas she and Gemma had shared. She loved working with Gemma. And she was really glad she hadn't let Sheriff Graystoke persuade her not to have anything to do with the girl and her boyfriend. She could see now that Eugene was just trying to protect her from people he thought less than honest. And it was true the lawman had managed to color her original perception of the two teens, but she was so happy she'd been able to see beyond their past and their outward appearance to the goodness of their hearts.

She had a sudden thought. Her uncle had hoped, by being honest about her past, to turn Reed away from her, because he bore some sort of grudge against the Malloy family. At the time she'd been hurt and offended. Now, looking back, Archer had actually done her a favor. He'd made it impossible for her to live a lie in this town. He'd forced her to admit the truth and hope people would accept her as she was.

And wasn't that exactly what Great One had wanted her to understand? She never needed to be an actor in a play. This life was her reality. By being herself, she knew a freedom she hadn't enjoyed in years.

She felt her eyes brim and blinked hard. Despite all that had happened, she was being given a second chance. Not just in business, but in life.

And maybe the strangest result of all this heartache was Archer's unexpected offer. Her uncle was making a real attempt to allow her and her son back into his life. Despite the shocking brutality she'd witnessed in him during the arrest of Glen, leaving her repelled and more than a little afraid of him, he seemed to have made a real turnaround in his attitude.

She clicked on the truck radio and began humming along to a happy song that had her tapping her fingers on the steering wheel. Maybe her mother's dream of being reunited with family could happen after all. For the sake of her sweet mother, she would give Archer another chance. After all, miracles sometimes happened. Just look at how far she'd already come.

CHAPTER TWENTY-THREE

When Ally drove up to the Malloy ranch, she spied several trucks parked near the back porch, alerting her that Reed's brothers and their wives were home. Once in the kitchen she was greeted by Yancy, who was being helped by Nessa and Ingrid. The two women were happily chatting about the progress being made on their building sites. Across the room Matt and Luke were drinking longnecks while sitting on either side of Great One.

"Matt thinks the south wall of the house should be mostly windows and sliding glass door walls, because of that spectacular view." Nessa held up her phone and showed them the photos she'd taken from the high ridge where they were building their house.

"Oh, that view is amazing." Ingrid passed the phone to Ally, who agreed.

Nessa accepted her phone back from Ingrid. "How about your place?"

"We're just in the planning stages." Ingrid sighed. "But Luke said he's been thinking about that spot for a place of his own for years now."

Like her sister-in-law, she held up her phone and passed around some photos she'd taken of their site.

"Oh, that's lovely." Nessa handed the phone to Ally, who nodded in agreement.

"What about your place, Ally?" Nessa caught her hand. "Tell us how Thorny is doing with the fire damage."

"I'm amazed at all he's managed to do." She accepted a glass of wine from Ingrid and leaned a hip against the counter. "By the time he left today, he decided I could open for business by next week."

"So soon?" Nessa caught her hand and led her to the low coffee table, where Yancy had set out a plate of cheese and homemade biscuits.

Ally nodded. "I can't tell you how happy I'll be to get back to work."

"And your apartment?" Matt asked.

"Thorny said it may be another week or more before I can move back."

Luke popped a cheese cube in his mouth. "That's a long drive from our ranch every morning."

"I know. I was wondering how I could manage, but Archer surprised me by offering to let me live with him until my apartment is ready."

Matt's brow shot up. "And you accepted?"

"It would certainly make things easier. Besides, it wouldn't be right if I refused his generous offer. Especially since he seems to be making a real effort to change."

"In what way?" Luke eyed her over the rim of his longneck.

"He said Sheriff Graystoke had a serious talk with him, and he's agreed to take sensitivity training."

Matt chuckled. "Using Archer's name in the same sentence as 'sensitivity' seems like an oxymoron."

Ally joined in the laughter. "I would have said the same thing before today. But he seemed sincere. Well..." Her voice lowered and she chewed her lower lip, deep in thought, before saying, "Except for a crude attempt at a joke."

"What was the joke?" Luke was studying her.

"Oh, something about asking in a polite way for a gunman to give up his weapon and giving him a chance to comply before knocking him senseless."

"Now there's the Archer Stone I know," Luke said dryly.

Yancy broke into their conversation by calling, "Dinner's ready."

Great One finished his martini before standing and offering his arm to Ally. As they made their way to the table, he said, "I'm glad you're able to return to your business. But it sounds as though you're serious about accepting your uncle's offer. If so, I'm sorry you'll be leaving us."

"I'm sorry, too." In an aside she said, "I shipped off that package via overnight delivery. It should arrive tomorrow before five o'clock. I asked Gaylen to phone you to confirm its safe arrival."

Nelson gave a satisfied nod. "Thank you, my dear." He closed a hand over hers. "As a character said in one of my favorite movies, I'll be on tenterhooks until I hear her verdict."

Ally returned from another satisfying day in town, watching the progress of her shop. In the past few days she'd been pleased to see how her building went from scorched and damaged to gleaming under new siding and fresh paint.

As soon as Thorny was able to confirm a day that she could open for business, she and Gemma had begun making plans for a grand reopening. And because all the folks in town had been watching the progress along with her, they were growing eager to begin shopping again. Dot and Barb had asked her to make up flyers announcing her plans, so they could post them on the door of their diner. Clay Olmsted offered to take one, as did Ivy and Trudy and Gert and Teddy Gleason. Every business in town was eager to do what they could to promote her reopening, including the medical clinic, where Dr. Anita Cross promised to hang a flyer on their bulletin board, while privately admitting that she hoped Colin would deliver it in person.

Ally's heart was lighter than it had been for weeks. These good people, who only months ago had been strangers, were now her friends, eager to celebrate with her.

Seeing several more trucks parked outside the ranch, her smile grew even brighter. She climbed down from the driver's side and hurried up the back steps.

Inside, she heard the quiet hum of voices and the higher pitched laughter of Lily and Kyle.

"Kyle."

At her voice the little boy turned and flew into her arms. She scooped him up and kissed his face over and over until he finally managed to say, "Okay, Mama. You have to put me down now so I can tell you all about our safari."

"I can't wait." She hugged Grace and Frank and Lily before turning to her son. "Tell me everything."

"We climbed a big mountain. And we slept in sleeping bags around a fire. And the first night I heard a coyote howl and climbed into Lily's sleeping bag."

Everyone joined in the laughter.

"I'd have probably done the same," Ally admitted.

She accepted a glass of lemonade from Yancy and sat down beside Grace while Kyle and Lily began an excited recitation of their adventure.

Kyle shoved his glasses up the bridge of his nose. "We saw deer and foxes and—"

"—even some mountain goats," Lily added. She turned. "Gram Gracie says we're lucky, 'cause not too many people get to see them. Didn't you?"

"Indeed." Grace nodded.

"And we found Gram Gracie's herd of mustangs," Kyle said. "A big white stallion. Grandpop Frankie says that's a daddy horse. And we took—"

"—hundreds of pictures," Lily finished.

The two were nodding in unison.

"We did. I've been searching for that stallion for years. I have a feeling spotting him means good luck." Grace caught Ally's hand. "And I've promised the children that I'll show them how to develop their pictures, and we'll make an album of their grand adventure so they'll never forget."

"I'll never forget," Kyle said solemnly. "And, Mama, there was a whole field of wildflowers, and I wanted to pick some for you, but Gram Gracie said they'd die before we got home."

"Gram Gracie's right. I hope you took a picture of them." He nodded.

"Good. A picture is even better. Now we'll be able to look at them forever, and those flowers will always be pretty and alive. They'll never die."

When Yancy called them to supper, the two children caught hands and danced along beside Great One.

The meal was a festive one, sprinkled with much laughter and dozens of stories about the mustangs, the wild animals, the spectacular sunsets, and the excitement of sleeping under the stars.

Grace glanced across the table at Ally's bright smile. "Yancy tells us the repairs to your building are coming along."

Ally nodded. "They're moving faster than I'd expected. Thorny gave the word today that I can definitely open next week. Gemma and I are planning a grand reopening Sunday, to catch the flow of ranchers who come into town for church and supplies."

"Oh, how grand." Ingrid clapped her hands. "I can't wait to see what treasures I'll find for our house."

"Which isn't even started yet." Luke turned to the others. "See what happens when a woman finds a new store? She invents reasons to shop."

While the men laughed, the women were in obvious agreement with Ingrid's sentiments.

Frank nodded toward his sons. "We'll need to head up to the hills. Reed's herd is going to be moved by cattle-haulers. The rest of the herds are ready to be driven to winter pastures."

Ally sighed. "I had so hoped Kyle and I could see a real roundup."

Frank shared a laugh with his sons. "You're not missing much, Ally girl. Roundup is hot, sweaty work. But it's necessary to button down the herds before the first snowfall."

"In August?"

He chuckled. "You're in Montana now. We see snow as early as August or as late as June up in the hills."

Ally stepped into the kitchen to find Yancy setting packets of food into a cooler. Burke was standing at the counter, holding a mug of coffee.

"Morning, Ally," the two men called.

"Good morning." She glanced at Burke. "Will you be seeing Reed?"

"I will. I figure he'll be grateful for the company, and for any news I bring him, since I keep getting a 'no service' notice on my phone."

"I've been getting the same message. It's frustrating. Will you let him know I'll be returning to my business Saturday, to prepare for a grand reopening on Sunday?"

"I'll tell him."

"There's one more thing." She lowered her voice, in case Kyle happened along. "I haven't said anything yet, because I know Kyle will be really disappointed. Tell Reed my uncle invited us to stay with him, and since it's such a long, tedious drive, I've agreed to move in with him just until my apartment is ready in another week or so."

Burke gave her a steady look. "When do you plan on telling your boy?"

"Today. I can't put it off any longer."

"He won't be happy with the news. He and Lily have become real close. You should have seen them in the wilderness. Like twins, joined at the hip."

She nodded. "I know. And I really hate separating them. Especially since he and Archer rub each other the wrong way."

"You could leave Kyle here. You know Grace and Frank would love having him."

"I know. But he's been gone for days now, and I've missed him too much to be separated again so soon." She took in a breath. "It's only for a week or two, and then we'll be back in our own place."

Burke set his mug in the sink and picked up the cooler. "Thanks, Yancy. Reed and the wranglers will be grateful."

He turned to Ally. "I'll give Reed your message."

"Thank you, Burke. And tell him I send my—" She stopped, aware of what she'd almost said. "Just tell him I send my best."

He grinned. "I'll do that."

She and Yancy stood at the back door and watched as the

foreman set the cooler in the bed of the pickup along with stacks of supplies. He secured everything with bungee cords before climbing to the driver's side and taking off in a cloud of dust.

Yancy filled two cups with coffee and handed one to Ally before touching the rim of his cup to hers.

When she looked up, he gave her a gentle smile. "I miss Reed, too."

She brushed a quick kiss on his cheek. "Thanks, Yancy." She stepped out the back door and sat on the step, watching as the sun slowly rose over the hills in the distance. The hills where Reed was saying good-bye to a herd in which he'd invested so much.

And all the while, she missed him with an ache that seemed to grow with every breath she took.

"I don't want to go, Mama."

Ally had anticipated Kyle's rejection and was quick to soothe. "I know. I don't want to, either. But I need to get back to work, and Uncle Archer was kind enough to offer us a room at his house."

"He doesn't like me. Why can't I stay here with Lily and Gram Gracie and Grandpop Frank?"

"Because I want you with me." She drew him close and pressed a kiss to the top of his head. "I missed you so much."

He looked up. "I missed you, too. But..."

"And this is only our temporary home. We knew we'd be going back to town when our place was repaired." When he opened his mouth to offer another objection, she quickly added, "I have an idea. Why don't we pack up some of our things and take them to Archer's before we go to work. And tomorrow, if Ingrid and Luke are okay with it, maybe they could bring Lily to town to spend the day at work with us, and you could show her all the new toys that have come in."

His eyes widened. "And could she spend the night with us, too?"

"If Luke and Ingrid don't mind."

"And could we take her to D and B's for grilled cheese sandwiches? And to I's for ice cream?"

"That would be fun."

"Oh, boy." His earlier disappointment was forgotten as he danced off to share his news with his best friend.

Ally quickly stuffed some of his clothes into a backpack and headed down the stairs. An hour later she and Kyle were driving toward town, while Kyle kept up a steady chatter about all the things he and Lily would do when she came to town to visit.

"And best of all, Reed promised when he gets back to the ranch he's going to teach me to ride a horse and be a real cowboy like him."

Reed turned his mount in the direction of the range shack when he saw Burke driving up across the meadow.

By the time Burke reached the cabin, Reed was there. He slid from the saddle and reached for the cooler in the back of Burke's truck.

"I'll handle this." He chuckled as he hefted it, testing its weight. "How many armies did Yancy think he'd be feeding?"

"He knows you and the wranglers have been making do with quick meals while you get the entire herd off this mountain. You know Yancy. If he could, he'd feed the world."

The two men shared a laugh as Burke held the door and Reed stepped inside.

"There's more," Burke added.

The two men worked companionably, returning to the truck several more times as they unloaded supplies and stored them on shelves.

Afterward, they helped themselves to a cold beer as they stood in the shade of a tree.

"These hills look bare, son. How're you feeling about letting go of your babies?"

"I'm feeling a lot of things. Relief. A little sad. They've been a big part of my life. But there's always next year's herd." Reed tried to keep his tone neutral. "How is Ally?"

"She's fine. She sends her"—the old foreman watched Reed's eyes—"regards."

Reed's lips curved. "You enjoying yourself, Burke?"

"Yeah. I notice the two of you are being real careful about what you say. But it's not the words you speak that matter. It's how you say them. Take Ally. She nearly slipped and sent her love, but she caught herself at the last minute."

"Thanks for telling me that. That sets my mind at ease. I'm sending"—he couldn't help chuckling—"kind regards her way, too."

"I'm sure you are. Oh, and she wanted you to know she's returning to work this weekend."

"So soon?"

Burke nodded. "Her apartment isn't ready yet, but Thorny and his crew have been working hard to get her back in business as soon as possible. I'm sure that little bonus you gave him was an incentive."

Reed flushed. "How'd you know about that?"

"I saw you hand him something when the two of you shook hands. Can't think of anything else you'd be giving him except maybe money."

Reed gave a negligent shrug of shoulders. "No big deal. I

just thought that might make things move a little faster. I'm glad he was able to make it happen. I just wish she didn't have that long drive every morning and night from our ranch to town and back."

"She won't be driving. Ally told me she and Kyle will be staying with Archer Stone until her apartment is ready."

Reed's smile faded. "Are you kidding me? She's had a taste of his temper. How could she put herself in his line of fire again?"

"She claims he's changed. The sheriff ordered him to take sensitivity training."

Reed stared at him with a look of disbelief. "I know how much family means to Ally. Archer is all she and Kyle have. She's desperate enough for family to believe anything he tells her. But I find it hard to believe a guy like that can change his behavior overnight." He gave a sigh of disgust. "Another week or more and we'd have the herds driven down for the season, and I could be there to chauffeur her back and forth so she wouldn't have to put up with Archer's hair-trigger temper." His voice lowered with feeling. "I want to support her decision, but I don't buy Archer's story that he's a changed man. Archer's a skunk. And even if you pour perfume on a skunk, it doesn't change his smell."

Burke was grinning from ear to ear.

Reed looked over. "What's that grin for?"

"You, son. You're complaining about Archer's temper, when your own is about to boil over."

"It's just that I'm worried about Ally."

"Sure you are." He made a sound that could have been a growl or a grunt of laughter. "You're sounding more and more like a man who, no matter what he says, has fallen head over tin cups for the lady."

* * *

As darkness settled over the hills, Reed sat alone beside the fire, brooding over Burke's words.

Head over tin cups.

It was the foreman's favorite expression for someone wildly, totally out of control, whether it was alcohol, temper, or love.

Reed tipped up his longneck and took a pull. There was no denying he was crazy about Kyle. That little freckled, redheaded kid with the big owl glasses had a way about him that tugged at Reed's heartstrings.

So did Kyle's mother. But that didn't make it love. There was no law that said just because he was worried about her safety and wished she was here with him right now, he was in love.

He had a right to worry about her. Look how much she'd been through. A guy who'd shamelessly used her, then refused to step up to his obligation. And then a guy so obsessed with her, he followed her all the way to Montana. It was true the stalker had been caught, and she was no longer in any danger from him. But sensitivity training aside, Archer Stone was still a loose cannon, and she was willing to place her trust in him. The guy didn't just get mad like other guys. He came unglued. Unhinged. Crazy mad. Always had. No doubt always would.

Reed rubbed at his temples. If he were honest, he'd have to admit that the trigger for Archer's temper wasn't Ally. She just happened to be in the line of fire. Archer's real trigger was a Malloy. Any Malloy. The very name set Archer's teeth on edge. At least for now, Ally should have smooth sailing with her uncle, as long as he didn't have to see a Malloy. The less Archer saw of Reed, the more he might be willing to forge a bond with Ally and Kyle.

Reed thought about all the hard work Ally had gone

through, getting that old building ready for her business and living quarters, only to have to start all over again after the fire. She deserved a chance to succeed.

She also deserved to be supported in her efforts. With the roundup of the rest of the herds well under way, if he pushed, he ought to be able to make it to town to surprise Ally on her grand reopening day.

The thought had his smile returning. His presence would catch her off guard. She wasn't expecting him. It would be fun to see the look on her face when she saw him standing in her shop. Those eyes going wide, and then that smile lighting all her features. And then later, when the crowd had left, and Kyle was asleep...

His eyes took on a faraway look as he stared into the fire. He couldn't wait to taste those lips. To inhale the soft, woman scent of her. To feel those gentle hands moving over him while he took her to bed and made wild, passionate love all through the night.

Just the thought of her there to greet him made these endless days and nights in the hills so much sweeter.

But it wasn't love, he told himself. It was...

Hell, he couldn't lie to himself.

It was love. Plain and simple.

Time to admit what he'd been working so hard to deny.

His poor heart took a hard, heavy bounce.

He was head over tin cups for Ally Shaw.

Ally filled a glass with orange juice and found herself thinking about the freshly squeezed juice Yancy provided at the ranch. How quickly she'd become accustomed to all his special treats. She would miss the comfort she'd found at the Malloy ranch. She'd discovered something amazing. The Malloy family didn't just share a name and a house.

They enjoyed each other's company. They talked, really talked, not just about important things, but about everyday things. They laughed together. Teased. Joked. Fought and made up. They were a real family. Not the imaginary family she'd carried in her mind. Not the sugarcoated family she'd conjured as a lonely child and an even lonelier woman. They were real, flesh-and-blood people who lived together, worked together, and accepted one another, warts and all.

Catching a glimpse of the clock, she poured milk over a bowl of cereal before heading up the stairs. In the cramped bedroom she shared with Kyle, she brushed a kiss over the top of her son's head as he struggled into his shorts. "There's juice and cereal on the table. I'll grab a shower and be downstairs in a little while."

Kyle turned. "Where's my shirt, Mama?"

She thought a minute. "Probably in the laundry basket. After working all day, and that long walk home, we were both hot and sticky. I tossed everything in Archer's washer. Afterward, I folded our things and left them in the basket."

"Okay." As Ally made her way to the bathroom, the little boy dashed down the stairs, carrying his shoes and socks.

As he passed Archer's room, he heard the strains of his uncle's usual loud, sad music.

The door slammed as he rummaged through the basket of clean clothes.

"Looking for this?"

At Archer's surly words, Kyle turned to see the glint of something shiny in the man's hand.

His eyes went wide. "My dog tags."

"Not anymore. You knew the rules. I warned you when you moved back in. I said drop them one more time and they're mine. So now I'm putting them in my room. You won't get them back until I say so." Seeing the tears welling up in the boy's eyes had his own narrowing. "Go ahead, you little crybaby. Maybe now you'll pay attention to my rules."

As Archer started down the hall, Kyle raced after him, his little legs pumping to catch up. The little boy paused in the doorway of his uncle's room.

Archer opened the bottom drawer of his dresser and lifted the lid of a box before dropping the dog tags inside.

As he straightened, his cell phone rang.

"Yeah?" He listened before saying, "Right, Sheriff. I'm on it."

Minutes later he slammed out of the house and drove off in his truck, tires screeching.

Ally descended the stairs and glanced at the kitchen table. The glass of juice and bowl of cereal lay untouched.

Kyle was sitting under the table wearing an expression she'd never seen before. He looked both sad and fearful.

"Something wrong, honey?"

Without a word he held up his shoes.

"Are those laces knotted again?" She caught his hand, helping him to stand, before setting the shoes atop the table and working out the knots in the laces. "You didn't eat your breakfast."

"I'm not hungry."

She touched a hand to his forehead. "You're a little hot. Are you feeling okay?"

Without a word he sat on the floor and slipped into his shoes.

Ally reached for her purse and the snacks she'd packed for midmorning. "We're late. I asked Gemma to come in and help me get an early start. Let's go, honey."

As they walked toward Main Street, Kyle lagged behind until she caught his hand. "I packed strawberries and string cheese and some peanut butter and jelly sandwiches. Whenever you feel hungry, help yourself. Okay?"

"Uh-huh."

"Here we are." She paused. Before she could fish her key out of her purse, she realized the door was unlocked.

As she stepped inside, Gemma waved from across the room. "I didn't expect to get here before you. Look at all the stuff that was on the doorstep this morning." She handed Ally an envelope. "This was taped to the biggest box."

Ally opened it. "Thelma Winter. She said she wants to sell all of it and will stop by tomorrow to talk about what I think it's worth." She set her purse on the counter and pulled on an old smock with deep pockets. Into each pocket she stuffed sheets of sticky labels and a pen. Gemma did the same before they began opening the boxes and bags. "Oh, my. Just look at all these household items. Won't they look great at our reopening? Oh, and, Kyle, look at this."

Ally pointed to a box of sturdy metal trucks. Instead of his usual enthusiasm, Kyle barely gave them a look before turning away to sit in a corner of the room.

Soon Ally and Gemma were busy sorting and labeling the assortment of household goods. And all to the chorus of saws and drills and hammers by the workmen in the apartment above.

"What ya doing, Gemma?" Kyle, still wearing his sad face, wandered into the girl's back room where she was seated on the floor, surrounded by bags of discarded clothes and handbags and jewelry.

"Jeremy brought these a while ago. When Thorny sent him to Bell City for some supplies, he stopped by a yard sale and the woman told him he could take everything that was left, or she was going to toss it in the trash."

"Wow." The little boy lifted up a gaudy red, white, and blue beaded belt. "Look at this, Gemma."

"Cool. I wish I could keep that for myself."

"Why don't you?"

She tousled his hair. "Because if I like it, somebody else will, too. And they'll be willing to spend money to have it. That's the name of the game. Jeremy and I are saving for our future."

"Oh."

"Come on, Kyle. Give me a hand with this stuff."

Soon he'd forgotten his earlier unhappiness as he and Gemma lost themselves in the wonder of their newfound treasures.

Ally started a new file on her computer and began typing in the description of each of the items left by Thelma Winter, her newest *client*. The very word had her smiling.

She and Thelma would go over the list together and decide on a fair price for everything. In the meantime, she'd labeled everything Thelma had brought in, so the proper client would get credit for the sale.

She was still smiling as the door to the shop was thrust open with such force it slammed against the wall. "I'm sorry. We're not open until..."

The words died on her lips at the sight of Archer, his face twisted in fury, eyes narrowed on her with a look of pure hatred.

"I told you my room was off-limits."

"Your room? I don't understand."

"Liar. You're not only a slut, but you're a filthy liar, too. The kid told you, didn't he?"

"Told me what?"

"Don't play cute with me. This isn't about your brat's damned dog tags anymore."

"Kyle's dog tags?"

"As if you don't know. Being his overprotective mama, you just had to go looking for them. And you spied on me, didn't you? And now you know the truth."

"You're not making any sense. The truth about what?"

He stormed across the room and caught her by the shoulders, lifting her off her feet with such strength, she cried out. "Archer, put me down. You're hurting me."

"Oh, I'll put you down all right. I'll put you down like a stray dog once and for all." He caught her by the wrist and dragged her across the room and out the door.

At the curb he wrenched open the passenger door to his truck and thrust her inside. In the blink of an eye he rounded the truck and stepped in, handcuffing her wrist to the steering wheel before taking off in a screech of tires.

CHAPTER TWENTY-FOUR

At the sound of Archer's voice raised in anger, Gemma and Kyle peered around the doorway in the back room, watching and listening in stunned silence.

The scene played out so quickly, there was no time to react.

One minute, Archer was shouting at Ally. The next he had grabbed her by the wrist and hauled her out of the shop.

Gemma and Kyle raced to the door to watch as the truck disappeared along Main Street. Gemma picked up Kyle and raced up the stairs.

The whine of a saw drowned out whatever she was trying to tell Jeremy. He took one look at her stricken face, and the little boy with his head burrowed into her shoulder, and hurried over to tap Thorny on the shoulder. The man turned off the equipment, leaving the room in sudden, shocking silence.

"Something's wrong." Gemma's breathy voice was the result of fear as much as her frantic race up the stairs. "Archer Stone just took Ally away."

"Away?" Thorny looked from her to Jeremy and back. "What do you mean he took her away? Where? Why?"

"I don't know. But he was really steamed about something. He was so hot, he didn't even notice us in the other room. Now this little guy's so scared, his teeth are chattering. I think we should take Kyle out to the Malloy ranch right away. Maybe they'll know what this is about."

They looked at the little boy, face hidden, body convulsed with sobbing, and Thorny gave a quick nod. "Jeremy, drive them to the Malloy place. I'll phone the sheriff and see if he knows what's going on. Maybe this is some kind of police business."

Jeremy was busy unfastening his tool belt as he led the way down the stairs. Minutes later he was driving along the interstate, while Gemma kept her arm firmly around the frightened little boy, doing her best to offer him some comfort.

Kyle sat in terrified silence, his little face buried against her shoulder.

"Well. Look who the cat dragged in." Luke looked up from mucking a stall as Reed slid from the saddle. "Looking good, bro. And smug. How does it feel to say good-bye to your prized herd?"

"It feels good." Reed ran a hand through his beard and grinned at Burke, who had accompanied him from the hills.

"You might want to think about a long, hot bath, son," the foreman said with a laugh.

Reed clapped a hand on Luke's shoulder. "Thanks for sending that crew of wranglers from Ingrid's ranch."

"No problem. Since I'm paying them to help with the roundup at her ranch next, I figured they could start earning their keep a little early."

"I'm grateful." Reed turned to greet Matt, who stepped out of another stall. "I hope Yancy has time to cut my hair. I need to make myself presentable before Ally's grand re-opening."

"Yeah." Matt shared a knowing look with Luke. "No sense having the girl of your dreams looking at you like you're her worst nightmare. And right now, bro, you're no dream lover."

They shared a laugh before Reed picked up a pitchfork. "Since I already smell like a trail bum, I may as well lend a hand with the stalls before I head into the house to clean up."

Matt slapped his back. "I like the way you think..."

They all looked up at the sound of a truck racing up the drive and spewing gravel as it came to a lurching halt.

"What the hell...?" Reed stepped out of the barn, followed by his brothers and Burke.

They watched as Gemma climbed down from the passenger side and lifted Kyle in her arms.

Jeremy stepped out of the truck and stood beside Gemma.

At that same moment the rest of the family began spilling out of the back door, gathering around in curiosity. Nessa caught hold of Matt's hand and gripped it tightly. Ingrid put her arm around Luke's waist while gathering Lily close to both of them. Great One, looking a bit shaky, stood holding on to Yancy's arm to steady himself.

Frank turned to his grandsons to explain the family's nervous behavior. "Sheriff Graystoke just phoned to say he doesn't have a clue what Archer is up to."

"Archer?" Reed looked from his grandfather to Gemma. "What's this about?"

As quickly as possible, Gemma described the scene she and Kyle had witnessed. "Deputy Stone didn't see us. And I guess he was so riled up, he didn't even think about Kyle. He was just really furious with Ally, though she didn't seem to know why."

Jeremy added, "So Thorny suggested I drive Kyle here to your place while he phoned the sheriff to see what he knew about this. We thought it might be some kind of police business. But now that the sheriff says he doesn't know a thing about it..." The young man's voice trailed off.

"Hey, little buddy." Reed reached out and tenderly took Kyle from Gemma's arms. For a moment he simply held him, feeling the tremors that rocked the little boy's body. Then he knelt and set Kyle on his feet before looking into his eyes. "I know you're scared and upset, seeing Archer take your mother. Is there anything you can tell me?"

Kyle sniffled and looked away.

Reed reached for his handkerchief and blew the boy's nose and wiped his eyes before saying gently, "Tell me about your morning. Was there anything different from other days?"

Kyle nodded.

"Want to talk about it?"

"Archer took my dog tags."

"Your dog tags? Why would Archer do that?"

"I forgot and left them on the floor with my clothes. He said I broke a rule and now they were his."

"And that's why he's mad at your mama?"

Kyle shook his head.

Reed struggled for patience. "Is there something else that happened, little buddy?"

Kyle looked down at the ground. "I saw Archer put my dog tags in his treasure box. He keeps one in his bottom drawer, just like me. Then he got a call from the sheriff, and he had to leave, and I did a bad thing, and now my mama's in trouble."

Reed tipped up his face. "After he left, did you go into his treasure box to find your dog tags?"

Kyle's lower lip trembled. "Archer said nobody could ever go in his room. He said he'd kill anybody who ever opened that door."

"But you went in there anyway?"

A chubby little fist wiped at fresh tears. "They're not his. He can't keep them. They're mine. Mama said they were my daddy's."

"Yes, they were. And now they're yours. So you went into his room. Did you get your dog tags?"

"Y . . . yes." His voice was soft as a whisper.

"Did you tell your mama?"

He shook his head. "She'd be sad. She said I should never go in Uncle Archer's room, 'cause he'd get mad and make us leave."

"So it was your secret. Where did you hide the dog tags?"

"I stuffed them in here real fast when I heard my mama coming down the stairs." Kyle reached into his pocket and pulled out the shiny tags. As he did, something sparkly was caught on the chain and slipped to the ground.

As Reed picked it up, his grandmother gave a loud gasp and took the item from Reed's hand. "Oh, sweet heaven."

While everyone stared at Grace, whose face had gone deathly pale, she turned to her father. "Look, Dad. It's Mother's ring." She placed it in Great One's palm.

For long minutes he merely stared at it, until his eyes were too filled with tears to focus. Finally he lifted it to his lips and kissed it before closing his hand around it.

Grace closed both hands around his before turning to the

others. "On the night of Patrick and Bernie's anniversary, Dad and I gave my mother's favorite ring to Bernie before leaving for town on the night she and Patrick..." She sucked in a breath. Seeing the blank look on their faces, she added, "Bernadette was so proud and happy. She was wearing it when she walked out the door."

As the enormity of it began to sink in, they were all shocked into silence.

It was Reed who asked what was on all their minds. "What in hell was Archer doing with a ring worn by my mother on the night she died?"

Archer, reeking of sweat and alcohol, turned the wheel of his truck, leaving the interstate and heading along a dirt road that snaked through the hills. Ally fought a rising panic as he drove like a madman.

If she'd thought his words, hurled like bullets, were frightening, his retreat into stony silence was much worse.

She waited as long as she dared, hoping the agonizing stretch of silence had somehow softened his attitude.

She fought to keep her tone reasonable. "Why won't you tell me what this is about?"

"Stop lying, you slut. You already know."

She wanted to scream at him. Instead, she was determined to keep from making things worse. "I don't. I swear, Archer, I don't understand any of this."

"You and your secrets. I should have known. You come to town with some phony story about leaving a big important career to start some stupid menial job in a backwater town like Glacier Ridge, and I bought into the whole lie."

"It wasn't a lie. I left for Kyle's sake. So he wouldn't have to spend years in day care and latchkey programs while his mother pursued a career. I wanted something simpler. I just wanted us to be a family. Why can't you believe that?"

"Liar!" His arm swung out and he backhanded her with such force, her head snapped to one side and she was forced to blink away stars. "I read the fax that came into the sheriff's office. I know why you're really here. You and those Malloys are all in this together."

Ally touched a hand to the blood that flowed from her split lip.

"You're just like her. You've lied so much, you don't know how to tell the truth anymore. But it doesn't matter now. Nothing does. Now that my secret's been discovered, all I can do is run as far and as fast as I can. But first I'll bury your miserable body so deep your bones won't be uncovered until the entire Malloy family is dead and gone."

He gave the wheel a twist, and they made a sharp turn to avoid a pile of rocks that had apparently slid from a cliff top into the middle of the road.

"Why are we way up here?" She hated the fact that her teeth were chattering and her voice was weak with nerves.

"My truck wouldn't get a mile on the interstate before it would be pulled over. By now, the sheriff will have the state boys joining in the manhunt. By using the back roads, I'll buy some time."

"Time for what?"

"To make a clean getaway. I'll stop at a small town, buy some hair dye, and get myself some wheels." He was talking to himself now, as though he'd already dismissed Ally as too insignificant to bother with. "I'll settle in a big city, where I can get lost in the crowd."

"What will you do for money?"

"I've got enough. Cash. No credit cards that can trip me up. I'll get a new identity. A job."

"Most employers run background checks before hiring."

"Shut up. I've got to think. I've made enough connections among the scum I've arrested over the years; one of them will be able to get me some documents with a new name." He floored the accelerator, pushing the truck to its limit. The vehicle flew along the narrow dirt road, leaving a cloud of dust in its wake.

As the truck climbed higher, Ally could see the Malloy ranch far below, with great herds of cattle darkening the pastures as they were being driven along trails, some in cattle-haulers, others in long lines of animals and wranglers.

Reed was somewhere in these hills. The thought brought a lump to her throat as she realized that he would never know what had happened to her or where Archer had buried her body.

He would do his best to find her. But in time he would move on with his life. He would have no other choice. He would marry. Have a family.

Family. Poor little Kyle. He deserved to be part of a loving family. Instead...

Once again, it was Kyle who would suffer the most.

Glen Lloyd had known that threatening to make her son an orphan was the perfect taunt. Nothing could hurt her more than the thought of Kyle growing up completely alone. No father or mother, no siblings, nor even a distant relative to offer him comfort and support.

One little boy, completely alone in this world.

The thought of it shattered her poor heart.

As the truck crested the hill and began its descent into a heavily wooded area of wilderness, Ally braced herself for what was to come. She looked longingly at the open window of the passenger side. How she would love to jump, if only she could get her hand free. She would prepare herself to fight if backed into a corner. She would do whatever it took to stay alive and return to Kyle.

But first, she had to try to stay one step ahead of Archer.

Desperate, she dipped her free hand into the pocket of her smock and felt the sheets of labels. She couldn't imagine anyone finding them in this desolate wilderness, but it was all she had. If she were to drop them at regular intervals, would they form a trail for someone to follow? Or would the breeze take them?

No matter. She had to do whatever she could. Praying Archer wouldn't hear the rustle of paper, she removed a sheet of labels and stuck her hand out the window, keeping it low enough that it wouldn't blow back inside the truck.

She held her breath, trying not to be caught staring at either Archer or at the back window of the truck. When they'd gone some distance, she removed a second sheet and did the same.

Her heart was pounding, afraid that any moment Archer would look in his rearview mirror and catch sight of the white sheets. But as they continued climbing, he seemed lost in his own plans for escape.

Though she knew it was a long shot, Ally continued dropping them at regular intervals, desperate to do something, anything, to mark their trail.

She would watch and listen, and pray. And whenever Archer decided to stop and kill her, she would have to be ready to fight with everything she had.

He was sick, of course. Absolutely mad.

But right now, as she dipped her hand in her pocket yet again and contemplated her next move, it seemed as if the whole world had gone mad with him.

CHAPTER TWENTY-FIVE

Sheriff Eugene Graystoke was ready for war. He drove his SUV equipped with all the bells and whistles at speeds up to one hundred miles an hour as he headed along the interstate. He slowed only when he turned off onto an asphalt side road.

He pulled up to the Malloy ranch to find the entire Malloy family on the back porch, passing around rifles and bullets.

"Hold on now." He slid out of his vehicle and strode authoritatively up the steps. "I know you're all feeling protective of Ally Shaw, but with my deputy involved, this is strictly police business."

"Like hell it is." Reed accepted a pouch of bullets from his grandfather. "With Archer on the run with a hostage, you need all the help you can get."

"The state police are on their way. They promised a team of sharpshooters and aerial surveillance as soon as they could be assembled."

"And in the meantime?" Reed asked. "Are we supposed

to just sit on our hands and hope they find Ally in time to save her life?"

"You don't know that Archer will hurt her."

"Are you talking about the Archer Stone we know? We're all aware of his hair-trigger temper, Eugene."

The sheriff turned to Frank Malloy. "Talk some sense into your grandson."

"Why should I? I agree. We need to get on Archer's trail as fast as possible, before he crosses into Canada and we're held up waiting for permission to hunt him down."

It was clear the older man had hit a nerve with the sheriff. "I've thought of that. I've already asked the state boys to check the border crossings."

"I doubt Archer will stop and ask permission to leave the country." Reed touched a hand to his grandmother. "You may want to stay with Great One and Yancy and the children, Gram Gracie."

She lifted her chin. "This may surprise you, Reed darlin', but Ally has come to mean as much to me as she does to you. Frankie and I have already agreed to take up the Cessna and see if we can spot Archer's truck."

Reed leaned close to kiss her cheek. "Thanks, Gram Gracie. I love you."

"I love you more. Now let's stop the chatter and get started."

Reed slung his rifle over his shoulder and started down the steps. "I'm going now."

Colin touched a hand to his nephew's shoulder. "I'll ride with you."

"Thanks, Colin. But if you don't mind, I need to be alone."

Colin nodded. "I understand. I'll follow in one of the ranch trucks." He trailed along behind.

The sheriff called to his back, "You don't even know where to start."

Reed never paused. "I'm starting on the back roads. I doubt Archer is dumb enough to try outrunning the state police on the interstate."

Frank took Grace's hand. "Come on, Gracie girl. The heavens are calling."

As they headed toward the barn that served as a hangar, Nessa and Ingrid stepped out the back door, dressed in denims and hiking boots.

Nessa caught up with Matt. "I'm riding with you."

"There's no telling how long we'll be on the road."

"It doesn't matter." She looped her arm through his. "I need to be there for Ally."

Ingrid stopped Luke. "Great One and Yancy will watch Lily and Kyle."

"What about you?"

She wrapped an arm around his waist. "We're a team. Remember?"

"Yeah." He draped an arm over her shoulder. "And don't you ever forget it, babe."

Burke turned to the sheriff. "I'm heading out, too, Eugene. Let the state police know we expect to be kept in the loop."

Sheriff Graystoke nodded. "I should have known I wouldn't be able to talk the Malloy family into letting me do my job without them."

"This is personal, Eugene."

"It's personal for me, too, Burke. Archer has been my deputy for more than twenty years. And now he's gone rogue…"

He turned to see Burke already striding away, carrying a rifle as he rushed toward the vehicle barn.

Even Jeremy and Gemma were running to Jeremy's truck to join in the search.

"What the hell." Eugene was muttering to himself as he climbed into his police cruiser and contacted the state police. "Sheriff Eugene Graystoke here. From now on, I'd like all means of communication turned to oh five hundred, our police call letters. That way, we'll all get the latest information at the same time."

From the Cessna he heard Frank Malloy acknowledge. Then he spoke into his cell phone and ordered those in trucks to keep their cell phones on speaker so he could relay any information.

From the various trucks came the voices of the other family members and friends as they acknowledged his instructions.

Alone in his truck, Reed muttered an acknowledgment as he steered toward a dirt trail that led away from civilization and snaked in a circuitous route to the very highest hills in the distance.

While he drove, he thought about what Kyle had accidentally found in Archer's treasure box. A ring once owned by his great-grandmother and given to his mother on the day she died. How had Archer Stone come by such a thing? What was his connection to the death of the two people so deeply loved by everyone in the Malloy family?

Maybe someday, when he had time to think about it, he would ponder what strange force in the universe had directed one little boy to the very place where such a treasure had been hidden for more than twenty years. It had to be fate that brought Kyle to come upon Archer's precious secret.

Was that the cause of Archer's hatred for all things Malloy?

For now, he was more concerned with what had happened to cause Archer to turn that hatred on Ally.

Ally.

Reed could see in his mind the gorgeous woman who had turned his life upside down. The minute they met, everything had changed. His carefree lifestyle had suddenly lost its charm. His obsession with becoming the most successful rancher in the state of Montana had lost its appeal. His love of solitude had morphed into a desire to share every minute of his life with Ally and Kyle. And the strangest fact of all was that he didn't mind the changes. He welcomed them.

He was happy just to be in Ally's presence. Hearing her voice. Seeing her smile. Making her son giggle. Spending time with the two of them felt right. His whole life felt right. He experienced a contentment he'd have never believed possible. But there it was.

She had forever changed him.

Because he simply loved her.

And right now, he was terrified that he would be too late, and the rare and wonderful light he'd found would go out of his life forever.

While Frank piloted the Cessna, Grace kept her gaze on the hills below.

This land, which had captured her heart all those years ago, held her so firmly she wasn't even willing to return to join her class for her college commencement. This land had brought her the man of her dreams and the family they'd made together. But right now, this land, with its hills and valleys, meadows and wooded hilltops, was hiding a monster and a frightened young woman who had come to mean so much to all of them.

"This all seems like a bad dream, Frankie. Ally kidnapped by Archer Stone. Her own uncle. Why? What could she have done to enrage him so?"

"The better question should be, what was Archer doing

with your mother's ring? Could it have anything to do with what's happening today?"

She shook her head, unable to fathom such a thing. "I know this much. Bernie was so thrilled with that gift, she told me she was never taking it off. There's no way she parted with it willingly."

"How could Archer steal it from her finger without her knowledge?"

Grace sighed. "That's what I keep asking myself. It simply isn't possible. So the logical answer is, he had to have taken it from her after..." Her voice trailed off. Even after twenty-plus years, she couldn't bring herself to speak of her son's death and that of his beloved wife. The loss to their family, the void in their lives, was always with them.

Frank caught her hand, lacing his fingers with hers. "Hold on, Gracie girl. We're going to find Ally alive. And then we're going to have our answers."

"Oh, I hope so." Tears filled her eyes and she blinked hard before returning her attention to the ground below.

"Believe it, my girl. We couldn't save Patrick and Bernie, but we've been given a second chance." He lifted her hand to his mouth, pressing a tender kiss to her palm. "No matter how slim this second chance is, we'll take it and make it work."

Reed drove across a meadow alive with wildflowers and wanted to curse every one of them for looking pretty and clean and ordinary on such a day. How could flowers bloom and birds sing when the woman he loved was being held by a madman? How could the sun shine on such a dark, cruel day?

For the first time in his life he felt like cursing the ranch that had demanded his time when he should have been with

Ally, keeping her safe. All his life he'd worked circles around his brothers, always keeping his goals plainly in sight. Stupid goals, he thought morosely. Doubling the size of the ranch. Raising the finest cattle in the land. Making the Malloy name famous the world over. And all to atone for the fact that his father and mother had died too young, without the chance to reach their own goals. Hadn't he always known why he pushed himself so hard? It had started with that terrible loss, and continued to this day.

And so he'd driven himself from the age of nine, thinking hard work and success would be an antidote for the pain of his loss.

Loss.

He couldn't lose Ally, too.

His childhood pain would be nothing compared to what he was suffering now and would continue to suffer the rest of his life if he didn't find her in time. If Archer hurt her...

He swore and turned up the volume on his cell phone, listening to the chatter among his family members and the state police already in the air and on the ground, crisscrossing the area, looking for any sign of Archer's truck.

"...Cloud of dust on Rooftop Ridge," Grandpop Frankie's voice intoned. "It could be coming from a vehicle moving fast."

"Circle that area and let us know how many ways we can get there," came Matt's voice over the phone.

"Will do." Frank's tone was thoughtful.

Reed turned his truck toward a distant road carved through the wilderness. It was little more than a trail formed by the wheels of some of their heavy equipment during roundup, when they brought in cattle-haulers to convey some of the herd to the lowlands.

As he started along the trail, his gaze swept the area,

searching for any sign of recent use. Tire marks. Crushed greenery. Anything that would hint of a vehicle having gone this way.

He passed a flutter of white and continued driving. When he passed a second, and then a third, he hit the brakes and leapt out of the truck.

He picked up a white sheet and studied it. It was too clean to have been outside for any length of time. He turned it over and over in his hands, tearing off one of the simple white squares with a wavy red border. It was clearly a sheet of labels, much like the kind used as name tags at church events. He'd seen these recently.

His heart nearly stopped. Of course he'd seen these.

At Ally's shop. On the day of her grand opening.

She'd been preparing for her grand reopening when Archer had abducted her.

He raced ahead and found another, and another.

He ran back to his truck and picked up his phone.

"This is Reed. Following up on the report of dust that could have been made by a fast-moving vehicle. I'm on a wilderness trail that leads to Rooftop Ridge, on the backside of my family ranch. There are no herds in this area, which means there are no wranglers. It's completely isolated."

He heard the buzz of conversation as the others began to comment, and the sheriff began issuing orders.

Reed broke in and there was a sudden, ominous silence as he added, "I've come across a trail of paper labels. They appear at regular intervals. I could be wrong, but I'm convinced Archer Stone has passed this way with Ally and that she's trying to signal their presence. Rooftop Ridge is the perfect place to commit a crime and hide the evidence, before getting away without a trace."

CHAPTER TWENTY-SIX

Reed drove like a madman, taking the twists and turns of the dirt trail without a thought to the fact that there were no guardrails, no protective fencing to keep a vehicle from going over the edge. The single track had a sheer drop-off of hundreds of feet into a steep, rocky ravine.

As he came up over a ridge, he saw the telltale cloud of dust in the distance, signaling another vehicle.

Archer. He had absolutely no doubt the deputy was up ahead. And with him, Ally.

After passing the information along to the others, Reed's mind was already working overtime to think of a way not only to catch up but also to force a confrontation.

Turning the wheel sharply, he veered off the trail and drove through a thick stand of evergreens, hoping to find a shortcut that might get him to the summit ahead of Archer.

* * *

Archer could feel his reflexes, always sharp and steady when fueled by liquor, beginning to dull. He craved another drink. There was a bottle stashed beneath the seat of his truck, but he couldn't risk losing his concentration as he navigated the narrow trail.

As he rounded another curve, he heard the sound of a plane's engines. Looking up, he saw the aircraft flying low in a circular pattern. With a vicious oath he hit the brakes.

Seeing a stand of trees to one side, he turned the wheel and drove slowly into the center of the woods, where his vehicle would be shielded from view.

He opened the door and stepped down before reaching under the seat for the bottle and taking a long, satisfying pull of whiskey. The familiar heat started low in his gut, burning a path of fire through his veins. And with it, a blaze of hatred.

The plane's engines could be heard directly above. His eyes narrowed. Police? Or Malloys? Not that it mattered. Right now, they were all banding together to stop him before he could hurt Ally. Being a lawman, he knew the drill. But they were too late.

Archer circled around to the passenger side and opened the door before uncuffing Ally's wrist and hauling her roughly from the truck.

She stumbled and quickly righted herself before trying to run.

"Why you—" He yanked her backward by her hair and pistol-whipped her until she dropped to the ground, dazed, blood spilling from the blow to her temple.

"You try that again, I'll beat you senseless. You understand?"

She fought back tears as she mopped an arm over her face to stem the flow. "Why are you doing this...?"

A shadowy figure stepped from the trees, causing both Ally and Archer to stare in stunned surprise.

"You're bleeding." Reed's voice was low with fury when he caught sight of Ally. He took aim with his rifle. "Drop your pistol, Archer."

In one quick move Archer wrapped an arm around Ally's neck, yanking her to her feet before pressing his gun to her head. "Now you drop yours, Malloy. Slow and easy." Archer's lips curved into a sneer. "You're talking to a man of the law. This ain't my first rodeo."

He watched with satisfaction as Reed tossed his rifle to the grass.

With a smile of pure pleasure, Archer took aim before calmly firing.

If Reed hadn't turned, it could have been fatal. Instead, Reed took a bullet to the arm.

Ally's screams filled the air as blood spurted from Reed's wound and ran in rivers down his shirt, his pants, and into the grass at his feet.

Pleased with himself, Archer thrust Ally aside before strolling closer to Reed and firing a second time, intending to finish him. A fountain of blood spurted, staining the front of Reed's shirt. The pain had him staggering to his knees and clutching his chest.

Out of the corner of his eye Archer saw a blur of motion and realized that Ally had taken that moment of distraction to run into the woods. He swore and started after her.

"You're not going to outrun me, you fool. You may as well give it up."

He paused in front of a giant fallen tree, layered with mounds of rotting leaves. A slow smile peeled back his lips. "You think you're so smart. That's the oldest trick in the books."

He kicked at the leaves and looked surprised when they

blew aside, revealing only empty ground beneath the fallen log.

When he turned, Ally was behind him, swinging a tree limb at his head. The force of the blow knocked him backward, and he fell over the log.

By the time he'd regained his footing, Reed was there, holding his rifle.

Archer appeared stunned. "You should be dead, Malloy."

Reed saw to it that Ally was safely behind him before saying, "You're a lousy shot, Deputy. Now it's your turn to toss aside your weapon."

Archer glowered at him before tossing his pistol into a nest of grass and leaves. "You think that's going to save the two of you, Malloy?"

"That, and this rifle, and the fact that the rest of my family are on their way here to back me up."

"You're going to need all of 'em. In fact, it'll take an army to stop me now, Malloy." Archer lowered his head and charged Reed, catching him in the midsection, knocking the rifle from his hands.

With a grunt of pain Reed shook his head to clear the stars that were floating across his line of vision.

The two men rolled around in the dirt, moaning in pain, exchanging blow for blow.

Ally picked up Reed's rifle. She'd never fired a gun in her life, and she dared not try to fire it now, for fear of hitting Reed instead of Archer.

She turned it around, intending to use it as a club. Above the sounds of the scuffle, she heard vehicles arriving, as well as several state police helicopters landing nearby. The whir of their blades sent the nearby trees into a frenzied dance. In the distance could be heard the drone of a Cessna as it landed somewhere out of sight.

Desperate, Ally raced from the woods, hoping to alert the new arrivals to what was happening.

Before she could say a word, the sheriff caught her by the arm and thrust her toward Frank and Grace, sprinting the distance from their plane.

"Here, Ms. Malloy." Eugene pushed Ally into Grace's arms before removing his gun from its holster. "See to her wounds."

"No. I don't need help. It's Reed. He's badly wounded, Gram Gracie." Ally turned to Frank. "You have to help him, Grandpop Frankie. Archer is trying to kill him."

Frank exchanged a look with Grace before hefting his rifle and joining the sheriff. A hurried exchange of words let Eugene know Reed was badly wounded and fighting for his life.

Eugene conferred with a cluster of state police in full gear who took up positions with orders to shoot the deputy if they saw an opening.

As they hurried into the woods, they could see both Reed and Archer bloodied beyond recognition.

The sheriff fired a shot into the air, hoping to put an end to the battle. Instead of drawing apart, Reed and Archer remained locked in mortal combat.

Those watching were aware that this epic battle could very well end with both men losing their lives, unless the deputy made an error and gave them an opportunity to take him out.

Sensing that Reed's wounds were taking their toll, Archer was on Reed like a feral animal, pummeling him about the head and face until Reed was blinded by his own blood.

Reed struggled to hold on. When he realized that Archer was frantically scrambling with one hand in search of his pistol, he made a valiant effort to roll free, but the gunshots had badly weakened him, and Archer's liquor-fueled strength proved to be too much.

Archer gave a snort of triumph as he suddenly pointed his police-issue pistol at Reed's head.

"I'm the one in control here." He looked around at the circle of sharpshooters. "You'll lower your weapons, or I'll blow his freaking head off."

At a single command from the sheriff, they did as he ordered.

"Now step back."

Again, they followed orders.

Archer glowered at the family and dragged Reed to his feet, his arm wrapped firmly around Reed's neck, using him as a shield. "If you don't want to lose another Malloy, you'll do the same."

Stunned by the amount of blood oozing from Reed's wounds, Frank, Matt, Luke, and Burke dropped their rifles, while the women, horrified by the sight of Reed's battered face, gathered around Grace to offer comfort and to draw strength from her.

Ally pulled away from the others, determined to distract her uncle.

It was Eugene who broke the silence. "What brought you to this, Archer?"

Archer turned to Ally, standing alone. "It didn't have to come to this, if the little slut hadn't meddled."

Ally moved instinctively closer to Archer and Reed. "If that's true, then let Reed go and I'll take his place."

At her words, Reed sucked in a breath and began struggling.

Archer seemed to be enjoying his new power. "Oh, I intend to kill both of you. But now that I know he's important to you, important enough that you'd give your life for his,

I'll just hold on to this Malloy and watch the rest of you squirm. And when he dies before you, you'll know it's all your fault, slut."

Ally held out a hand pleadingly. "I told you, Archer. You're not making any sense. I swear I don't know what this is about."

"Liar."

"She doesn't know, Archer." Reed looked at Ally and fought for breath as Archer's arm tightened on his throat. "Archer took Kyle's dog tags away and put them in his room. After Archer left, Kyle slipped into Archer's room and found his dog tags in Archer's treasure box. There was something else in that treasure box. Damning evidence that caught in the chain of Kyle's dog tags without his knowledge. When Archer got home and found it missing, he knew his secret had been discovered."

"What was it?" Ally took another step, hoping for the chance to touch a hand to Reed. Just a touch.

Despite the pain of his wounds, Reed managed to say, "A ring. A ring worn by my mother on the night she and my father died in the accident."

At the mention of Bernadette's name, Archer's face contorted with rage and pain, causing his trigger finger to twitch. "Don't you speak of her. Don't you dare speak her name." His eyes filled with tears and, to the amazement of all watching, he began sobbing. "Bernie was the love of my life. She was mine long before she ever met Patrick Malloy. Then he came along and dazzled her with his big ranch and fancy life. From the first time she saw him, she never even looked at me again. I hate Patrick for stealing my girl. And I hate him for being the son of a rich rancher. If I'd had all that, it would've been me all those years instead of Patrick."

At his words, the Malloy family stared at him with matching looks of astonishment.

"What about the night of the accident?" Eugene's voice had gone deadly soft. The voice of a professional interrogator, hoping to keep a man on the verge of insanity from going over the edge and doing something drastic.

Archer flinched, and for a moment those standing around feared he might snap and pull the trigger.

Instead his voice wavered. "I was at Clay's, drinking with Lon Wardell. Patrick and Bernie came in and started snuggling in a back booth, blind to everyone. I knew it was their anniversary. I'd counted every day, every year she'd been with Malloy. I sent them a round of drinks so they'd invite me over. Patrick said he didn't want to drink because he was driving his grandfather's Rolls." Archer sneered. "This was the guy who used to be my drinking buddy before he stole my girlfriend." His voice rose to a whine. "So I picked up the beer I'd ordered for Patrick and downed it in one long swallow before setting it down and walking back to my own table. It was Lonny who said it was too bad I couldn't get Patrick drunk so I could have an excuse to drive him home. That way I'd get a chance to drive his grandfather's big, fancy car, as well as time alone with Bernie. So I ordered another round and had it sent to their table, and then another. Later, when I saw Patrick hadn't touched any of the beers, I went over and drank all of them and left the empty bottles on his table."

"You wanted everybody to think Patrick was drinking?" The sheriff's voice remained soft and easy. "Were you setting him up to be killed?"

"It was an accident." Tears rolled unchecked down Archer's cheeks. Though he kept an arm around Reed's throat, he seemed unaware of anyone now. His voice rose higher with each memory. "I saw Bernie get up from the table and start toward the ladies' room, and I rushed over and dragged her onto the dance floor. I just wanted a chance to have my arms around her. But she said I was drunk and tried to push past me. Then Patrick walked over, and I was itching for a fight, to show Bernie what kind of real man she could have married. Instead, the two of them just headed for the door, after Patrick told me to leave his wife alone."

Archer's eyes blazed. "His wife. His wife. What about the fact that she'd been my girl before they met?"

Eugene stepped slightly closer, keeping his hands where Archer could see them. "Then what happened?"

"I wanted to hit him. He cheated me out of a satisfying, knock-down, drag-out fistfight so I could show him up in front of my girl."

"So you followed his car?"

"Huh." Archer puffed himself up. "That was a no-brainer. Nobody but a Malloy ever drove a Rolls in Glacier Ridge. Besides, anybody with any sense wasn't out on the roads in a snowstorm like that."

"But you were. And Patrick. Is that when you decided to kill him?"

"I swear I never intended to kill him. Maybe I would have, if he'd been alone. But I just wanted to smash that fancy car so Patrick would be in trouble with his rich old grandfather. So I stayed behind until I realized we were coming up toward that big old tree that stood on the turn just as you pull off the interstate. Then I speeded up, and as I pulled up alongside the car, Patrick saw me and hit the gas, trying to get away while waving me off. At the moment of impact, when my truck sideswiped the Rolls, it hit the tree with such force, I couldn't believe the wreck."

Archer went very still, returning in his mind to the scene.

"I ran around to the passenger side and dragged Bernie from the car. She was so still. I laid her in the snow and pressed my mouth to hers, hoping I could force her to breathe. When I realized she was gone, I guess I went crazy. I saw a pretty ring on her finger, and I slipped it off and told her it would always be a gift from her to me."

"What about Patrick? He'd once been your friend."

Archer's eyes went hard as flint. "He was all bloody and still. I knew he was dead. He deserved it, after killing my girl."

"So now he killed your girl?" Eugene moved closer. "How did you explain the damage to your truck?"

"You know. You filed the report."

"I know what you told me at the time. Why don't you tell me again."

"A couple of wranglers from a nearby ranch arrived on the scene, and one of them asked about the damage to my truck. I told them I'd just arrived, and it was snowing so hard, I couldn't stop on the snowy, icy road, so I bumped into the crushed Rolls. After that, they repeated what I told them, until everybody on the scene believed it."

"What about your drinking buddy, Lon Wardell? How did you keep him from talking?"

Archer's voice grew agitated. "That piece of…" He looked over at Luke Malloy. "Lon promised to always keep my secret. Then, when his life was on the line and he tried to use that information to save his miserable life, I saw my chance to get rid of him once and for all."

"So it was you who gave that order to the police sharp-shooters to open fire in Ingrid's barn?"

"Yeah. Served him right for thinking he could spill the beans on me."

"And you figured your last tie to Patrick and Bernie's death had been severed."

"Yeah. And then my niece and her brat had to come along and start poking into my life, and they ruined everything." He turned to Ally with a look of supreme confidence. "I read the fax from your big, important security company, saying they had proof that a crash from twenty years ago may have been deliberate. You're just like my sister. A traitor to her own family. You had to come back all these years later and say you wanted us to be a family again. I should've stuck to my guns and had nothing to do with you or your brat. As for the Malloy family"—he turned to Frank and Grace and actually smiled—"now you get another funeral."

As his finger closed over the trigger, Reed brought his booted foot back with such force, Archer dropped to his knees with a grunt of pain.

Ally caught Reed's hand and pulled him so hard he slammed into her, and the two of them fell into the grass.

Seeing their opening, the sharpshooters let out a deafening volley of gunfire that rang out in the still summer air.

CHAPTER TWENTY-SEVEN

Ally heard the hail of bullets resounding in her own chest. Or was that her heart pumping so furiously? She heard a moan. Fearing Reed had been shot in the cross fire, she was screaming as she freed herself from his weight and knelt over him.

Reed lay in the grass, blood oozing from a half dozen wounds, staining the grass beneath him.

"Oh, Reed. Hold on. Please, Reed. I love you so much. Please don't die."

Through thick layers of fog, Reed tried to say something that would reassure her. But though his lips moved, no words came out.

Grace knelt beside Ally, fighting tears.

Reed saw the pain and grief in his grandmother's eyes and struggled to comfort her. But though he fought to lift a hand to hers, his arm refused to move. He stared dumbly at it, wondering why his body was failing him.

The sheriff touched a hand to Archer's throat before getting to his feet and leaning over Reed.

He straightened and shouted, "We need a medic here. Now."

A team of state police medics raced over, checking Reed's vitals, injecting something to ease the pain while hooking him up to a bag of intravenous fluids.

The blades of the state police helicopter were already beginning to spin as the team lifted Reed to a gurney and raced toward it.

Ally covered her face and began weeping. "This is all my fault. If I'd never come here..."

Frank came up behind her and lifted her to her feet before giving her a shove toward the waiting copter. "There's no time for that now, girl. You go with Reed."

She was shaking her head. "It isn't my place to do that. You and Gram Gracie..."

"We have a plane to fly. Go." Grace put her hands on Ally's shoulders and began steering her toward the team of medics.

One of them offered Ally a hand up, and she climbed in behind the gurney. There was no time to utter a word of thanks or good-bye to all the family members and police who had teamed up to save her.

The helicopter lifted into the air and headed toward the medical clinic of Glacier Ridge.

Dr. Leonard Cross and his niece, Dr. Anita Cross, had grown accustomed to the chaos that always seemed to accompany anything even remotely connected to the Malloy family. As soon as they received the call from the police that Reed Malloy was being transported to town, they began preparing for the coming pandemonium.

Agnes, their devoted assistant, set up extra chairs in the exam room, knowing the Malloys would refuse to remain in the waiting room like other families. She even prepared an armchair for Nelson LaRou, esteemed patriarch of the family, who would no doubt try to direct the entire operation in that rich baritone he always used to his best advantage.

Patients who would have been discharged later in the day were being signed out as soon as their family members arrived to drive them home.

Still, despite all their attention to details, the doctors were surprised by the depth of emotion they could sense in the entire family as they began arriving. They realized that something monumental had occurred.

Instead of the usual shouting and teasing that seemed a necessary element of anything involving the Malloy family, this crowd seemed unusually subdued.

By the time Yancy pulled up to the entrance and helped Nelson, Lily, and Kyle from the truck, the others had assembled in the examining room. They stepped inside to join Frank and Grace, Burke, Matt and Nessa, Luke and Ingrid, and Ingrid's foreman, Mick, as well as Gemma and Jeremy.

Leaning on Yancy's arm, Great One refused the use of an armchair to stand with the others. Lily hurried over to hug her sister, Ingrid. Kyle walked up beside his mother, who had refused all medical help until Reed was taken care of. Like the rest in the crowded room, Ally was watching and listening intently as Dr. Anita examined Reed, describing aloud each wound to her uncle, who stood on the opposite side of the bed, making markings in a chart.

"Gunshot to the right arm. Clean entrance and exit. Gunshot to the right shoulder. Bullet still lodged in muscle. We'll treat for possible infection after removal of the bullet. Cheek swollen. No bones broken there. Eye blackened. Again, no bones damaged. Knuckles swollen and bloody. Minor damage." She moved to Reed's torso. "Several broken ribs..."

As she continued her litany, Kyle tugged on his mother's arm.

"Who hurt Reed, Mama?"

"Archer."

At the mere mention of that dreaded name, the little boy buried his face against her leg while the doctor's voice droned on.

At last Dr. Leonard turned to the crowd. "We'll be taking Reed to OR now to remove the bullet from his shoulder and repair any other damage as needed. If you folks care to go over to D and B's or Clay's, you'll have a couple of hours before you can see the patient." He turned to Ally. "As for you, young lady, you'll come with me now before you collapse."

Ally followed the old doctor from the room.

Instead of protests or complaints, the rest of the group filed from the room in silence and settled themselves in the waiting room, where they would remain until Reed and Ally would be taken to recovery rooms.

Anita pulled Colin aside and studied the pain in his eyes. "What's wrong, Colin?"

"I'm worried about my nephew."

"You've seen worse." She shook her head. "This is about something other than his wounds. I've had the opportunity to observe your family during a crisis. They're loud and more than willing to express their feelings. Tell me what's happened."

He sighed and drew her close, pressing his face to her temple. "You're right. It's much more than Reed's gunshot wounds or the fact that he was just in the fight of his life. But if you don't mind, I'd rather wait until the surgery is over.

Our family is reliving a loss that's more than two decades old, and deeper than anything we've ever suffered."

She put a hand on his cheek. "That's when you lost your brother."

He nodded.

"Let me operate on Reed and get him comfortable. There will be time enough for explanations later."

He brushed a quick kiss over her lips. "Thanks for understanding."

He caught up with his parents and offered his mother his arm. She shot him a grateful look as she leaned into him.

He glanced beyond her to Frank, holding Grace's hand. For the first time in his life, his father and mother looked their age. Both were bone-weary.

As he glanced around at the rest of his family, seated in silence, he wondered if his own face reflected the emotions he could read on all of them. They were shell-shocked. And trying desperately to process all that had happened this day.

It had become so much more than an attempted murder. It had ripped open raw, gaping wounds that, though decades old, had never healed.

Reed kept fading in and out of consciousness. He struggled to see the faces that occasionally hovered over him, but they were a blur. The pain came in waves, but mostly it was dulled by whatever the doctors were giving him through his IV.

Mostly he slept. His dreams were fragments of scenes from his childhood. Riding up to the hills with his father. Struggling to keep up with his brothers as they rode ahead, leaving him in their dust. His father telling him that one day he'd be as big as Matt and Luke, and they would look up to him the same way he looked up to them. His mother making

his favorite grilled cheese sandwich and telling him she'd
added something special: love. Bits and pieces of voices and
laughter and genuine tokens of affection that he'd thought
would always be there, but were now carried only in his
memories.

The sudden shocking void left after one cold, snowy
night, when his parents were taken away without warning.

His eyes flew open and he looked around the sterile hospital room until his gaze settled on Ally. She was in a
reclining chair positioned beside his bed, lying on her side,
her red hair spilling over one eye.

She bore the bruises of Archer's fists.

His heart contracted, experiencing fresh pain.

As if sensing he was awake, she suddenly sat up, shoving
hair from her eyes.

Reed struggled to speak. "How long have you been
here?"

She glanced at the big clock on the wall. "A day and a
night."

"Is Kyle with my family at the ranch?"

She nodded. "He wanted to stay here. Everyone did. But
Anita said you'd be out for a good long time. They finally
gave up and left."

He studied the heavy drapes covering the window. "Is it
day or night?"

"Midnight."

"You should have gone with them."

"Too late. They left hours ago."

"That chair looks uncomfortable." He patted the side of
his bed. "Join me over here."

"Anita won't like it."

"She's probably home and sound asleep. Come on, Red.
I want you here."

She reluctantly slid out of the chair and settled into bed beside him. When he tried to put an arm around her, he was forced to suck in a breath on the sharp burst of pain.

"See? This isn't right..." She started to slide away but his hand snaked out, closing over her wrist.

"I've still got one arm that works. Besides, if you had any compassion at all, you'd wrap your arms around me."

"Like this?" She snuggled close and did as he suggested.

"Oh, yeah. Now that's a lot better." He turned his head until his breath feathered the hair at her temple. "Do you mind filling me in?"

"On what?"

"I've got some blank spots in my memory. Is Archer dead?"

"Yes." Her voice was little more than a whisper.

"Did he admit killing my parents, or did I dream it?"

"He admitted it."

He sighed and fell silent for so long, Ally thought he'd fallen asleep.

"Was Archer the one who ordered the police to shoot Lon Wardell?"

"Yes."

"Bastard."

Ally went very still. When there were no more questions or comments, she drifted off to sleep. When next she awoke, Reed had turned away from her, lying as still as death.

She stared at his broad back, his muscled arms and shoulders, and absorbed a series of tremors along her spine. They'd had so little time together. And now...

He'd turned away.

She slid silently out of his bed and walked to the window. Outside, the first faint ribbons of dawn were streaking the sky.

She pulled on her boots and let herself out of the room before making her way down the empty hallway to a small kitchen, where she plugged in a coffeepot. A short time later she sat alone in the staff kitchen, watching the sun climb from behind the hills.

The Malloy family would be arriving today, since Dr. Anita had said they could take Reed home.

Home.

Everyone, it seemed, had a home. Where was hers?

She'd come here hoping to reunite with family and had been coldly rejected.

She'd found a warm and loving acceptance with the Malloy family and had thought, for a while, Reed's family could be hers, as well.

And now?

Now her family had brought pain and heartache to the Malloy family.

It wasn't something any of them would soon forget. As for her, it was branded into her memory for all time.

CHAPTER TWENTY-EIGHT

It was late afternoon when Burke walked into the clinic waiting room. Seeing Ally, he quickly removed his hat. "They tell me Reed can come home." He looked past her to where Agnes sat behind a reception desk. "Is he ready?"

The assistant nodded. "Dr. Cross is giving him last-minute instructions right now. She's already signed his release papers."

Minutes later Reed was pushed out in a wheelchair. When he spotted the ranch foreman, his smile grew.

"You're looking good, son." Burke leaned close, and the two clasped hands.

Burke stepped up behind the wheelchair and pushed it out the clinic doors to where the ranch truck was parked. While Ally held the passenger door open, Burke helped Reed inside. Ally climbed into the rear seat.

As they started toward the ranch, Burke said, "Yancy's been cooking and baking since he got up this morning. I hope you're bringing an appetite."

Reed put on sunglasses, shielding his eyes from view. "I doubt I'll eat much."

"Make an effort, son." Burke glanced in the rearview mirror and noted that Ally had put on sunglasses, as well. Which wouldn't be unusual, except that the day seemed to match their moods. Cloudy and overcast and threatening rain.

"Kyle and Lily are baking up some surprises of their own."

"They are? Well, I guess I'll have to fake an appetite."

"See that you do." Burke grinned.

As they left town behind and turned onto the interstate, Reed leaned his head back and covered his face with his big hat.

Out of respect for his need to sleep, Burke and Ally fell silent.

When at last the truck pulled up to the house, the entire family spilled out the back door and down the steps to welcome home their hero, with Lily and Kyle leading the parade.

Frank and Grace were the first to hug Reed.

"Oh, how grand to see you up and around," Grace managed to say through her tears.

"Don't cry, Gram Gracie." With his good arm Reed drew her close. "You know what that does to me."

"Welcome home, sonny boy." Frank started to give him a bear hug, then remembered his grandson's injuries in time to give him a more gentle embrace.

"Hey, bro." Matt slapped his back, while Luke tugged on his hair.

Their wives laughed and hugged him fiercely.

Great One, standing on the back porch, held out his arms, and Reed hurriedly climbed the steps to embrace him.

Yancy pumped his hand. "I'm sure you're sick of hospital food, so I've made all your favorites for your homecoming."

"Thanks, Yancy." Reed turned to find Colin coming up behind him.

"I'm glad you're home where you belong," his uncle said.

"Me too. I figured you'd pick me up at the clinic so you'd have an excuse to see Anita."

"I wanted to. Chores," Colin said by way of explanation. "Thank the heavens Anita's as busy as me, and understands."

"Well." Grace noticed Ally standing back and looped her arm through the young woman's. "Come on. It's time we gave Reed a real Malloy welcome."

The kitchen was perfumed with the most wonderful, mouthwatering fragrances. Over the table hung a hand-lettered banner that read: WELCOME HOME. It was obvious that Lily and Kyle had spent hours decorating it with drawings of horses, cattle, and even a dog and her puppies. And in the middle of the banner stood a tall stick man that was undeniably Reed.

Reed took long minutes to examine every drawing.

"What do you think?" Lily asked.

"It's the best homecoming banner I've ever had."

The two children were beaming with pride.

While the men tipped up frosty longnecks and the women sipped cool white wine, Yancy and the children began carrying trays and platters to the ornately decorated table.

When Yancy summoned them to eat, they began passing platters of slow-roasted beef in gravy and steaming bowls of mashed potatoes, as well as tender peas and carrots from the garden and baskets of hot rolls fresh from the oven.

"I see you fixed all my favorites."

"This is a celebration." Yancy circled the table filling goblets with ice water.

Luke turned to his wife. "I guess it pays to get into a

brawl every now and then, just so Yancy remembers our favorite foods."

Ingrid closed a hand over his. "Your brawling days are over, cowboy."

Everyone was chuckling as they dug into their meal.

If Reed was silent, allowing the others to carry on a conversation, it didn't seem unusual. He was, after all, still recovering from an exhausting, painful ordeal.

Kyle looked across the table at the dressing on Reed's shoulder. "Does that hurt?"

"Not much." Reed moved the food around his plate before draining his beer.

When the meal ended, Kyle turned to Lily. "Want to give Reed our surprise now?"

The little girl looked at Yancy. "Is it okay?"

He nodded and the two children pushed away from the table, returning with a plate of cookies.

"They're your favorite," Kyle announced.

Reed pretended surprise. "Chocolate chip?"

"Uh-huh."

He chose the biggest one, causing the two children to giggle. He bit into it, then made a terrible face and pretended to gag. Seconds later, when they realized he was having fun with them, they both broke into laughter.

"You were just teasing, weren't you?" Lily scolded.

"You bet. These are the best I've ever tasted." He indicated the plate. "Want to pass them around, or are you saving them all for me?"

Lily and Kyle circled the table, offering their special treats to everyone and smiling proudly at all the compliments.

After emptying the plate of cookies and drinking their milk, Kyle turned pleading eyes to his mother. "Can me and Lily go and see Molly's puppies now?"

Ally shrugged. "I'll leave that up to Ingrid."

Ingrid smiled. "You two have been so good, and I know you're dying to get to the barn. Go ahead."

The boy and girl caught hands and flew to the door.

While the men sat around the table, bringing Reed up to date on the progress of the last of the roundup, the women helped Yancy clear the table.

A short time later, they all strolled out to the barn to admire Molly's brood.

Kyle was cuddling his favorite pup as he walked over to Reed. "Look how big Toughie's getting."

"If he keeps on growing like that, you'll soon be able to ride him like a pony."

"I won't need to." Kyle nodded toward the pasture. "You said when I'm big enough to ride, Freckles will be just the right size, too."

"I did promise you that, didn't I?" Reed dropped his good arm around the boy's shoulders. "I can't wait to take you riding, little buddy."

"Me too."

"All right," Ingrid called. "It's Lily's bedtime."

Kyle set Toughie in the pen with its mother and the other pups before taking Ally's hand.

As they walked to the house, he was talking a mile a minute. "Me and Lily . . . Lily and I had the best day. We colored that banner for Reed. And then we baked cookies. And we picked the peas and carrots from the garden." He looked up with wide eyes. "Yancy even let me dig some of the carrots. Then me and . . . Lily and I got to take turns mashing the potatoes. Yancy said we're getting so good that pretty soon we'll be able to cook right alongside him. And you know what's the best thing of all today?"

"What?" Ally said softly.

"Seeing Reed back home with us. Isn't that the best thing of all?"

Ally nodded and was forced to swallow the huge lump that was lodged in her throat. "Yes, it is."

He was still smiling as they climbed the stairs to his bedroom. And when he'd undressed and put on his pajamas and climbed into bed before saying his prayers, he was still smiling. When his eyes finally closed and he'd fallen fast asleep, the smile was still on his lips.

As Ally made her way downstairs, there was a knock on the door, and Eugene Graystoke stepped in.

"Evening, folks." He whipped his hat from his head and paused in the kitchen to shake Frank's hand. "I wonder if I could have a few minutes of your time."

"Sure thing, Eugene." Frank indicated the great room, where the rest of the family had gathered.

Grace smiled. "Good evening, Sheriff. Would you like some coffee and dessert?"

"Just coffee." He looked around at the family. "I finished meeting with the state police detectives." He turned to Great One. "Nelson, they were grateful for that report you received in the mail from Ally's former employer."

Everyone turned to look first at Great One, and then at Ally.

Great One merely smiled. "It came while you were at the clinic. I passed it along to Eugene."

The sheriff nodded. "And I passed it along to the state police. Now I'll try to give you their summary."

Yancy handed him a cup.

Eugene sipped before setting it aside. "Those state boys did a thorough search of Archer's house." He looked down at his feet, choosing his words carefully. "I know that what I say will be painful for all of you to hear, but it has to be said.

They reported that Archer's bedroom looked like some kind of shrine to Bernadette. His desktop and dresser were lined with framed pictures of her, many of them with someone cut out, probably Patrick."

Everyone went silent.

"He had an old boom box, loaded with music from the eighties. Kenny Rogers singing 'Lady.' Rick Springfield's 'Jessie's Girl.' The lead detective said they were badly worn, as though he played them a lot. He also said this is a classic behavior of arrested development. Archer was stuck in another time and place." The sheriff began turning his hat around and around in his hands, looking distinctly uncomfortable. "The state boys think once Archer made that fatal decision that caused Patrick and Bernadette's death, he couldn't move on. He wanted her back, but he wanted her as he'd first known her. It's a sad testament to his sick mind. He's been living in his own private hell for all these years, loving her and knowing he'd caused her death. And none of us put it all together. We just thought his drinking and temper tantrums were part and parcel of who he was." He coughed, hoping to hide his discomfort. "I made a serious error in judgment all those years ago by accepting my deputy's word about the damage to his truck. The report sent from that security firm to Great One corroborates what Archer admitted to."

He picked up his cup and drained it. "I'm really sorry to cause you folks all this pain a second time around, but you deserved to know the full story. And at least now"— he stared pointedly at Great One—"your long-held theory has been proven true. Their deaths all those years ago on a snowy road weren't caused by alcohol or because of driving an unfamiliar vehicle."

He jammed his hat on his head. "I'll say good night now."

"Thank you, Eugene." Grace's good manners forced her to speak over the lump in her throat.

The family sat listening to the sound of his footsteps as he crossed through the kitchen. The back door opened and closed.

In the silence that followed, Ally got slowly to her feet. "I'm sorry. I'm so very, very sorry for what my uncle did to your family."

Reed lumbered to his feet. "Ally, this isn't about you…"

She backed away. "Archer was my uncle. And what he did to all of you is unforgivable."

"Ally…"

When Reed started toward her, she held out a hand. "Please. Don't say a thing." She looked around wildly. "I'll…I'll leave you all now. You deserve some privacy as you grieve."

She hurried up the stairs. Moments later they heard the closing of her door.

Grace gathered her family close and hugged each of them in turn, though they exchanged few words before going off to their separate rooms to process in private all they'd heard.

When Reed passed Ally's room a short time later, he could hear the sound of crying. But when he tried her door, it was locked.

"Ally. Let me in. Please."

Though he knocked several times and called softly to her, his pleas went unanswered.

He moved stiffly on to his own room, where he lay fully dressed on his bed, too weary to bother undressing.

The wounds to his heart felt deeper than any inflicted by Archer.

CHAPTER TWENTY-NINE

Kyle and Lily bounded into the kitchen, their faces wreathed in smiles.

"We've named all the puppies," Lily announced.

"All of them?" Yancy turned from the stove. "Do you think that's fair? What about the people who might want to adopt them?"

The two children seemed stunned by his question.

"Can people 'dopt them if they're ours?" Kyle asked.

Lily shook her head and turned to Frank. "They can't, can they, Grandpop Frank? Aren't they our puppies?"

He shared a grin with Grace. "Well, technically, Molly is Luke's dog, so I guess they're yours, too. But I'm not sure Luke and Ingrid want that many dogs. Usually, when neighbors hear about a new batch of pups, they drop by to see if they may want to adopt one or two."

The two children looked stricken.

The rest of the family struggled to hold back their smiles.

Reed, freshly showered, put an arm around Kyle's shoulders. "How many do you want?"

The little boy's eyes grew round. "Can I have more than one?"

Reed glanced at his brother, who was grinning like a fool. "It'll be up to Luke. But I might put in a good word for you, little buddy."

"Oh, boy. Come on, Lily." He caught her hand and the two of them headed for the stairs. "Let's go tell my mama."

When they were gone, Grace turned to Reed. "Did you get a chance to talk to Ally last night?"

He shook his head. "She was asleep." He thought it best not to mention what he'd heard or the fact that her door had been locked against him.

Colin poured himself a cup of coffee. "I was worried about her reaction to Eugene's report, so I phoned Anita. She said she's not surprised that a sensitive woman like Ally bears the burden of guilt for what her uncle did."

Reed was instantly alert. "What's Anita's advice?"

Colin frowned. "She didn't have much. Just that the two of you need to open up and be completely honest. If there's any lingering anger on your part, you need to deal with it."

Reed's tone hardened. "I've got plenty of anger. But not toward Ally. All my anger is directed toward that lowlife uncle of hers."

Before he could say more, Kyle and Lily came running into the kitchen. Kyle's eyes were red with tears.

"Hey, now." Reed dropped to his knees. "What's wrong?"

The little boy removed his glasses and rubbed the back of his hands over his eyes. "Mama's packing our things. She said we're leaving."

"She has a business to run in town."

Kyle shook his head. "No. She said we're leaving Montana and going back to the city."

Reed stood up and looked at his family, who had gone ominously quiet.

He held out his hands. "Come on, Kyle. Lily."

"Where are we going?"

"To the barn." Over his shoulder he called, in a tone that left no doubt of his pain, "When Ally comes downstairs, tell her where she can find us."

Ally carried her overnight bag and Kyle's backpack down the stairs. Before stepping into the kitchen, she paused and dragged in a quiet breath, prepared to face the Malloy family. From the chorus of voices, it seemed all of them were present.

"Morning, Ally." Frank was the first to greet her.

"Good morning." She set the baggage in the corner of the room before straightening.

Ingrid and Nessa walked up to stand on either side of her, forming a wall of support.

"How are you feeling today?" Ingrid touched a hand to her arm.

"Fine." Ally jerked back. "My injuries were nothing compared to Reed's."

"Oh, I don't know about that." Great One set aside his cranberry juice, which, at his request, Yancy had spiked with a splash of vodka. "Sometimes the wounds you can't see are the deepest."

Ally blinked at the tone of his voice.

Before she could say a word, Yancy handed her a glass of orange juice. "How about some eggs, Ally?"

"No thanks."

"You need protein to start the day."

She shook her head and touched a hand to her midsection.

"I couldn't eat a thing. Really." She looked around. "Where is Kyle?"

"Out in the barn with Reed."

"Well, then." She swallowed and began speaking quickly, so she wouldn't lose her nerve. She'd spent half the night rehearsing what she would say. "I want to thank all of you for what you've given Kyle and me. We were homeless, and you took us in and made us feel so welcome. I can't tell you what it has meant to me to see Kyle belonging to a family like yours, if only for a little while. And again, I realize I can never atone for the horrible crime my uncle committed against your family. I'm sure you understand why we have to leave."

"Oh, Ally." Grace was crying softly.

"All I ask is that one day you can forgive me."

"Now, Ally girl…" Frank cleared his throat, struggling to find the words.

The others began offering protests.

"I quite agree." At Great One's booming voice, the room fell silent.

Ally's head lowered and she stared hard at the floor.

"Dad…"

Great One hushed Grace's words with a withering look before turning the full force of his formidable energy on Ally. "Do you recall a conversation we had one late night?"

Her head came up. She nodded.

"I told you about two impossible love matches. Two completely unsuitable couples who, beyond all rhyme and reason, meshed their lives, their ambitions, their hearts, into happily-ever-afters. Do you want that, Ally?"

"I don't deserve…"

"That's not what I asked. Is that what you want?"

Her voice was a whisper. "You know it is."

"Then go get it."

"But Reed..."

"Is a mere man, hopelessly in love with a woman who holds all the power." He pointed to Luke and Matt. "Ask his brothers."

As the old man's tough-love strategy dawned, the two were suddenly grinning like fools.

"He's right," Luke said. "I'm putty in Ingrid's hands."

Matt followed suit. "I'd walk through fire for Nessa. And she knows it."

Like the iconic director he was, Great One lifted an arm and pointed his fingers in imitation of the character Moses he'd directed in one of his finest films. "If that is what you want, Allison Shaw, go. And seize your impossible dream."

The entire room went silent as Ally strode out the door.

Ally stood in the darkened entrance to the barn, not quite certain how she got here. Great One's words had propelled her, despite all the guilt and fear that had taken over her senses. And now here she stood, watching Reed, who was kneeling beside Molly's pen with Lily and Kyle. A half dozen balls of fluff wriggled and danced around them.

Kyle's voice rose in a plaintive wail. "Who's going to 'dopt Toughie when I'm gone?"

"I'll take care of him." Lily had her arm around the little boy, trying to soothe. "And when you come back—"

"Mama says we're going away for good. Even if I come back when I'm old enough to leave my mama, Toughie won't even know me."

"He'll know you." Lily turned to Reed. "Won't he?"

Reed gathered them both close. "Toughie will never forget you, little buddy. A dog's heart is a special thing. Once he loves, that person is imprinted on his heart forever. No matter what you do, or where you go, he will know you and love you. You're his special person. Don't you forget that. Just the way you're special to me."

"You're my special person, Reed." Kyle started to cry. "I can't leave you and Lily and Grandpop Frankie and Gram Gracie, and…and… everybody else. You haven't teached me to ride a horse yet. Or how to be a cowboy. Please don't let my mama take me away."

"Hey, now." Reed got to his feet and picked up the little boy, wrapping him tightly in his arms.

For a moment Kyle's eyes were too filled with tears to see. As he slipped off his glasses and wiped them with his fists, he caught sight of a figure in the doorway. He quickly slid on his glasses, and the figure came into focus.

"Mama."

Reed turned.

Ally had to blink several times before her own eyes were clear.

Reed stayed where he was. "Did you come to say goodbye?"

"That was my intention. But then Great One told me that was wrong. What I should be doing is seizing the impossible dream."

Reed set Kyle on his feet. At once the little boy ran over to Lily and clutched her hand in his.

While the two watched, Reed took several steps closer to Ally, until they were inches apart.

"What's your impossible dream, Red?"

"A year ago, I would have said I wanted a clean slate. A chance to start over. But your great-grandfather pointed out that it would mean not having my most precious gift, my son. So now this is my impossible dream." She swept her hand. "This. Land so big and grand, it takes my breath away. Horses and puppies for my son. His best friend, Lily. A family like yours, that loves unconditionally. But most of all...you, Reed. A man so good I don't deserve you."

"And all along I was the one feeling unworthy." He touched a big, rough palm to her cheek. "From the time I was a kid, all I've ever cared about was this ranch. And the herds. I've been obsessed with making it all bigger, better, more important. Since meeting you, I realize my focus is too narrow. I've fallen head over tin cups for a freckle-faced kid and his mother, and if you ever leave me..." He shook his head. "Please don't go, Ally. I need you in my life. You and that little cowboy." He turned to beckon to Kyle.

Puzzled, the little boy kept his hand firmly tucked into Lily's as the two walked up to Reed.

Reed knelt down and whispered something to Kyle.

The boy solemnly nodded.

"You're sure?" Reed asked.

Kyle shoved the round glasses in place before giving a wide smile.

"All right then." Reed stood and turned to Ally. "Now that I have your son's permission, Ally, will you marry me?"

She was struck speechless.

"Mama." Kyle tugged on her hand. "Pleeease say yes."

"Yes." She knew her eyes were filling, and she didn't want tears to mar the moment, but there was no way to stop them. Instead of words, she wrapped her arms around Reed's neck and hugged him fiercely.

"Was that a yes?" came a chorus of voices from the doorway.

Reed and Ally turned to find the entire family gathered around the entrance to the barn.

Kyle and Lily were dancing up and down while shouting, "She said yes."

Reed looked happier than anyone could ever recall as he stood with his arm around Ally, while the family came rushing toward them, calling out their good wishes.

Taking up the rear was Great One, leaning on Yancy's arm.

"Well." He was looking smug. "Since I feel I had a hand in this, I would beg a favor."

Ally caught his hand. "Anything."

He winked at his great-grandson. "I believe I should like to be the one to give the bride away."

She leaned close to press a kiss to his cheek. "Nothing would make me happier."

As the family began making their way back to the house with visions of a grand party in their minds, Reed caught Ally's hand, holding her back.

When they were alone, he gathered her close and kissed her, pouring all his feelings into it until they were both breathless.

When at last they came up for air, he framed her face with his hands and stared hungrily into her eyes. "I'm willing to celebrate with the others right now, as long as you promise me a private celebration after Kyle's asleep tonight."

"It's a promise."

"And one of just many, I hope."

As they turned to join the family, he kept his arm around her waist. Glancing at the brilliant blue sky, he started to chuckle. "For the first time in my life, I'm looking forward to winter. Maybe, if we're lucky, we'll be socked in by a blizzard, and we'll have to come up with all sorts of ways to pass the time."

"I like the way you think, cowboy."

He nuzzled her ear. "Anything to please you, Red. Pleasing you is what I want for the rest of my life."

EPILOGUE

T ake a deep breath, Gracie girl. You can smell the crisp air of autumn." Frank Malloy stood on the back porch with his arm around his wife, watching the activity going on around them.

The highlands were bare of herds. Some had been shipped by cattle-haulers, others moved to lower elevations for the winter.

There was a rare sense of endings and beginnings rippling through the family as they gathered for the wedding of Reed and Ally.

Tables and chairs had been set under a huge tent in the yard. Baskets of flowers appeared mysteriously overnight. A side of beef had been cooking over a fire pit all night. The wonderful perfume of barbeque permeated the air.

Yancy, directing an army of wranglers who'd been pressed into kitchen duty, was in his element.

Grace leaned close. "Look at that sky."

Puffy white clouds floated in a sea of blue. A gentle

breeze ruffled the branches of the ponderosa pines growing in profusion all across the hills.

Frank nodded. "I think Mother Nature is smiling on us in honor of this special day." He kissed her cheek. "And lucky for us, all our chicks are here in the nest."

"It's been a long road, Frankie."

"That it has, Gracie girl. But such a happy one."

"I wouldn't have traded it for any other." She patted his arm before turning away. "I'm needed upstairs."

"And I'm heading over to the meadow."

With a kiss, the two went their separate ways.

Reed, looking handsome in a starched white shirt and string tie, his boots polished to a high shine, sauntered downstairs to find Yancy in the kitchen, frosting a huge cake.

When the cook spotted Reed, he shooed him away. "You can't see your wedding cake until it's ready."

"Okay." Reed looked around. "Where is everybody?"

Luke stepped into the kitchen. "The women are upstairs in Ally's room having a hen party. Nothing like a wedding to get their juices flowing. Grandpop Frankie said to get our hides over to the gravesite for our manly ritual."

"Speaking of manly, I'd better get our little man, Kyle."

"He's already there. He was the first one dressed today."

Reed grinned. "You think he's a tad excited?"

"He's not the only one, bro. Where's your brain this morning?" Luke pointed to Reed's boots. "They're on the wrong feet."

With a stupid grin on his face, Reed sat on a bench in the mudroom to switch his boots to the proper feet before the two brothers walked, punching each other's shoulders and laughing like loons.

When they reached the family burial plot, Matt produced

a bottle of good Irish whiskey and a tray of tumblers. After passing them around, they solemnly turned to the simple headstone of Patrick and Bernadette.

Frank lifted his drink. "Here's to the two lovers gone too soon, yet always with us in spirit. I know they can finally rest in peace, knowing we've uncovered the truth. And I believe they're smiling down on their youngest son this day, as he adds more love to our family."

They drank before Matt refilled their tumblers.

Great One's voice was strong as he lifted his glass. "Here's to love. It's the glue that binds us all."

They drank again.

Matt turned to his uncle. "And here's to Colin, the last holdout. Let's drink to some of that glue sticking to him."

With a chorus of laughter, they all drank.

Lily, wearing a frilly dress of pale orchid, came dashing up the hill. She was out of breath as she announced, "Ingrid says Reverend Townsend is here."

As the men turned away, Reed offered his arm to Great One.

"You look happy, sonny boy."

Reed laughed. "Happy is too tame a word, Great One. Right now I feel like the luckiest guy in the world."

When they reached the ranch house, Reed left Great One in the kitchen, chatting with Yancy, while he signaled for Kyle to follow him.

"Where are we going?"

"Upstairs, to see your mama."

Kyle's eyes rounded. "Lily said we weren't allowed upstairs before the wedding."

"Is that so?" Reed winked. "Don't quote me, but some rules were meant to be broken. Come on." He caught the boy's hand, and the two of them climbed the stairs.

Outside Ally's room, Reed knocked on the door and the sound of feminine laughter inside faded.

The door opened a crack, and Nessa peered around. "Is it time to go?"

"It is."

The door closed. Moments later it opened and Nessa, Ingrid, and Grace stepped out, looking flushed and happy.

As Reed started into the room, Ingrid caught his arm. "No. Wait. You can't see the bride until—"

Seeing the determination in his eyes, she stepped away, calling, "Ally. There are two eager gentlemen here to see you."

As the women descended the stairs, Ally called, "Come in."

Reed and Kyle stepped inside and then stopped, staring at the vision in an old-fashioned white dress with a high lace dog-collar, long, tapered sleeves, and a scalloped hemline that fell to her ankles.

Reed shook his head. "You look like a picture in my grandmother's album."

"That's because this is Gram Gracie's wedding gown." She stared down at herself as though she couldn't quite believe what she was seeing. "When she first offered it, I said I didn't feel I should. But then I admitted that it was gorgeous and told her I'd love to wear it, and she and I both cried." Her lips quivered. "I seem to be doing a lot of that lately."

"Maybe this will dry your tears." Reed nudged Kyle, and the little boy brought his hand from behind his back to present her with a lovely nosegay of white roses.

"Oh." She lifted them to her face to hide a rush of fresh tears.

Lily poked her head in the door. "Great One said you're holding up the show."

Reed laughed and offered Ally his arm, while Kyle moved to her other side and did the same.

The three of them walked down the stairs together and found Great One, looking elegant in one of his many custom-tailored tuxedos from another era, waiting impatiently.

Reed pressed a kiss to her cheek before whispering, "Kyle and I will see you in the yard."

When they walked away, Great One stared at Ally, blinking furiously. His famous voice sounded strained. "I've seen that dress before."

"It was Gram Gracie's."

He nodded. "But I only got to see it in pictures. I was such an arrogant prig, I never made it to her wedding to Frank." He offered his arm. "Now I get to do what I was too foolish to do for my own daughter. And that makes you my other daughter."

As she tucked her arm through his, he leaned close. "Welcome to our family, Allison Shaw. I hope you know how much we all love you."

"It can't be more than I love all of you." To the strains of a guitar playing a tender love song, with Lily walking in front of them, she began to walk with Great One, down the porch and into a day filled with sunshine.

In the crowd she saw Dot and Barb Parker, heads bent, gathering as much gossip as they could for those who couldn't be here. Every little detail would be repeated a dozen times or more by the end of the day. Ally nodded and smiled as she walked past Gert and Teddy Gleason, Clay Olmsted, Trudy Evans, Gemma and Jeremy, and so many of the citizens of Glacier Ridge who were delighted to be invited to this grand event at the Malloy ranch.

When they reached the preacher, Great One kissed Ally's

cheek before placing her hand on Reed's. Her other hand was caught firmly by Kyle, who looked up at his mother with shining eyes.

With Matt and Nessa and Luke and Ingrid standing on either side of them as witnesses, Reed and Ally spoke their vows.

Afterward they accepted the warm wishes and embraces of friends and family before leading them to the tables groaning under the weight of enough food to feed the entire town.

There were toasts to the bride and groom and dancing to the music of a little country band of musicians from Glacier Ridge.

As the family stood in a circle watching the activities, Gemma and Jeremy hurried over to catch Ally's hand.

The two young people were beaming as Gemma said, "I still can't believe you're going to let us live in your new upstairs apartment and run your business."

Ally laughed. "It's your business now. But you'll have to pay me rent."

Gemma leaned close and hugged her. "You're too generous, Ally. Nobody's ever given us something so fine."

Ally squeezed her hands. "I'd know a thing or two about generous people. The Malloy family taught me a lesson I'll never forget."

When they walked away, the others fell silent as Great One said, "Well done, girl."

Ally flushed. "Thank you. I'm just paying it forward."

"It was a brilliant idea. You said yourself Gemma is a natural in retail. And those two young people will never forget your kindness. You've given them a future."

Ally turned to indicate Kyle and Lily dancing and having the time of their lives, surrounded by so many good neighbors. "There's the future. My heart has never felt this light. As if the weight of the world has suddenly shifted."

"It has for me, too. Speaking of the future..." Reed gathered her close and pressed his mouth to a tangle of hair at her temple. "I told Kyle he could spend the night with Lily. Ingrid promised them popcorn and a movie."

"What about us?"

He gave her that rogue smile that had her heart dancing. "I thought it was time for you to see where I spend so much of my time. It's a little shack in the hills."

"A shack? On our wedding night?"

He gave a rumble of laughter. "City girl, it's time you see just how we cowboys rough it out there on the range. Now don't you worry. We have an indoor bathroom and shower. And to make you comfortable, I've asked Burke to have one of the wranglers deliver some champagne and a couple of steaks for the grill."

"All of that for poor little me?"

He chuckled. "I may have been thinking of my own comfort, too. But at least you'll get the flavor of a cowboy's life."

She lifted herself on tiptoe to brush his mouth with hers and felt the quick sizzle of heat along her spine. "I wouldn't care if we had nothing more than a blanket and the cold ground, as long as you were with me."

The hungry look he gave her said more than words.

"Come on, wife. Dance with me." He brushed his lips over hers before leading her into the circle of friends. "And pray our guests leave soon, so I can start enjoying my very own family."

Family.

She'd come to Montana desperate to connect with her last remaining family member. Instead, she'd found so much more than she ever could have imagined. This rowdy, amazing, diverse family. And though she'd thought she had nothing in common with them, she had what mattered. Love. Despite their differences, they were bound by a deep and abiding love for one another. Not the kind of needy love she'd come seeking, but the steady, rock-solid love she'd discovered in this man. Her husband. Reed Malloy. The love of her life.

LILY AND YANCY'S 7-LAYER STRAWBERRY CREAM TORTE RECIPE

TORTE

- 4 cups granulated sugar
- 6 cups all-purpose flour
- 4 teaspoons baking powder
- 2 teaspoons kosher salt
- 1 cup canola oil
- 6 large egg whites
- 4 teaspoons vanilla extract
- 3 cups whole milk

Directions

Preheat oven to 350°F, butter 4 round cake pans, and line the bottoms with parchment paper.

Combine the dry ingredients in a large mixing bowl of a stand mixer fitted with a paddle attachment.

Whisk together the wet ingredients in a smaller mixing bowl.

Pour the wet ingredients into the dry ingredients and mix until just combined.

Divide the batter evenly between cake pans (8 inch) and bake for 35 to 40 minutes.

Allow the cakes to set for 10 minutes in pans before inverting onto a cooling rack to cool completely.

Or

If you prefer, use two boxes of your favorite white cake mix to fill four layer pans.

When completely cool, use a sharp, serrated knife to smoothly slice each cake into two thinner layers. Set each layer aside after wiping clean of crumbs.

Note: This will give you 8 layers, but since these are fragile, if one falls apart, you will have a backup. A good cook always plans for an emergency.

Beginning with the bottom layer, and continuing to the top, spread each layer with buttercream frosting.

BUTTERCREAM FROSTING

- 3 cups confectioner's sugar
- 1 cup butter, softened
- 1 teaspoon vanilla extract
- 2 tablespoons heavy whipping cream

Directions

In a stand mixer, whisk or mix the sugar and butter on low speed until blended, then on high speed for 3 minutes.

Add the vanilla and the cream and continue to mix for 1 minute. Note: Add more cream if needed to make the frosting spread easily.

Spread buttercream frosting atop each layer, allowing some to drift down the edge and sides. When all layers are frosted, add a cup of whole or sliced fresh strawberries for garnish on the top layer.

Serve with a dollop of whipped cream or strawberry-vanilla ice cream.

Enjoy.

Yancy and Lily will be proud of your accomplishment. So will you and your family.

After a two-week business trip, Matt Malloy only wants to put on a pair of jeans and ride his horse up to the cabin for some alone time. The last thing he needs is a big-city lawyer invading his privacy—even if she is the most beautiful woman he's ever seen…

An excerpt from *Matt* follows.

CHAPTER ONE

Rome, Italy—Present Day

A limousine glided toward the sleek, private jet parked on the tarmac of Rome's Fiumicino Airport. The uniformed driver hurried around to open the door as two men exited.

Matt Malloy extended a handshake. "Thank you for your hospitality, Vittorio. And please thank your lovely wife for the tour of her family's vineyards. That was a bonus I hadn't expected. Tell Maria I hope I didn't overstay my welcome."

The handsome, white-haired man gave a vigorous shake of his head. "You know how much we enjoy your company, Matthew. The vineyard was all Maria's idea. She said to expect a case of her family's finest wine in time for your summer holidays. You do take a holiday from ranching, don't you?"

Matt chuckled. "Ranchers like to say our only day off is our funeral."

"Do not say that, even in jest." The older man shook his

head before closing a big hand over Matt's shoulder. "It is always a pleasure doing business with you, my friend."

"The pleasure is mine." After a final handshake, Matt turned away and greeted the crew at the bottom of the steps before ascending to the plane's interior.

Within minutes the steps had been lifted and the hatch secured; then the pilot announced their departure.

As soon as they reached their required altitude, Matt unbuckled and retreated to the small bedroom in the rear of the aircraft. When he returned to the cabin, he had already shed his suit and tie and replaced them with denims, a comfortable flannel shirt with the sleeves rolled to the elbows, and a pair of well-worn Western boots. Just as easily he shed the attitude of a worldly, successful businessman and became once again a rancher, a man of the soil, eager to return to the life he loved.

Matt leaned over the shoulder of his pilot as the plane cast its shadow on the vast herds darkening the hills below. "Now there's a sight I never grow tired of."

"Can't say I blame you." Rick Fairfield, with his trim build and graying hair cut razor short, could never be mistaken for anything but a former military pilot. He adjusted his mirrored sunglasses. "After nearly three weeks out of the country, it's got to be a good feeling to be home again." He glanced at Stan Novak in the copilot's seat. "Let's bring this baby down."

Matt returned to the cabin and fastened his seat belt for landing. A short time later, after thanking the crew, he deposited his luggage in the bed of a truck that stood idling beside the small runway and climbed into the passenger seat.

Behind the wheel was Burke Cowley. Burke had spent

his younger years tending herds on ranches from Montana to Calgary, until he'd settled on the Malloy ranch, working his way from wrangler to ranch foreman. With his white hair, leathery skin from a lifetime in the weather, and courtly manners, he was a cowboy in the traditional mode. Strong, silent, watchful.

"Welcome home, Matt."

"Thanks, Burke. I see the weather's turning." Matt slipped into a battered parka.

"Springtime in Montana. Shirtsleeves one day, winter gear the next. Was it a good trip?"

Matt shrugged. "Satisfying. Is everyone home?"

"You bet." Burke nodded. "By now they've finished their chores and they're just waiting for you so they can enjoy the special dinner Yancy's been cooking all afternoon."

Matt was smiling as they drove along the wide gravel driveway that circled the barns before leading to the rear of the ranch house.

As Matt stepped down from the truck, he turned. "You coming in?"

Burke grinned. "Wouldn't miss it. I'll just park this in the barn and be back in no time."

Matt hauled his luggage up the back-porch steps, experiencing the same little thrill of pleasure he always felt whenever he returned to his family home.

"Matthew." His grandmother was the first to greet him as he stepped inside and dropped his luggage in the mudroom.

Matt simply stared. "Gram Gracie, you never age."

"Go on. Look at all this gray hair."

Despite the strands of gray in her dark hair, she was as trim as a girl. She was wearing her trademark ankle-skimming denim skirt, Western boots, and a cotton shirt the color of a ripe plum, the sleeves rolled to the elbows.

She flew into his arms and hugged him before drawing a little away to look into his eyes. "I missed you."

"No more than I missed you."

Matt kept his arm around her as they made their way into the kitchen. "Hey, Yancy."

At his words the cook and housekeeper, who stood all of five feet two, his salt-and-pepper hair cut in a Dutch-boy bob, set aside a pair of oven mitts before hurrying over to extend his hand. "Welcome home, Matt."

"Thanks. I've missed this. And missed your cooking. Something smells wonderful."

The cook's face softened into a mile-wide smile. "I've fixed your favorite."

"Yancy's Fancy Chicken?" Matt used the term he'd used since childhood to describe the cook's special chicken dish that never failed to bring compliments. "If I'd known, I'd've had the pilot get me here even faster."

They were enjoying a shared laugh when a handsome man with a lion's mane of white hair entered from the dining room. Gracie's father paused for a moment. Standing ramrod straight, his starched white shirt and perfectly tailored gray pants brightened by a cherry-red silk scarf knotted at his throat, Nelson LaRou looked exactly like the director he'd once been, who had commanded an array of Hollywood's rich and famous.

He hurried toward them. "Welcome home, Matthew."

"Thanks, Great One." Matt ignored the outstretched hand and gathered his great-grandfather into his arms for a bear hug.

Though the old man remained straight backed, his stern countenance softened into a smile. It had taken him years here on the ranch to accept such casual signs of affection. In truth, he was still learning. And he liked it more than he would ever admit. Just as he loved the nickname the boys had given him all those years ago. *Great-grandfather* was just too long. They'd shortened it to Great One, but he sensed that it was more than a title. It spoke of the esteem in which they held him, which tickled him no end.

He cleared his throat. "How was Rome?"

"As amazing as ever. I wish you'd have come with me. Vittorio's wife took me on a tour of her family's vineyards. Every time I sampled another wine, I thought of you and all those fancy wines you brought from your places in Connecticut and California."

Nelson crossed to his favorite chair. "I hope you thought enough of me to bring some home with you."

"I'm having it shipped."

"It flipped?" He turned, cupping a hand to his ear. "Can you flip some my way?"

"*Shipped*, Great One. It's being shipped from Italy."

"Good. Good." Nelson settled into a comfortable easy chair in front of a huge stone fireplace just as the rest of the family began arriving.

The family's often-absent son Luke ambled in from the barn and rolled his sleeves, washing up at the big sink in the mudroom. Where Matt was tall and lean, his dark hair cut short for his trip to Rome, Luke was more muscular, honed by his never-ending treks to the mountains that called to him. Thick, long hair streamed over his collar.

He hurried over to welcome his brother back. "Another tough assignment, right, Matt?"

"Right. But somebody has to do it. And I manfully accepted the challenge."

The two were still sharing grins when Reed strolled down the stairs and clapped Matt on the shoulder. Tall, wiry, with his long hair tied back in a ponytail and his rough beard in need of a trim, their youngest brother looked as though he'd just come in from months in the wilderness. "You're alone? I was hoping you'd bring a couple of Italian beauties with you."

"Wishful thinking, little brother. You'll have to go to Rome and do your own shopping."

"That works for me. Next time you're heading to Italy, you've got a traveling companion."

"You always say that, until it's time to actually go. Then you realize you'll need to wear a suit and tie and get a real haircut, and you find way too many things that need your attention here on the ranch."

Reed gave a mock sigh. "The trials of a cowboy. Never enough time for the ladies." He looked up. "Speaking of which, here's the ultimate cowboy now." He grinned at the handsome man in faded denims and plaid shirt strolling into the kitchen. "When's the last time you took a pretty lady out to dinner, Colin?"

His uncle was already shaking his head, sending curly dark hair spilling over his forehead. "So many females, so little time." He grabbed Matt in a bear hug. "'Bout time you got your hide back here. I was beginning to think you'd been seduced into moving to Rome permanently."

"I did give it some thought. But then I wondered who'd handle all the family business if I just up and relocated."

Matt's grandfather, Frank, chose that moment to walk in from the hallway. It was easy to see where his son and grandsons got their handsome Irish looks. From his twinkling blue eyes to his towering frame, he was every inch the successful rancher who'd tamed this rough land with sheer sweat and tears. Though his hair was streaked with gray and his stride was a bit slower, he was still able to work alongside his wranglers without missing a beat.

With a wink at his wife, he reached up and ruffled Matt's hair the way he had when his grandsons were little. "Any day you get ready to walk away, don't you worry, sonny boy. I can still negotiate contracts on behalf of the family business."

"Or hire a staff of lawyers to handle it for you."

At Matt's words, Frank pretended to groan. "You think it would take a staff to replace you, sonny boy?"

"At least a staff. Maybe an army." Matt grinned good-naturedly before accepting a longneck from Yancy's tray.

The others followed suit. Nelson accepted a martini, which Yancy had learned to make to the old man's specific directions.

When old Burke walked in, the family was complete. They touched drinks in a salute, and tipped them up to drink.

Matt looked around and felt his heart swell. He never grew tired of this scene. His brothers, his uncle, his grandparents, and his great-grandfather all here, as they'd been since he was a kid, surrounding him with love. Yancy cooking. Burke standing just slightly outside the circle, like a fierce, vigilant guardian angel.

Outside the floor-to-ceiling windows, the tops of the mountains in the distance were gilded with gold and pink and mauve shadows as the sun began to set.

Life, he thought, didn't get much better.

"Dinner's ready."

At Yancy's familiar words, they circled the big, wooden harvest table and took their places. Frank sat at the head, with his Gracie girl at his right and their son, Colin, to his left. Matt sat beside Colin, with Burke beside him. Luke and Reed faced them on the other side, with Nelson holding court at the other end of the table.

After passing around platters of tender, marinated chicken, potatoes au gratin, and green beans fresh from the garden, Yancy took his place next to Reed.

Matt took a bite of chicken and gave a sigh of pleasure. "Yancy, after all that great Italian food, this is a real treat. I can't tell you how much I've missed this."

The cook's still-boyish face creased into a smile of pleasure at Matt's words.

"Okay." Luke pinned his older brother with a look. "Enough about the food. I want to know what happened with Mazzola International. Are they in?"

Matt put aside his fork before nodding. "They're in."

"They signed a contract?"

"Their lawyers still have some work to do. But Vittorio and I shook on it. And that's good enough for me."

Luke reached over to high-five his brother.

Matt laughed as he looked around the table at the others. "I figured that news would make Luke's day."

Colin shot a meaningful look at his nephew. "Does this mean you intend to give up all those reckless pursuits and settle down to raise cattle?"

"Reckless pursuits?" Luke arched a brow.

His uncle narrowed his gaze. "I caught a glimpse of you on your Harley, heading into the wilderness. You were doing one of your daredevil Evel Knievel imitations, as I recall."

Luke gave one of his famous rogue grins. "The way I see it, jumping a motorcycle off a cliff, or hiking through the mountains with nothing more than a camera, a rifle, and a bedroll"—he turned to his grandmother—"searching for that elusive white mustang stallion you've been tracking for years, is no distraction from work. They help prepare me to be a better cowboy."

"Or an aimless drifter," his great-grandfather muttered.

Luke's grin widened. "There's nothing aimless about it, Great One. It's preparing me for whatever life throws at me." He turned to Matt. "Enough about me. Tell us more about Rome."

Matt paused for dramatic effect before saying, "I brought back a little something for you, too, Reed."

Their younger brother looked up in surprise before narrowing his eyes in suspicion. "Okay. Give."

"I know how you've been hoping to make a mark in the green industry..."

Reed nodded. "Organic. Pure beef with no hormones, no antibiotics."

"Exactly. Leone Industries has agreed to a limited contract, to test the market. If they can see enough profit, they'll sign for the long term." He studied the excitement that had leapt into his brother's eyes. "Just remember. It's only a limited contract until they test the market."

"It's a foot in the door." Reed sat back, too excited to finish his meal. "And there's an entire generation of buyers out there just waiting for this. If Leone Industries will give it a fair trial, this will become the gold standard for prime beef. And we'll be there first."

"Hah." Nelson sipped his martini and frowned. "Food fanatics. That's what they are. Now in my day—"

"Not now, Dad." Grace kept her tone light, but there was a hint of steel in her words. "Let Reed enjoy the moment. This is something he's been preparing for since he was barely out of his teens."

"You got that right, Gracie girl." Frank Malloy patted his wife's hand before turning to his grandson. "You realize this means you'll have to work twice as hard to see that you have enough healthy cattle to fulfill this contract with Leone."

"I don't mind the work, Grandpop."

"I know you don't, sonny boy, and you never have. You've been tending your own herd since you were knee-high to a pup."

Reed flushed with pride. "I'll need to get busy segregating one herd and seeing that they meet all the requirements to be truly organic."

"And I'd like to get in one more trip to the mountains and see if I can spot a herd of mustangs for Gram Gracie before I settle down and do my lonesome cowboy routine."

At Luke's deadpan expression, they all burst into laughter.

"Yeah. That'll be the day, sonny boy." Frank squeezed his wife's hand.

All of a sudden, with so much good news springing from Matt's Italian trip, everyone seemed to be talking at once.

Matt sat back, looking around the table, listening to the chorus of voices, and smiling with satisfaction.

He'd missed this. All of it.

He'd grown impatient to get back to his roots.

But now, seeing the animation on their faces, hearing the excitement in their voices, he knew without a doubt it had all been worth waiting for.

Fall in Love with Forever Romance

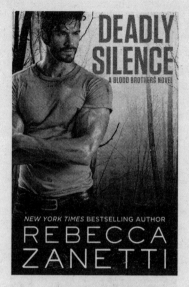

DEADLY SILENCE
By Rebecca Zanetti

Fans of Maya Banks, Shannon McKenna, and Lisa Jackson will love this sexy, suspenseful romance from *New York Times* bestselling author Rebecca Zanetti. Paralegal Zara Remington wants to keep things casual with private investigator Ryker Jones. But when a secret military organization starts to hunt them down, her true feelings for him surface—just as their lives are being threatened.

Fall in Love with Forever Romance

TOO HARD TO FORGET
By Tessa Bailey

The "Queen of Dirty Talk" is back with the third book in the Romancing the Clarksons series! Peggy Clarkson is returning to her college alma mater with one goal in mind: confront Elliott Brooks, the man who ruined her for all others, and prove she's over him for good. But she's in for a surprise when this time Elliott has no intention of letting her walk away.

Fall in Love with Forever Romance

IT HAPPENED ON LOVE STREET
By Lia Riley

Lawyer Pepper Knight finds herself stranded and unemployed in Everland, Georgia, and she turns to the sexy town vet, Rhett Valentine, for help. But when she starts to fall for him, she has to decide: Will she be able to give up her big city dreams for love in a small town? For fans of Kristan Higgins, Jill Shalvis, and Marina Adair.

Fall in Love with Forever Romance

"R. C. Ryan delivers it all with page-turning romance!"
—NORA ROBERTS

NEW YORK TIMES BESTSELLING AUTHOR
R.C. RYAN

REED
By R.C. Ryan

In the tradition of Linda Lael Miller and Diana Palmer comes the latest from R.C. Ryan. Cowboy Reed Malloy is Glacier Ridge's resident ladies' man and now his sights are set on the beautiful Allison Shaw. But a secret feud between their families threatens their love—and their lives. The heartwarming conclusion to R.C. Ryan's Western romance series, the Malloys of Montana.